PRAISE FOR BARBARA WOOD
AND *PERFECT HARMONY*

"Sharply realized . . . beautifully detailed . . . compelling to untangle."

—Publishers Weekly

"An accomplished storyteller."

—John Jakes

"Barbara Wood's writing is flawless, spiritually uplifting. . . . She has a complete grasp of her characters and narrative."

—CompuServe Romance Reviews

"A master storyteller."

—Tulsa World

"Bright, slick, and pleasing. . . . As ever, Wood shows herself a wizard at juggling action and romance, maintaining the momentum and sparkle of both."

—Kirkus Reviews

Novels by Barbara Wood

The Prophetess

Virgins of Paradise

Green City in the Sun

Soul Flame

Domina

Childsong

Yesterday's Child

The Magdalene Scrolls

Hounds and Jackals

Night Train *(with Gareth Wootton)*

The Watchgods

Curse This House

Vital Signs

The Dreaming

BARBARA WOOD

PERFECT HARMONY

WARNER BOOKS

A Time Warner Company

The characters and events in this book are fictitious. Any similarity to real persons, living or dead, is coincidental and not intended by the author.

The author is grateful for permission to include the following previously copyrighted material:

Excerpts from "Two Sunrises" by Jonathan Cheyne. Copyright © by Jonathan Cheyne. Reprinted by permission of the author.

WARNER BOOKS EDITION

Copyright © 1998 by Barbara Wood
All rights reserved.

Cover design and illustration by Tom Tafuri

This Warner Books Edition is published by arrangement with Little, Brown & Company.

Warner Books, Inc.
1271 Avenue of the Americas
New York, NY 10020

Visit our Web site at
http://warnerbooks.com

 A Time Warner Company

Printed in the United States of America

First Warner Books Printing: January, 1999

10 9 8 7 6 5 4 3 2

To Linda, dear friend, with much love
(Lucy and Ethel forever!)

Acknowledgments

A very big thank you goes to the following people, who gave so generously of their time and knowledge:

In Singapore: Doris Chew of Raffles Hotel for a private tour of the museum and a fascinating account of the island's colorful history.

In San Francisco: Nancy Chung, M.D., and Sam Li, herbalist, for enlightening me on two different views of Chinese medicine; and Rosemary Chin for a fun and insightful tour of Chinatown.

In southern California: John Teng, L.Ac, Ph.D., Judy Lin, *feng shui* practitioner, and Dr. Kaz Yamatsu, professor of Asian studies, for opening a previously mysterious and unknown world to me.

Special thanks to Jim Settle, CEO, Settle Services in Technology, LLC (and formerly manager of the FBI's National Computer Crime Squad), for shedding light on the hacker community and computer crimes, and for patiently answering the questions of a "newbie."

To Jonathan Cheyne for permission to use his poem "Two Sunrises."

And to the staff of the Lordston Corporation for once again keeping me happily connected and online.

Lastly (although you really do come first), hugs and kisses to my agent, Harvey Klinger, my editor, Fredrica Friedman, to dear friends Carlos and Sharon, and, most important, my husband, George. I could not have done it without your support, encouragement, and faith in me.

Love to you all!

PERFECT
HARMONY

PART
ONE

6:00 P.M.—Palm Springs, California

The phone jarred Charlotte out of a deep sleep.

As she reached to answer it, she looked at her bedside clock. Six P.M. She hadn't slept well the past few nights, so she had come home from the lab and stretched out for a short nap. To her surprise, she had slept through the rainy afternoon.

The caller was Desmond. His words dropped like bombshells: "Charlotte, you'd better get down here right away. There's been another one."

She was instantly awake. "A *third?*" The room was dark; she turned on the bedside lamp. "How bad?"

"Like the others. The victim died."

She closed her eyes. *Dear God.* "I'm on my way."

"Charlie. One more thing. There are picketers out front."

She squinted at her rain-washed window. "In this weather?"

"Some of them are holding up the Chalk Hill picture."

Her stomach did a somersault. "Oh no, Des," she whispered.

"I just wanted to warn you so it didn't come as a shock."

She hung up the phone and hurried into the bathroom, as if trying to run from Desmond's shocking announcement. They had the picture. The Chalk Hill Research Lab incident. Charlotte's waking nightmare.

As she stood beneath the coldest shower she could tolerate, the spray set on full force, Charlotte pushed thoughts of Chalk Hill from her mind — *the picture had come back to haunt her, as she had feared that someday it would* — and tried to analyze the strange dream that had visited her during the nap: her grandmother saying, *"We descend from a long line of motherless daughters. Always, at one time in our lives, our mothers guide us from Beyond. Someday, Charlotte-ah, you will hear your mother's voice speak to you, as I once heard mine."*

"But how will I recognize it?" Charlotte had asked in the dream. *"My mother died when I was a baby. I've never heard her speak."*

"You will recognize her with your heart, not with your ears."

"And when will this happen?"

"When the time comes."

It hadn't been only a dream; it was also a memory. Charlotte's grandmother had spoken those prophetic words over ten years ago. Charlotte was still waiting to hear her mother's voice.

As she dressed hastily but with care, choosing a cream wool suit, white silk blouse, and modest pumps and drawing her long black hair into a gold clip, Charlotte looked out the window at the desert valley spread before her, barely visible in the dying day. A demonic rain fell from a sky black with thunderclouds; in the west, explosions of lightning illuminated the horizon in brief, sulfuric bursts. She thought: If Grandmother were alive, she would be able to read the signs. She would say, "Those clouds, like cranes, urgently flying home. A happy omen. It means good luck is coming."

Charlotte had never learned to read the signs well, although her grandmother had certainly tried to teach her. Maybe I am too American, Charlotte thought. Just as Grandmother was too Chinese.

As she shielded her eyes from a flash of lightning, she thought: *Palm Springs has three hundred and thirty days of sunshine in a year. How can this tempest be considered a good omen?*

It was a bad omen. Three deaths caused by Harmony products within one week. It *had* to be product tampering, like the Tylenol case, because Harmony Biotech manufactured herbals under the strictest quality control. But if it was product tampering, then were the deaths related, or had only one of them been the intended target and the other two innocent victims? Or was Harmony House the target?

She clicked on her bedside radio and caught the evening news: flash flood warnings in the low deserts . . . power outages in Pomona, Manhattan Beach, and areas of the San Fernando Valley . . . mudslides in Malibu. . . .

She turned it off. Not good omens at all. . . .

Suddenly something her best friend had once quipped popped into her mind: "A good omen is when your blind date shows up with a pulse."

Charlotte was mortified at herself. How could she think humorous thoughts at a time like this? "Self-defense," Naomi would say. "Humor is chocolate cake for the soul. Without humor we might as well live in Tarzana."

Naomi! Charlotte looked at her watch. She had forgotten. Tonight was Naomi's séance.

Picking up the bedside phone, she quickly dialed her friend's number. Although Charlotte wasn't sure she believed in contact with the dead, she always attended Naomi's séances because, as Naomi had put it, the spirits were drawn irresistibly to Charlotte's rich Chinese vibes. "You're a ghost magnet," Naomi had said with a grin.

She got the answering machine. "Hi," sang Naomi's cheerful voice. "You have reached *the* psychic friend. No network, just me! I can't come to the phone right now because I'm attending a reunion with my past lives. You don't have to leave your name and number. Just press the phone to your forehead and I'll get back to you."

Charlotte didn't like the long beep at the end of the
recording because it meant the message machine was almost
full. Naomi was very popular. "Naomi? It's me. About
tonight —"

The machine cut her off.

Deciding to try again from the car phone, Charlotte hurried through her spacious hillside house and into the kitchen,
where the live-in housekeeper was preparing dinner. Retrieving her oversized leather handbag that served as a briefcase and a tote, Charlotte grabbed her keys, and said, "I have
to get to the plant, Yolanda. There's an emergency. I don't
know how late I will be."

"Pedro should drive you," the housekeeper said, referring
to her husband, who worked as a handyman on Charlotte's
thirteen-acre desert estate. "The storm is bad."

"I'll be okay. Don't worry." The Sanchezes had been with
Charlotte for eight years. They had followed her down from
San Francisco "when the medicines moved," Mrs. Sanchez
liked to tell the cashier at the grocery checkout at Ralph's.
"We could not leave the *señorita* alone. She needs looking
after. Except she does not know it."

"But what about your dinner?" Yolanda asked, sweeping
her arm over the bubbling pots and pans, the countertops
strewn with vegetables and spices.

"I'll grab something in the cafeteria," Charlotte said, and
she vanished through the door that connected to the garage.

Cafeteria! Yolanda thought in sudden alarm. This must be
a very big emergency indeed for the *señorita* not to care
about what she ate. Yolanda knew better than anyone the
strange eating habits of her employer.

Tonight, at Miss Lee's instructions, Yolanda was preparing lotus root salad. She was making it not because Miss Lee
liked the taste of lotus root but because, as she had once explained to Yolanda, the Chinese words for lotus root and the
expression "achieve more each year" sounded almost iden-

tical, and so it was considered helpful to one's finances to eat a lot of lotus root. Yolanda had long ago gotten used to her employer's eating habits, which were governed less by rules of taste than by curious rules such as "sounds like" — Miss Lee ate a lot of long rice because it sounded like "long life" — and selecting good luck food, like bok choy, and avoiding bad luck food, such as corn.

So many rules! Yolanda thought as she went back to her cooking. As far as she was concerned, if you felt like tamales, you ate tamales.

Charlotte used the remote to raise the massive garage door, the motor grinding as overhead lights went on. She slipped behind the wheel of her Corvette — a gift she had bought for herself the year before, when she had turned thirty-eight — and started the engine. As she reached for the car phone and pressed a single button that auto-dialed Naomi's number at the college, she contemplated the formi dable storm that was turning her driveway into a river.

She always backed into her garage so that, in an emergency, she could drive out quickly. She was facing the driveway and thinking: Flash floods in the low deserts . . .

When she heard the busy signal at the other end, indicating that Naomi was still at the school — besides being a licensed psychic, she was also a professor of paranormal studies at a desert college — Charlotte cut the connection and regarded the driving rain. She went everywhere in the Corvette; it was her baby. But now she felt vulnerable and at the mercy of the elements in such a small, low-slung car.

Giving the other car in the garage a quick glance — a monster Chevy Suburban she had bought for rare forays into the mountains when pressures at the lab got to be too much — she made a snap decision. Slipping out of the Corvette, she hurried around the utility vehicle and climbed into the driver's seat. The keys were tucked in the sun visor; Pedro started the motor occasionally to keep the battery charged and washed and waxed the onyx paint job.

Charlotte felt strange in such a big car. She couldn't remember when she had driven it last. Turning the key, she was pleased to hear the engine jump instantly to life — Pedro was a very reliable handyman. She gripped the wheel with confidence. This tank with its mammoth wheels would get her through the worst flooded intersection Palm Springs could throw her way.

With the headlights turning the rain into a curtain of diamonds, Charlotte shifted into gear and eased the Suburban forward.

The crash was sudden and deafening. Charlotte screamed as the windshield exploded in a galaxy of shattered glass, just a split second after a deafening jolt rocked the vehicle and plunged everything into darkness.

2

Voices . . . from far away. "*Dios mio!*"

"What has happened?"

"*Señorita?* Hurry, Pedro!"

As Charlotte felt herself float up from a dark place, she saw two pale faces — the housekeeper and her husband, their eyes big and frightened, their mouths twisted in shock and fear. Charlotte wondered for a moment where she was, but then, as the couple's feet crunched over broken glass and as she saw their shaking hands reaching for her, she remembered that she was in the Suburban and that she had been about to leave for the lab. When her eyes focused on the caved-in windshield, just inches from her face, she cried out.

The garage door was protruding through the shattered glass.

"Are you okay?" Pedro said anxiously as he pulled the driver's door open. "We heard a noise, *Dios mio!*" He crossed himself.

"What . . ." Charlotte could hardly find breath. "What happened?"

"The door, it fell!" It crashed down on the car. Are you okay? Shall we call a doctor?"

"No. . . ." She raised a hand to her forehead, shards of safety glass cascading from her arm. She looked down at herself. She was covered in glass. "How did it happen?" Accepting Pedro's offered hand, she tried to slide out of the seat. But there was no strength in her body. Charlotte realized she must be in shock.

"I do not know," Pedro said, with worry etching deep wrinkles in his leathery face.

"I need . . . I need to change my clothes."

"You need a doctor!" Yolanda protested, wringing her hands and biting her lip. "Holy Mother of God, we heard the sound. We thought it was thunder!"

Charlotte twisted in the seat, her head clearing, her eyes coming into focus. The garage door rested on the Suburban, leaving enough room for the Guatemalan couple to have walked under if they stooped. Charlotte frowned. Wasn't the electronic safety, which she had had installed a few months ago, supposed to prevent this very thing from happening?

She put trembling fingertips to her face. Had she been cut? Was she bleeding? But her hands came away clean. By some miracle she had escaped being injured by flying glass.

"I'm all right," she said as she let Pedro assist her from the car. But as soon as her feet touched the cement floor, her knees gave way. Supporting her around the waist, the elderly handyman helped Charlotte over the broken glass and back through the door that led to the kitchen. "I need to change, and then I have to get to the lab."

"No," the older woman protested, fussing over Charlotte, brushing glass from her, muttering a frantic prayer in Spanish. "You do not worry about your clothes. You need a *doctor*."

"Pedro, please see if you can raise the garage door. I'll have to take the Corvette after all."

"Sit." Yolanda persisted. "I make you some nice tea. I call the doctor for you. You are as white as flour."

"I'm all right, really," she said, drawing away from Pedro to show she could walk on her own. "I'm fine." It was a lie, but Charlotte didn't want them fussing over her. And she had to get to the lab. The reporters would be there by now, and maybe more picketers — with that terrible picture. . . .

She would try Naomi again. If there was one thing Charlotte needed right now, it was her best friend's solid strength and wry humor.

The line was still busy.

As she replaced the receiver, she turned to the sliding glass doors that led from her study to her private rock garden, and she saw a large, old desert tortoise making its way slowly through the rain. Charlotte had found the animal at the side of the road a year ago. Someone had ill-treated it, so she had brought it home and fed it a diet of special Chinese herbs. She had expected it to wander off when it was better, but the old thing had stayed, even though it wasn't penned in.

"You rescue animals," her grandmother had said, "instead of having babies."

Charlotte had laughed. "I have one very big baby, Grandmother. Harmony House is child enough for me." But Charlotte's laughter had been hollow. She would soon be forty. Had she missed her chance to have a family? The company had always come first in Charlotte's life. There was always something new she wanted to try, something innovative she needed to persuade her grandmother to adopt. Somehow the years had slipped by and the issue of a family always took backseat. And now there was this new calamity: someone poisoning Harmony products.

Quickly changing her skirt and jacket — selecting this time a black business suit to give herself a more in-command appearance — Charlotte swallowed two Harmony tablets containing natural calming herbs. She was still shaken from the accident with the garage door and she was going to need to be steady and in control when she reached the lab.

As she passed the small atrium where she grew rare herbs and flowers, she felt a cold draft. Turning, she saw that the glass door to the patio had blown open.

Hurriedly making her way through the delicate palms and fragile ferns to close the door, she felt something crunch underfoot. When she saw what it was, she put her hands to her mouth and, in a brief reversion to her childhood, cried, *"Aii-yah!"*

The glass wind chimes that had hung in the atrium for two years had fallen and shattered.

She bent to touch the pieces. The chimes had been a gift from Jonathan, the last time she saw him, ten years ago. For an entire decade these delicate glass circles had kept the good *chi* flowing wherever she lived, the tinkling music reminding her with bitter-sweet sadness of the one great love in her life, and how she had lost him.

Her grandmother had approved of this remembrance of sadness and loss. "Now you will never be completely happy, Charlotte-*ah*, *Yin* and *yang* are balanced in your life."

What a concept! To approve of misery because balance and harmony were more important than complete joy.

The outer glass circle had shattered so that it no longer enclosed the smaller ones. You can't hang broken wind chimes, Charlotte thought as a lump gathered in her throat. The voices would be wrong. The *chi* would flow backward.

Staring for a moment at the shattered luck and wondering if anything would ever be right again, Charlotte hurried back down the hall to her bedroom, where she opened her dresser and brought out a silk scarf richly textured in aquatic blues and woodsy greens — another gift from Jonathan. He had given it to her at their last meeting, when he had dropped shocking news on her and she had felt her life shatter on the spot, like the broken chimes, like the Suburban's crushed windshield.

Returning to the atrium, she gently gathered up the chimes and pieces of glass and wrapped them in the scarf. Pedro appeared then, in a dripping raincoat, to tell her that he had raised and secured the garage door.

As Charlotte was about to leave, Yolanda stopped her at the kitchen door and said, "For you," and she pressed something into Charlotte's palm. "Very old," said Yolanda, who came from Chiapas in Mexico and therefore had Maya blood. Charlotte saw that it was a small talisman, a chunk of green jade carved into a sleeping serpent. "Very good luck, very very old," Yolanda assured her.

But as Charlotte curled her fingers around the relic, she wondered if her luck had finally run out.

3

Charlotte slowed her car as she turned onto Joshua Tree Drive, where the low-profile buildings of Harmony's science park occupied a vast expanse of lawns, palm trees, rock waterfalls, and a lake that was churning with whitecaps in the rain. The sign — Harmony Biotech Laboratories — and the smaller sign below — Harmony House Herbal Products — were as low profile as the buildings. The rich and elite who came to the Palm Springs golf courses and exclusive resorts did not want to be reminded of sickness and mortality.

As she passed first the building that housed the labs and factory, Charlotte saw members of the local police, in yellow rain slickers, cordoning off the entrances and keeping people out. At the main building, she was dismayed to see news crews already in the parking lot, vans from local stations, the three networks, CNN. Before getting out of her car, she said a silent prayer for the innocent life lost. She felt sick at heart to know that her company — which was dedicated to wellness and saving lives — had *killed* three people. She was glad her grandmother wasn't alive to witness this shame and dishonor.

Then she saw the picketers clustered under umbrellas and holding up angry signs. Desmond was right. They had gotten hold of the picture. But it was easy to, the news photo, taken eight years ago, was a matter of public record. The problem was, the picture didn't tell the true story. *The charges were dropped*, Charlotte wanted to shout as she tore her eyes away from the black-and-white image of herself, her bloodied arms raised, a look of fury twisting her face.

Stepping from the Corvette, she felt the wind shift, driving rain into her eyes, but sending also a brief whiff of delicious cooking aromas from the nearby employees' cafeteria. Although Harmony employed many Anglos and Hispanics, the food served was mainly Chinese, a tradition begun long ago by Charlotte's grandmother, who believed that food was medicine. Tonight, for the appetites of the evening shift, it was braised cod cooked with *dangshen* and *huangqui* — Chinese herbs that increased body energy and aided digestion.

"Ms. Lee," the reporters called out through the rain, thrusting microphones at her as she hurried toward the main building, "do you think it's still an accident? *Three* deaths now?" As she wordlessly pushed through, another reporter blocked her path. "What about the allegations that your company has been using animal parts from endangered species in its products?" She gave the man a startled look. Then she sidestepped him, delivering herself into the sheltering arms of Desmond, senior vice president in charge of marketing. Desmond was her cousin. He had also once wanted to be her lover. She suspected he still did.

"This is such a nightmare!" he said as he hurried her through the spacious lobby, where the security staff was trying to keep everyone else out. "Good God, you're as white as a sheet!"

"I had an accident, Des." She quickly recounted the incident with the garage door.

"Holy shit, Charlie! Are you all right?" Eyes hidden behind Ray-Bans ran a diagnostic of her from head to toe.

"I was shaken up but I'm okay now."

"Is there anything left of the Corvette?"

"That's the scary part, Des. I wasn't *in* the Corvette. I decided to take the Suburban at the last minute. If I had been in the 'Vette I could have been seriously hurt, maybe even killed."

"Holy shit," he said again, more softly. "If ever the gods were watching over you, it was tonight."

"Des, what is this about illegal animal parts in our products?"

Charlotte noticed that he looked beleaguered, so unlike Desmond, whose concern about his appearance, she often thought, sometimes bordered on obsession. Which alarmed her even more. For Desmond to be so upset that, for once, his hair wasn't perfectly combed meant the news might be even worse than she suspected. "I don't know," he said. "Apparently several TV stations and major newspapers received an anonymous tip. Now the FDA is investigating charges of putting tiger penis into our tea!" When they reached the elevators, Desmond's frown deepened, marring his attractive features. "There's more bad news," he said. "The federal agent who was on the other two cases —"

"Yes. Johnson."

"He's been pulled. Guess who his replacement is."

Charlotte didn't have to guess; by Desmond's unhappy expression she already knew. Valerius Knight, an agent with Food and Drug who was building his career by attacking herbal manufacturing firms. This did not bode well.

"What about Adrian and Margo?" she asked.

Desmond took advantage of the wait for the elevator to correct his image — fingers fluffing out his brown, moussed hair, hands smoothing down the black merino-wool V-necked sweater and black nylon pants. Charlotte noticed that his black leather coat was dry, which meant he hadn't yet been outside to face the reporters. He even, she noticed, took a moment to settle the gold chain around his neck into a perfect curve. "Mother and Father are on their way down," he said. "They've taken the corporate jet."

As they continued to wait at the shiny elevator doors, Charlotte regarded her own reflection. With her long black hair rain-drenched and plastered to her skull, she knew she did not look like the CEO of a multimillion-dollar herbal and pharmaceutical company. Her expression was so taut that her Asian cheekbones, normally not so noticeable as to make her look anything other than American, were prominent now and dewy, and her skin was cast in an ivory pallor that reminded her of the ancient ivory statue of the goddess Kwan Yin that stood in her office. Her eyes were haunted by the dark circles of a week of sleepless nights. "Secret eyes," Jonathan had once called them, long ago. Because they were eyes that guarded hidden knowledge, things that no one else knew, even the fact that Charlotte wasn't her real name.

She glanced at the other face reflected in the polished

chrome. Desmond was a handsome man with even features and a carefully cultivated look. He, too, had secrets. Was that why, she wondered, he was always wearing sunglasses, even now, with it dark out and pouring with rain?

"Christ," Desmond said, pounding the elevator button again. "This is unbelievable! I swear this is worse than that time you were abducted by aliens!" He quickly gave her a sheepish look. "Sorry. Bad joke."

Desmond hadn't intended it as a joke. Charlotte knew he had meant it. She had never known Desmond to pass up an opportunity to refer to an incident he seemed to have been preoccupied with for the past twenty-four years.

It had happened when she was fifteen years old and Des was fourteen: Charlotte vanished mysteriously for three weeks one summer and when she wouldn't tell anyone afterward where she had gone — especially Desmond, who kept asking, "Did my randy old grandfather take advantage of you like everyone's saying?" — Desmond started making a joke of it, quipping, "Nah, that couldn't be true. You must have been abducted by aliens."

She could not believe it. Even after all these years, and in the midst of a company crisis, Des still wanted to know where she had disappeared to that summer. What Desmond didn't know was that he was closer to the truth than he realized: she *had* been abducted.

"Give me the details of this latest incident," she said as they rode up to the third floor where the corporate offices were.

"Preliminary analysis of the capsules found on the scene —"

"No," she said, gently laying a hand on his arm. "The person who died. Was it a man or a woman?"

"A thirty-year-old woman. Lawyer. Divorced, with two kids."

"I am sick at heart, Desmond. So sick at heart."

"Charlotte, it wasn't your fault."

"Are the children being taken care of? There is family?"

"Um, I'll have to look into it. I'm afraid my mind has been on the company. I mean, how the hell did those capsules get contaminated?"

She frowned. "Capsules?"

"Oh God, that's right. I didn't tell you. It wasn't the tonic this time. It was Bliss."

The elevator came to a halt and the doors whispered open, but Charlotte didn't move. "Bliss?" she said. "You mean this death was caused by *another product?*"

He nodded gravely.

"Oh my God, Des!" The implications took her breath away.

Every day, Harmony House shipped hundreds of products to thousands of drugstores and health food stores all over the United States and around the world. The three victims had used three different products; how many other products had been tampered with? *All of them?*

"Pull everything. Withdraw all Harmony products from the shelves immediately," she said as they stepped into a chaotic reception area where phones were ringing and everyone seemed to be talking at once.

As people rushed up to her with questions, Charlotte scanned the area for Federal Agent Valerius Knight. He possessed some vital information and she wanted it. But she paused first to speak to a short, plump woman in a wet raincoat, her round Asian face framed by a floral scarf, her eyes filled with worry. "Tell your crews I will meet with them in the morning, Mrs. Wong," Charlotte said. "Tell them there is nothing to worry about. Everyone will continue to get paid, no one will be laid off."

But Charlotte knew there was a bigger question behind Mrs. Wong's frightened eyes: the promised bonuses, announced four weeks ago.

The bonuses had in fact made news around the nation, including the cover of *Time* magazine. Charlotte's personal brainchild, it was a new profit-sharing plan based on values taught to her by her grandmother and in keeping with the tradition that Harmony House had always treated employees like family. When Harmony's profits for the previous year had reached record-breaking figures, instead of slicing the pie among herself and other members of the board, Charlotte had decided to share with the nearly one thousand workers in the company. Some of the checks were going to be in the six digits, the profits were so good. Executives at other companies regarded Charlotte's plan as an unwelcome threat to the employee compensation status quo. But Charlotte's rebuttal was simply to point out that Harmony's employees were loyal and tireless, and that turnover was less than one percent a year.

The checks were to have been processed this weekend. But the new turn of events threatened that.

When the lights suddenly flickered and everyone moaned, Charlotte said to Desmond, "Have maintenance check the emergency generators. We might have a power failure."

"Already done," he said.

Her secretary came hurrying up. "Charlotte, I've got someone from KFWB on the line, and KRLA is calling. They want statements."

"Put them off as long as you can. Margo is on her way. She'll handle the press. Have you seen Mr. Sung?" she asked, referring to the company's chief counsel.

"I saw him around a while ago."

"Find him for me, will you, please?" Charlotte turned to Desmond. "We could be facing product-liability litigation. I want Mr. Sung on top of this."

"Don't worry, Charlotte. We'll be able to prove outside tampering."

"Not if Valerius Knight is on the case," she said, finally

espying the FDA representative across the room, standing a head taller than everyone else. "That man has a hidden agenda. He would like nothing more than to destroy Harmony."

Charlotte's chief chemist came up, wringing his hands, his face pale and agitated. "They've locked me out of my lab. I need to get in."

She put her hand on his arm. "I'll see what I can do. Don't worry. Everything is going to be all right." Charlotte turned to her secretary. "Find Mr. Sung. I need to see him at once."

"I have four others on hold," the young woman said, holding up pink message slips. "Via-tek Corporation is on the line, and Chang How Imports. Mr. Lopez at the Gilroy Farm is upset about something —"

"Take messages, tell them I will get back to all of them as soon as I know something." She turned to Desmond. "The first thing I have to do is talk to Knight and find out what information he has."

"Good luck," Desmond muttered as he watched Charlotte hurry across the crowded reception area.

She found the FDA agent near the supply room, helping himself to a desk and setting up a personal laptop computer. Valerius Knight was an imposing African American of commanding stature, with a thick black mustache and smoothly shaven head and a deep, resonate timbre in his voice — a man known for seeking the limelight and going after the more spectacular cases. His presence at Harmony set off alarms at the back of Charlotte's head.

"Agent Knight," she said without preamble, "what information can you give me on the victims?"

"Ah, Ms. Lee," he said, turning a charming smile on her. "So sorry we have to meet under such circumstances."

"Is the FDA positive that Harmony products were the cause of death?"

"In all three cases, the very last thing the victims ingested was one of your products. I'll need to question all employees who had contact with those products, from chemical processing to the guy who drove the truck to the distributor." He held out a pack of spearmint gum, offering her a stick.

She shook her head. "Why do you think the tampering was done here?"

"We talked to the latest victim's brother," he said, carefully unwrapping a stick of gum and examining it as if it, too, might be contaminated. "He said his sister was very scrupulous about making sure safety seals weren't broken, always checking expiration dates, that sort of thing. Well, she *was* a lawyer." He smiled as he folded the gum into his mouth. "Besides, we found the outer cellophane wrapper on the kitchen counter, and only four capsules of Bliss were missing, which means she had just opened a new bottle. If those capsules were altered *after* they left your plant, then the perpetrator is a very clever person."

"What was the cause of death?"

He chewed modestly. "The first victim, cardiac arrest. The second, a seizure."

"And the third?"

"We prefer to keep that classified for now."

"Agent Knight, if my company is under suspicion then I have a right to know how the woman died."

He weighed it for an instant. "Cerebral hemorrhage. Stroke. But that is not for public consumption."

"I can keep a secret, Agent Knight."

"Yes, I imagine you can." He smiled.

"Have you found any connection between the three women?"

"We're working on it. But we're also considering Harmony Biotech as the possible target. Have you received any threatening letters? Phone calls? Anyone demanding money?"

"No," Charlotte said. "Nothing."

"What about . . ." He reached into his expensively tailored sport coat and brought out a small notebook. "This Norman Thurwood, the man you took the drug company from?"

"We did not *take* anything. It was an amicable acquisition."

"That's not what I heard. He didn't like being bought out. Might he carry a grudge?"

"Agent Knight, Harmony was not purchased from Mr. Thurwood. Only this science park and the biomedical research end of his company. Harmony House is *my* company, it has been in my family for generations. Our products are based on my great-grandmother's herbal remedies."

"Yes, I am familiar with those so-called remedies, Ms. Lee." He forged a cold smile. "Could these killings be an inside job?"

"We are a family, Agent Knight."

"No, I mean an employee, maybe."

"That was what I meant. This company *is* a family, Mr. Knight. Most of my people have been with us for years. We have a very high level of employee loyalty."

"The kind of loyal employees who would withhold information, or lie for their employer?"

She ignored the comment. "Have the results of the chemical analysis come back yet? Do you know if it was the same ingredient in all three products that was the cause of death?"

"We don't have the results yet. I expected them any time. Which reminds me, I'll need the formula for Bliss, so we can run a comparison."

Charlotte gave him a hard look. She had requested samples from the first two products so that her chemists could run independent tests, but the FDA had denied her request. "I'll see about obtaining that formula for you, Agent Knight. It might take some time, though."

His smile widened. "I have every confidence, Ms. Lee,

that you and your staff are going to give us your full coop-
eration in this investigation, and in a speedy fashion."

As she started to turn away, he said, "I understand, Ms.
Lee, that your labs were inspected three times last year by
the FDA. Isn't that rather unusual?"

She leveled her gaze on him. "Agent Knight, our products
are manufactured under the strictest guidelines, above and
beyond what the FDA requires. Each lot of raw materials
that arrives at this plant is sampled and tested before being
used. Our products are then manufactured according to
strictly written batch records, with qualified chemists and
pharmacists measuring, checking, and rechecking each step
in the process. The batch is sampled, tested, and approved
before it is shipped to drugstores and health food stores. We
are not a shoddy operation, Agent Knight."

"Well, I never said —"

"It is no secret that the FDA and Harmony do not see eye
to eye. They have been pressuring us to run clinical tests on
animals. And Harmony has a policy against animal experimentation."

His smile looked suspiciously like a smirk. "Yes, I know
how you feel about animal experimentation."

Her guard was suddenly up. The Chalk Hill incident was
rearing its ugly head, as she had feared it would, from the
picket signs outside to Knight's innuendo. That picture was
going to hurt her and the company. And what was worse,
some determined reporter might dredge up even more, dark
secrets best left hidden. . . .

They suddenly heard a commotion near the emergency
stairwell, voices calling for security, Desmond shouting,
"Get that damn camera out of here!"

"What about this new drug, GB4204?" Knight said when
the commotion had died down.

She met his eyes, trying to read a hidden threat there.
"What about it?"

"I understand two other companies have similar formulas currently before a secret advisory board."

She arched her eyebrows. "Are you suggesting these deaths are due to industrial sabotage?"

"Or something made to *look* like industrial sabotage. Say, by an insider within your company, to discredit those other two drug manufacturers." He shrugged and quickly added, "But I'm probably wrong." He flashed her a self-effacing smile that Charlotte did not for one second believe.

She regarded him for another moment, taking the measure of this man she had heard so much about — a man of mighty ambition, it was said, a maverick among federal agents who, it was rumored, would stoop to any means to further his career. His personal crusade was herbal manufacturers. He had been responsible for closing down two smaller companies, and Charlotte suspected that bringing down Harmony House would be the springboard he needed for his next career advancement.

"Are you going to shut us down?" she asked bluntly.

"Just temporarily," he said, the smile still charming, as though he were on her side. "Just long enough."

"If you will excuse me, Agent Knight, I have a lot of things to see to. My secretary will provide you with anything you need."

"Sure," he said. "You go ahead. I'm not going anywhere."

She found Desmond talking to Mr. Sung — Desmond looking distraught, the older man gazing back with an implacable expression. Taking her cousin to one side, Charlotte said, "Put together radio and TV spots alerting people to a problem with Harmony products, that they are not to purchase any, not to use any they already have. And make sure everything is pulled from the shelves."

"What about the employees?"

"We'll keep a skeleton crew and send everyone else home on paid leave."

He shook his head. "This is bad, Charlotte. Very bad."

"And tell those reporters out there that I will be preparing a statement." She paused to put her hand on his arm. "Give me a few minutes, okay? I need to collect myself. And," she added, glancing over her shoulder at Agent Knight, who was plugging his laptop computer into a wall outlet, "keep *him* occupied. But whatever you do, don't cooperate. I have a strong feeling that man is here to crucify us and the company. He'll twist all the facts to make it look like it's *our* fault. He's done it before."

As Desmond went off into the crowd, Charlotte turned to Mr. Sung, who stood patiently at the edge of the pandemonium, calmly surveying the scene.

In his late seventies, Mr. Sung was not only the company's chief counsel, but had been Charlotte's grandmother's adviser and close friend as well. Mr. Sung was the one who had brought the casket home; he had been the last person to see her grandmother alive.

"Charlotte," he said in his soft-spoken voice. "Such a mess."

"I'm going to really need your help in this."

He gave her a sad look. "Listen to the noise, to the disharmony. There is only bad luck here." He shook his head. "I bring unfortunate news. The families of the victims are suing the company."

Charlotte groaned. Six days ago she had been on top of the world, with the FDA on the brink of approving her new anti-cancer formula, GB4204 — the result of her twenty-year dream. Now, her whole world was shattering into a billion irretrievable fragments, like the crushed windshield of her Suburban and the broken wind chimes, which she had tucked carefully into her bag, fearful of leaving her shattered luck behind.

Who was doing this? *Was* it a personal grudge against Harmony House? A disgruntled employee? Industrial sabotage? Or had the killer simply chosen Harmony products to carry his instrument of death, and it really had nothing to do with Charlotte or her company at all?

It was a moment before she realized Mr. Sung was holding something out to her. She recognized it at once: a small box made of light wood and inlaid with intricate marquetry — a Chinese puzzle box that had once belonged to her mother.

"I haven't seen this in years," she murmured in wonder as she took it from him. "I remember the shelf where Grandmother kept it." She gave him a baffled look. "Why did you bring it now?"

"I thought it might help in your hour of need. And now, if you will pardon me, I have much to see to. I will be in my office if you need me," he said, adding, "Charlotte-*ah*," affectionately.

As she watched him thread his way across the reception area, a small elderly man for whom everyone respectfully made way, Charlotte gave the puzzle box a gentle shake. To her surprise, there was something inside.

Turning from the chaotic scene, where Desmond was trying to deal with upset supervisors and department heads, and Valerius Knight was typing away on his laptop, and secretaries who had been asked to stay on were trying to handle the overloaded phones, Charlotte went down the hall where her office occupied a corner suite.

The silence that engulfed her as she delivered herself through the double oak doors and closed them behind her was an instant panacea. She looked at the two statues that flanked the door: Aesculapius, the Greek god of Western healing, with an inscription on the pedestal that read "First do no harm." *Hippocrates*. And Kwan Yin, Chinese goddess of mercy: "Harsh hands make harsh medicines." *Mei-ling*.

Charlotte sent a brief mental prayer to the ancient god and goddess, asking for their guidance and strength.

Except for Kwan Yin, there was nothing Asian about the decor of Charlotte's gray-and-burgundy office. Very corporate America — a look Charlotte purposely cultivated. Most people, when they met her for the first time, did not know she was one quarter Chinese, or that her name Lee was not American but had its roots in South China. In fact, it was Charlotte who, having inherited the position of CEO upon her grandmother's death six months earlier, had shifted the emphasis of the company from the manufacture of Chinese herbals to the research and development of Western pharmaceuticals. The name change, from Harmony House to Harmony Biotech, had been her doing.

The phone on her desk was ringing — all ten lines were lit up. She would let her secretary handle the calls. Right now she had more pressing things to attend to. First of which was to get hold of Naomi.

This time she got her friend's machine at the school. "I've been trying to get hold of you," she said. "I can't make the sitting tonight. There's been another death, this time from Bliss. It's chaos here at the lab. And I had an accident at home. The garage door came loose and fell on my car. Thank God I was in the Suburban and not the Corvette." She paused to massage the bridge of her nose. "There's something more. There are protesters outside with signs. They're dredging up the Chalk Hill thing again. I thought you should know, in case it shows up on the evening news." Charlotte suspected Naomi hadn't told her superiors at the college about the massacre and her part in it. Especially about the arrest.

After hanging up, Charlotte went to the wet bar and, forcing herself to use slow, thoughtful movements, she poured water into the electric kettle and brought out a special cup and saucer, made of the finest bone china and decorated with symbols of good luck. Despite the two tablets she had taken earlier, her nerves were still quivering from the garage door accident. *What if I had been in the Corvette?* She placed in the cup a small cloth bag filled with chamomile tea. As she waited for the water to boil, she practiced slow breathing and mental exercises to bring her racing heart back under control, and to calm her nerves.

As her breathing slowed, Charlotte placed her hand on the necklace that rested just below her collarbone. At the end of a silver chain strung with amethyst beads, the Shang dynasty silver pendant and golden amber teardrop was in fact a locket. Charlotte had placed something inside it twenty-four years ago, sealing it with a fifteen-year-old's tears. She had not opened it since.

When the tea water was ready, she poured it into the cup and instantly the aroma of the rising steam soothed her, bringing up a memory: how her grandmother had had a series of teapots, each for a different purpose: "for the tea that prevents misunderstanding," "for the tea that brings luck," "for the tea that improves *chi*." How often her grandmother had chided Charlotte for boiling all her tea water in the same kettle and then dunking the tea in a bag at the end of string. Very bad luck. When instant tea had appeared on the supermarket shelves, Charlotte's grandmother had declared, "Instant worthlessness."

Feeling a sudden, sharp stab of grief, Charlotte regarded the statue of Kwan Yin and tried to recall what her grandmother had once told her about *another* statue of the Queen of Heaven. But all she could remember was that it had been a strange, exotic story about how the goddess had come a great distance across the ocean with treasures hidden in her body, and how Kwan Yin had brought good luck once, and bad luck later. But Grandmother hadn't expounded on that; she had kept from Charlotte the stories of bad luck and good luck, which made Charlotte think that her grandmother's

grave must be very crowded, she had taken so many secrets
to it.

As she put away the box of tea bags, she glimpsed the
label with its warning: "Caution — This product contains
chamomile, a member of the ragweed family. Can cause allergic reaction or asthma attack." And she thought of Agent
Valerius Knight and a remark she had once heard him make
on *Nightline:* "Herbal medicine is nothing but quackery and
a way to bilk innocent folks out of their hard-earned money.
It is also dangerous because companies aren't required to
warn the consumer of possible adverse side effects."

Harmony was the only herbal manufacturer in the United
States that included warnings on its labels, something the
FDA did not yet require of nondrug companies. Harmony
was known for exceeding federal guidelines; the company
had a history of high morals and ethics. Contrary to the reporter's allegation, Harmony House did not use animal parts
in its products, nor did it test products on animals. Nor, despite increased pressure from the government, was it ever
going to.

As she started to sip the tea, she suddenly stopped and
frowned.

Bliss.

Setting the tea down, she reached into the cupboard and
brought out another box. Bliss was an herbal compound,
natural and safe, that offered, according to the label, "a cool-
ing of hot nerves, a restoration of the balance of *yin* and
yang." Bliss consisted mainly of *dong quai*, Chinese for
"compelled to return," a feminine herb cultivated primarily
for women's health, and Charlotte often added two capsules
to her tea or juice on those days when she needed to quiet
her nerves.

The innocent victim who had ingested this product had
sought peace. Instead she received death.

Why?

Feeling her anger start to bubble to the surface again, Charlotte fought for control as she brought the teacup to her lips. She paused when her eyes settled on the puzzle box that Mr. Sung had given her. She picked it up and shook it again. There was definitely something inside. Yet she could have sworn that it had stood empty on Grandmother's shelf for years.

As she set her teacup down and turned the box over and over in her hands, looking for the starting place to open it, her eye caught on something else — the computer on her desk. She frowned. The monitor was turned on. She distinctly recalled shutting it down when she had left the office earlier.

Slipping the puzzle box into her leather tote, she went to her desk and saw, as she drew closer, her private e-mail account displayed on the computer screen, the folder containing new mail standing open — a folder that could be accessed through a protected password known only to Charlotte.

She clicked on Read.

A message came up:

You murdered those three women, Charlotte. You *killed* *them.*

4

Charlotte stared at the message, then she quickly sat down, clicked on Reader in the toolbar, then on Show All Headers.

Return-Path:rrabbit@guidenet.com
Received: from nova.unix.com

(root@nova.unix.portal.com)
[156.15.1.0]
Comments: This message is NOT from the person listed in
the From line.
THE PORTAL SYSTEM DOES NOT CONDONE OR APPROVE
OF THE CONTENTS OF THIS POSTING
X-PMFLAGS:2244560

She frowned. What on earth was *this*? A prank? Who had
turned her computer on, dialed her modem so that she was
online, and then accessed her e-mail account and set it up to
receive?

As she was reaching for her phone, the mail alert sounded,
indicating that a new message was coming through. She
clicked on New Mail and read the new title: *Me again.*
Clicking on the title, she brought up the text of the message:
*Just joking! You didn't really kill those women. I did. And in
case you think I'm not legit, here's proof — the woman who
drank Bliss died of a cerebral hemorrhage. Classified info
known only to the feds and, of course, to me, her killer.*

Charlotte was immediately on her feet and out the door.
At the end of the hall, she observed the same chaotic scene
in the reception area, the rows of secretary desks where
nearly all the computer terminals were in use. She could
even see Mr. Sung, through his partially open door, staring
thoughtfully at his monitor. She looked for Valerius Knight.
His laptop screen was glowing but the federal agent was
nowhere in sight.

Charlotte returned to her office, sat at her computer,
clicked on Reply, and hastily typed, *Who are you?* hitting
the keys so furiously that she mistyped and had to go back
and correct it. She hit Send and watched as the message
went to her mail host. A moment later a warning appeared
on the screen:

**MAIL DELIVERY SUBSYSTEM: Your Message Could Not Be
Sent. Host Name Look-up Failure.**

She typed again, *What do you want?* hit Send, and
chewed her lip as she watched the screen.

But the message came back undeliverable.

She stood up. The person was clearly a crank. Someone
taking advantage of the bad situation, the kind of sorry bastard, Charlotte suspected, who preyed on victims at an accident scene. She would mention it to Knight, let him handle
it, since the person had obviously managed to get hold of
classified data.

In the next instant, the alert sounded and a new message
appeared on the screen: *Too bad about your windshield.
Good thing you changed cars.*

Charlotte became rooted to the spot.

The message continued: *Time for business, Charlotte.
You are going to make a public statement. You are going to
publicly confess that Harmony House uses unethical practices, puts endangered animals in its products, and knowingly commits fraud. If you do not comply, the consequences
will be on your head. Others will die . . . thousands.*

She was still in shock when the addendum came through:
You have exactly twelve hours to prepare your statement.

Her eyes riveted to the screen, she felt her body turn to
ice. *Good thing you changed cars.* She always drove the
Corvette, a small car with a vulnerable fiberglass body. If
she hadn't decided at the last minute to take the tank-like
Suburban, when the garage door came down — She shuddered. The sudden, sickening jolt to the car, the deafening
crash, the glass splintering, flying everywhere.

Good thing you changed cars. What was this person implying? That it had been done on purpose?

No. It was too monstrous to even consider.

She began to shake, and a dark foreboding stole over her.

Something evil and lethal was gathering around her, she
could feel it shifting, moving, like an invisible snake, coil-
ing to strike.

She had to tell the FDA agents, Desmond, the police —
But her mind had already made the decision.

The wall safe was hidden behind a nineteenth-century
Chinese scroll; only Charlotte and Desmond knew the combination. She opened it now and brought out a slender
leather-bound book. The title was stamped in gold: *Silver
Laurel Wreath Prize Poetry, 1981.* Charlotte had kept it all
these years, but she had not opened it since that day in 1981
when she had felt her world come crashing down around
her.

She opened it now, just lifting the cover so that a business
card whispered out, fluttering to the carpet like a feather.
When she had received this card in the mail, unexpectedly,
nine years ago, she had put it inside the book and locked it
away. She now brought the cream-colored card back to her
desk and held it under the lamp:

Jonathan Sutherland
Technology Security Consulting
London: 71-683-4204
Edinburgh: 31-667-9663
email: TSC@atlas.co.uk

The card had opened a wound so painful that Charlotte
had immediately locked it away and forced herself not to
think about it. It had taken her years to come to the point, finally, of not thinking about him every day, to a point of *accepting,* as her grandmother would have advised. Long ago
she had solemnly vowed never to let Jonathan back into her
life; she had renewed that vow nine years ago.

But now she needed him. There was no one else she could
trust, no one she knew who was skilled enough.

She looked at the computer screen: *You have twelve hours*. But Jonathan was eight thousand miles away. He couldn't get here in time. Maybe she could get advice over the phone, maybe he could tell her how to trace her anonymous mailer, or maybe he could do it remotely from his own computer.

As she reached for the phone, she calculated the time difference. It was 2:00 A.M. in London. The card, she noticed, did not include a home phone number. Perhaps he had call-forwarding.

With a racing pulse she began to dial. Jonathan, after all these years. . . . Would she be able to stand the pain? Would he even want to talk to her?

She listened to the phone ring at the other end — the urgent double rings peculiar to British telephones. She tried to picture Jonathan. He would be asleep next to his wife.

When she heard a soft knock at her door, she thought, Not now, Desmond. Give me a few moments to learn how to talk to Jonathan again.

But he was persistent. "Come in, Des," she finally said.

The door swung open and there he stood, wearing a damp raincoat and a familiar smile. "Hello, love," Jonathan said.

5

Charlotte wasn't prepared for the emotional tidal wave that swept over her when she saw him standing there, as if he had materialized from her thoughts.

The love she had once felt for this man — a deep, desperate love that she had kept buried for so many years — came rushing back with all the force of a Singapore monsoon. "Hello, love," he had said, and her heart skipped a beat. He had called her "love." But then she remembered that London shopkeepers, when handing over change, said, "There you go, love."

It took every ounce of her will not to rush into his arms. When she saw the familiar smile, she was flung back to the first time those lips had touched hers. She and Jonathan had been in his secret hideaway; he had been crying. In the comforting, the "Don't worry, Johnny," the awkward embrace, their mouths had somehow met, and in that instant fifteen-year-old Charlotte had pictured two tall candles, like tapers, leaning toward one another, flames coming together until they were just a single flame, hot and consuming.

After that one passionate adolescent kiss, when she and Johnny had breathlessly pulled apart because they both had seen the brink they had reached and it frightened them, Charlotte had felt herself become only half of what she had been just moments before. It was as if Johnny had completed her; without him she would never be whole again.

And Johnny had felt it too. He hadn't said so, because Johnny had never been able to put his emotions into words. But his eyes spoke. They both just *knew*. Jonathan and Charlotte were soul mates; there could never be anyone else in their universe.

"I know I should have telephoned first to see if you even wanted my help," he said with a dark, brooding look that reminded her of passions from long ago. "But I thought you might refuse my help and then I would have to come anyway and it would have been awkward."

He's gotten very British, she thought. As though he worked at it. She remembered how he had fought his father's attempts to turn him into an American, even though, technically, Jonathan Sutherland *was* American — it said so on his birth certificate. Charlotte recalled that the first thing she had learned about him was that his heart was not in this continent. It was what had made her fall in love with him.

"How did you know I needed help?"

Closing the door behind himself, he removed his wet rain-coat and said, "I watch the news. When I heard about the deaths, I made a few phone calls." He flashed her a wry smile. "I still have friends at the Agency. The packaging of the products in the first two deaths did not appear to have been tampered with prior to the victims opening them. Pre-liminary gross analysis of the uningested products revealed that the entire contents within the package were altered, not just what the victims ingested. I call that a good indicator that the products were tampered with at the plant here. Now," he said as he set his black nylon carry-all on her desk and unzipped a side pocket, "I happen to know that chemi-cal processing and manufacture here at Harmony are all computerized —"

"You've done your homework," she said, amazed at how he still possessed the ability to take over a situation, a man in command.

"So we're going to find the perpetrator, or at least his tracks, somewhere in your computer system. Now, I happen to be the best damned technical investigator on the face of this planet —"

"You can do better than a team of federal agents?"

He released a short mirthless laugh. "That lot don't know a hard drive from a hard-boiled egg. All right, what else can you tell me about this case?"

She met his challenging gaze and realized that Jonathan's presence here had to do with much more than just finding a killer. Jonathan had brought twenty-six years of history with him — *their* history, and she had a sudden fear that a very nasty beast was about to be let loose.

She wanted to say, "I'm glad you came." But the words wouldn't come. Instead, she filled him in on what she knew so far, telling him about the accident with the garage, and then she showed him the e-mails.

He frowned at the computer screen. "Who knew about the garage thing?"

"My housekeeper and her husband. I told Desmond, too. But someone could have overheard us. Surely it was an accident, Jonathan, and this person is just trying to frighten me."

He gave her a noncommittal look. "What is the purpose of this public statement you're supposed to make in twelve hours?"

Charlotte studied his profile, recalling a time when Jonathan had felt self-conscious about his large nose. But of course he had eventually grown into it, developing also a strong jaw and a forehead she had always thought sexy. His dark brown hair was still thick and untouched by gray, even though he was soon to turn forty. His body looked fit. "Blackmail, I assume," she said, realizing that old desires were rushing back. "Such an announcement would destroy my company. This person clearly is hoping I will offer to buy him or her off."

"The cause of death for the third victim, the cerebral hemorrhage, . . . you're sure no one knows about this?"

"Agent Knight told me he was withholding that information. I didn't even tell Desmond. So who else could know about it except for the killer?"

"There are ways of obtaining classified information," Jonathan said thoughtfully, his eyes fixed to the monitor. "So," he said softly, "Desmond is still with the company?"

"He's a board member," she said, recalling the days of bitter rivalry between Jonathan and her cousin, the times when she had had to intervene as peacemaker.

"Is there a way to trace these letters?" she asked.

"No. They came through an anonymous re-mailer. It would be nearly impossible to trace the path back to the sender." Jonathan looked around the office. "Who could have gotten in here to turn your computer on?"

"Anyone. All they have to know is where they keys are kept."

"Who knows your password?"

"Only me, and there is no way anyone could find it out. I don't have it written down anywhere."

She saw how Jonathan continued to look around the office, as if searching for clues and answers. She remembered how he had always done that, searched his surroundings for answers that eventually came from inside himself. When she saw his gaze settle on the wall safe, standing open to expose the leather-bound volume of poetry, she saw something flicker in his eyes, and for a moment she was startled: she thought it was pain. But it couldn't have been. *She* was the one who had been hurt.

As she watched him rake back his wet hair with long, tapered fingers, she thought of the innocent beginnings of their love, years ago, when they had been physically inseparable, two kids jumping off a diving board together, or hugging each other, helpless with laughter, or Jonathan's hand encircling her wrist as he had finally led her into his secret, astonishing sanctuary — they had been thirteen, fourteen, and fifteen years old then.

For an instant, on this stormy, nightmarish evening, with the lights flickering and federal agents swarming all over her property, her whole world threatened, Charlotte wanted to go back and sit in the shadow of the Golden Gate Bridge and count the ships sailing into the bay while Jonathan wove a bracelet of grass for her. But when she noticed how he was dressed — Savile Row tailoring, the French-cuffed shirt and silk tie knotted perfectly in place — she was yanked back to painful reality. What had she been expecting? Torn jeans and a Grateful Dead T-shirt? *That* Jonathan no longer existed. *This* Jonathan, wealthy and successful, was a stranger. They could never go back.

He turned now, started to say something. But when he

stopped and regarded her with solemn eyes, Charlotte knew that he, too, was remembering.

He reached out, lifted the pendant necklace that lay on her chest. "You still wear it," he said.

"To remind me." Jonathan was the only person who knew the truth about her disappearance during the summer of her fifteenth year. He was the only one who knew what the locket held.

Releasing the silver-and-amber pendant, he said, "Harmony Biotech."

She knew what he meant. She had changed the name when she had taken over the company after her grandmother's death. "It was time to come into the modern age," she said now, a little defensively. "Herbs aren't enough. People need serious drugs, too."

"The most important medicine your grandmother had to offer didn't come in a bottle," he said softly, his deep brown eyes reflecting memories. "Her strongest medicine was compassion. She understood that caring was an important part of curing."

"*Caring* for cancer doesn't cure it. Harmony is on the verge of coming out with a new drug that can fight cancer. Clinical testing of GB4204 on volunteer human subjects has boosted survival rates nearly fifty percent. Think of it — fifty percent!"

He smiled. "After all these years, your dream is about to come true."

Her look turned dark. "Or it is about to be shattered."

He addressed the monitor again, and the last threatening e-mail. "Maybe that's our friend's motive. After all, GB4204 will mean a lot of revenue for Harmony." He unfolded the cellular phone he had taken out of his black bag and punched in a number.

"You think this is the work of a competitor?" Charlotte said.

"If someone wanted to destroy Harmony House, the three deaths are a pretty good start."

"*If*," she said, "Harmony is the target."

He listened as the line at the other end rang. "The big question is what exactly our friend here plans to do in twelve hours if you don't agree to that ridiculous public statement." He held up a hand and said into the phone, "Thorne, please. Yes, I'll hold." Then he placed his hand over the mouthpiece and said to Charlotte, "This FDA agent on the case. What did you say his name was?"

"Valerius Knight."

"What's he done so far?"

"I don't know. We aren't exactly communicating. I don't trust him, Jonathan. I happen to know that Knight has put in a bid for a big promotion. He has a personal agenda that makes him very biased in this case. It worries me."

"Who have you told about these e-mails?"

"No one, yet."

"Good," he said, speaking rapidly, his hand over the phone. "Right now the feds aren't interested in your computer system beyond maybe checking production logs and formula files. But if they find out about these e-mails, and if these threats are crossing state lines, or if the feds determine that the formulas were tampered with by a cracker in another state, then it becomes a federal case. They will do a takeover of your network. They'll shut down the system and there will be no way we can get in after that. If this fellow has hacked into the Biotech network, then this system is our only link to him, our only hope of ever catching him. But once the feds take over, we'll never catch him."

"Which means I have another time clock to worry about besides this twelve-hour deadline!" she said, snapping away from him, pacing the floor as if she wanted to charge through the solid wall. She turned back around. "Can you do it? Can you catch this guy working on your own?"

"I work best alone, you know that."

As she was momentarily caught in his gaze, Charlotte was surprised to find herself suddenly remembering Jonathan's comical laugh. It had sounded like a car starting on a cold morning. Ga-*haw!* Ga-*haw!* Ga-*haw-haw-haw!* She used to think up funny things just to make him laugh so that she would get laughing, too, until the pair of them were howling and clutching their stomachs because it just felt so good and nothing hurt anymore, not even the slingshotted stones and dog shit and shouts of "Chink!" on California Street.

Charlotte wondered if Jonathan still laughed that way. And she suddenly wanted to hear it, she wanted to say, "Have you heard the one about. . . ?" But she couldn't think of anything funny.

He looked at her. "What's that for?"

"What?"

"The look on your face. I could always tell when you were thinking something."

That was then, she wanted to say; my face has changed. You don't know it anymore.

He held up his hand again. "Yes, Roscoe. Jonathan Sutherland here. Fine, thank you. I need a favor. I have a profile that I would appreciate your running through your database."

Charlotte resumed pacing as Jonathan said, "Targets pharmaceutical companies, specifically herbal manufacturers. Sends threatening e-mails using anonymous rerouters. Some familiarity with computers, possibly knowledge of pharmacy or biochemistry. Possible connection to Harmony Biotech. Yes," he said. "Doing some private work. Not for general knowledge. Pardon? Yes, I'll hold."

As he waited for Thorne to return to the line, Jonathan watched Charlotte march the width and breadth of her spacious office. He allowed his eyes to trail down her back. He recalled how she had always complained about her wide hips. But Jonathan loved the way the black skirt flared out snugly from her small waist. He would have liked at that moment to put his hands on those generous hips and feel their rhythm again.

"Yes, Roscoe," he said into the phone. "Yes, thanks. That's the number where you can reach me. I appreciate it. Cheers."

When he snapped the phone shut, he said, "I'll need blueprints of the facility — the plant, the grounds, the offices — showing phone and electrical wiring." He spoke quickly, as if his mind were racing ahead of his words. "And a plan, if you have one, of all modems and computer terminals. Your network server is in the main building, I assume?"

"Yes, on this floor," she said, realizing that some things about him hadn't changed. Jonathan had always been impatient. If things didn't go his way quickly enough, he would make them go his way and to hell with the consequences. She felt that same impatience now, and the familiar bulldog determination that meant Jonathan was going to get to the bottom of this mystery no matter what it took.

He glanced at his watch, then quickly sat at her computer. "How secure is your system?"

"We have firewalls, passwords, encryption."

"High priests of false security." He tapped a few keys, regarded the screen, and murmured, "Dianuba software. Good." He turned to her. "Do you allow remote access maintenance by Dianuba Technologies?"

"You would have to check with my system administrator. But he's gone home already."

"Does your network have auto-answer modems? That's how most intruders get in."

"No, we have call-back modems."

"Right. Now, our friend here will no doubt be contacting you again. I'll set up a trap-and-trace. How well can you trust your system administrator?"

When she hesitated, he said, "Never mind. We'll work without him. It's safer and faster that way."

"Jonathan," she said, "his threat that others will die. How can he make that threat? We are pulling all our products off the shelves. We'll be broadcasting TV and radio warnings. How can he make sure people will still take one of our products? And thousands of people at that."

"He even seems to think," Jonathan said as he looked at his watch again, "that he can withhold it or cause it to happen in twelve hours. Charlotte, I need a station where I can work privately, one that has peer-to-peer on your network."

She had to think. The whole building complex was swarming with federal agents and police. There was nowhere he could —

"Yes," she said suddenly. "There *is* one. I don't think anyone even knows it exists."

"Good." He stood up and, returning the cellular phone to his black carryall, zipped the compartment shut. "No one saw me come in. It's pure bedlam out there. I waved to Desmond but he dismissed me with a remark about not answering any more damn questions. I don't think he even looked at me. I want you to go out there and tell Desmond that you're going to be busy for a while, out of sight. Can you do that?"

"Yes. Wait here a minute." Charlotte went out to where her cousin was being besieged by ringing phones, harried agents, employees in a panic. She pulled him to one side and said that she was going to go back through employee records, to see if she could spot a likely suspect. She was also going to go through the books and financial accounts, and see if there was anything suspicious. She did not mention the threatening e-mails or Jonathan. "I need you here to hold the company together, Des."

He patted her hand and said from behind dark sunglasses, "Don't worry, Charlotte. I'll take care of things."

Back in her office she said to Jonathan, "Okay. We can slip out the back way, using the fire stairs. Hurry!"

6

They followed a covered pathway that led from the main building and then branched to other areas in the park. As Jonathan followed Charlotte, stepping around puddles and moving in and out of circles of light, he stopped suddenly and peered through the downpour. "What's that?" he said.

"A greenhouse. We grow rare herbs there."

He squinted at the ghostly structure glowing green in the rain, a faint light inside creating dark green silhouettes of twisted trunks and gigantic leaves. "I need to get inside," he said.

"The greenhouse? Why?"

"Can you get me in?"

"Yes." They hurried along the gravel path, making sure they weren't seen, and then Charlotte punched a six-digit code on the keypad, causing the door to swing open. Immediately they were hit by warm, moist air and thick, loamy smells. Jonathan delivered himself into the jungle of plants, flowers, and trees, inspecting each one, in particular their bases. He paused before a shrub heavy with pink, fragrant blossoms. "What's this?"

"Tree peony. We cultivate it for antiseptics, diuretics. Jonathan, what —"

He wiped his perspiring forehead. "Will anyone be working on it?"

"No. We don't harvest the roots until autumn."

To her surprise, he dropped his black bag, quickly knelt, and, unzipping a compartment, withdrew three metal objects wrapped in plastic. To her further shock, she saw Jonathan gently scoop earth away from the base of the trunk and bury the objects.

As she watched him replace the soil, making sure he left no traces, Charlotte felt her head fill with the warm scents of the greenhouse — summer smells — and she was reminded of the summers long ago when Jonathan would leave each June. She recalled how she would tell him all the things she was going to do while he was gone, chatting excitedly, making it sound somehow as though his absence was gong to free her to do the things she really wanted to do. Charlotte had not intended for it to come out that way, to sound as if she were relieved that her jailer was going away. But she was hurt. And she wanted to hide it. She would list Giants games and Renaissance fairs and horseback riding in Golden Gate Park to cover up her sadness at his leaving, to clothe her naked fear that this time he might not come back. Look how happy I will be, her tone and smile boasted, while her heart cried: Don't leave me, Johnny, I will be a shell without you.

And he would stand there with soulful brown eyes, his lips mute, his voice silent. But she would see the vulnerable throb at his pale, thin neck, and she would know that his emotions were struggling against his muteness. So she, chatty and giggly, and he, silent and bewildered, would say good-bye and wonder when things were ever going to be right.

As Jonathan scooped earth over the metal objects, patting the soil down, dried leaves broke away from the shrub and floated to the ground. They made Charlotte think of broken promises. Her father had died before she was born, her mother when she was a baby. And then she had watched her uncle Gideon die. "They all left me, Johnny," she had said when they were nineteen. "Promise me you'll never leave me."

He promised. And then he left her.

He stood up from the tree peony, brushing his hands. When he saw her questioning look, he said, "It's a gun, dismantled. I brought it, just in case. But it's illegal, so I can't be caught with it. Let's go."

Charlotte took him back to "old China," or so it seemed to Jonathan as he followed her through a heavy door and Charlotte flicked the wall switch, causing soft lights to illuminate a scene from another time, another world.

"This was my grandmother's project," she said in a subdued tone as he stepped away from the door and looked around this museum that stood at the edge of Harmony Park, a few hundred feet from the main offices.

"It used to be open to the public," Charlotte explained. "But after Grandmother's death I closed it."

The lighting was subtle. Glass cases housing precious memorabilia seemed to glow with an otherworldly incandescence, almost as if, Jonathan couldn't help thinking, these objects had been transported here by a time machine, and were held in fragile time fields, possibly to wink back into the past at any minute. "Incredible," he murmured.

"It was my grandmother's attempt to hold on to the past. I told her that Harmony House must move into the twenty-first century. We exchanged bitter words —" Charlotte looked briefly away. "I regret that now," she said softly. "But it doesn't alter the fact that Grandmother lost sight of the vision she once had for this company. I told her that I don't believe in clinging to the past — *any* past," she added, returning her direct gaze to Jonathan. "I'm sorry that, when she died, we were not on good terms."

Jonathan surveyed the remarkable collection that represented, literally, the history of Chinese medicine. He knew that much of the history of the Lee family was here as well, in these porcelain bowls, lacquer screens, bamboo baskets, jade figurines. He was not surprised to see a giant stone Chi-

nese temple dog and realized that it was familiar — he had
seen it before, many years ago. There was a story attached
to the statue, just as there were stories attached to every one
of these incredible treasures.

When he saw, on a nearby wall, a map of San Francisco's
Chinatown, he realized with a jolt that part of his *own* past
must also be represented here, for his path had linked up
with that of Charlotte Lee and her family when he was thirteen years old.

"The work station is there, in Grandmother's office," she
said, turning to lead the way. "She never used it, of course.
She never even learned how to type."

He followed her across the soft carpet, between rows of
glass cases filled with exotic mementos from a vanished
past. When he suddenly came upon a tall man outfitted in
handsome silk mandarin robes, Jonathan gasped, the mannequin was so lifelike. He didn't have to read the small
plaque to know that this would be a representation of Charlotte's great-great-grandfather, a wealthy Singaporean doctor. He recognized the emerald silk gown and black satin
jacket from a photograph Charlotte had shown him long
ago.

"I locked this place up the day after Grandmother died,"
Charlotte said when they reached the small office. She
flicked a wall switch. "Everything is just as she left it." She
turned to face him, to observe him with the clear green eyes
he remembered so well. "Grandmother was ninety when she
died, and still running the company. But most of her time
was spent here, tending her memories, nurturing the past."

The office, also softly illuminated by recessed lighting,
had the feel of not having known a human presence in a long
time. Charlotte's grandmother had died six months before
— Jonathan wondered if Charlotte had received the flowers
and sympathy card he had sent from South Africa.

She pointed to a small TV console in the corner. "I had

this installed," she said, turning it on, "so Grandmother did not have to walk around the grounds. She never used it. Even at ninety she still personally visited every department daily, as she had done for years. . . ." Charlotte hit some keys on the control panel and the main parking lot came on the screen, showing a commanding Valerius Knight standing dramatically in the rain, making a grave statement to the TV cameras. She clicked again and the bottling room came into view, the employees milling about in confusion as the machinery stood silent.

Going to her grandmother's desk, she drew the plastic cover off the monitor, booted the computer, and, a moment later, the screen came to life.

Jonathan set his black bag on the desk. It was a large nylon-and-leather case with many zippers and side compartments, and when he opened it, Charlotte saw a crammed but orderly collection of floppy disks, coaxial cables, alligator clips, coils of telephone wire, power cords, cassette tapes, patch cables, a computer headset, desktop microphone, microcassette recorder, antenna, rubber gloves, Baggies, tweezers.

He removed his jacket and draped it over the back of the chair. Charlotte watched him roll up his shirtsleeves in the crisp, decisive movements that had always made her feel that everything was going to be okay. Jonathan was taking control.

But in other ways he was a stranger. He was so perfectly groomed now, and fresh looking, not a man who had just stepped off a twelve-hour flight and then driven over a hundred miles through a storm. She wondered if the look was staged, if it was part of his putting clients at ease. He was, after all, in the technical security business. His appearance as a man of supreme capability would be vital.

The polish, Charlotte realized, was the end result of a metamorphosis she had seen begin ten years ago. She imagined him no longer eating an apple in his hand, but carefully slicing into it with a knife, European style. She suspected he no longer dipped french fries in gravy or made sloppy sandwiches of pork and beans and Wonder Bread. She had a suspicion about the cause of this change. It hadn't come from within. A man who hadn't discovered socks until he was in his twenties did not suddenly become this polished overnight. Jonathan had clearly been subjected to ten years of a strong external influence.

His wife, of course. Adele.

When he raised one side of the case, Charlotte saw a strip of plastic affixed along the top edge, bearing the words: *"Any sufficiently advanced technology is indistinguishable from magic."* — *Arthur C. Clarke.* She also saw a paperback novel tucked into one of the pockets. *I, Robot,* by Isaac Asimov. Charlotte found herself drawing comfort from these two things. Jonathan was still interested in science fiction, and still a reader, which meant that if at least *some* things about him hadn't changed, then maybe others hadn't also.

"I'll need to familiarize myself with your network," he said, "and determine the level of your security. If our friend is an intruder, he is familiar with Biotech's internal system."

"Intruder! You mean a hacker?"

He frowned and smiled at the same time. "Hackers are the good guys, remember? We were proud of our ability to go for forty hours without food or sleep in order to fine-tune a program no one was ever going to use to the point where it couldn't be fine-tuned any further. The media stole that title from us and gave it to the bad guys."

How could she have forgotten? That rainy night in Boston, seventeen years ago, when a bearded, ragtag, antiestablishment Johnny had declared with passion, "I'm going to MIT, Charlie. The best hackers on the planet. . . ."

And all she could think was: Johnny was going to be in America!

"Would you log in for me please?"

She dragged herself back to the present. "I can give you my password."

He stepped away from the desk, holding the chair out for her. "I want you to do the log-in."

"But Jonathan, *you* can know my password."

"I don't want to know it." He turned his back to the computer. "Please, log in for me."

"All right," she said, and she sat down and quickly typed a word. "There," she said, standing up and relinquishing the chair.

"Thanks," he said, and sat down.

Charlotte marveled at how Jonathan was immediately transformed. She had witnessed this change in the past — as soon as his fingers met a keyboard, as soon as his eyes connected with a monitor, his brain shifted into high gear with an intensely focused single-mindedness, and nothing could distract him after that.

"What's the password to your e-mail account?" A moment later, a new message appeared on the screen. "Well, well," Jonathan said. "He's written to you again."

Charlotte peered over Jonathan's shoulder and read the newest message: *Getting to those three women was easy, Charlotte. I can get to you even easier.*

"He called you Charlotte," Jonathan said. "He seems to know you."

"Or wants me to think he does. If he called me by my *real* name, then I would be impressed."

Jonathan lifted coiled telephone wire, bridge clips, and wire cutters from his kit. "I'll need to get into your communications array as soon as you get me those blueprints." He spoke in the clipped tones she knew so well from long ago, a staccato speech that meant Jonathan was furious. But at what? At the situation? At her?

After all, she had walked out on him ten years ago. She

was the one who had left him sitting there with a stunned look on his face.

"Can you lay hand to those plans?" he said.

"Yes. They're in my office." She seized her leather bag and turned away. "I'll be quick."

Jonathan watched her as she went back through the museum, and when she suddenly stopped at one of the displays, he continued to watch her, unable to take his eyes away.

Charlotte was still beautiful after all these years, with the straight black hair of her Singaporean ancestresses and lively green eyes of her American grandfather. But the blunt-cut bangs he remembered were gone; now her hair was parted in the middle, swept back behind each ear and held in a gold clasp at the nape of her neck, to lie flat, like a wide black ribbon, between her shoulder blades. She was taller than her Chinese relatives, but she had inherited the wand-like body of her grandmother, a figure more suited, Jonathan had once remarked, to a silk *cheongsam* than blue jeans.

He was suddenly remembering the day they met, a meeting that shimmered in his memory like one of the softly spotlighted mementos in the glass cases. It had taken place in the Pacific Heights district of San Francisco, twenty-six years ago. Jonathan had passed the house with the moon gate and two stone temple dogs many times, a house shrouded in mystery, until one day he had seen a face at the window, steadily watching him. She wasn't always there after that, only sporadically, watching him as he walked past on his way to the Academy, leaving him with an impression of solemn eyes over high cheekbones.

It was on the day he couldn't carry his sadness any longer, when it had become heavier than his knapsack, that he had sat down in the nearby park, put his head on his knees, and wept his heart out. He had sensed her before hearing or seeing her, her shadow falling over him like a caress. He still remembered the look in her green eyes as she had stood there gazing down at him. She asked, What's wrong? even though she never actually said anything.

He ran his sleeve under his nose and she sat next to him, folding her arms into her lap like graceful wings. "I miss my mam," he blurted. "I try not to cry, but I canna help it."

Almond-shaped eyelids slipped down over the jade-green irises. She was silent for a moment, then she was looking at him again. "My mother is dead, too," she said.

That had startled him. He had said nothing about his mother being dead. But it was true, she had died the year before, and his father had sent for him, to make him live here in this strange country. "I'm from Scotland," he said, not really knowing why he said it. But he had felt instantly better, as if her knowing this fact eased his pain.

"Would you like some lemonade?" she asked, rising.

That was when he had entered the remarkable house filled with exotic treasures and a strange, palpable silence.

"I'm Charlotte," she had said when they reached a vast living room with windows filled with a view of the Golden Gate Bridge.

"Jonathan," he had said. Correcting it to "Johnny."

"I like your accent." And she had smiled.

He watched her now in her grandmother's museum, this monument to the contention between grandmother and granddaughter for as far back as he could remember, and she did a startling thing: Charlotte unlatched the back of one of the glass cases, and reached in to bring something out.

Leaving the computer, he went to join her, to see what had caught her interest, and he saw in her palms two beautifully embroidered silk slippers.

"These were my great-grandmother's," Charlotte said in an awe-filled tone.

"When she was a little girl?"

"When she was a grown woman." The slippers were no more than three inches long.

Replacing them in the case, Charlotte reached into the leather tote slung over her shoulder, and when Jonathan saw what she brought out, he said, "I remember those. That's a puzzle box."

"It was my mother's. Mr. Sung gave it to me a few minutes ago. He said it might help me in my time of need." She held it to Jonathan's ear. "Listen. There's something inside. This box was always empty. Someone has put something in it."

"Can you open it?"

"It's been a long time. . . ." Charlotte turned the box around and around in her hands, gently pushing here, pulling there, pressing certain points to find the starting place. "I remember the first puzzle box my grandmother ever gave me," she said quietly as she found the first panel and slid it sideways. "Grandmother explained that a puzzle box is an illusion. They appear to be seamless, with no lid, no way inside. She showed me how to open it, the patience that was required, the way to feel the wood, to test one panel and then another, and never to assume that because this slides this way, this other panel will be freed. She showed me how the whole depended upon the precise movements of its parts, that each panel depended upon the movement of the one before it. It took me a week to open that first box, and I think it was a simple one, only twelve moves. But when I looked inside, I was disappointed because it was empty. I thought I should receive a reward for so cleverly figuring it out."

She slid back another panel on the small box, and then felt about for the next. "Grandmother said that the pleasure is in the seeking of the treasure, not the obtaining. She kept doing it to me, year after year, empty boxes."

Jonathan listened as he watched Charlotte's slender fingers gently work the box, finding the movable parts, testing them, sliding them back and forth like a cautious explorer in a treacherous maze. He remembered the first time she had shown him how to open a puzzle box, they had stood like this, their heads together, Jonathan fighting an overwhelming impulse to kiss her.

"Grandmother was trying to teach me the joy of opening the box. She didn't understand that without the hope of reward, there would be no effort. Finally, one Christmas, I guess I was seventeen or eighteen, I looked at the newest box and didn't bother opening it. Grandmother was very hurt. She had always delighted in watching me eagerly open each box. And now I wouldn't play her game."

Charlotte's fingertips skated over the smooth marquetry, finding the hidden seams, exposing the optical illusion, moving panels this way and that, up and down. "The next year she gave me a box and said, 'Something inside.' So I opened it and found a pearl ring. But it wasn't the same anymore."

The last panel gave way and the lid slid all the way open to reveal the interior of the box. It contained a small piece of paper.

"There's something written on it," Jonathan said. "Chinese characters. Can you read them?"

Charlotte's grandmother had taught her to read and write Chinese, patiently demonstrating the brush strokes, showing her how to write the characters for "sun" and "moon," and demonstrating how writing them together became the word "tomorrow."

"It's been a while," she said as she held the scrap of paper to the light. "My Chinese is rusty."

"I remember the peculiar conversations you and your grandmother used to have."

She raised her head. "Peculiar? How?"

"She would speak to you in Chinese and you would answer in English."

Charlotte frowned.

"You don't remember that?"

"I wasn't aware of it."

"I'll tell you, it sounded very odd to the observer!"

Did we do that? Charlotte wondered as she studied the mysterious Chinese characters on the scrap of paper. Did Grandmother and I speak two different languages? Or do all grandmothers and granddaughters, even if they're both speaking English?

"This character," she said, pointing it out to Jonathan, "shows a snake in a house: *danger*. And this one is two faces: *deception*."

"Mr. Sung is warning you that someone within the company is betraying you."

"Or someone within my *house*," she said, her gaze sweeping over the glass cases that contained the history of her family.

"Seems a strange way to give you advice, putting a hidden message in a puzzle box. Why not just say, 'Charlotte, I think we have a traitor in our midst'?"

"Chinese way," she murmured.

Jonathan smiled. He used to be very familiar with Chinese ways.

"There is a lot I don't know about my family," she said, her eyes gliding over the display cases, a small furrow between her brows. "We were whisperers, keepers of secrets. Grandmother most of all. And yet she created this museum, this monument to closets filled with skeletons. This place is filled with the past, it's filled with clues. I wonder . . ."

"You wonder what?"

"The person who tampered with the products and who sent those e-mails. Maybe it isn't industrial sabotage. Maybe the intruder isn't a stranger. He might be someone close to me, someone with a personal grudge against me or my family — an old score to settle."

Jonathan glanced around at the glass cases. "I'm in here, too, you know," he said softly.

"Yes. I know."

Their eyes held for a moment. Then she said, "I'm going to look around in here. I told Desmond that I would be going through employee records and financial accounts. But I didn't tell him *where* I would be. We can monitor the campus from Grandmother's office and keep tabs on everyone's whereabouts. If anyone should come looking for me, I can suddenly appear."

Charlotte reached back into the glass case and brought out the three-inch slippers again. "You know," she murmured, regarding the tiny shoes with exquisite gold-and-silver embroidery that had hidden mutilation and pain. "I used to know all the stories. Grandmother told them to me. But I stopped listening. And then I took a broom and swept those old stories out of my head. But you know?" She lifted her green eyes to Jonathan. "Looking at these slippers, I can almost hear Grandmother again, telling me about her mother, Mei-ling, who wore these. Do we really hear our grandmother's voices, Johnny? Or do we just want to so badly that they seem real?"

He put his hand on her arm, a firm touch as if to create a bridge from him to her. But as he was about to speak, a sound suddenly tore the silence.

"What's that?" Charlotte said.

"It's an alert on the computer. Someone is hailing."

They hurried back into the office, where they saw an icon flashing on the screen.

"Someone knows we're here?"

Jonathan shook his head. "I rerouted incoming transmissions from your office computer to this one. Sort of like call-

forwarding." He double-clicked on the icon and a picture
filled the screen. "It's a video transmission."

Charlotte sucked in her breath. "Jonathan, that's my study
at home!"

He gave her a puzzled look. "Are you sure?"

"Of course I'm sure! Those sliding glass doors lead to my
rock garden."

"Where is this being shot from?"

"It would be my desk. My computer."

"Do you have a camcorder hooked up?"

"No. I don't even own one." Her eyes widened. "That's
Yolanda, my housekeeper!" The Hispanic woman came into
view, smiling and appearing to be saying something to a
second party, who was off screen. "Turn up the volume,"
Charlotte said.

"It's turned up. The video is being transmitted without
sound."

"I don't understand. Why is someone taking Yolanda's
picture? And why are they in my study?"

"Your housekeeper seems to know the person. She's acting as though it is natural for whoever it is to be there."

"And filming her?"

"She doesn't seem to be aware of the camera. I don't
think she knows she's being filmed. Hello, what's this?"

They saw Yolanda extend her arm beyond view, as if she
were reaching for something, and when her hand came back
into view, they saw that she held a cup. She was smiling and
nodding, and then lifting the cup to her lips.

"Oh, Jesus," Jonathan said.

"What? What is it?" Charlotte watched her housekeeper
take a few sips, talking without sound, seeming to be very
relaxed with the person off-screen. Yolanda appeared to like
the beverage, as her smile widened and she drank some
more.

"Oh my God," Charlotte whispered, suddenly realizing

what they were watching. "Oh my God!" She reached for the phone and quickly dialed her home number.

The line was busy.

She tried her back line, one that only her closest friends knew about.

It, too, was busy.

Yolanda's smile suddenly vanished. She put her hand to her forehead and seemed suddenly not to feel well. The cup fell from her hand.

"Oh God, no!" Charlotte cried. "He's poisoning her! He's murdering Yolanda!"

"Let's go," Jonathan said as he grabbed his jacket. "I'll drive."

"No," she said as she punched in three numbers: 911. "Wait," she said into the phone. "Don't put me on hold —" She whispered an oath as she heard silence at the other end. Then she stared in horror at the screen. Yolanda was turning away from the camera, clearly in distress. She staggered to the door, slumped against it, and sank to the floor, out of view.

"Yes!" Charlotte shouted into the phone. "A woman is being poisoned. Send paramedics. Hurry!" She gave them her address and then disconnected. "I'm going alone, Jonathan," she said as she snatched up her leather tote.

"Charlotte —"

"Jonathan, I need you here. I need you to find the son of a bitch who's doing this."

Before he could protest, she was gone. As she ran through the museum, her pulse pounded in her ears — *Please God, let me reach Yolanda in time* — she barely missed the glass case where the three-inch slippers lay. . . .

7

Even before she felt the pain, the little girl began to scream.

With her arms pinned down by her aunties, the six-year-old was forced to sit on the stool, her little legs stretched forward so that her bare feet were propped on Mei-ling's knees. It was when she saw the stiff bandages that she began to scream, but when the true pain came — when Mei-ling took hold of the girl's right foot and swiftly bent the four toes down and back, pressing them toward the arch, the toes breaking with a muted crack — the child stretched her mouth open wide, but no sound came out.

Stiff and trembling, she was held suspended over the stool by aunties who told her how brave she was, how beautiful she was going to be, and all the while Mei-ling's swift fingers applied the bandage tightly, securing the broken toes in their new crushed position, leaving the big toe free.

Everyone agreed that the child was lucky to have Mei-ling doing the binding. Of course, foot binding was never painless, since it involved crushing the bones, but Mei-ling had special herbal pain relievers, and elixirs to calm the terrified spirit. And there was a way about her — just her presence could be calming.

Mei-ling was in fact a legend on the island, a book-learned young woman who touched diseased bodies; yet her feet were bound, which meant she was high-born.

The child emitted unearthly wails and the candles burning at the altar of Kwan Yin flickered, as if to show the goddess's sympathy. Outside, beyond the high courtyard wall, Singaporeans were celebrating a noisy festival in honor of the dead.

Mei-ling worked with a divided mind, half on the foot binding, the other on an omen that had visited her a few days ago and how the fortune-teller had interpreted it. "Ghost festival is coming," the old woman had said. "It brings more than spirits of the dead into the life of Lee Mei-ling. It brings a foreign devil."

A man, the fortune-teller had gone on to say, from across the ocean, fair-haired and green-eyed.

"Is he British, venerable one?" Mei-ling had inquired. Like the rest of her family, who were aristocratic Chinese tracing their line back to the creation of the world, her feelings for the English were a mixture of tolerance, curiosity, and impatience.

But the fortune-teller had said, "American."

And so the ghost festival was now upon them, with the streets of Singapore alive with feasts, puppet shows, and Chinese operas for the entertainment of the dead. It was the seventh lunar month, when tradition held that the Gates of Hell were open to allow the souls of the departed to visit their descendants. Families held great banquets in their homes, honoring the dead who visited them, but the souls of those without descendants wandered the streets, hungry and envious, and so they were appeased with food and entertainment. Candles and incense burned throughout the city, the rich scents drifting over the high garden wall and settling down upon Mei-ling and the women gathered there.

When she was done with the binding of both feet, the little girl was in shock, silent and quivering, so Mei-ling showed the child her own bound feet, tiny and precious, in three-inch-long embroidered slippers.

After the family claimed their daughter, carrying her back into the house to exclaim over her new feet, Mei-ling slowly made her way through the crowded streets where jugglers entertained the dead and the living, and people feasted, sharing their bounty with wandering ghosts. Her faithful servant at her side, to carry the box of medicines and instruments that she never traveled without, Mei-ling kept thinking of what the fortune-teller had said about the American stranger who was coming into her life. But when? Where? How would she know him? And was it for a good purpose or bad? Was the omen meant to warn her *away* from him or to encourage her to go *to* him?

Mei-ling hadn't told anyone, and it had been a difficult secret to keep, for she lived in a very populous household. Situated in Singapore's wealthy district, the magnificent house on Peacock Lane was home not only to Mei-ling and her widowed father, but to numerous female relatives who otherwise had nowhere to live — widows and maiden aunts and young nieces and cousins, plus Golden Elegance and Summer Dawn, the wives of Mei-ling's two brothers, First Young Master and Second Young Master, as well as Moon Orchid and Moon Cassia, the babies born to her father's Third Wife, who had died in childbirth. A house filled with women, but it was Mei-ling, whose name meant Beautiful Intelligence, who commanded her father's heart. So un-Chinese, the older women would say, especially those with grown, unmarried sons, to dote on a daughter so, to allow her such freedoms, to let her live to be twenty years old and still unmarried! But Mei-ling's father turned a deaf ear to their complaints and criticisms and prided himself that he had taught his eldest daughter well, for she knew the art of writing and the skill of medicine as well as himself or any respected doctor.

Of course, she could only attend to women — mostly Mei-ling performed foot binding, as she was known to have the most gentle touch in all of Singapore, and attended childbirth, for women said she had good luck and knew how to coax a baby painlessly from the womb.

"Help! Help!"

Mei-ling stopped on the crowded street. "What was that?" she said to her servant.

They listened to the music and laughter and fireworks exploding against the night sky. "What is it, *Sheo-jay?*" the older woman asked, using the polite address of "Young Mistress."

"Didn't you hear —"

"Help!"

"Someone is in distress!" Mei-ling looked up and down the street, filled with Chinese and Malaysians in their holiday clothes. She saw no foreigners, and yet the cry had been in English.

"Oh God —"

"There!" she said, pointing down a narrow alley. "A man is in trouble!"

"But *Sheo-jay —*"

"Hurry!"

Mei-ling moved down the alley as fast as her tiny feet and tiny steps could take her. The servant, being older and stouter, and bearing the heavy ebony medicine box, puffed behind. They reached the rear alley behind a string of shops and saw a group of thugs kicking a fallen man.

"*Aii*," cried Mei-ling's servant. "Turn back, *Sheo-jay!* This is bad luck! The Night of Ghosts —"

But Mei-ling pressed forward, calling out and waving her arms. The thugs ignored her at first, but when she passed into the light of swinging lanterns and they saw her silk dress and tiny feet, her hair dressed in the combs and ornaments of a rich man's woman, they turned and fled, padding off down the alley on bare feet.

Mei-ling let them go. Quickly kneeling at the man's side, she saw that he was unconscious and moaning, blood staining his white jacket, white shirt, and trousers.

"A foreign devil, *Sheo-jay!*" the servant said, quickly tracing a sign of protection in the air. "Bad luck!"

But Mei-ling laid her hand on his bloody forehead. He had blond hair. And when she lifted one of his eyelids, she found a green iris underneath.

The American who was prophesied.

"Don't touch!" her servant cried. "Bad luck!"

But Mei-ling was calm, more fascinated than afraid. "He is hurt," she said. "We must help him."

"I'll fetch police."

But Mei-ling stayed the servant, saying, "This man was prophesied in a dream. I was brought to him for a reason."

"To call police!"

Mei-ling straightened and surveyed the alley. There were few people about; the only life came from shadows that danced over the cobblestones as paper lanterns swung in the night breeze. "Over there," she said, pointing to the silk shop of Madam Wah. "Go there. Ask Madam Wah to send her strongest son."

The servant obeyed for fear of disrespecting a prophecy sent by the gods, but she went reluctantly, glancing back over her shoulder to see her mistress bend again over the fallen stranger.

Madam Wah sent her biggest son to bring the unconscious stranger back to her shop, and then had him take the man up to a small room that overlooked the alley. She did it not for the foreigner but for Mei-ling, who had given her a secret herb tonic last winter, when her monthly cycle had ceased for two months after the visit of a special houseguest. Madam Wah's husband had been away; she could not have deceived him into believing the child was his. Mei-ling's tonic had restored the moon's phases to Madam Wah's body, and for that she would be forever grateful.

"Now we call the police?" the old servant said after the foreigner had been laid on a bed and they were alone with him.

"Hush," said Mei-ling as she quickly opened her medicine box. "You would defy a prophecy of the gods?"

"But perhaps that is what is meant — that you are to call the police."

But Mei-ling shook her head as she began to clean his wounds. Any passerby could have called the police. Her path had been made to cross this stranger's for another, more important, purpose. When he wakens, she thought, then I will know.

When Mei-ling started delicately to unbutton his shirt, the old servant sat on the floor and began to wail. To see her high-born mistress debase herself so, to see an aristocratic daughter of Singapore dishonor her modesty by looking at a man's body, and then to touch it!

Mei-ling stared at the pale, bruised flesh. "What they did to him," she whispered in outrage. "How they hurt him." Tears fell from her eyes onto his bare chest.

"Perhaps he deserved it!" the old servant wailed. "Perhaps he is a bad man, *Sheo-jay!* A thief, an adulterer, or worse!"

But Mei-ling stroked the blond hair back from his forehead, touched each of his closed eyes, and she knew he was not a bad man.

She had to work quickly. She was expected home soon and the family would be wondering where she was. First she washed his wounds with a soothing antiseptic made of the roots of white peony and sprinkled them with powdered cuttlefish bone to stop the bleeding, then bound them with bandages. She felt his pulses the way her father had trained her, each of twelve pulse points reflecting the condition of his twelve vital organs, her sensitive fingertips on the stranger's wrist, neck, and feet, detecting the struggle between his failing *yin* and his frightened *yang*. She lifted his eyelids and observed his pupils, she laid her hands on his bare skin and calculated the degree of emptiness, the lack of heat, the places where his spirit was trembling.

Madam Wah brought up a steaming bowl of pine seed broth for the injured stranger, and for Mei-ling and her servant, curried rice with spicy shrimp, almond cakes, and green tea. Madam Wah did not ask questions as she set out the bowls and lit a small brazier to keep the tea warm. If it had not been for Mei-ling's safflower menstrual restorative, Madam Wah would have died at the hands of her husband. Instead, he gave her gifts of pearls and perfumes for her faithfulness.

That the stranger did not wake up worried Mei-ling. She wondered if the wound to his temple had caused an irreparable imbalance of the winds that blew through his head. She laid her hands along his ribs, down his waist, feeling for internal imbalance. She studied his handsome face. She applied drops of clove oil to his lips. Then she pinched his cheeks to snap his spirit back into his body, and gently slapped his arms to wake up sleeping strength.

Finally, she could delay no longer; she had to leave. "You will stay with him," she said to her old servant, who had calmed considerably after a feast of shrimp and rice, none of which her young mistress had touched. "Tomorrow I will bring the fortune-teller and she will tell me what I must do."

It was at that moment, as the old woman was about to protest, that the stranger awoke, eyelids fluttering up, pupils trying to focus. He blinked at Mei-ling. "Am I . . ." he began, "am I dead?"

Because Mei-ling's father moved between two worlds, Chinese and British, priding himself on being modern and having cultivated friendships and business relationships with Englishmen, the house on Peacock Lane frequently offered hospitality to people from the West. Mei-ling had learned English from her father, for those occasions when she poured tea for important visitors. But it was not the best

English, and she had to digest the stranger's question before she could form a reply.

"You are safe," she said, and instantly his eyes focused on her face.

"Are you an angel?"

She smiled. "I am Mei-ling. My servant and I brought you to this house. What is your name? And whom should we summon to take you home?"

His eyebrows came together in a frown. "I . . . I don't know," he said. "I haven't the faintest idea who I am."

"*Aii*," cried the old servant. "A ghost has stolen his memories and now inhabits his body!"

"Be quiet," Mei-ling commanded in Chinese. "Do not upset him." She laid her hand on his cheek and bent close to peer into his eyes.

The old woman trembled with fear as she watched her young mistress relinquish her soul to the foreign devil — for he gazed back at Mei-ling with such intensity that the old servant knew he was stealing her spirit. He whispered words —"You are so beautiful" — and she heard a familiar, ageless tone in his voice. Disaster had struck on this ominous night — she knew by the way her young mistress looked at the stranger. She had seen that look many times in her years, on the faces of sisters and daughters, and on her own face once, long ago. It was a timeless and universal look.

Mei-ling had fallen in love.

Mei-ling returned the next day with the fortune-teller, who studied the stranger's palms while he slept. Then she cracked open an egg, and when she saw the double yolk, she exclaimed that this was bad luck. "He is two men, *Sheo-jay*. One will love you, one will deceive you."

Then I will love the one who will love me, Mei-ling decided. And I will not look for the one who will deceive me.

*   *   *

She went every day to the secret room above Madam Wah's
silk shop, taking warm bowls of health-giving food that she
prepared herself: fennel beef for balancing the *chi* and reducing cold excess, truffle rice to reduce *yang* excess, carp
soup to nourish the blood. She washed his wounds, applied
ointments, and changed the bandages. She applied soothing
compresses to his bruised flesh to appease the angry blood
beneath. She had him drink restorative tonics and wines, all
made from the roots of ginseng and yam and licorice, which
Mei-ling had harvested herself in the private garden of the
family home.

She bathed him in bed, preserving his modesty under a
sheet, and supported him around the shoulders when he was
too weak to sit up and eat. She burnt incense to Kwan Yin
and purified the air with special prayers. Every day she
asked him his name. And every day he said he did not know.

She asked about the ring on his right hand. Heavy and
gold, the design appeared to be two English letters intertwined. "*RB*," he murmured, frowning at the ring. "I don't
know what they mean."

The old servant continued to watch and tremble with fear,
for her young mistress was performing forbidden things —
touching a man's nakedness, a man who was not a relative,
not even Chinese! If Mei-ling's family were to find out, they
would put her, and the old servant, to death. But there was
nothing she could do to prevent this calamity. Her young
mistress was under an enchantment.

When Mei-ling sent the stranger's clothes away to be
cleaned, she first went through the pockets, and although
she found no papers, no form of identification, there was an
enormous amount of cash in American dollars and British
pounds. "I don't know where that money came from," he
said. When Mei-ling asked if she should send for the American authorities, he said, "What if I am a criminal?"

And so they kept him a secret above Madam Wah's silk shop, waiting for his memory to return.

Finally, one morning Mei-ling and the old servant arrived to find the man already sitting up in bed, looking stronger, and smiling. While the old servant squatted in the corner, praying to her ancestors, Mei-ling opened wide the shutters to admit the balmy sunshine, then she helped the stranger to bathe and shave, and then she set out his breakfast, placing the tray in his lap.

The entire time, from the minute she had walked through the door, he had not once removed his eyes from her face.

Now he looked down at the food and frowned. "Is this what I have been eating?"

She picked up chopsticks and pointed to each dish: "Wonton soup, sesame chicken, stir-fry noodles, fresh pineapple."

"Quite a variety," he murmured with a dubious look on his face.

"Opposites that balance the *chi*."

He gave her a questioning look.

"This dish is hot," she said with a smile. "This is cold. This one smooth, this crispy. These produce harmony."

He laughed and his green eyes danced. "If it's all the same with you, I sure could go for some old-fashioned bacon and eggs and black coffee."

She puzzled over his words. She had never heard the American vernacular before. "Eat this now and tomorrow I will bring eggs."

As he picked up a crunchy piece of chicken with his fingers, Mei-ling gently took his hand and placed the chopsticks in it. For a moment he looked down at her hand cradling his, then he lifted his eyes and a silent communication passed between them. "I don't know how to use these," he said softly. "I don't suppose you could wrangle me a knife and fork?"

"Tomorrow knife and fork," she said, looking down at their two hands — hers small and pale, his large and sun-browned. "And black coffee," she added with a shy smile.

His own smile faded then as he gazed at her. Propped against the pillows, the sheet drawn to his waist, leaving his chest bare, he studied the young Chinese woman who sat on the edge of his bed. "You saved my life," he said. "Why?"

"Should I have let you die?"

He glanced over at the medicine box — a black lacquer case painted with red-and-gold dragons, its many drawers and compartments open to reveal small bags of herbs, vials of liquid, packets tied with string. "Are you a nurse of some kind?"

"My father taught me the ancient healing arts," she said modestly.

"Pretty powerful art," he said with a wry smile. "The last thing I remember, as I was on the ground and those thugs were kicking me, was that I *knew* I was about to die."

She watched him with solemn eyes. When he reached for her hand, she did not pull away. "You are so very beautiful," he said.

Mei-ling and her servant brought bacon and eggs the next day, cooked the way the chef at Raffles Hotel had described to her, and the stranger was so thrilled to see a familiar breakfast that he devoured it all — fried eggs, strips of bacon, hash brown potatoes, buttered toast and hot coffee — without saying a word. When Mei-ling saw the empty plates, she smiled. They were words enough.

"How long have I been here?" he asked as he shaved himself with the soap and razor she had brought.

"Three weeks."

He looked at the old servant woman, who sat in the corner with a worried expression. "I wish I could tell you what happened," he said to Mei-ling. "I wish I could tell you who I was and what I am doing in Singapore."

And yet he knew some things. He knew that he was American; he even knew that the president who currently ruled America was a man named Theodore Roosevelt. He told Mei-ling about a city named San Francisco, and that he thought he lived there because he could tell her about cable cars and flower vendors and his favorite restaurant on Powell Street. But of himself — who he was, who his family was, what he did for a living — he knew nothing.

"My memory has started to come back in dreams," he said. "But when I wake up, the dreams vanish."

Mei-ling understood the power of dreams, for it was a dream that had brought her path to his. "Perhaps if I were to be here while you slept. . . ," she said.

"It wouldn't be proper for you to spend the night with me."

"You would be sleeping and I would be watching. When you dream I will waken you and you will tell me what you saw in your dream."

"The truth is, Mei-ling, I would not be able to sleep with you here."

"I would be very quiet."

"That's not what I meant," he said softly.

The old servant, who did not hear the words they exchanged, knew nonetheless what was being said. She read their eyes, their bodies, the tones in their voices. And she knew that the catastrophe she had been dreading was nearly upon them.

Mei-ling chose the eighth night of the eighth month to stay with him, for eight was the luckiest number and a double eight was doubly lucky. For the first time, she left her father's house without the company of the old servant, stealing into the night while the household slept. "I go to help him bring back his wandering memory," she told the old woman. "I go to help him call back his spirit from the mists where it has gone."

But the old woman knew why Mei-ling was going, and all she could do was curl up on her sleeping mat, draw the blanket over her head, and wail in fear for the bad luck that was to come.

When Mei-ling and the American stranger made love for the first time, a gentle monsoon held Singapore in a sweet embrace.

Mei-ling knew that what she was doing was punishable by death. A woman was permitted only one man in her life — her husband, should she marry. An unmarried woman was allowed no man. On the other hand, a man was permitted by law and tradition as many wives and concubines as he could afford, for the rationale was that "a teapot must have many cups."

As she lay in the arms of her handsome American, whose vigor and virility had been restored to him through her gentle care, as she watched him sleep, marveling at this beautiful stranger whom the gods had brought into her life, Mei-ling asked herself, what was a death sentence where love was concerned? She would gladly die for one embrace with him.

She left him while he still slept, returning to her house before the servants wakened. And then she went again the next night, and the next. She helped him to take a few steps out of bed, slowly pacing the floor while she supported him, Mei-ling herself taking tiny painful steps on her deformed feet. She would report to him news from the outside world, and then he would remove the pins and combs from her long hair and tell her how much he loved her.

During the day, Mei-ling made discreet inquiries whether anyone was searching for a missing American. And during the night, as she lay at his side, she watched him toss and turn in dreams, speaking names and words that were foreign to her. When she woke him, he had no memory of the dreams. When she said, "Who is Fiona?" he said he had no idea.

"Perhaps I should take you to an English doctor," she said one afternoon as the sun slanted through the shutters. "You have been too long without memory. Your family will be worried. You need to find your home."

But he took her hands and said with passion, "You are my home, Mei-ling. You are my family. I want to marry you."

"But what if you are already married?"

"I don't *feel* married. Shouldn't I *feel* married?" Then he said, very tenderly, "I do feel married, Mei-ling. When I am with you."

She lowered her eyes. "I can never marry you. I must marry Chinese."

"We already are married, Mei-ling." He removed the gold ring from his finger, with the intertwined initials *RB*, and took her left hand in his. "With this ring I thee wed." And he slipped it onto her finger. "We are married, my dearest. In the eyes of God and in our hearts, we are husband and wife."

And then Mei-ling committed her fatal error.

Distinguished guests of her father came one evening to the house on Peacock Lane, Englishmen who exclaimed with delight over the gardens and courtyards and curved eaves of this very Chinese home. As Mei-ling served tea and almond cakes, she inquired of one of the guests, who was a doctor specializing in disorders of the mind, if it was possible to lose only part of one's memory while retaining the rest. And it was while the foreigner explained to Mei-ling how little was known about the human mind that her father observed the scene with a studied expression. It was not that Mei-ling should ask questions of a stranger — he had always encouraged her to seek knowledge — nor was it the nature of the questions, for he himself found the human mind a topic of great fascination. It was the way the Englishman looked at Mei-ling that opened her father's eyes to a truth he had been trying to avoid: that his beautiful daughter could no longer remain unmarried.

The aunties came from a great distance, the ancestral village in a South China province. And even while she smiled and served tea and pretended to be honored that they were examining her as a future bride, Mei-ling had already made the decision: for the love of her American, she would bring dishonor to her family.

She packed the next day with care, so that the servants would not get suspicious, taking only the barest necessities and personal items. And her medicine box. She told Golden Elegance, her sister-in-law, that she had been called to a house on the other side of the island, to deliver a child.

Then she left her father's house, where she had been born and had grown up; she turned her back on her life and her family and her culture, and hurried as quickly as she could to the silk shop near the harbor.

But when she arrived, her American was not there.

He had left a letter: "Dearest Mei-ling, Forgive me. I waited as long as I could. But now the sun is setting and you aren't here yet. I have remembered who I am and I must go. I have taken the money because I must buy a boat ticket with it. I am comforted to know that you will be living in your father's house until I return. I will come back, my dearest, and I will marry you. But there is something I must do first. . . ."

She ran to the window and looked out. Which way? Where was he in those crowded streets? She cried out, scattering doves that had gathered under the eaves. *Was this her punishment for dishonoring her family?*

She looked at the ring on her hand — not a real wedding

ring at all. And now she had no husband. She read again, through eyes filled with tears, his letter, and his signature at the bottom — Richard.

Then she placed her hand on her abdomen . . . for that is where *I* was, that is how *I* began, how I know this story, and how I am able to report the private thoughts and feelings of people and events that happened so long ago. It is because my mother told me these things. For the American named Richard not only left Mei-ling a letter and a ring, but he left behind another gift: myself, their daughter. I was born eight months later, and my mother named me Perfect Harmony, to ensure that I would have good health and a long life.

This is where the story of our family begins.

8

7:00 P.M. — Palm Springs, California

Charlotte saw the flashing red lights through the rain. The paramedics were already at her house. "Thank God," she said to Valerius Knight, who was driving. "Just pray they got here in time."

When she had run from the museum, after watching Yolanda drink from a cup and collapse, Charlotte had encountered Knight in the parking lot. Hearing that her house-keeper was in danger, he had signaled to two of his men and then offered to drive. Charlotte accepted. She was frantic, and she wasn't sure the Corvette could handle possible flooded intersections.

Knight now guided his car through the wrought-iron gates that protected her estate, and as they neared the end of the long drive, Charlotte jumped out of the vehicle before it

came to a complete stop. She flew up the flagstone steps and
through the front door. "Yolanda!" she called out. She heard
voices in the kitchen.

But when she reached them, she stopped short.

A very much alive although slightly bewildered Yolanda
was waving a wooden spoon at two equally perplexed paramedics, telling them they were in the wrong house.

"Yolanda!" Charlotte said. "Are you all right?"

"Miss Lee! Why are these men here?"

Charlotte put a hand on the housekeeper's arm, as if to sat-
isfy herself that this was no apparition. "Are you all right?"
she repeated.

"I am fine, *Señorita*. Why should I not be?"

Agent Knight came through, his mere presence making
the paramedics retreat a step. "Ma'am," he said to Yolanda,
"Miss Lee said you were in some kind of danger. That she
saw you drink something and then collapse to the floor."

Yolanda's eyes widened. Dark pupils flitted from the
agent's face to Charlotte's, back to the agent. "I do not understand, *Señor*. I drink nothing."

"But," Charlotte began. She *had* seen it, hadn't she?
"Yolanda, you were in my study. You were talking to someone. They handed you a cup and you drank from it."

The housekeeper presented a blank expression.

Charlotte left the kitchen and hurried down the hall to her
study, where she found everything as she had left it. There
was no video camera attached to her computer.

"Ms. Lee," Knight said as he joined her, "you said you
got a message on your computer that your housekeeper was
being poisoned. And then you said something about seeing
it happening. Exactly *how* did you see it?"

She bit back her response. She did not trust Knight; to tell
him the truth would reveal Jonathan's presence, and for now
secrecy was on their side. Besides, she wasn't exactly sure
now what she had seen.

Charlotte wrapped her arms around her waist, trying to get a grip on herself. She was shaking and her heart galloped. This was the second terrible shock she had received in less than two hours. Although she lived only a short distance from the facility, the drive had seemed endless; she had been so afraid she would find her housekeeper lying dead on the floor.

"I received an anonymous e-mail," she lied. "A letter saying that my housekeeper was being poisoned."

"But you said you *saw* it happening. You mean as in a psychic vision?" he pressed, a smile playing at the corners of his mouth. "You 'saw' it figuratively?"

Gathering her wits — she could not allow herself to fall apart — she met his challenging gaze with her own equally challenging one. She did not appreciate his patronizing tone, a man who obviously gave short shrift to such concepts as women's intuition. "The e-mail alarmed me. I believed my housekeeper was in danger. It appears I was the target of a prank."

"Well," he said in an avuncular manner, "I can understand why you'd be hysterical at a time like this, with your company under attack and all. I'll have my men take a look around the grounds, see if they find anything suspicious."

Like mice in the attic? she wanted to say. "Thank you," she said, and she headed back to the kitchen.

But as she followed the gallery where her art collection was displayed, Charlotte felt her body betray her again. Seeing Yolanda on the computer screen, and then the frantic drive through the rain —

Charlotte slowed her steps until she came to a standstill, putting her hand on the wall for support. As she peered ahead into the shadows and listened to the sounds all around her — voices in the kitchen, the storm rumbling in the distance, her prize grandfather clock chiming the hour — she realized that something was wrong with the house.

Built of adobe and stucco and *saltillo* tiles, the ten-thousand-square-foot villa overlooking Palm Springs had been designed and decorated in Southwest style, complete with weathered beams, hand-painted glazed tiles, and life-sized wooden sculptures of howling coyotes. Although there was not a hint of the Orient anywhere in the house, not a single Chinese object, Charlotte had nonetheless, before she moved in, hired a geomancer to go through the rooms and check for proper *feng shui* — the Chinese practice of adjusting one's surroundings so that they brought health, happiness, and prosperity.

The *feng shui* practitioner had found some horrendous flaws in Charlotte's interior design. Her bed, for example, had been placed directly under an exposed ceiling beam so that the beam ran horizontally across the bed, certain to cause aches and pains and "cut in half" the life of the sleeper; the bed was moved to a luckier position. The guest bathroom faced the front door, which meant that any good *chi* that entered the house would be flushed away; a small mirror at the base of the toilet to deflect the *chi* away from the drain corrected the error. And the pond in the garden curved away from the house, creating a bad luck "arrow" aimed right at the living room; the pond was altered to curve toward the building, thus protecting it.

And so for two years Charlotte's house had felt lucky and healthy. But now it was different. Tonight something was wrong. And she was certain it wasn't her imagination.

When she returned to the kitchen, she saw that the paramedics were gone and Yolanda was keeping a keen eye on Agent Knight, who stood on the steps of the open doorway, looking out at the rain.

"Yolanda," she said quietly. "I want you and Pedro to go and stay somewhere else tonight."

The housekeeper gave Charlotte a look as if she had just proposed something outrageous.

"There is danger here," Charlotte said. "Someone wanted me to think that they had hurt you, and maybe next time they really will. Go to the Camino Real Hotel. I'll call them and have them put the room on my —"

"Ah no, *Señorita!* Pedro and I, we cannot leave if there is trouble."

"I insist, Yolanda. Please. I'm having problems at the lab. I can't be worried about you as well. I need to know that you are safe."

Yolanda tipped her chin proudly and folded her arms across her ample bosom. But Charlotte saw the flicker of fear in her eyes. "We can go to my sister's," she said finally. "In the morning."

"No, I want you to go now. We'll lock up the house together. And then we'll lock the gates across the driveway. Hurry, Yolanda. We haven't much time."

Charlotte saw one of the other agents come up to Knight and hand him something, talking in a low voice. Then Knight came into the kitchen. "Ms. Lee," he said, holding up an object in his hands, "why didn't you tell me about the accident with your garage door? I am told it did considerable damage to your utility vehicle."

"Why should I have told you?"

"Do you have any idea what made the door fall like that?"

"No. It isn't supposed to be able to. We have a lot of wild animals in this area — coyotes and occasionally mountain lions. I once accidentally killed a bobcat when I closed my garage door. So I had a safeguard put in."

"This?"

She looked at the green plastic case in his hand and recognized it. "Yes. It emits a red beam a few inches off the ground. If the door is coming down and something breaks the beam, such as a car or an animal, or a person, the door will stop. But it works when the door is *moving*, Agent

Knight. It doesn't *make* the door move. And the door was not moving. It fell."

"When did it fall?"

She thought for a moment. It was when the Suburban had started to roll forward.

"Ms. Lee, your vehicle cut the beam, causing the door to fall."

"But how is that possible?"

"Because this safeguard was reprogrammed."

"What? Are you sure?"

He pointed to the short copper wires sheathed in red and green insulation. "These have been switched. And you can see by these scratches here on the patch screws that they were switched recently."

She stared at the box and then at the FDA agent.

"That's right," he said, nodding gravely. "That garage door didn't come down by accident. It happened on purpose."

9

"I'm sorry, Charlotte," Jonathan said once she was back in her grandmother's office, the outside door to the museum securely locked. "By the time I realized this was a video and not a live transmission, it was too late to stop you."

"Knight looked at me as if I were a crazy fool," she said, throwing down her tote bag and shedding the raincoat she had brought from home.

"Come and look. I recorded it."

Charlotte studied the scene on the monitor as Jonathan played it back. "That's my housekeeper all right, and that is definitely my office. But Jonathan, I questioned Yolanda about it. She said she couldn't remember accepting a drink from anyone, and she certainly would remember if she had passed out."

"Maybe it happened a while ago and she doesn't remember."

"You're saying someone sneaked into my house, gave Yolanda something to drink, and filmed it?"

"They didn't necessarily have to sneak in. Maybe they did it while you were there. Have you had any parties in the last few months?"

She tugged at her right earlobe. "There was *one* gathering. It wasn't exactly a party. After Grandmother died, Naomi — she's my best friend — said I wasn't grieving properly so she insisted I sit *shivah*."

"Shivah?"

"It's like a wake, only Jewish."

"And there was food? Beverages? A large crowd?"

"Grandmother had many friends. And, yes, there was plenty to eat and drink. So you say this could have been done at that time?"

"It fits. Especially judging by your housekeeper's actions in the video. She definitely knew who the person was. And she doesn't seem to find it odd that they are in your study."

"Then why doesn't she remember passing out?"

"Watch this." He ran the playback frame by frame until it was like watching a series of snapshots. "See here? Where Yolanda turns away?"

Charlotte gasped. "The falling woman isn't Yolanda!"

"Correct. This segment was filmed elsewhere and added on. It's a good piece of editing but doesn't stand up to very close scrutiny."

Charlotte straightened. "What's the purpose of this? To scare me?"

"Possibly. Or to discredit you in the eyes of Agent Knight. Make you look like a hysterical woman."

"He did use that word. God, what a nightmare!" She spun away, paused, then turned back. "Something else happened."

He looked up at her.

"Agent Knight said my garage door had been tampered with."

"What!"

She explained about the reprogramming, her voice shaking as she added, "If I had been in the Corvette, I might have been killed. So if it was done on purpose — Knight positively grilled me on the way back! He asked me who might have rewired the garage door. Did I have enemies? Why did I think Yolanda was being poisoned?"

"What did you say?"

"I said I don't know. Because I *don't* know!"

"We know one thing," he said grimly. "We know this isn't random — the three women who died, the Yolanda video, the garage door. And we know these aren't impulsive acts. This appears to have been months in the planning. And there is no doubt in my mind, Charlotte, that you are the target."

"But why?" she cried. "What does this maniac want from me? It certainly can't be that ridiculous press announcement I'm supposed to make."

Jonathan thoughtfully shook his head. "I agree. He wants something else from you. This threat, this deadline, is simply a weapon to fray your nerves, to render you vulnerable and weak when he makes his final move."

"And the garage door and this video?"

"To demonstrate that he can get to you, and those close to you, anytime he wants."

Jonathan's words hung in the air like a dark cloud as they both considered this new turn of events. The risk factor had gone up many notches; the stakes were now much higher.

He abruptly stood up from the desk, reaching for his jacket.

"Where are you going?"

"To retrieve my gun. I want you to have it."

"No."

"Damn it, Charlotte —"

"Jonathan, you know how I feel about guns."

"Then I want you to get away from here, somewhere safe."

"You can't be serious. I can't leave."

"It's for your own safety." He slipped his arm in a sleeve. "I can continue to work here. As long as no one finds me, I can catch this bastard in a matter of —"

"I'm not leaving. If anything, I'm going to fight back."

He let the jacket hang from one arm as he regarded her. Charlotte stood pale-faced and with trembling hands, but her chin was firm and her eyes clear. She was scared but not about to lose control. And she wanted to attack, *now*, when she was vulnerable.

A special woman.

He draped his jacket back over the chair. "All right. For now. I don't like it but I can't physically remove you. By the way," he said, suddenly remembering, "a message came on this phone while you were gone. I didn't pick up. I didn't think I should."

Charlotte pressed the rewind button on the answering machine. "Before I locked up my house, I put my private phone on call-forwarding. I had the calls directed to this phone because I didn't want to risk my secretary or any of the others picking up."

As the message began to play, Naomi's lilting voice brought light into the room. "Char, I got your message. We have *got* to get together. Listen to me, you are in *personal* danger. I read your Tarot — read it three times to be sure — and it's as plain as vanilla ice cream. The Fool card is you,

Char, the young man who represents a quest, naïveté, and unawareness. But then the Magician appears. He represents manipulation and trickery. Now, *he's* the one tampering with the medicines. But don't be fooled. He could be a woman."

Charlotte exchanged a glance with Jonathan.

"But here's something that mystifies me," Naomi continued. "The Lovers card keeps turning up, joining all your life-force aspects with an overwhelming connection with the Divine and, get this, with erotic love! You are in danger from all sides! God," she groaned, "and I managed to catch part of the evening news. They showed picketers outside Harmony Biotech. You're right, they've plastered that picture to their signs. It's come back to plague us, Char. Listen, I'm still on campus, stuck for now. As soon as I can, I'll come to your office. I'll swing by home first and grab my yarrow stalks. Keep the faith, girlfriend. Everything will be all right."

Jonathan gave Charlotte a questioning look. "Yarrow stalks?"

"Her I Ching sticks. They give warnings and advice." When Jonathan's look turned skeptical, she said, "Naomi's a psychic. We met during the Chalk Hill incident, eight years ago." She watched him and gathered by his silence that he was familiar with the grisly episode. "She and I were handcuffed together. That's when our friendship began."

"She sounds like an interesting person."

"Naomi is a Jewish New Ager, the only one I know. She is a genuine sensitive. And a lifesaver. Naomi has kept me sane more times than I can count. She used to force me to take a rest when I worked eighty-hour weeks in the lab. She once even kidnapped me. I went to her house for dinner and fell asleep. When I woke up, we were in a cabin at Big Bear, surrounded by snow. She had put something in my wine and then dragged me to her car. We spent four days indulging in pizza, jug wine, and videos. Grandmother would have had a stroke. But when I returned to the lab, I felt refreshed and vitalized."

"Sometimes pepperoni is the only cure," he said with a smile.

"And humor," Charlotte said, also smiling, and enjoying the feel of smiling with Jonathan again. "The very first time I laid eyes on Naomi, she was arguing passionately with someone about, of all things, whether dogs were smarter than cats. And Naomi shouted, 'Have you ever seen eight cats pull a sled through the snow?' "

Jonathan laughed softly.

Charlotte met his eyes. "So you know about the Chalk Hill massacre?"

He nodded.

"Did you know that I was never convicted? That the charges were dropped?"

"I know, Charlotte," he said, "I know."

"But they're going to use it now. The whole nightmare is going to be dredged up and they are going to use Chalk Hill to crucify me and my company. And Naomi will be hurt by it, and other innocent people. My God, Jonathan, how did it come to this?"

He reached out and massaged her shoulder. But at his touch, she quickly backed away. "I'm sure Grandmother had some tea around here." She opened cupboards in the small kitchenette that was part of the office. When she pulled open a drawer, she paused. Then she reached inside and brought out what appeared to be an antique book. As she started to open it, a photograph slipped out.

A very old photograph . . .

"What the hell is going on?"

Charlotte and Jonathan turned toward the private security monitor that showed the rain-swept parking lot. "Why haven't the police done anything yet?" Adrian Barclay

boomed as he emerged from a white stretch limousine, the
chauffeur sheltering him with an umbrella. When a long
shapely leg appeared from the back of the limousine, the
chauffeur abandoned Adrian Barclay and rushed to shelter
the thin, tanned woman who delivered herself into the rain.

Jonathan let out a low whistle. "I see Margo has kept herself in good condition."

But Charlotte, holding the newly discovered photograph
in her trembling hand, looked at the two new arrivals and
thought: Now the trouble really begins.

10

When the Barclays moved out of the camera's range,
Jonathan punched keys on the console and picked up the
husband and wife again as they crossed the foyer in the main
building. Dressed in white slacks and pastel shirts, tanned
and fit, they looked exactly like what they were: wealthy
Palm Springs socialites who played golf with retired U.S.
presidents. Adrian Barclay, short and compactly built with
iron-gray hair, was talking into a cellular phone, while his
wife, Margo, taller, with ash blond hair swept back from her
cosmetically lifted face, snapped at the guards to tighten security at the main entrance.

"Do they know about this private monitoring system?"
Jonathan asked as he punched another button and the security camera in the third-floor reception area came on.

"I'm sure I must have mentioned it, but I doubt they listened. Since it was for Grandmother, they wouldn't have
cared. There was no love lost there."

Jonathan nodded. "A curious relationship, as I recall." He
turned up the volume when the elevator doors opened and

the Barclays stepped out. "I remember how it was twenty-five years ago. Very bizarre."

"It got worse," Charlotte said quietly, as if the people on the TV screen could hear, "after Mr. Sung read my grandmother's will."

"Where the hell is Charlotte?" Adrian barked as Desmond met them at the elevators.

Charlotte watched as her cousin, still wearing his black leather coat over black sweater and nylon pants, quickly whipped off the sunglasses he always hid behind. "She said she was going to go through employee records —"

But Adrian walked past him, and for a moment Charlotte felt a stab of pity for her cousin. Adrian was Desmond's father. He treated his chauffeur better. But Margo gave her son attention, kissing him on the cheek and smoothing back his hair. This time it was Desmond who was unresponsive.

Margo's secretary suddenly appeared, a small woman who had to hurry after her boss, who continued to stride down the hall, tossing orders over her shoulder, most of which Charlotte and Jonathan were able to hear: "Get Schaeffer and Schaeffer on the phone. Use their back line. Tell Tom Schaeffer to handle this personally. Then call Judge Batchelor, tell him it's personal. Call over at Aphrodite, find out if Simone is available. If not, see if they can send Jason or Nikki. And bring me something from the cafeteria. None of that Chinese stuff. A plain salad with lemon juice, black tea, whatever fresh fruit is available. Find Charlotte. Tell her I want to see her right away."

Jonathan was back at the computer desk, quickly lifting things out of his black bag. "Margo is summoning *you* to her office? Doesn't she know you're the company CEO?"

Charlotte murmured, "It's always been a mystery to me why my grandmother linked herself with that family, especially after the horrible things they did to her."

Jonathan paused in what he was doing and looked at

Charlotte's profile, the tight jaw and trembling lower lip, and he was struck for the first time by how much she resembled her grandmother, Perfect Harmony. Certain beauty runs in the family, he thought, and then he wanted to ask if she got the flowers he had sent for the funeral. He had been so upset when he read news of Harmony's death, particularly the shocking way she had died, that he had almost flown out of Johannesburg that day. But because of the secret government job he was on, he had been unable to leave, and so he had sent flowers and a telegram instead. Charlotte had never acknowledged them.

As Adrian vanished down the hall, cellular phone to his ear, his secretary running after him, Charlotte and Jonathan saw Margo bypass her office and go straight to Agent Valerius Knight, who immediately rose from his chair, straightening his tie and cuffs. When Margo delivered her hands into Knight's, giving him a warm smile, Jonathan said, "Does she *know* him?"

"Not that I was aware of," Charlotte said. "This is very strange."

Jonathan resumed his task of laying out a camera, gloves, a black leather zippered pouch. "You said you don't trust Knight. Why?"

"He isn't an impartial investigator," Charlotte said, her eyes on the pair on the screen. Agent Knight, towering over Margo, his smoothly shaven head shining like polished ebony in the overhead lights, inclined himself toward Mrs. Barclay, a little too closely, Charlotte thought. "Two years ago a Kansas City woman became very sick and almost died after using a face cream that was laced with mercury. Knight went after the manufacturer with both barrels. Even though they were ultimately proven to be faultless, and even though an ex-boyfriend eventually came forward and admitted to tampering with the cream, the company was ruined. Knight sees himself as sheriff, judge, and hangman. He passes sen-

tence and asks questions later." She added: "I'd give anything to know what he and Margo are talking about right
now."

"We soon shall," Jonathan said decisively. "Charlotte, I
want you to call a meeting."

She turned to him. "Now?" Then she saw the pouch he
had hooked onto his belt. "What for?"

"I need to get into their offices and I can't risk them seeing me. It's been a while, but one of the Barlcays might still
recognize me."

"You want me to call everybody?"

"Not the secretaries. They don't know me."

"But if one of them catches you in an office, she'll wonder what you're doing."

He reached into his back pocket and produced an ID wallet. He flipped it open: she saw a card and a badge. "A sou-
venir from my days with the NSA," he said with a smile.

She hesitated. Jonathan's smile was bitter. It reminded
her of the last time she had seen him, ten years ago in San
Francisco, when he had told her he was "out of the spy
game." That he had even been a spy had come as a surprise,
but that he had left it, and didn't explain why, had deepened
the mystery. She hadn't had a chance to ask further, because
that was when he had dropped the news bombshell that had
severed their relationship. "All right," she said now, setting
down the antique photograph she had been holding. "I can
think up a few things to say."

"Here," he said, holding out his hand.

She saw a small metal button in his palm. "What's that?"

"It's how you and I are going to communicate. Put it in
your ear — it's a transmitter as well as a receiver. And it's
an open connection, so I will be able to hear everything you
say. I will not, however, be able to hear the others, as it only
transmits the wearer's voice." After inserting an identical
button in his own ear, he whispered, "Can you hear me?"

Charlotte gave him a startled look. It was almost as if Jonathan were inside her head. "Yes, I can hear you very well. What are you going to do?"

"Plant listening devices in the main offices so we can hear what's going on." He reached out and loosened the gold clip to brush her hair forward over her ear. "Better hide this, just in case," he said.

Charlotte almost jumped. Jonathan's touch was still electrifying.

As they headed out, Jonathan glanced down at the console and saw the antique photograph she had left there. He recognized it from long ago: it was a picture of Charlotte's grandmother when she was a little girl in Singapore — a pretty child in a school uniform, smiling shyly for the camera, her face framed by two long black braids. There was writing at the bottom — Chinese characters, and then English: *"Perfect Harmony, age 10, 1918. St. Agnes Missionary School."*

As they paused at the entrance to make sure the way was clear, Jonathan thought of the first time he met Charlotte's grandmother. He and Charlotte were thirteen and had known each other only a few weeks. Charlotte had introduced him as "my friend from Scotland."

"Aii-yah, you come from so far away," the grandmother had said, "your family so far, far away," saying it softly and sadly, as if in that one instant she had read his pain and understood it. Charlotte had told him her grandmother owned a medicine company. "The company is named after my grandmother. Her name is Perfect Harmony." By the compassion in the grandmother's voice — as though she knew exactly how he felt — he wouldn't have been surprised if she had a medicine that cured homesickness.

And in a way she had, although thirteen-year-old Johnny hadn't known it at the time. She had invited him to stay and have dinner with her and Charlotte that night and, as the fog rolled into San Francisco Bay, Jonathan had tasted Chinese food and Chinese compassion for the first time.

Charlotte's grandmother had asked him about himself, placing questions gently to him as she had placed bowls of steamed dumplings and noodles before him. She poured forth her curiosity about his life as she poured small cups of green tea. She had probed delicately about his family as she probed a platter of fried shrimp, choosing the plumpest and tastiest to offer him. And before he knew it, as he was taking in the grandmother's curative dishes of balance, harmony, and luck, he was releasing his unhappiness, resentment, and grief.

That was also the day Charlotte had told him her own real name, the one on her birth certificate, and Jonathan, who secretly liked the name but didn't want to hurt her feelings, had agreed with her that Charlotte was a much nicer name, even if it *had* come from a storybook.

After a run through the rain, Charlotte and Jonathan arrived at the main building and quickly mounted emergency stairs. At the third floor they peered out at the reception area, where they could just see Margo.

It amazed Jonathan: Margo Barclay did not look her age. The invisible stamp of an expensive plastic surgeon lay upon her tanned, smooth face. Jonathan calculated she was in her late sixties. He recalled rumors from long ago of a voracious sexual appetite. He wondered if it was still true. Did she ever think of that day during his last spring in America, when he was nineteen and swimming in the pool at Charlotte's house? Charlotte had gone inside for lemonade and Mrs. Barclay, a woman nearly thirty years his senior, had appeared in a hot-pink bikini. A smooth, silent dive into the water had delivered her right to where Jonathan was sitting on the steps in the shallow end. She had torpedoed straight to him, suddenly tugging at him. He had barely scrambled out of the pool in time.

He never told Charlotte about the incident. By the time she had come out of the house with a tray of lemonade, Mrs. Barclay was on a chaise lounge, calmly lighting a cigarette, while Jonathan was burning with the memory of her rapacious mouth at his groin.

He shook the memory away and turned to Charlotte. "I'll wait here until you've got them all in the boardroom. You give the signal by asking one of them to close the door. Then I'll get to work. I need about ten minutes. Don't let them out until I give you the all-clear."

She felt his hand on her arm, his fingers squeezing her flesh. She looked into his dark eyes and saw a familiar courage and intensity. "Yes," she whispered, thinking of shattered wind chimes wrapped in a sea blue-and-woods green scarf. Jonathan had come back to her when she had thought she would never see him again.

11

As Charlotte approached Margo, she recognized her perfume: Tuscany by Estée Lauder. Charlotte knew that Margo never used Harmony products. Her bathrooms at home and the private bathroom attached to her office here were filled with Clinique, Lancôme, Elizabeth Arden — as if to demonstrate how much she despised the very company she wished she owned.

When Margo turned around, Charlotte saw the hard lines of fury around her eyes. The smile was there for public consumption — Margo was a past mistress of putting on a good appearance, which was why she was vice president in charge of public relations. But the anger lay just below the surface.

When Charlotte saw Margo's eyes flicker down, she knew exactly what the older woman was looking at. Charlotte did not wear the Shang dynasty locket all the time, only on days when she needed spiritual strength. She knew that, like her son, Desmond, Margo was dying to ask what happened that summer when Charlotte vanished; she also knew that, unlike Desmond, Margo would remain silent.

She had asked only once.

Charlotte would never forget the surprise invitation from Margo to go shopping, the only time she could recall Margo being nice to her. Charlotte, only fifteen then, had been flattered and had not suspected a thing. But then, over lunch, when Margo had artfully brought the conversation around to Charlotte's curious absence for three weeks, she had realized what the luncheon was all about.

"Charlotte, dear, where did *you and your uncle go?"*

Charlotte hadn't known at the time the ugly word that was being whispered about: *incest.* It wasn't until years later, when Desmond, in one of his cutting moods, had said, "You *do* know what the family think went on between you and my grandfather, don't you?" that she had understood. She hadn't told him what he wanted to know, just as she hadn't told Margo at that luncheon, or Aunt Olivia, or anyone. The only person she had told was Jonathan.

"Charlotte, darling," Margo said now as she air-kissed Charlotte's cheeks. "This is terrible, simply terrible! Adrian and I have decided that this is just too great a burden for you to carry on your own. Let us help you. Shift some of your responsibilities to us. You must admit it makes sense during this terrible crisis that you temporarily step aside and allow more experienced people to take over."

"I can manage, Margo," Charlotte said, remembering Margo's rage and indignation when Charlotte had inherited the company's top position. Margo had been certain she or Adrian would get it.

"But my dear, those terrible picket signs outside. That whole nasty animal business is going to come out into the open. Are you sure you want to go through all that again?"

Despite the appearance of caring and concern, Charlotte saw behind Margo's facade, and thought: She still hasn't forgiven me for keeping that secret from her.

"Margo, I'm calling a meeting."

"A meeting! When?"

"Right now. You, Adrian, Desmond, and Mr. Sung. In the boardroom."

Margo released a weary sigh. "I don't suppose it can wait, dear?"

"No, it can't. Will you please tell Adrian?"

Before Margo could protest further, Charlotte continued on down the hall, rounding up the others. She found Agent Knight in the employees' lounge, helping himself to coffee from the machine. When she invited him to sit in on the meeting, he accepted in a way that let her know he would have been there anyway, invited or not.

As they finally gathered at one end of the long, polished table in the boardroom, Charlotte cleared her throat and, reaching up to feel the electronic plug in her ear, said, "Desmond, would you please close the door?"

As she began to address the small group, praying that Jonathan worked swiftly and unimpeded, Charlotte's thoughts went back to the photograph of her grandmother as a schoolgirl in Singapore. She wondered if Jonathan remembered the day she first introduced him to her grandmother, and how he had stayed for dinner that night and ravenously devoured her grandmother's cooking as if he hadn't eaten in ages, talking about himself under her grandmother's clever coaxing. That was when Charlotte had learned his tale, which she had thought so wonderfully tragic and romantic.

Although Jonathan had been born in America, he had

grown up in Scotland, on the eastern edge of the Highlands, in a small village north of Dundee. His father was a wealthy American businessman who had been traveling through Scotland on a whim, searching for his clan roots. During the idyllic summer Robert Sutherland had met and fallen in love with pretty Mary Sutherland — no relation, except perhaps centuries ago. The honeymoon in scenic Inverness had boded well for the marriage: within two months Mary was pregnant. And then Robert had brought his pregnant bride back to the United States, to his Manhattan penthouse and corporate dinners and seasonal tickets to the opera, and Mary had lasted until the baby was six months old. When she had announced that she wanted to go home, Robert did not argue, because their love had died somewhere between the heather and the New York skyline.

The divorce was quiet and amicable, and Mary was allowed to take "the boy." Jonathan saw his father only on holidays after that, when a private jet came for him and he spent two weeks in San Francisco or Honolulu or Chicago, usually in the company of valets and bodyguards, after which he was flown home with suitcases full of useless expensive gifts for the simple folks back in the Highlands. When he was twelve, he finally refused the invitation to spend Christmas with his father. Robert Sutherland did not press it. When Jonathan turned thirteen, his mother grew ill and died of an undiagnosed congenital heart ailment, and the father dutifully claimed his son, bringing him "home" to San Francisco, where the rough Highland boy was enrolled in an expensive academy in Pacific Heights, to make him a "proper" American. That was when Charlotte first found him, crying in the park because he didn't know where he belonged. And she had consoled him by saying neither did she, because she didn't know if she was supposed to be Chinese or American.

Charlotte pictured him now as he had looked when he arrived an hour ago. His gray three-piece suit, with such fine hand-tailoring details as working buttonholes on the sleeves — a quiet sign of the wearer's taste and wealth — reminded Charlotte of dinners with Jonathan's father, when Robert Sutherland would take the two teenagers out to the most expensive restaurants in the Bay Area. Over caviar and crumbled egg, chateaubriand with béarnaise, and the desserts always flambéed, Mr. Sutherland would clear his throat and say, "Charlotte is a name rich in literary history. Charlotte Brontë comes to mind." Or: "The Chinese have a rich and ancient culture. They gave us spaghetti, you know, yes it's true, Marco Polo. . . ." And he would deliver a gentle lecture to fill in the space between himself and the two kids who perplexed him.

Robert Sutherland was forty when he went to Scotland, Charlotte recalled now. A self-made millionaire, childless and a bachelor, who had decided to search for his roots. He didn't find roots but planted a seed instead. Charlotte was amazed now how like his father Jonathan had become. No trace remained of the long-haired anti-establishment rebel who had been tracked by the FBI for "phreaking." Now he worked *with* them, showed them how to catch international hackers.

You turn forty this year, Johnny, she wanted to say. Where will your midlife crisis take *you?* Into whose arms. . . ?

When she saw the impatient faces before her, she realized she was starting to sound as if she were stalling for time, filing the others in on details they already knew. She looked at the clock on the wall. How much time had passed? Was ten minutes really enough for Jonathan to plant bugs in the offices? But he had also taken a camera with him. What was that for?

"Okay," she said, "we have to take action. Desmond, I want you to contact all of our field reps and tell each of them to personally visit every distributor in their area. Have the reps ask if they noticed anything suspicious, if any customers seemed to complain about Harmony —"

"Charlotte," he said with a heavy frown behind his sunglasses. "That's a job for the FDA, not us!"

"I want us to conduct an investigation of our own, Des. It's just possible someone saw something, a customer tampering with packages."

She turned to Margo and paused, waiting to hear Jonathan's all-clear whisper in her head. "Margo, I will be making a press announcement first thing in the morning. I want you to arrange as much coverage for me as you can."

Margo didn't respond. Margo did not take orders, not since Charlotte, a woman nearly thirty years her junior, had become CEO.

Charlotte glanced at the clock again. She saw that Agent Knight also looked at the clock. No whispers from Jonathan.

Desmond stood up. "If you don't mind —"

"Adrian, I want you to make sure the bonuses will still be processed. The employees will take that as a sign that the company is not in any danger."

"Yeah," he said, "but it *is*, isn't it?"

Hurry up, Jonathan, she thought as she saw Desmond move toward the door.

"Desmond, we aren't finished here. Adrian, it's important that we make every effort to show our employees and our private investors that Harmony is a healthy company and that we have control of the situation."

Muttering something about important phone calls he had to make, Adrian began to stand up. Margo followed suit.

Charlotte tried to cast about for something further to say. "I thought you would have some input —" she began.

Desmond had his hand on the doorknob. "The only input I'm interested in right now is putting a thick steak inside me, juicy and rare, drenched in ketchup."

Agent Knight pushed away from the wall he had been leaning against and said, "I'll second that steak request."

Desmond yanked the door open, revealing the outer reception area, the corridors, and doorways leading to offices.

Charlotte felt her heart rise to her throat.

And then —

Hey, Charlotte. Where are you? I'm halfway to China by now.

12

When they got back to the museum, Charlotte quickly unrolled the blueprints she had picked up from her office and anchored the edges with a stapler and coffee mugs. She was trembling with rage. "You should have seen them, Jonathan! How they treated me! They never would have dared to walk out on one of Grandmother's meetings."

"Don't let that lot get to you, love," Jonathan murmured as he scrutinized the plans of the facility. He tapped a corner of the drawing. "Here it is. Not easy to get to."

She looked to where he was pointing — a complex diagram of the plant's communications array.

"I'll have to get in there," he said, "but first . . ." He went to the desk where he had earlier set up his own laptop computer and quickly got to work installing a small black box with a green digital display. "This is the receiver for the transmitters I planted in the offices. By combining it with that" — he pointed to the security monitor — "we'll be able to eavesdrop on any conversation going on. And this," he added with a smile, holding up a smaller device that had a cable coming out of one end, "is my present from Father Christmas this year. Agent Knight!" he said triumphantly as he plugged the box into the back of his laptop. "Observe." He pointed to the security monitor, where they saw Valerius Knight take a seat at his desk and begin to type on his keyboard. Instantaneously they heard the tapping come through Jonathan's laptop, and on the screen a series of letters began to appear.

Charlotte's eyes widened.

Jonathan smiled with pride. "A little software I wrote myself. I slapped a transmitter on Knight's laptop. This receiver picks up the signal and forwards it to my computer, where my program translates the keystrokes into letters."

"Johnny, you had a camera. What was that for?"

"You'll like this bit." Sitting at her grandmother's computer, he pulled the palm-sized camera out of the pouch on his belt. "I installed the software earlier," he said as he plugged the camera into a port. A moment later, black-and-white photos of a naked blond woman in seductive poses appeared on the screen.

"What is *that*?" Charlotte said.

"That, Charlotte, is what Desmond was doing when you called for the meeting. When I planted the bugs, I also took pictures of all active monitors. Now we can get a look at who was doing what at their computers."

When Charlotte saw the look on Jonathan's face, a mixture of victory and amusement, she was suddenly hearing another voice, belonging to a younger Johnny, saying passionately, "They're the best bloody hackers on the planet, Charlie, and I intend to be one of them."

It was the spring of 1980 and he had been referring to the Computer Science Lab at MIT. While Jonathan had gone on to sing the praises of the Massachusetts Institute of Technology, twenty-three-year-old Charlotte had cradled her cold coffee, oblivious of the rain pouring down onto the Boston street beyond the café window, because all she could think was: He's coming back to America!

Four years earlier, after they had graduated from high school, Johnny had told her that his father wanted him to go to college at Cambridge in England. After years of trying to turn his son into an American, Robert Sutherland suddenly wanted him to study mathematics in England. "He's opening up a new office in London," Johnny had said glumly. "I don't want to go, but I think he's lonely."

"Go with him, Johnny," she had urged. It was the most painful thing she had ever said to him. "We can find ways to see each other." So to Cambridge he had gone, and although they wrote and occasionally telephoned, they had seen each other only twice in the four years since. When she had gotten the letter asking her to come to Boston to see him, she had had no idea what he was going to say. She had assumed he would do post-grad work in England.

Instead he had said, "I've chosen MIT." He would be on the same continent, no longer an ocean away.

As she watched him now work swiftly and energetically with gadgets and wires and keyboards, first typing on her grandmother's computer, then rapidly switching to his own, his words from that rainy day in 1980 came flooding back, bringing his youthful passion and zest into her grandmother's office.

"These hackers are the best, Charlie! Met one bloke who told me there wasn't a system he couldn't get into." Johnny had talked between bites of hamburger, occasionally running the back of his hand across his chin. "This bloke sat there in the pub talking as calmly as if we were discussing football scores! Lists of all the break-ins he's done: Teradyne, Fermilab, Union Carbide. I said, bugger me! Then he tells me he goes to East Berlin and sells individual accounts from these places, passwords and log-ins! Bragged that he got over a hundred thousand Deutsche marks for a password and log-in at the Jet Propulsion Lab in Pasadena!"

And then Charlotte had had a sudden fear. "Johnny, *you* aren't going to do those things, are you?"

"No worries, love." He had taken a long draw on his beer. "Can't risk it, can I?"

Charlotte knew about his last two brushes with the law, when he had stumbled into the system at University College in London and accidentally found a gateway to a link that had led, astoundingly, to a classified U.S. military database at the Anniston Army Depot. Johnny had managed to get off by declaring innocence. His father's good name had helped. The second arrest had been for breaking into the private e-mail system at rival school Oxford, where he had singled out a particularly disliked professor, catching his computer mail on the fly, changing the text and rerouting it. The faked letters had gone to Amnesty International, generously offering large donations. When they came to graciously collect, the startled professor had been so embarrassed that he had given them the money; and then he had also been so mortified that he had had to be embarrassed into making a charitable donation that he had had the whole matter dropped.

Charlotte had wondered if Johnny really could stay out of trouble while at MIT. He just couldn't seem to help himself. If there was a computer and a system that couldn't be broken into, Johnny had to go at it tooth and claw until he did.

Relishing the memory that, because of events that came afterward, she had worked hard to suppress, Charlotte recalled something now that she had forgotten . . . the federal agent at the other table in the café.

"Johnny," she had whispered, leaning close, "I know it's my imagination, but I would swear that man is eavesdropping."

Johnny turned around and waved congenially at the man. "Not your imagination, love. He's FBI. They think I'm stealing government secrets."

"What!"

"No worries, love, my kind of stealing doesn't hurt anyone. If anything, I'm doing them a favor." Johnny's brown eyes had danced with mirth. "The electronic universe is growing, Charlie, and it's full of gaping holes. The pranks I pull alert these yobbos to the weaknesses in their networks. They should thank me, really." He laughed and ran the last of his hamburger bun around his salty plate. "I've already had one Russian come up to me and offer me vast amounts of money for American software. I turned the bastard down flat."

Then he had raised his eyes to hers and she had felt two electric bolts shoot right to the back of her brain. "But mainly," he said quietly, "I chose MIT because I wanted to be closer to you."

That was *the* day, Charlotte realized now. As they had sat in that smoky café with only a scratched table between them, that was *the* most perfect day she and Johnny had ever spent together. Even more than all the autumns and springs in San Francisco, the nights of making love — better than all of those put together, this one day, this one moment, with Johnny finally opening up and baring his feelings, was the zenith of their relationship.

Because after that it all fell apart and, like Humpty Dumpty, could not be put back together again.

"That's it," Jonathan said now, suddenly standing up from the computer. He began to quickly undo the buttons of his vest. "I checked your system security — it's excellent. Your internal phone system isn't hooked up to your computer network and you're not using the default security specifications that came with the software. You also don't have access to the sensitive material from just anywhere on the network, not even from your grandmother's station. Whoever installed your security did a top-notch job. I couldn't have done it better."

Carefully folding his vest over the back of the chair,

where his jacket already hung, he reached into his black kit and pulled out a ball of black nylon that, when he shook it out, turned out to be a windbreaker. "I ran a check on the employees' e-mail logs. Our blackmailer's messages weren't sent internally — unless it's from a hidden modem. And I checked the formulas in the database against the backup logs — everything seems normal, nothing altered. So if the tampering was done here at the plant, then it was done during another step of the process."

As she watched him shrug into the black windbreaker, a million questions crowded her mind. She wanted to know what he had done every single day for the past ten years — what did he have for breakfast, what movies had he seen, was he still fond of scones and jam? But how could she ask? Where could she even begin? "Where are you going?" she said at last.

"I need to install an electromagnetic pulse monitor on your communications array." He reached into the kit and brought out gloves, flashlight, and wire cutters. "You attach it to a circuit and it picks up the different types of signals going out — in this case, keystrokes in a specific band spectrum. If anyone is doing any secret work on the Internet, we'll know."

He gave her a confident smile, but his eyes remained serious, making her wonder if questions crowded *his* mind, too.

"You seem to be laying traps all over the place," she said.

"Next comes the cheese and the box propped on a twig," he said with a wink. "Lock the door behind me —"

The mail alert suddenly sounded on the computer.

A question, Charlotte: on the evening news tonight there was no mention of how many capsules of Bliss the victim ingested. But it was more than two, wasn't it, Charlotte? Because two would have only made her sick. She needed to take three or more to receive a lethal dose. Am I right?

Jonathan looked at her. "Is that true?"

"Agent Knight said there were four capsules missing from the bottle."

"What's the recommended dose for Bliss?"

"Two capsules."

"So he only intended to make her sick?"

"Perhaps, I don't know. Since herbal products are not federally regulated, people think it's safe to double or triple dosages, thinking they'll get even better results."

Jonathan's look darkened. "Our friend here knows that and was counting on someone to do exactly that. Which means the dead woman was not his intended target but rather a random victim. And you, as I suspected, are who he is after." He fell silent, and moody eyes settled on her. "Charlotte, I wish you would take my advice and go somewhere safe —"

"If only we knew *how* he did the tampering!"

Jonathan gave Charlotte a look that broadcast both being annoyed with her and being proud of her. "That'll be the next step," he said, realizing she wasn't going to hide. "When I return, I want you to show me the labs and the plant."

"Why?"

"I'll tell you when I get back."

"Okay, I'll watch for a break when there's no chance of anyone seeing you. If I know Margo, she'll head straight for her office and her private bathroom, where she'll shower and redo her entire hair and makeup before facing any more people. She also told her secretary to call Aphrodite to send over a masseuse. Adrian we can count on to talk on five phones at once, which will leave Desmond tied up with the mess. That will give us the break we need to get you over to the labs."

"In the meantime," Jonathan said as he hooked coils of red and blue wire to his belt, "I want you to try and find out the common denominator among the three products that were tampered with, whether it's a chemical, or the day they were packaged, or maybe they all went out on the same truck. Are those records kept in your database?"

"Everything that goes on in Harmony Biotech is in the computer system."

"Do you know yet what killed those women?"

"Agent Knight said he would let me know as soon as the analysis came in. But I don't think we can rely on him to be prompt in reporting."

"You have no samples from those batches?"

"The FDA took every last bottle and package. I even tried buying one at a health food store, but couldn't find any. We distribute all over the country — all over the world."

"I know," Jonathan said, recalling a painful memory from two years before, when he had been on a security consulting trip in Paris. He had known that Harmony products were distributed globally, that they even put out a catalog and had a chain of small, classy stores. But he had not been prepared for the shock when he had seen, on the corner of the rue de l'Odéon and boulevard Saint-Germain, a small shop with a sign that said: *Parapharmacie et Herboristerie*. And in the window, a display of Harmony herbal products.

"All right," he said, starting for the door. "We have less than eleven hours." He paused, and then he turned back, stepping closer to her, to swim for a moment in her clear green eyes. He saw her pupils flair, he heard the breath catch in her throat, and he knew the old hunger was still there, because it was the same as his own. "Charlotte," he said with sudden passion, "I'm sorry I had to come back this way, I'm sorry it took a tragedy for us to see each other again. But by God I'm glad I'm here and I swear to you by everything that I hold sacred and dear that I will stay with you until this whole sorry mess is ended."

He saw her lips part slightly, pink and moist, like the lush peonies where he had buried his gun, and he thought about how years ago, when they were very young, he would fantasize about kissing Charlotte. There had been opportunities, and there had been times when he had thought she was inviting his mouth to come to hers, when they had chased each other in Golden Gate Park and he would catch her and she would spin around so that her face was uplifted to his, her mouth offered up like the exotic peony. At fifteen Jonathan had not had the courage to go that extra step. But a year later he had, when she had taken him into her arms because he had been crying, and he had felt her soft body against his, her warm breath on his cheek as she had whispered, "Don't cry, Johnny, it'll be all right."

Suddenly rocked by an unexpected shock of desire, he stepped away from her and ran his hand over his eyes, to break the spell. "I shan't be long," he said, and then he was gone.

She watched him leave, and when the door clicked shut behind him, she stood for a long moment, spellbound.

Less than two hours ago she had felt all alone in a world that was rapidly falling apart. And now Johnny was here. He hadn't asked. He had simply come.

The silence of the museum closed in around her, echoing another silence from long ago, when she would come home from school to the big house that smelled of wood polish and perfection, with the maid saying, "Good evening, miss," and the cook proudly showing Charlotte the potstickers she had made, just for her. Charlotte would sit at the kitchen table and read her grandmother's note apologizing for not being there because a shipment of rare herbs had arrived and it needed her personal inspection. Charlotte would listen to the foghorns out in the Bay and she would regard her plate of potstickers, made especially because they were her favorite and because the cook felt sorry for her, and the loneliness would make Charlotte's throat close up until she couldn't eat.

Few of her schoolfriends ever came back a second time — they found her house too alien, especially when her grandmother would appear in one of her *cheongsams*, her hair done up Chinese-style with combs and ivory pins. The girls had all seen *The World of Suzie Wong*, and they all watched old Charlie Chan movies on late-night TV. "Does your grandmother smoke opium?" one girl had innocently asked.

Charlotte hadn't been able to find the bridge that could bring her American friends into her grandmother's Chinese world. They always seemed uneasy in that big house, as if they expected the evil Fu Manchu to spring out from behind a curtain. Only Johnny had made the transition easily, practiced as he already was in moving between two worlds.

And Johnny had made her loneliness vanish. Johnny with his impulsiveness and prankster nature, suddenly calling her up and saying, "Hey, I have a fantastic idea!" They might spend the day seeing how many cable cars they could ride without paying, hopping off before the conductor reached them, and hopping on to the next, for no other reason than to "beat the system." Or they might spend the day making free phone calls to Cairo or Athens by using the whistle from a Cap'n Crunch cereal box because it had a pitch of 2600mhz, the same tone that activated the AT&T long-distance switches.

Johnny not only shooed loneliness away, he made life exciting, spontaneous, and definitely worth living.

And now he was back, bringing all his passion and urgency with him, filling her with a consuming curiosity about how his life had gone for the past ten years. But she wouldn't ask. Charlotte knew he would have to leave, to return to his wife and his life in another world.

Pressing down her pain and her fears — she would not think about the garage door and Knight's speculation that

someone had tampered with it — she turned and looked into
the museum, where relics in glass cases beckoned. Wondering if indeed, as she had thought, the clues to who was attacking her and her company were hidden somewhere in all
this memorabilia, she approached one of the illuminated displays, where a small card read *"The goddess Kwan Yin,
circa 1924. Singapore."* She knew that her grandmother had
told her the story of the small porcelain statue that sat alone
in the glass case, but Charlotte had forgotten it.

Now, however, as her fingers curled around the delicate
figurine, she felt the story coming back, the strange fate of a
goddess whom not even a thief would take. . . .

13

1924 — Singapore

We watched the last ship sail into the harbor, watched the
passengers come down the gangway, go through the customs sheds, and disperse. My mother turned to me and said,
"This is the last time I come to the harbor, Harmony-*ah*. I
will come no more."

My mother had visited the harbor every day for seventeen
years.

After I was born, she came with me in her arms, and she
watched the ships sail into the harbor as she waited for her
beloved Richard to return. He had promised he would come
back. She never gave up the hope that he one day would.

When I could walk, she would take my hand and bring me
here, to watch the ships with the mighty sails and masts, the
boats with the smoking stacks and deafening horns. We
would take our usual place on the quay, where we were a fa-

miliar sight to the fishermen and dock workers, and we would train our eyes on the horizon, like twin lighthouses, watching as the cargo vessels, ocean liners, private yachts, warships, junks, and tugboats all carved their various ways through the green water. We would bring humble meals of rice gruel and fish heads and study the face of every passenger who stepped down to the dock; we would scan the faces of those who remained at the railings, if the ship were moving on to another port. My mother would ask those passing by if they knew of an American traveler named Richard who was coming back to Singapore. She would go to the customs shed and passport office and harbormaster and ask her questions. Everyone was kind, but they all said, "No."

She never gave up hope.

Even as her feet began to grow crippled from so much walking and standing, for we could not afford a rickshaw, my mother would make the journey to the harbor. I became her cane, her hand rising up on my shoulder as I grew taller and stronger, and she grew smaller and more bowed, even though she was not an old woman. At night I changed her bandages, scraping away the rotten skin and bathing her feet in sweet-smelling oils.

Now, just weeks after my sixteenth birthday, we had come to the harbor for the last time, because my mother could make the journey no more.

She said, "The goddess visited me in my sleep last night, Harmony-*ah*, and she told me that I will die soon. It is time for you to leave Singapore, my daughter, and go to your new life."

I had known this day was coming. I had known that it was my destiny to leave the place of my birth. But still, I protested.

She said, "There is no future for you here. Once I am gone, you will be alone, the illegitimate daughter of an outcast. You know what you are here, Harmony-*ah*," she added with great unhappiness.

I knew the contemptuous word that described me: *sten-gah*, which was Malay for "small whiskey." It literally meant "half," for I was Eurasian, the very lowest of the social castes.

"It will be different in America," my mother told me. "There you will be accepted." In Singapore it was like China, she explained, where to be born a girl was hardship enough. But to be born to an outcast, a girl could have no future. "In America you can change your luck. In America a farmer's son can become a king. And an illegitimate daughter can gain respect."

I could not imagine what that would be like.

I had grown up invisible. We were "non-people" — the outcast woman who had once been the cherished Eldest Daughter of a scholar and his First Wife — and her illegitimate daughter, sired by a foreigner. We belonged nowhere, had no family, no clan, no ancestors. No caste would accept us, and because everyone must look down on someone, we were at the lowest social level, just above the beggars and lepers.

She finally turned her back on the harbor and its ships and said, "We will go home now and make preparations."

My mother and I lived on Malay Street, nicknamed the Blood Alley of Singapore. Here among the open-air shops, the drink stalls, the shooting galleries and bordellos, was the worst of the island's crime, and also the best of its entertainment. Here you could find Chinese theaters filled with shopkeepers and rickshaw boys or pantomime artists performing plays in the street or Indian gully-gully men piping cobras out of baskets.

In our small room above Abdul Salah's bordello, my mother and I would prepare the medicines that we dispensed or sold. From my mother I learned the secret of Golden

Lotus Tonic, named for Lady Golden Lotus, a poet who lived in the eleventh century. It is said she received the recipe from a water spirit, and that she drank it every day and lived to be a hundred and twenty, bearing her last child when she was well into her sixties. The tonic, a magic blend of just the right herbs harvested during the correct phases of the moon and year, acted upon the reproductive system, as well as bringing vitality to the heart, liver, hair, and mental state. It was sales of our small bottles of Golden Lotus that kept a roof over our heads and rice in our bowls.

My mother's main clients were the prostitutes who came to her seeking contraception creams, teas for restoring menstruation, good luck charms against sailors' diseases, aphrodisiacs for themselves and their customers, endurance tablets, penis wax. My mother also read their fortunes, told them when they were pregnant, and dispensed good listening as well as herbs and advice.

But she had other patients as well. No longer the highborn daughter of a nobleman, my mother was not restricted to foot binding and midwifery. Now she treated also the shopkeepers and their wives, the fishermen, the dock workers, blacksmiths, pawnbrokers, opium sellers, the harbor ferrymen, bricklayers and basket weavers, as well as beggars, vagabonds, and thieves. Occasionally white "mems" secretly sought my mother's services, refined upperclass ladies who came seeking the same advice, cures, and sympathy as the low-caste prostitutes.

By making herself an outcast, my mother had also cast off rules that had once governed everything she did. She defied tradition and the laws of our ancestors and did not bind my feet. By the time I was sixteen, foot binding had been outlawed, and so only older women were now seen hobbling with mincing steps through the streets of Singapore, as my mother did, her hand on my shoulder for support, walking as if crossing a stream on wobbly stepping stones.

She sent me to the Christian Missionary School, where I learned English and Western ways. Each night I would come home to our small place above the bordello, where I would speak to my mother in English and show her how to drink tea with milk. My mother would speak to me in Chinese and teach me *feng shui*. At the mission the English ladies taught me how to play soccer; at home my mother taught me to behave with flower-like modesty. I learned to eat ice cream during the day, and potstickers in the evening. I prayed to Jesus on Sundays and to Kwan Yin the other days. I celebrated both Christmas and the Festival of Ghosts. I learned to lower my eyes the Chinese way and raise my chin the American way.

But mostly my mother passed on to me the ancient healing art of our ancestors. She taught me how to carefully record in a book the formula for each medicine, in Chinese characters and in English: "For *yin* emptiness — one part *sha shen* root, three parts wolfberry fruit, two parts powdered tortoise shell. Boil softly, not to let steam rise too quickly."

She also explained about the harmony of *yin* and *yang*. "*Yin* is feminine — dark, wet, symbolized by water and the moon. *Yang* is masculine — bright, hot, symbolized by fire and the sun." When I pointed out that *yang* was superior, my mother said, "Have you ever seen fire extinguish water? Given time, water wears down the hardest rock. Which is more superior?"

And now, on this day that was to be our last visit to the harbor, my mother had said, "Your education is complete. Now you go out into the world."

We had arrived at Malay Street and stopped at a food stall, where my mother spent precious coins on bowls of rice with curried shrimp, which we ate standing at the stall while dock workers and rickshaw boys squatted at the curb, rapidly scooping noodles and dumplings into their hungry mouths. My mother did this as a treat, for it was a luxury we could ill afford. And when she had eaten only very little, she complained of being full, she even complained to the stall owner that she had given us too much food, and then my mother emptied her bowl into mine, giving me her plump untouched shrimp and the moistest part of her rice. "Need strength, Harmony-*ah*," she said, "for long journey ahead."

When I finished eating, delighting in the rare treat, the stall owner gave me a large papaya, saying, "No pay, no pay! Gift for you. *Aii-yah!*" the woman declared to my mother, "your medicine worked miracles! My two babies, no more cough, they sleep through the night! You come and see!"

She showed us the crib intended for twins. It was empty because her babies had died twenty years ago during an influenza epidemic. Her neighbors and customers believed it was kinder to play along rather than force her to see the truth, and so once a week my mother gave her a bottle of tonic to mix in the babies' milk.

"Remember this, Harmony-*ah*," my mother said, and I realized she was teaching me a final lesson.

But before we reached home, on this last day at the harbor, my mother said, "*Aii-yah*," softly, leaning on me. "I can go no further, my feet pain me so."

I led her into the shade, so that she could rest against a wall.

And while we waited, as I watched the pedestrians pass us by — Chinese women shopping, Malay women laughing, Arab men strolling, Englishmen in a hurry — a tall, dignified gentleman paused before us.

Although he was Chinese, he wore the white jacket and white tropical trousers of a respectable Englishman, with small round glasses over intelligent-looking eyes, and on his head the kind of hat the Reverend Peterson at the mission wore to protect his fair skin from the sun. The gentleman

looked at us for a moment, and then he dipped his hand into
his pocket and brought out a coin.

I realized to my great shame that he thought we were beggars.

But when he looked at my mother, he stopped. His gaze
beheld her for a long moment, and then, with a look in his
eye that I did not at first understand, he pocketed the coin
and continued on his way.

"Why did he not give you the money?" I asked, even
though I knew my mother would have refused him anyway.

"To preserve my dignity," she said, her eyes following his
tall figure down the street until he had disappeared in the
crowd. "To be a beggar, Harmony-*ah*, when you have once
been a nobleman's daughter, is a loss of face that is worse
than death."

"But why did he stop?"

"He recognized my need for honor as greater than my
need for money."

"How could he know that?"

"Because, Harmony-*ah*, that man is your grandfather . . .
my father."

That was when I learned the true story of my mother's
sacrifice, for she told me then, as we slowly made our way
back to our little room above the bordello on Malay Street.

Seventeen years ago, when Mei-ling had returned to the
room over Madam Wah's silk shop to find the American
stranger gone and the new life stirring in her womb, she
knew she could have gone home and begged for mercy from
her father. Perhaps his heart could have been moved and he
might have hidden her away, and my mother might have
continued to live in the house she had so loved, and stayed
there until her American returned for her. But Mei-ling
could not bring dishonor to her father.

Instead she witnessed her own funeral.

She had sent her old servant to the house on Peacock Lane

to report that her young mistress had fallen into the bay while trying to rescue a drowning child. The servant had bribed dock workers and coolies to attest that they, too, had witnessed the heroic act. The father, the servant reported back to Mei-ling, had gone into a state of deep grief, for he had loved his daughter, and he held an elaborate funeral for her, even though her body had never been recovered from the water. Mei-ling had been sorry to bring him such pain, but she knew it was far less than the pain the truth would have brought him — a dead daughter with honor was better than a live daughter with no honor.

That was when I understood the look in the gentleman's eyes when he had gazed at my mother, first in vague confusion, then in shock, and then in admiration, for when he saw me, and recognized my features — I was, after all, his granddaughter — he realized in that moment what Mei-ling had done, and the sacrifice she had made to save her family's honor.

By the time she had finished telling me this astonishing tale, we had reached our room on Malay Street. A man was waiting for us. I recognized him from the mission. He had brought a packet from the Reverend Peterson — the papers that were to take me to America, all officially stamped by the U.S. consul in Singapore. I even had a proper birth certificate that listed my father as an American citizen. This was because my mother had learned from the Reverend Peterson that there was a law in America that said the children of Americans, no matter where in the world they were born, were citizens of the United States. When I saw the marriage license between Mei-ling and Richard, my mother said, "Your father and I *were* married, Harmony-*ah*. In our hearts we were married. Reverend Peterson is a kind man who understands the plight of women. With these papers, which took me many years to obtain, many favors, Harmony-*ah*, and money, the gates of Gold Mountain will open for you."

Gold Mountain . . . the name for the land on the eastern edge of the ocean.

But my mother cried out when she examined the papers. "*Aii-yah!* They have made a mistake! They have changed the year of your birth."

I looked at the papers and saw that she was right. They all said I had been born in 1906 instead of 1908.

"You are Dragon! They have made you Tiger! This is bad luck! You will walk a confused road, tugged this way, tugged that. Dragon is happy and lucky and finds a good husband. Tiger lacks caution and has no patience, she will never find a husband." She shook her head, sadly. "Cannot be helped. Too late for new papers. You are two years older now. You must remember that for the rest of your life."

And so it was by a strange twist of fate that I was to live forever two years in the future.

"Bring me the goddess, Harmony-*ah*," she said finally as the last of the sunlight vanished from our shuttered window, and smoke from cookstoves drifted up and reminded us once again of our hunger. I brought the goddess and I also brought a knife, for we would feast on the papaya given to us by the mother of ghost twins.

My mother had shown me when I was very little how to talk to Kwan Yin, Goddess of Mercy, and how to light incense sticks so that the smoke carried our prayers to heaven. But tonight we did not pray to Kwan Yin. Instead, when I removed the small statue that had stood upon its altar for as long as I could remember, my mother took the porcelain figurine from me and said, "Now I am going to tell you a secret."

My mother doled out secrets the way the Reverend Peterson handed out sweets. So I listened with both ears, just as I used to receive the sweets with both hands.

"The goddess has protected us well, Harmony-*ah*. When your father went away, he left me with no money, only his ring. I could not return to your Chinese grandfather's house. What was I to do? A week after your father had gone, I received a visitor in that small room over Madam Wah's house. He was from the Bank of London, on Orchard Road. He asked me to identify myself, and when I did, he gave me an envelope. In it were two letters. The first was sealed. It contained a note from your father and it was written on bank stationery. He was writing in haste, he said, because he had a boat to catch. He had established a bank account for me. He said he had done this under secrecy, for reasons he would explain when he returned to marry me. But he said the account was mine to do with as I pleased. The other letter was from the bank manager, telling me my account number and how much had been deposited. It was a lot of money.

"I went to the bank that same day, with you only six weeks old in my womb, and I withdrew all those paper notes and exchanged them for money that does not burn. Look." She turned the statue over and showed me where a hole in the base had been plugged with wax. "Open it," she said.

I did, and out tumbled a rain of sparkling green stones.

"Emeralds," my mother said. "The finest."

Thus did I learn that I and my mother were actually rich and could have lived well all these years. "But these stones were your legacy. For your future. Take them," she said. "Go to America and find your father."

I could only stare at the beautiful gems and marvel at my mother's cleverness. For though our little room had been robbed many times over the years, no one had thought to steal a humble goddess statue.

14

8:00 P.M. — Palm Springs, California

Are you taking me seriously, Charlotte? Are you preparing that public statement? Or are you wasting your time searching for me? Give up. You will never find me. Schedule the press conference, Charlotte. Otherwise I shall have to show you another demonstration of my powers.

Charlotte hit a key and closed the offending window. She looked at her watch. Where was Jonathan?

Going to the security console, she pressed buttons that brought up different views. Offices and halls, outdoor walkways, parking lots, labs, manufacturing and shipping rooms, came onto the screen one after the other, revealing in one area a nervous Adrian Barclay pacing the floor with two cellular phones at his ears; in another, Margo admitting into her office a woman carrying a tote bag and a folded massage table; in a third, Desmond, pointing something out to Agent Valerius Knight at the shipping dock. These two had been there for the past half hour. She wondered what had caught Knight's interest so. Unfortunately, Jonathan had not planted a listening device at the shipping dock.

Glancing in the direction of the museum entrance, she wondered what was keeping him. Jonathan had left over half an hour ago to install an electromagnetic pulse monitor in the communications array panel. He should have been back by now.

She was getting jumpier by the minute. She couldn't put the garage door out of her mind. Had someone really tampered with it? Could Agent Knight really be a hundred percent certain it wasn't just an accident? She shuddered. If it was intentional, then whoever it was might try again. And

Charlotte would have no idea where or when he might strike next.

She punched a key on the console and when the side entrance to the main offices came into view, she saw a figure emerge into the rain and then hurry for shelter. Mr. Sung. She wondered where he was off to in such a hurry. He looked upset. Very unlike him. . . .

She glanced again at the museum entrance. This was the window of opportunity she had been looking for; while everyone was preoccupied she could take Jonathan to the labs and processing areas. But she hadn't heard from him.

She contemplated the two computers crouched like strange beasts on her grandmother's desk. One displayed the last screen Jonathan had photographed, Margo's — it showed her e-mail account open. Had she been about to send an e-mail? The other computer was flashing text on its screen as a search program zipped through the company's database — an AI, Jonathan had explained, Artificial Intelligence, his own creation, a software program that learned as it went along.

Was it going fast enough? she wondered as she tried to keep from trembling. How could Jonathan be so confident about catching this maniac? Maybe they *should* tell Knight about the e-mails. No, Jonathan was right. It was best that they run their own secret investigation. As far as she knew, the FDA team was making little headway. And if the person who tried to kill her with the garage door made another attempt, Charlotte doubted he would let federal agents get in his way.

The main door suddenly blew open and Jonathan came in, shaking off the rain and saying, "That's done. Anyone logging on to the Internet and we'll know it. Any word from our anonymous friend?"

She saw how his hair was curling slightly with the damp. It made her recall the feel of it, when she would run her fingers through those curls, long ago. But now that privilege belonged to another woman. "Just the one that came a while ago. I turned it off. I couldn't stand seeing it on the screen. Jonathan, this is a good time to go to the labs."

"Good," he said as he quickly gathered up his gear, zippered his black bag, and slung the strap over his shoulder. "Just remember, we have to be extra careful that we don't get caught. This facility is under official federal investigation and we could be charged with anything from obstruction to tampering with evidence."

Jonathan's warning was unnecessary. Charlotte had been arrested before — she had had a taste of crowded jails, indifferent police, the degradation of a body search — and she was not going to risk it again. And being handcuffed . . . she would never forget the feel of that cold metal on her wrists, as if she were some dumb beast being led to slaughter. The arresting officer hadn't even let her wash the blood off her hands. He had seemed angry, as if he wanted her to wear the evidence of her unspeakable act. She had tried to explain, but he hadn't listened. No one had. Except Naomi. Out of all the players in the Chalk Hill nightmare, only Naomi with the frizzy red hair and slight lisp and plump body — Naomi Morgenstern, who lived with two cats named Rodeo and Juliette, and who chatted on a regular basis with dead people — only she had understood why Charlotte had done what she did.

15

When they reached the exit of the museum, they heard muffled thunder in the distance, and a moment later the building shook. Jonathan opened the door a few inches. It was dark out, the falling rain illuminated in the glow of lamps along the walkways. When thunder cracked again, louder and closer, Jonathan looked back toward the office and said, "Is there a power backup to that computer?"

"There is on all our equipment. Two hours, I believe."

"Not much time if the power fails. Ready?"

They dashed into the rain and hurried along the covered walkways, watching out for anyone who might be out in the storm. But the paths and lawns were deserted, with puddles forming as the rain came down harder and water rushing noisily along unseen gutters. "This way," Charlotte said, leading Jonathan to the entrance to the main building, where they ducked under yellow police tape that barred the door.

They made their way down a silent corridor until they reached the outer area of the main lab, where they quickly slipped into white disposable coveralls, paper shoes covers, and bonnets over their hair. "Keep this handy, just in case," Charlotte said, handing Jonathan a surgical mask. "If anyone should suddenly show up, you can hide your face."

Charlotte went first through glass doors that read Authorized Personnel Only. She paused to look and listen. The lab appeared to be deserted. She proceeded forward and Jonathan followed as they passed among chrome workbenches, refrigerators, incubators, sterilizing equipment. "Very impressive," Jonathan said as he took in the mass spectrometers, oscilloscopes, electronic microscopes, state-of-the-art apparatus. "Not exactly like the old days, when your grandmother had Chinese ladies sitting at wooden tables sorting roots and berries by hand."

He paused at a work station crowded with test tubes, petri dishes, and flasks, and picked up a clear plastic bag containing dark green leaves. "Or maybe I should take that back."

"That's our latest success," Charlotte explained, keeping a lookout for anyone who might suddenly walk in. "Saint-John's-wort. For years Harmony offered products containing this herb, but they were for external treatment of cuts and burns. However, the plant also contains the chemical hypericin, which is an antidepressant. When I read in the *British Medical Journal* that pharmaceutical companies were researching the herb's use in depression disorders, I saw a wide-open market for a no-drug preparation from us. So last year we came out with a hot new product — Saint-John's-wort in ingestible form, useful for anxiety, tension, and insomnia."

Jonathan set the bag down. "Sort of an herbal Prozac?"

"We received a tremendous response, bigger than we expected. Orders were coming in faster than we could fill them. We had the plant going night and day to keep up with demand."

"Good for you," he said quietly, in an old-Johnny way, his dark eyes radiating admiration and praise.

"Des deserves credit, too," she said. "He launched a brilliant marketing campaign."

"I'll wager it made him bloody obnoxious. He hasn't changed, you know. I've watched your dear cousin on the security monitor."

"Desmond can't help the way he is," Charlotte said as she paused suddenly when they heard a sound. "Shh. What was that?"

Jonathan listened. "Just thunder," he said. He looked down at her hand on his arm. He could feel the gentle pressure of her fingertips through the paper sleeve of his coveralls. As he watched her green eyes do a slow sweep of the lab, Jonathan said quietly, "Still defending poor old Des after all these years?" But she didn't respond.

They continued on until they came upon a glassed-in room protected by a series of doors with warning signs. "What's in there?" Jonathan said.

"That is one of our controlled-environment chambers. An ultra-high-security area."

"Limited access?"

"Extremely. In addition to ID tags and a keypad requiring an entry code, we installed biometric identification."

Jonathan leaned close and examined the security panel. "Facial infrared imaging. Security did a good job here, too. Is this where GB4204 was developed?"

"And others that are in various stages of research and development."

He nodded. "A lot of money tied up in here, a lot of future money as well."

"We invited private investors."

He turned to her with a surprised look. "This isn't just Harmony money?"

"We needed capital."

"And whose job was it to raise this capital?"

"Adrian's."

"So he has a bigger stake in this than I thought."

"So you suspect the Barclays."

"Charlie, I've been suspicious of those people ever since the day Adrian walked into your grandmother's house without even knocking and demanded to know what the heck she was doing by keeping nonworking employees on the payroll."

"I remember that day. Adrian wanted to downsize the factory staff, but Grandmother wouldn't lay off any of her workers. Some had been with her for over thirty years — Wait! Did you hear that?"

They both listened and heard footsteps in the outer corridor.

"This way!" Charlotte said. "Hurry!" She led Jonathan to a metal door marked No Admittance and pushed on the bar. "This will get us to the processing plant."

"What I couldn't get over," Jonathan said as they slipped into a dimly lit passageway, the door whispering shut behind them, "was the way Adrian just barged in, unannounced, as if he owned the house. He practically knocked me out of the way . . . but then I was just a thirteen-year-old kid."

"Don't take offense, he treated his own son the same way."

"Yes, and turned the poor bastard into a clone of himself." Jonathan decided that two decades had done nothing to modify the arrogance Desmond seemed to wear like his ostentatious leather coat and sunglasses. Perhaps he couldn't help imitating his adoptive father, Jonathan conceded; after all, Desmond's own DNA was a mystery to himself. Charlotte's cousin appeared to be a totally self-invented man, like Frankenstein, Jonathan thought, a composite of bits and pieces he had found in magazines and films.

Jonathan kept this opinion from Charlotte, who he suspected would hasten to Desmond's defense. What he really wanted to say was: "Is Desmond still in love with you? Did you two ever become lovers?" It was no secret, after all, that Desmond wasn't Charlotte's real cousin, that he wasn't even really a Barclay. Jonathan often wondered if Adrian's treatment of Desmond sprang from a hidden resentment of his failure to produce a son of his own.

They reached another doorway, where Charlotte paused to listen. "This is our visitor area," she said quietly. "We sometimes allow groups to come through, or private investors." She pushed the door open and peered in. "All clear," she said.

The visitor reception area was a showcase for Harmony Biotech products, with glass cases displaying bottles and packages, elixirs, tonics, potions, and pills. Jonathan said, "I remember when you were embarrassed by all this."

"Not so much embarrassed as I thought it was all useless and hopelessly old-fashioned," Charlotte said when they reached the opposite door. She produced a magnetic security card from her pocket and paused before slipping it into the slot. "My God, I was arrogant in those days. I remember when I came home from summer camp. I was eleven and I had a bladder infection. The camp doctor had given me antibiotics, but Grandmother started pouring bitter teas into me to restore my *chi*. She said I was suffering from liver stagnation descending as damp heat. I told her the doctor had said it was bacteria. And she said, 'Maybe so, Charlotte-*ah*, but something must be out of balance in your body that allows these bacteria to grow.'"

Jonathan smiled gently. "You know what I think? I think you believe in all this.' "

"Of course I do. Five thousand years of healthy, long-lived Chinese is proof of something! My *grandmother* was proof. She wouldn't have died at age ninety-one except by accident. She was over ninety and yet you would have believed she was twenty years younger. She still came to the plant every day, just as she did sixty years ago. She knew most of the employees, their names, their families. That's why that monitoring system I had installed went unused."

"You know," Jonathan said as he watched Charlotte put her ear to the door, "I never did learn how your grandmother died. I read her obituary, but it didn't give details."

"It was an accident. She was in the Caribbean following a lead she had heard about a rare African herb purportedly brought over by slaves and supposed to have great healing powers."

"What happened?"

"She was traveling to one of the outer islands. The boat capsized. Mr. Sung was with her. He was the one who brought her body home." Charlotte averted her eyes. "Her funeral was very well attended. Hundreds of people —"

Too many flowers, then, Jonathan thought. Hundreds of floral arrangements, too many to acknowledge. Did she get the telegram, though? Couldn't she at least have acknowledged that?

"Did you know that Grandmother left all her shares in the

company to me? Everyone had expected she would distribute them evenly, giving no one person controlling interest. Yet she left them all to me."

"How did the others react?"

"I thought Adrian was going to have a stroke, right there in Mr. Sung's office. And Margo . . . well, the look she gave me could have frozen hell over."

Charlotte slipped her card into the security lock. "Here is where we control the many different production parameters, using microprocessor-based control systems. Before we installed this system, our quality control was subject to human error. There won't be anyone in here. Agent Knight had all the buildings cleared and sealed off before I even got here."

But they both received a shock. There *was* someone there. Jonathan quickly tied the surgical mask over his face.

Mr. Sung spun away from the desk, startled. "Charlotte!" For a moment he was flustered. And then a shutter seemed to click and he was his usual calm self. "I needed to access some information and that federal agent, Mr. Knight, was hovering outside the door to my office. I had the impression he could read what was on my computer screen."

She looked at the desk. "Did you get what you needed?"

"Yes, Charlotte-*ah*," he said softly. "I did." He glanced at Charlotte's masked companion.

"I'm checking security," she said. "I was worried about the isolation lab."

"Yes, must be protected," he said. Then he gave her a small bow and started to leave.

"Mr. Sung," she called out after him.

"Yes?"

"Why did you give me that puzzle box?"

"It was your mother's. Now it is yours."

"But —"

And he was gone.

As soon as the door clicked shut, Charlotte turned to

Jonathan and said, "He lied! Valerius Knight wasn't standing outside his office! When I saw him leave the main building, Knight was talking to Desmond at the shipping dock!"

She looked at the closed door and recalled the letter Mr. Sung had proudly displayed in his office, framed and lighted. The date was 1918 and it was addressed to Mr. Sung's father, praising him for his patriotism and Americanism. Also in the frame was a yellowed newspaper article from the same year, reporting how a Chinese immigrant in San Francisco had named his child after the U.S. president. The letter was signed by President Wilson. The newborn boy who made the news was Woodrow Sung.

"Do you trust him?" Jonathan said.

"He was my grandmother's close friend and adviser for many years. Yes, I trust him. But there *is* something . . ."

"What?"

"I don't know. Just a feeling. Jonathan, I went to Europe last year on a tour of pharmaceutical manufacturers. I was gone for a month, and when I returned . . ." She shook her head. "It was nothing I could put my finger on at the time, and I still can't, but I had the strangest feeling that Mr. Sung's attitude toward me had changed. I've known him all my life, but I would swear that when I came back he was different."

"How so? Good? Bad?"

"Just . . . different."

Jonathan looked at his watch. "We'd better hurry."

They crossed the small office to the large plate-glass window that overlooked a vast processing and bottling-packaging plant, the enormous steel tanks, metal pipes, conveyor belts, forklifts, walls, and floors all spotlessly clean and shiny. The place was eerily silent and deserted, even though all the lights were on and bottles sat waiting in their hoppers.

"How fully automated is the manufacturing process?" Jonathan asked as he set his black bag on the desk.

"There is a dedicated hardware panel that reads the database — this is what controls the machinery."

Jonathan got to work unzipping compartments, pulling out floppy disks. "And who gets that going?"

"The senior technician. The first thing he does is log in to the computer and read the day's production order. Then he sets up for, let's say, two hundred bottles of Golden Lotus. Then either he or an assistant will go down to the machinery, where there are panels with touch-sensitive controls. He punches in the batch order number to be printed on the labels and then presses the 'go' button. The conveyor belt and carousel start, the product is dispensed into each bottle — in this case, Golden Lotus Wine, which would already be in the overhead vats. After that is automatic capping and labeling. Then they're taken to shipping, where they are boxed by hand and sent out."

"I assume there are checkpoints along the way?"

"Yes, the first bottle of Golden Lotus would be removed and brought back to the lab for mass spectrometry analysis that produces a signature of the molecular structure. This is checked against the main database for irregularities. If there is an anomaly, the batch is halted and the system shut down."

"And this analysis is recorded?"

"Every step of manufacture is recorded and double-checked. So you see, it would be pretty difficult to tamper with the product at this stage. Those conveyor belts move fast, and as you can see from here, the bottles are beyond human reach. Even if someone were to manage to get close enough to drop in an additional chemical, he would be observed by others. And anyway, he would for certain get his fingers smashed."

"Could you give me a quick demonstration?"

She thought for a moment, surveying the various machines and conveyor belts that seemed to go forever. "That one there," she said, pointing to a compact mechanical assembly close to the control booth. Compared to the rest of the equipment, this one was small and, Charlotte knew, relatively quiet during operation. "It's our newest acquisition — a Computerized Ampoule Measured Dosing System. What it does is fill and seal glass ampoules."

"I didn't know Harmony manufactured injectible drugs."

"We don't. I came up with this idea myself when we were having problems with our rose oil. Natural essential oils are a big part of our business; we're one of the few manufacturers who haven't switched to synthesized substitutes. But the problem is with their volatility. Essential oils evaporate quickly, and when you are dealing with rose oil, which requires four thousand pounds of rose petals to distill one ounce of rose oil ... well, you can see why the high cost would compel us to find a better way of storing the oil to slow down the evaporation."

"Sealed ampoules."

"Watch." Charlotte moved to a panel covered with lights, buttons, gauges, and levers. Flicking a switch to get a motor started, she then hit a key that set the assembly into motion. Jonathan watched as the robotic arm came to life, gliding on a smooth track as it conducted a three-step operation: first, large needles shooting down and squirting oil into the ampoules; then, flames heating and melting the tops of the vials; finally, metal pincers sealing the hot glass and pinching it off.

"I can see what you mean," he said. "Anyone attempting to tamper with that stuff would either get stabbed, burned, or get a finger chopped off."

Charlotte flicked the switch and the robotic arm was stilled.

Jonathan eyed the shining steel overhead vats. "What precedes all this, before the bottling begins? I assume a night crew does some sort of cleanup and preparation for the morning?"

"All the vats and tubes are cleaned every morning. Whatever of a certain product was remaining in the vats and tubes is noted down. This is for reordering purposes. Reorder levels are based on bulk factors, not what went into the bottles."

Jonathan sat at the desk, booted up the computer, and switched on the monitor. "Who does the recording? The senior technician?"

"No, another man takes care of that."

"And intake and outgo of all supplies are monitored and recorded?"

"To the last drop. For Golden Lotus, for example, we order tincture of valerian from a medical supply company. Let's say we receive twenty gallons, which goes into the vat to be mixed with other herbal compounds. We calculate what was bottled and combine that with the spillage, and it comes out to twenty gallons. Ever since we had problems with theft some years back, we have used a check- and double-check procedure. Every drop is accounted for."

When thunder suddenly cracked overhead, causing the lights to wink, Jonathan said, "I'd better copy those files while we still have power. Will you log in, please?" He stood up and offered her the chair.

Charlotte sat at the computer and, using her ID and pass phrase, accessed the production logs. She relinquished the chair and Jonathan immediately sat down. He whistled. "Harmony certainly puts out a lot of products! Right, Bliss, Ten Thousand Yang, and what was the other?"

"Beautiful Intelligence Balm."

Snapping a floppy into the a-drive, he typed in commands that would begin the downloading of the data. "Keep an eye out," he said as he typed. "If we're caught, we'll have a bastard of a time explaining ourselves."

As Jonathan looked at his watch to time the download, he

saw the clipboard hanging beside the desk, listing the day's production log: *Formula 8, The Eight Heavenly Herbs*. And it made him recall how Charlotte had explained long ago, as they had sat in their favorite tea shop in Chinatown and devoured pork and mushroom potstickers, that eight was the luckiest Chinese number. "Chinese love homonyms," she had said, and Jonathan smiled now at the memory because he had asked her what kind of food that was and she had tossed back her long hair and squealed with laughter, so that the other patrons looked up from their rice and noodles to frown. "A homonym is a sound-alike word, Johnny! And if one word sounds like another word — a lucky word — then the other word is lucky, too!"

"Sounds daft," he had said teasingly.

"In Cantonese the word for eight is *baat*, and in Mandarin it's *pa*. These sound like *faat*, which means prosperity. So, if your address or phone number has an eight in it, it's lucky. Even luckier if you have *two* eights, because then it sounds like you're saying 'prosperity and more prosperity.' See?"

"You aren't Chinese anymore," he said out loud now, unintentionally.

Charlotte gave him a surprised look. "I beg your pardon?"

He shook his head. "Nothing. I was just thinking."

"Well, I never was Chinese."

"Yes you were. When you were young, when we were friends together in San Francisco, you were Chinese, Charlotte. I remember how, when you saw behavior you didn't like, you would blurt, *'Chow mah!'* Didn't that mean 'positively disgraceful' or something like that? And when I took you to my house and you saw my room, you made me move my bed because you said it was in the 'death' position. And you made me drape a black cloth over my TV screen because you said it would disturb my spirit while I slept."

She paced the small control room, watching the door and

the security monitor over it. "That was my grandmother's influence. I outgrew all that."

"And now you're one hundred percent American," he said softly, irony in his voice.

He kept his eyes on her for a moment longer, and then turned away. The memories were rushing toward him at breakneck speed. He had not expected such a deluge from the past. When he had heard, through his inside sources, of the third victim of a Harmony product, he hadn't given it a second thought — he had packed an overnight bag, retrieved the computer kit he always kept in readiness for emergencies, and informed his housekeeper and secretary that he was going away for a few days. Adele, his wife, he had telephoned from the plane, giving her the same message without going into specifics. She had taken the news with the same aplomb as his housekeeper and secretary. It had once been a source of contention in their marriage, Jonathan's sudden departures on top-secret errands. But Adele had grown used to it. "Let me know when you're back," was all she had said.

And then on the flight over he had reviewed what he knew about pharmaceutical companies and their special computer security needs, drafting a customized security profile analysis in case Harmony's system had been invaded. But he hadn't let himself think about Charlotte, hadn't allowed memories to tiptoe in between thoughts of industrial espionage and encryption algorithms. In focusing on the checklist he brought up on his laptop monitor, he had been able to keep thoughts of Charlotte out of his mind. Even when they had finally come face to face, just two hours ago, he had managed to keep the barriers up. He was here to do a job. Granted, he hadn't been hired, he wasn't being paid, it was more of a favor, really — but there was nothing more personal involved than the fact that he and Charlotte had once been friends.

"Grandmother is sooooo upset!"

The voice, from twenty-three years ago, sounded as alive
and fresh as if sixteen-year-old Charlotte were standing
there in the control booth with him. He wanted to say to the
phantom, "Leave me alone"; instead he heard his own
sixteen-year-old voice saying, "What's the matter, then?" in
the Highland burr he had yet to get rid of.

"It's these new area codes! Grandmother just found out
that San Francisco's is *415*."

They were in Charlotte's secret sanctuary, one of the
places they went when they needed to escape from the
world. She had first brought him there when they were thirteen, when he had seen boys following Charlotte down the
street, calling, "Chinky chinky Chinaman!" and lobbing
stones and dog dirt at her with slingshots. Charlotte had
maintained her dignity, walking with her chin up, tears
streaming down her cheeks, but Jonathan had gone ballistic,
flying across the street to take out all three, right there and
then, knocking two of the boys down and sending the other
one running. He received a cut above his eyebrow and Charlotte had taken him into her house, the way she had done a
few weeks before, when she had given him lemonade and
told him her mother was dead, too. She had taken him into
the kitchen and washed his wound and then she had shown
him her private sanctuary where only she went.

And so they were there, three years later, that day in 1973
when they were sixteen and Charlotte was saying how upset
her grandmother was that San Francisco's area code was
415 because "Four is the *unluckiest* number for Chinese. It
sounds like the word for 'death' so Chinese never, *ever* use
the number four. *Aii-yah*, she's writing letters right now to
our congressmen and senators and to President Nixon!"

While she had talked, he had just sat there dumbly watching the way the wind played with her hair, how the sun
shone on her smooth skin. Charlotte's secret place was a

small garden on the roof of her grandmother's mansion, where someone had built a frail gazebo long ago. Now it was forested with potted plants and tiny trees and even a birdbath that Charlotte kept filled with water, and they could see the Golden Gate Bridge from up there, and the Bay and the city and the edge of the world.

After the first time, when they were thirteen, and Charlotte had shyly said, "Would you like to see my secret place?" Johnny had awkwardly reciprocated by showing her *his* private sanctuary — she was the only person he ever took there, and he would never forget the shocked look on her face when she first saw it.

Just as, he thought now, darkly, he would never forget another shocked look on her face sixteen years later, the last time they met, in San Francisco. He had gone hoping for a mending of the break that had occurred between them six years earlier, after he had been at MIT for a year — 1981, the year his world had shattered when she had said on the phone, "I need my freedom."

He had thought she would marry him, that black year of 1981. Instead she needed to go her own way. And so, six years later he had gone to San Francisco hoping she had changed her mind, that she wanted to be with him after all.

Instead, she had walked out, leaving him sitting there.

"Jonathan?"

He blinked. The Italian restaurant and Charlotte's shocked look vanished. She was regarding him with a small frown as she stood there in the paper coveralls with a paper bonnet on her head. "How is the download going?" she said, as though she had had to repeat herself.

"Information moves at its own speed," he said thickly, his throat constricted from the memories. He had almost run after her that day. He had almost called after her, "Tell me not to marry her, Charlie. Tell me it's you I should be marrying."

"Oh my God!" Charlotte said suddenly, pointing to the security monitor. A figure had entered the adjoining lab. "It's Knight and he's heading this way!"

Jonathan quickly shut off the monitor and sprang to his feet.

"Over here!" she said, and they quickly slipped into a supply closet, where brooms and mops and buckets left little space. "Just pray the system doesn't decide to do some de-fragging," Jonathan whispered as they watched the door.

"Why?"

"Knight will hear it, so he'll know it's running."

Through the crack in the door they saw Knight come in, raincoat dripping, his bare head glistening. He looked around, eyes pausing on the dark monitor.

Charlotte felt her heart pound in her ears. Could he hear the hum of the computer under the desk?

Jonathan also kept an anxious eye on Knight, but his thoughts were elsewhere. Charlotte stood very close to him, almost touching him, filling his head with the scent of her shampoo and body cream — the subtle, delicate perfume of Harmony Primrose Collection.

"*Jonathan!*" she hissed suddenly. And then she nodded toward the desk, where his black computer case stood on the floor by the chair.

"Oh Christ," he said. If his mind had been on his work, he never would have made a mistake like that.

"If he sees it —"

They both held their breath, Charlotte moving closer to Jonathan. He put an arm about her waist as they watched Knight slowly scan the control room, his eyes trailing over the desks, monitors, control panels. When he walked over to the large plate-glass window to survey the processing plant, his left foot nearly kicked the computer case.

Charlotte tried to remain calm, telling herself that she owned this company, that she had a right to be in here, that she also had a right to hire an outside consultant. Why was she being made to feel like a criminal? It was Knight. If it were anyone other than he, she might tell him what she knew. But she did not trust this man. Especially after the way he and Margo had appeared so cozy together.

She felt Jonathan's arm around her waist, felt the warmth of his body penetrate her coveralls and skirt and blouse. She wanted to lean into him, rest for a while in his strength. But she had done that once before, and he had stepped away to let her fall.

She turned her head slightly, to look up at him, and almost instinctively he turned to look down at her, their faces inches apart, each able to delve into the other's eyes. And suddenly the small utility room was a vortex of hot passions and fiery memories. Jonathan's arm tightened around her waist; Charlotte's breath caught in her throat. Valerius Knight was forgotten, the black bag on the floor, the computer, the bottling plant, the whole world — all vanished as Jonathan and Charlotte connected for one quick, electrifying moment.

He bent his head, she raised her lips.

And then they heard the outer door clicking shut; the moment shattered, they pulled apart.

"He's gone," Jonathan said, and he pulled himself away from her to return to the computer. As Jonathan retrieved his disk and shut down, Charlotte managed to find her breath. Suddenly she needed to say something, to fill the silence created by their old passions, to bring them both back to reality. "You had a long flight," she said. "Are you tired or hungry?"

He looked up at her. He opened his mouth, hesitated, then said, "It's nothing that coffee directly into a vein won't cure."

"I'll go to the cafeteria. A lot of my employees are still here, at least to have their dinner before going home in the

storm. Smoked salmon soup tonight," she added with a
weak smile. "Improves nervous functions."

His eyes met hers and suddenly she was like the old Charlotte, sounding like her grandmother.

16

They hurried back to the museum, making a run through the
rain, ducking at one point into a dark doorway when a policeman in a yellow slicker suddenly appeared.

When Jonathan was situated once again at the computer,
Charlotte regarded his broad back, the way his dark hair
curled over the collar of his shirt She could almost feel the
energy in his body, as if it radiated out and filled the room.
And she found herself thinking of the men she had been with
over the years: the professional athlete who was great in bed
but a manipulator; the ad executive who never argued fairly,
always getting his side voiced and then quickly kissing her
and saying, "Let's not fight," before Charlotte could argue
her side; the news anchor who believed so strongly in the
equality of women that he had once remained in the car
while she changed a flat tire; the accountant who always
whipped out his calculator in a restaurant and figured the tip
down to the penny. They had all had their good points — for
the most part Charlotte had managed to find gentle men who
were kind and humorous — but they had had their faults,
just as she knew she had faults of her own that had ultimately driven the men away from her: impatience, obsession with Harmony House, keeping secrets, and putting up
barriers. No one had cared enough to want to change her or
to stay around and pull those barriers down. Her worst fault

was that she could not break the habit of comparing every man she met to Jonathan.

It wasn't that Jonathan was better than every other male on the planet; it was the single inescapable fact that Jonathan's mere presence always made her feel better.

He had flown to her aid without even asking.

Charlotte turned away and went to the doorway to look into the museum. While Jonathan had been working on the communications array, she had done more research on her family. She hadn't known that her grandmother's parents were never married. Or that her grandmother and her mother had been social outcasts in Singapore, or that her great-grandfather never returned. Her grandmother had traveled to America on her own, when she was sixteen years old. She had gone in search of her father. Had she found him?

As Charlotte's eyes shifted to the glass cases, housing the dusty mementos of a forgotten history, her eyes rested on a mannequin dressed in a lavender silk *cheongsam* — a form-fitting, knee-length dress with mandarin collar and slit skirt — and she tried to imagine what it had been like for that young girl to arrive in a new country, all alone, hoping to find her father.

"What's this?" Jonathan said. He was pointing to the answering machine by the phone. "The message light is flashing."

"I didn't notice it," Charlotte said as she hit the rewind button. "It must have come through while we were in the production plant."

Naomi's energy rode into the room on her voice. "Char! I'm still stuck on campus. The storm knocked a tree across the entrance to the parking garage. It's been cleared away now, and as soon as I can get out, I'll come to you. But oh, God, Char, the most awful thing has happened! I went through the staff lounge a few minutes ago and the news was on TV. It was all about you, Char."

"Oh no," Charlotte moaned, bracing herself.

But it was worse than she had expected. "They're not just showing that godawful picture," Naomi said, her voice rising with tension. "They ran a segment of that blasted interview!"

Charlotte felt her heart stop. The televised interview when she was released from jail after the Chalk Hill incident had harmed her reputation far more than the photograph of her with bloody arms raised. The reporter had guaranteed a fair interview, and it had gone well. But it had been edited so that Charlotte's words were twisted to make her out to be a demented sadist.

"Char," Naomi said heatedly, "I hope you're braced for this. You're in for a shock. I mean, we haven't talked about Chalk Hill in a long time. We've both worked hard to put it behind us. So I didn't make the connection when the news first came out last week. And I know you've forgotten, too."

Jonathan gave Charlotte a puzzled look. "Connection?"

She spread her hands; she had no idea what Naomi was leading to.

"They weren't running that interview tonight for the hell of it! Some clever twit made the connection and dug it out of the archives. Char, that witch who interviewed you and made you look like Lucrezia Borgia — Charlotte, are you aware that she was the first victim? Oh Jesus, Char. *She* was the one who died after using Beautiful Intelligence Balm."

17

1924 — San Francisco, California

We were taken to an island called "angel" although it was run by devils. Here was where I heard about the Exclusion

Act, an invisible wall to keep Chinese out. But I was lucky. My father was an American. Only the year before, the wives and children of Chinese men living in America had been allowed in. But then there was a new law called the Immigration Act of 1924 that forbade even the families of legal immigrants living in America to join them. These women and babies who made the long voyage with me were sent back to China, back to poverty and sickness, never to see their husbands. One young woman hanged herself in her bride's dress because the man she loved was allowed in while she was sent back.

The barracks on Angel Island were plain wood and we could see the city of San Francisco from the barred windows. We were locked in all day and night, and women wrote poems of anguish on the walls. I did not know why we were being held in jail. We had been taken from our ship and ferried to the island where we waited, we unwanted Chinese who had the proper papers and who longed to be in the city across the water.

I waited forty-two days. Each day, women I had made friends with left the barracks. Some returned to tell the rest of us about the interrogation, some never came back. I do not know if they went into the city or if they were sent back to China. When my turn came, I was asked only one thing: what was my father's name, address, and occupation. Because my mother didn't know these things, she had made them up with the Reverend Peterson's help.

When the jailers on Angel Island could not find a Richard Smith who resided on Powell Street and worked as an accountant, I explained that my father left Singapore sixteen years ago and we had lost contact with him. Perhaps he is in New York, I said, or New Hampshire, or New Orleans. I chose those names because the "new" sounded lucky. In the end they let me in because my papers bore the stamp of the

U.S. consul in Singapore. Not even the devils on Angel Island could ignore that.

Finally I set foot in the city where my father lived, and I am ashamed to say I was filled with joy. My mother was dead, and I had not been there to bury her and mourn for her. I had made arrangements with the Reverend Peterson to take care of my mother after she died. I left him with plenty of spirit money to be burned at her funeral, and I asked him please to hire the best mourners in the city. Although my mother was alive when I kissed her good-bye and walked onto the ship, I saw the clouds of death on her face.

I had mourned as I sailed across the Pacific Ocean, on a crowded ship where women frantically memorized information they would need at the interrogation, and then threw the sheets overboard before the officials could see them. I searched the horizon each day and wondered if this was the day she had died, alone, an outcast. While the ship sailed east, I faced west and I thought of my mother, our life together, everything she had taught me. But when I finally set foot on the soil of America, I turned my eyes east, toward my new beginning.

The Reverend Peterson had told me about Chinatown, which was where he said I should look for lodgings. "Don't try to find a room anywhere else in the city," he cautioned me, "because they won't rent to Chinese."

At the time his words were like feathers on the wind. America was the land of equality. I could live anywhere.

Nonetheless, I did look for a room in Chinatown, because I wanted to be among familiar people. As I searched for a place to live, I thought about how my whole life had been a saga of homelessness, my mother and I always on the move as she told me stories about the big house on Peacock Lane where she had grown up, where generations of our family had been born, lived, and died. I yearned to live in such a house. Perhaps when I found my father, I thought, he would invite me to stay with him. I pictured a large house on top of one of the San Francisco hills, overlooking the water and the sky. I would go there to live for the rest of my life.

Chinatown, I learned, had been burned down eighteen years earlier, after a big earthquake. It had been rebuilt by someone whose idea of Chinese architecture was not at all Chinese. But the people were! Crowded into these few blocks were people who had come from Canton and Peking, from all the provinces, with many different dialects riding the breeze like New Year's streamers. My eyes widened at the sight of the shops, where barbecued ducks hung in windows and bountiful crates of onions, eggplants, and oranges enticed the shopper. For the hungry there were tearooms and food stalls, displaying their offerings of sesame cakes, steamed dumplings, and chicken buns. I smelled familiar smells, I saw and heard the sounds of home. I had thought America would be a strange and foreign place and that I would be very homesick. But I encountered people on the sidewalks who smiled with my smile and looked at me with my eyes. We were from all over Asia, we "Celestials" as the Americans called us (some even called us "yellow peril"), but we were like one large family, sharing culture, gods, and noodles.

I knew I would be happy here.

As I walked with my suitcase, which had been a gift from the Reverend Peterson, and my mother's black lacquer medicine chest, I looked at the For Rent signs along the streets. The signs were written in Chinese and placed in the windows of the Happy Laundry, Yin-Fei Tearoom, Ping Huang Trading Company, but the streets were named Grant, Stockton, and Jackson. I scrutinized the numbers of the addresses, watching for good luck numbers. I found a building on Grant Street. Number eight-nine. A lucky address.

The landlady was Mrs. Po, who owned the Happy Laundry. She had a gold front tooth and she spoke a dialect of

Chinese I was not familiar with, so she asked me in English, "You all alone? No family?"

I showed her my papers, and she looked closely at me. "You look younger than eighteen." She shook her head. "Girl all alone not good. Men come around, give my house bad name."

But I wanted to live there. She had told me the apartment was the one in the front, on the third floor, and I saw how the morning sunlight struck the open window. Good for *chi*. And the street door had been painted red, for keeping out bad luck. So I offered her twice the rent and she became very friendly, taking my suitcase and saying what a respectable girl I looked. "No men," she admonished me, however, when we reached my apartment. "Plenty of whores in Chinatown, but not in my house."

As soon as the apartment was mine, I changed the number on my door to eight, until I saw that three other tenants had done the same. We could not all live in number eight! So I changed my number to two, which stands for abundance.

It was a nice apartment with a tiny kitchen and bathroom, enough for me, and soon I furnished it with new curtains and a new rug. I brought in plants, and an aquarium because water brings prosperity, and an angelfish for companionship. I pulled the bed away from the window, because otherwise all my hopes would have drained down into the alley below. I placed the head to the East, where luck comes from, and my feet to the West, so that I wouldn't miss my destiny. I bought a lamp and placed it on the left side of my bed so that the left chambers of my heart received the first heat in the morning. And I set a pan of water under my bed, to drown bad dreams.

In the kitchen, where I intended to spend my days cooking my meals, and my nights my herbal medicines, I cleaned the small gas stove because clogged burners block a family's income. And when I saw that the stove was next to the sink, which placed two conflicting elements side by side — fire which is *yang* and water which is *yin* — I remedied the problem by placing a wooden cutting board between the two. Then I purchased two Yixing teapots, one for boiling morning tea, "for luck," one for evening tea, "for good dreams." Lastly I hung crystal wind chimes by the open window to keep good *chi* swirling.

Compared to our humble room over the bordello on Malay Street, this was a palace. I had rented such a place that I might honor my father when I brought him here.

I sold one of my emeralds and bought lovely new dresses — a Taiwanese silk *cheongsam* with hand embroidery — and fashionable shoes with matching leather handbags. I wanted to look my best when I met my father.

And then I went to find him.

It was his ring that would lead me to him, for in a city so large, how else would I find him?

The ring had clearly been custom-made, the intertwined initials *RB* done by an artist's hand. So I would inquire among jewelers to see who remembered creating such a unique ring.

Onboard the ship I had learned to keep my most precious possessions on my person, so I wore my father's ring on a long chain around my neck, hiding it under my dress, and as I visited jeweler after jeweler, I would modestly draw out the necklace and hold out the ring, but never did it leave my neck.

I began first around Chinatown, making the acquaintance of my new neighbors. Already the shopkeepers liked me because I never argued over price, always buying the best quality, never counting my change when they handed it back. "Very nice girl," Mrs. Po told the neighbors. "From

Singapore. Very wealthy family. I have only the finest tenants in my house."

When jewelers near Chinatown did not recognize the ring, I went farther out, riding the cable cars until I was dizzy, aware of people staring at me as though they had never seen a Chinese before. When I went to a restaurant for lunch and they would not give me a table, although there were many empty ones, I began to understand the Reverend Peterson's admonishment to stay close to Chinatown. And the farther I strayed from my own world, the more hostile the other one became.

Everywhere I went, the policemen said, "Move along." Or they stopped me and asked questions, demanded to see my papers, asked me if I was a prostitute. I learned about racial hatred. I learned that Chinese were the only race not permitted into the United States. I learned that there were laws saying, "No more Chinese." We were not allowed to own property, to marry whites, or to enter white men's hospitals. And when a Chinese ventured into a white neighborhood and was beaten and robbed, the police said, "Why did you go in there?" But I was American. When I tried to explain this, however, they only looked me up and down, and when they saw the *cheongsam* that I wore, I knew they saw the villainous Chinese ladies they saw in American films.

But I would not give up. The ring was my only connection to my father. I did not know his last name or what he did for a living or where his family was. The ring would lead me to him, and to identifying the ring, I needed to go out into a city that did not want me.

Finally, after days of bad luck, with my feet aching and blistered from so much walking, my spirits low, my hunger sharp, the policemen watching me, good luck came my way. I went into Sadler and Sons on Market Street — I was far from home — and saw at once the flicker of recognition in the jeweler's eyes when he saw the ring.

"Let me take a look at that more closely," he said, reaching.

But I drew back. "Please," I said, "I need to know what these letters stand for."

"I don't know," he said, and his eyes shifted. "Let me show this around to some of my colleagues."

I told him I would return, and I realized in excitement that he might even contact my father, that I might meet him in this very shop.

I returned the next day in my finest dress of lavender silk, my long hair coiled up and held in place with expensive ivory combs. My heart raced ahead of my hopes, but I approached the shop cautiously.

How should I greet my father? How should I address him? Would he receive me with joy and exclaim how like my mother I was? A thousand doubts suddenly assailed me. He never returned to Singapore. Had he forgotten the woman who saved his life? When his old memory returned, had his new Singapore memory been pushed away? Would he look at me and say, "Who are you"?

Before going into the shop, I peered through the large window to see if my father had come. Instead, I saw a handsome young man in there, and a young girl with him, maybe my own age, with yellow hair and white skin. But it was the young man, who was a few years older than I, who captured my attention. He was leaning casually against the counter, talking to the jeweler, laughing. I heard his rich voice, I saw the striking profile that could have made him a film star. And when he turned suddenly, as if he sensed me watching him, our eyes met.

It was in that moment that my life changed forever.

I had seen plays and films in which a hero and heroine fell in love at first sight, and had not my own mother fallen in love with my father when she first set eyes on him? But I did not really understand it until that instant, when I peered through the shop window and locked my gaze with the sparkling gray eyes of the handsome young man at the counter.

I reached deep down for my courage, swallowed it whole, and went inside, hoping the jeweler had news for me.

The young man, whose smile seemed frozen on his face, kept his eyes on me as I stepped in. I tried to look away, but could not. I hesitated just inside the doorway, feeling the enchantment surround me. The shop, I think, was full of silver and gold and glitter and polish, shiny display cases and crystal lamps. But I saw only two piercing eyes the color of morning mist, and a smile that seemed to want to say more.

"That's her! That's the thief!"

I looked at the jeweler. He was pointing at me. And suddenly a policeman materialized from the back room. As I turned to run, I heard the handsome young man say, "Wait! Let's talk to her first! Maybe she just *found* my father's ring!"

"They're all thieves, Mr. Barclay!" the jeweler shouted. "The lot of them!"

I ran all the way home, down one street and up an alley, down another, and up another, to the cable car, from the cable car, until at last I was safe among people I recognized, people in padded blue jackets and black silk pants, people reading Chinese newspapers pasted to the walls, people selecting a duck for dinner or arguing over the weight of a melon. I was home among my own kind; the policeman did not follow.

My thoughts were a whirlpool of confusion. "Mr. Barclay," the jeweler had called the young man. "Your father's ring." Which meant he was my half brother. I had already known my father had a First Wife because he wrote that in the letter he left for my mother. The letter signed only "Richard" and a promise to return.

Why did he not return? Had First Wife convinced him to forget his Chinese concubine?

My heart was heavy as I climbed the stairs to my apartment. How was I to find my father if a policeman lurked behind every corner?

When I saw the door to my apartment standing open, I thought Mrs. Po had come to visit. And then I saw my furniture in disarray.

A burglar had visited.

My mother's black lacquer medicine case was gone. The mattress on my bed was torn open, and my American dollars, which I had tucked into the stuffing, were gone. My aquarium lay smashed on the floor, my angelfish dead. This was the worst of it, the shattered fish tank, and the fine white sand spread on the floor.

My eyes traveled to the humble statue of Kwan Yin, which my mother had said no thief would steal. It was still there. But because I had thought Kwan Yin had carried the burden of my mother's emeralds for too many years, I had given her a rest by removing them from her body and hiding them elsewhere.

I had thought: What better place than beneath the sand in a fish tank?

I would have wept at that moment for all that I had lost. But then I thought of the ironies fate can deliver because, while everything was being stolen from me, two gifts were being given — gifts that could never be stolen. The first was that I had learned my father's name: Barclay. Now I could find him.

The second was a newborn love. But it was love of the wrong kind, because the handsome young man I had just fallen in love with was my brother.

18

9:00 P.M. — Palm Springs, California

Stay tuned, Charlotte. I have a surprise for you in a little while and I wouldn't want you to miss it.

"Charlotte," Jonathan called out, "we got another message."

Replacing Richard Barclay's ring in its display case, Charlotte hurried back into her grandmother's office, where another e-mail seemed to mock her on the computer screen.

"What kind of surprise, do you suppose?" Jonathan said.

Charlotte felt her stomach tighten. Ever since hearing Naomi's telephone message about the first victim being the news reporter who had practically crucified her on national television, Charlotte's nerves had danced like live wires. It was only a matter of time before Valerius Knight found out the connection, if he didn't already know, and then he would start questioning her about the other two victims.

"Are you sure you don't know them?" Jonathan had asked.

But Charlotte was certain she had never heard of the other two women. Their names were not remotely familiar, and they didn't live in California. She was praying that the reporter was only an incredible coincidence, because she knew how it looked: the woman had nearly destroyed Charlotte's reputation, which gave Charlotte a clear motive for murder.

In the meantime, the last line of the e-mail said, *here's a little something to keep you entertained*. And a document file opened up on the screen.

"What on earth is all *this*?" Charlotte said as she leaned closer to read the rest of the message. Her eyes widened as she scrolled down the list of numbers that appeared on the screen. "That's my checking account number! And my American Express card! My social security number, my PIN —"

Jonathan was already typing, pulling down the message headers and scrutinizing the route of the e-mail.

Charlotte wrapped her arms around herself. "Do you know what he can *do* with this information? He could wipe out my bank accounts, ruin my credit, get me into trouble with the IRS."

Jonathan copied the address of the re-mailer, pasted it in a new message, addressed it to the administrator of the mail host, and typed: *We are being harassed and threatened by the attached. Can you provide us with the source of the message?* He had already sent the appeal to the previous re-mailers, with no results so far.

Then he checked the receiver for the electronic pulse monitor. Nothing. The transmitter he had placed in Knight's laptop was also silent. "Good, that tells us something," he said as he picked up the disassembled cellular phone he had been working on when the e-mail came through. "We'll get him, Charlotte, don't worry," he said, snapping the cellular case shut. Swiveling around in his chair, he quickly plugged the phone into a port in his laptop. "Watch this," he said as a map suddenly sprang to the screen.

Charlotte leaned forward to look, her long hair brushing the back of his neck. "What is it?"

"This little device will track every phone call made from the building. Watch." Using his own cellular phone, he dialed a number, and immediately blue lines began shooting across the screen, with the names and locations of switchers and nodes cropping up as red dots. "Unfortunately, it doesn't work in reverse, but if our anonymous e-mailer is working with an accomplice on the inside, we'll catch him when he makes a call."

"This is so frustrating!" she said. "You're building this complex web, all these traps, and yet he still eludes us."

"In a cat-and-mouse game, love, the one with the most patience wins. I learned that when I spied for the NSA."

Charlotte abruptly turned away and, snatching up her raincoat, headed for the door. "I'm going to have a talk with Agent Knight. I need to know what he's found out so far, if he knows about my connection with the reporter, and if he has the lab report on the latest victim."

"There are thousands of production logs in here," he said, tapping the computer screen. "There isn't time to run a check on all of them. We need to know the common denominator. Something to work from. We need to know the lethal ingredient."

"I'll wring it out of Knight if I have to."

"Just don't get arrested," he said with a smile, and when she gave him a startled look — how could he joke about her Chalk Hill ordeal? — she realized he wasn't referring to that arrest, but to another one long ago, which she had almost forgotten about, when they had *both* been arrested and carted off to jail.

And then she saw a look of waiting in his eyes, as if he had questions but he wanted *her* to start. But she didn't know how.

"Be careful," Jonathan said finally, turning away so that she could leave before the moment of silent questions went on too long.

"I'll be back in time for our e-mailer's little surprise," she said softly, and then she was gone.

When he heard the outer door close, Jonathan got up from the desk and went to the security monitor. He hit a key on the console and the covered walkway to the main building came into view. At first all he saw was the steady downpour, and then he saw a figure emerge from the right side of the screen — Charlotte, hurrying through the rain. From the back, with her long black hair lying flat between her shoulder blades, she almost looked like a teenager again.

"I swear my grandmother doesn't like me," Charlotte had said in her high, sing-songy voice, which Jonathan sometimes thought was a subconscious way of imitating the way her grandmother talked. Charlotte, at sixteen, worked hard to be American, but her grandmother's Chinese influence was strong. "She was always trying to give me nightmares when I was little. Like the story she told me about the naughty little girl who stamped her foot so hard the ground cracked open and the little girl fell in and the ground closed up on her. It gave me nightmares for ages afterward."

"She just wanted you to be a good girl," Jonathan said as he concentrated on soldering a component to the circuit board in his lap. He was sitting cross-legged on the floor, surrounded by electronic gadgetry and scattered copies of *Popular Electronics*, while Charlotte sat on his bed, in tights and an oversized Greenpeace sweatshirt, her knees drawn to her chest, arms hugging her legs. When he had first brought her here, when they were thirteen, he hadn't thought anything about Charlotte sitting on his bed. But now, at sixteen, it was all he could think about. The concentration on his new project was a sham. His entire mind was focused on Charlotte on his bed, thinking how much he loved kissing her, and wondering if he was ever going to get the courage to take the next step.

"Grandmother used to tell me that I wasn't really a girl-child, that I had originally been a duck, plucked and cooked and hanging in Ah Fong's Market on Stockton, but that I was so worthless no one would buy me, so she traded him a melon for me and raised me as a human. She actually said that, Johnny. She thinks I'm worthless."

He reached for micro-pliers, his eyes on his delicate work. "She thinks you are more precious than her own life. She doesn't want you stolen away from her."

Charlotte gave him a wry smile. "How do you know that?"

"Because Chinese grandmothers don't have a monopoly on ways of keeping evil spirits away, y'know."

She regarded the contraption in his hands. "What are you making?"

"A computer."

"What will it compute?"

"Different ways," he said in all seriousness, "of keeping evil spirits away."

He hadn't been able to tell her how much he envied her having a grandmother who loved her enough to scare away the evil eye. His own gran in Scotland had done the same thing, telling him she'd exchanged a cabbage for him from a passing gypsy. It was a way of letting the fairies know that he wasn't worth stealing.

But he wasn't in Scotland anymore, he was in America, and his father didn't seem to know anything about the evil eye or fairies. He didn't seem to know about love either, or how to be a father to a son. Jonathan didn't really blame him. And the man did try — Jonathan didn't lack for anything he asked for or needed; this private sanctuary attested to that. When the first hand-held calculators came out, too expensive for most people to afford, fourteen-year-old Jonathan had received several to play with.

"Someday, Charlie," he said as he tossed his long hair off his shoulders, "every household is going to have a personal computer."

She laughed. "Not *my* house! Grandmother won't even allow a TV remote control because, as she puts it, anything that can change a television channel can change a person's *chi*. Grandmother doesn't even trust electric clocks because she says how do you know how fast the electricity is flowing? 'Clock might be slow, might be fast.' "

Charlotte had unfolded herself from the bed and pulled a

Snickers bar from the enormous tote bag she carried everywhere. Unwrapping it, she broke the candy bar in two and handed, as she always did, the bigger portion to Jonathan. Then she slipped down onto the floor next to him and munched on the peanuts and caramel as she watched him hook up the circuit board to a Teletype with a paper-tape reader. She sat so close to him that his palms had gotten sweaty. He had also, to his mortification, sprung a healthy erection.

Charlotte had had that effect on him for as far back as he could remember.

She still did.

19

Charlotte found Agent Knight at the work station he had set up at a vacant desk. Now he not only had a laptop up and running, Charlotte noticed, but a printer as well. He also had two phones next to the monitor. She wondered what he would think if he found out that an ex-spy for the NSA was secretly monitoring his keystrokes.

He was eating a cheese burrito, with extreme delicacy, Charlotte thought, meticulously dabbing his thick black mustache between bites, taking care to use the napkin that was draped over his large thigh. He had removed his jacket and loosened his tie.

Charlotte noticed the shoulder holster and gun. She wondered where he'd gotten the burrito.

"Ah, Ms. Lee, there you are!" he said with great geniality, setting his burrito down and gently brushing off his fingertips. "I was just about to come looking for you." He ripped a sheet off the computer printout and handed it to her.

"The final analysis," he said with a smile. "The culprit is ephedrine."

"Ephedrine," she repeated out loud. And instantly, through the electronic plug in her ear, she heard Jonathan say, "Ephedrine! Got it!"

As Charlotte scanned the report, Knight said, "We are familiar with the formulas for Ten Thousand Yang and Beautiful Intelligence Balm, and neither of those calls for ephedrine. May I assume the same of Bliss?"

"Yes," she murmured, her eyebrows knotting in a frown. "There is no ephedrine in the Bliss formula."

"But your company does use it?"

She looked up at him. Knight towered over her. "Quite a few of our products contain ephedrine. It's used for chest ailments. It is also a stimulant."

"Well, I wonder how ephedrine got into these three products. And you will notice that it was added in very precise amounts. This was no hasty job. And judging by those careful measurements, this was not something that was done after the products left this factory, either. Would you agree?"

She read the results again. Each Bliss capsule contained the same precise amount of ephedrine. Every sampling of Beautiful Intelligence Balm, from different areas in the jar, contained the same trace of ephedrine. It was harder to tell with the Yang tonic, since it was a liquid, but the report attested to the fact that the bottle had been new, part of the safety seal still on the cap.

Agent Knight was correct. The tampering most likely had not been done off the premises. So Jonathan was right. The production logs held the key.

"Now, this is either gross negligence," Knight continued after taking a sip of coffee and carefully replacing the cup on the desk, "or someone has done this deliberately. And I am thinking that it is someone who knows what he or she is doing." He paused, dabbed the napkin to his lips. "I am curious though. . . . I understand that Ten Thousand Yang is a formula for men. Yet the second victim is a woman. Why is that, do you suppose?"

"We found that, in smaller doses, Yang works as a hair restorer in women in certain cases."

"And if a woman were to, say, overdose herself, could this have a harmful effect?"

"No."

He considered this. "The balm, though. Now don't you find that odd?"

"What do you mean?"

"Well, Bliss and the Yang tonic are ingestible products. The balm is a topical product."

The thought had already crossed Charlotte's mind: it *was* strange that the balm had been tampered with. That ingestible products such as a tonic or tea additive should have been altered made sense because there was a guarantee of a result. But adding ephedrine to a topical agent was generally useless unless the product was applied to an open wound, in which case the ephedrine would be absorbed by the bloodstream and cause adverse reactions. "This woman was using the balm to cure leg ulcers," Charlotte murmured thoughtfully. "Agent Knight, could *she* have been the intended target?" She searched his face for signs of game-playing. If he suspected the TV reporter had been the target, and he knew Charlotte's connection to her, he was hiding it well.

"That possibility is already under investigation, but if she were, then there would have to be some connection to the other two women, don't you think?"

Were they connected? Charlotte felt an arctic shiver rush through her. And were the three somehow connected to *her?* "So you think my company is the target of whoever tampered with the products and these women are random victims?" she said as calmly as she could.

"Your company," he said, "or yourself."

She held up the report. "May I keep this?"

"Certainly. Perhaps you can look it over when you have a minute and see if you can come up with any theories."

"Thank you," she said and started to walk away.

He sat back down, draped the napkin over his thigh, and picked up the cheese burrito. As he was about to take a bite, he said, "Oh, and where will you be in case I need you?"

She gave him a look. "I am going to the cafeteria, Agent Knight. If you need me, I shan't be hard to find."

He offered a polished smile. "I should imagine you won't be."

Charlotte stopped again and felt her anger rise. "Agent Knight," she said, "may I please have the name of your superior?"

"May I ask what for?"

"I believe you are prejudiced against my company. I do not believe you are acting on behalf of the public, but rather in your own self-interest."

His look darkened. "In that, Miss Lee, you are absolutely correct. I do have a personal interest, and I do mean to protect myself and the public from quack operations such as this."

She relented a little. "Agent Knight, I know about your son and I am sorry —"

He held up a large, spatulate hand. "My son is with the Lord. You will please not call his memory up in this place."

She started to say something, then, with a quick nod, turned and walked away.

My son! he thought as he watched Charlotte vanish down the hall. What do *you* know about my son? he wanted to shout. What do you know about doctors telling you that there was nothing they could do, that it was a rare form of cancer that just somehow began to grow in a six-year-old child?

Valerius Knight closed his eyes and wrestled with the memories that haunted him every minute of his life: the long drives down to Mexico and the clinic there, the sending away to Sweden, Taiwan, and Beijing for "miracle cures," the turning away from God and praying to nature instead.

Herbals! Their desperate search for a cure had turned a God-fearing Christian woman into a plant-worshipping pagan! False hope was worse than no hope because it stripped the soul of true faith and turned you away from the Lord.

The night the boy finally died, Valerius hadn't been able to pry the little body from his wife's arms, and so instead he had rampaged through their Santa Monica home, collecting all the bottles, jars, packets, and needles of false hope, scoured all shelves, drawers, and cupboards of the demon herbals, harvesting every pill, leaf, and root of mumbo-jumbo healing, and burned the lot in the backyard barbecue, sparking the fire with his tears while the paramedics tried to talk his wife into relinquishing her son's stiff body.

She had never returned to God after that. False hope in heathen elixirs had drained her soul of the Lord's faith and left the Devil's darkness there instead. Do I have a personal interest in this case? he wanted to shout at Charlotte Lee. You had better believe that I do. For every one of these evil citadels I bring down, my little boy lights a new candle in Heaven.

20

With the toxicology report tucked into the waistband of her skirt, Charlotte hurried down the hall toward her own office, where she found the cold cup of tea she had abandoned earlier. Retrieving the box of teabags, she slipped them into the pocket of her raincoat, and left.

Instead of going straight to the elevators, she took a brief trip along the corridor where the senior offices branched off. Pausing to listen at Margo's door, she heard soft music and muted speech. At Adrian's office, she heard him saying, "Don't worry about your goddamn investment. You'll get your money back, trust me." The door to Mr. Sung's office was standing open, with no sign of the elderly lawyer. And the one at the end, Desmond's, was also open. But the lights were out, and she thought he had gone.

"Hell of a thing, huh?" he said from the darkness, startling her.

"Are you trying to sleep?" she asked, when her eyes adjusted and she saw him sitting in his executive chair, staring out at the rain.

"Nope. Just sitting here wishing I drank."

Desmond had never been able to handle alcohol. Charlotte would never forget the New Year's Eve when he had had some champagne and he had said to her, his words slurring, "Becky's leaving me. Can you believe it? This'll be my third divorce and I'm not even thirty-five."

"I don't blame her," Charlotte had said. "The way you treat her. Why do you do it, Des? Why are you so nice at first and then you turn nasty?"

"It's because, dear cousin," he had said, "I can't respect someone who'd fall in love with *me*."

Even in the darkness, Charlotte could see all the trophies that adorned Desmond's office. Her cousin was driven to win — winning was his drug of choice, and his aphrodisiac as well. He would tackle and master one skill until he got the ribbons, cups, and recognition, and then move on to another. His eclectic prizes embraced tennis, fencing, race car driving, and Korean kickboxing. If he could, he would have had a glass case to display women as well, because they, too, were trophies to be won, and once won, were no longer of interest.

"You know what I think?" he said softly in the darkness, barely visible because his clothes were the color of the night. "I think we're under a curse, Charlie. I think we're being punished."

She stared at him. Desmond was even wearing the sunglasses in the dark, as if he were afraid evil forces might invade his soul through his eyes. "Punished for what?" she said.

He rolled his head to the side. She saw a pair of black lenses staring back at her. "You know what for, Charlie," he said. "You know."

21

As soon as the wind and rain delivered Charlotte into the museum, she made sure the door was locked, then she hurried across to the office, her arms cradling warm bowls and dishes.

"Any word from our e-mailer? Has he pulled his little surprise?" she said breathlessly as she deposited everything on the kitchenette counter.

"Nothing so far. It might just have been an empty threat."

"Anything on the ephedrine?"

"The search is running," Jonathan said as he typed on his laptop. When Charlotte heard the modem dial, she gave him a surprised look. "Are you going on the Internet?"

He shook his head. "Making a phone call." He consulted his watch. "Bad news, Charlie. While you were in the cafeteria, I picked up a transmission from Knight. He called for an emergency response team. There's going to be a takeover of your computer network."

"How much time do we have?"

"It depends. If Knight has called Washington, then his men won't be here until tomorrow. But if the response team is coming from Los Angeles —"

A face suddenly appeared on Jonathan's laptop screen — a balding man with wire-rimmed glasses. He did not look happy. "Roscoe," Jonathan said, "I need to know about an FDA emergency response team. What can you tell me?"

"Got problems here, John. An intruder has brought down the MCI gateway in Dayton, Ohio."

"Jesus!"

"Yeah. The SOB has effectively blocked twenty-five percent of all e-mail going to Europe."

Jonathan was thoughtful for a moment. "Sounds like the Jaguar gang."

"That's what we think, too. Hey, sorry about that profile, John. I haven't had time to run it through our computers. We're going bonkers here."

"Is Pogo still in prison?"

"He was the first one we checked out. The kid's doing bathroom duty in maximum security. We'll get 'em, though," Thorne added with a weary smile. "They always try something and we always manage to catch 'em."

"Good luck," Jonathan said, and he signed off and reached for his cellular phone.

Charlotte lifted lids off steaming dishes. "I hope you still like stir-fried shrimp and pork dumplings."

"No time to eat, love. As soon as Knight's agents get here, we'll be locked out of the system." He punched a number on his phone and cradled it to his ear while he typed again on his laptop.

She looked at him. Just like the old days, Jonathan was

constantly in motion, his hands always busy, his body moving with endless energy. "You have to have food."

He smiled. "You sound like your grandmother."

"I sound like everybody's grandmother. Didn't *your* granny always make sure you had plenty to eat? Wasn't she always forcing tattie soup on you?"

"My gran never had to force me to eat her tattie soup!" he said with a laugh. "Special Agent Varner, please," he said into the phone.

"Every September, when you came back, it was all you could talk about — haggis this and scones that."

He put his hand over the mouthpiece. "That's not all I talked about."

"Trout fishing and mountain climbing! You had such fun summers, while I stayed at home and learned to be a good respectful Chinese girl."

"Until I returned in my tartan and my kilt and corrupted you all over again."

"I never once saw you in a kilt," she said, quickly turning away. Did he know how painful those absences were for her? Did he really understand what happened to her that summer when she was fifteen and he left her — alone and vulnerable?

While Jonathan held a brief conversation with the special agent, Charlotte dished steaming rice into a blue porcelain bowl. "Here you go," she said after he hung up. "It isn't finnan haddock, but it'll have to do."

"No word on the FDA response team," he said as he frowned at the phone.

As Charlotte reached for the bottle of soy sauce, she glanced up at the security monitor and saw Mr. Sung in the reception area of the corporate offices, talking to Adrian. Desmond's father seemed agitated, his arms going up and down, while Mr. Sung faced him placidly. "I wonder what he was doing in the control room," she murmured.

Jonathan looked up. "Mr. Sung?"

"It's not like him to be secretive."

"You said he had changed when you came back from Europe last year."

"I thought it was my imagination. But there is something different about him now. . . ." Charlotte opened a drawer, looked inside, closed it and opened another.

"Charlotte, he and your grandmother were close friends. Do you think there might have been more to it?"

She turned around, her eyebrows arched. "Do you mean were they lovers? I don't think so. Grandmother was ten years older than Mr. Sung." Besides, Charlotte wanted to add, the women in my family have notoriously bad luck in love: my great-grandmother, whose handsome American never returned; my grandmother, who fell in love with her half-brother; my mother, widowed before I was born; and me, falling desperately in love with a boy who was only to pass briefly through my life.

"No forks," she said as she opened the last drawer and brought out a pair of chopsticks. "Can you manage?"

"I should," he said with a look filled with remembrance and painful nostalgia. "I had the best teacher."

As Charlotte placed egg rolls in the pristine microwave oven, she saw an image of her smooth hands over a pair of callused, awkward ones — chopsticks lessons of long ago, when touching Johnny had set her on fire. "You know," she said, using words to push the memory away, "my grandmother worked in this office for almost a year and never once used this microwave. She was so mistrustful of technology. I told her microwaved food wouldn't harm her, it's just convenient because it cooks faster. She said food cooked too quickly digests too quickly and upsets the balance in the body."

"She might have had a point."

Charlotte noticed how Jonathan approached his dinner as

if he were dining with the queen. It made her think of the days she had spent in his private retreat in his father's big house on Jackson Street. It had been so exotic for Charlotte to come from her grandmother's old-fashioned technopho-bic world and enter Jonathan's world of advanced electron-ics, where the floor, bed, and all surfaces were littered with Twinkies wrappers, Coke bottles, hardened triangles of pizza. The first time he had brought her here, when she was thirteen, it had shocked her. And she remembered now the day Jonathan called her and told her to come over right away. It was the year they were both to turn eighteen, the year they were facing high school graduation and an un-known future. Charlotte had run the two blocks to his house, where the maid had let her in, and then down the stairs to the basement, which Jonathan had converted into his private den, a world cluttered with radios, dismantled hi-fi sets, tele-vision parts, wires, electronic gadgets. He had installed a bed and a hotplate, a tiny refrigerator, and a color TV set that was always on, sound turned off. Charlotte remembered the three familiar faces on the screen — Haldeman, Erlich-man, and Mitchell — who had just been sentenced to prison for their roles in the Watergate cover-up. She had found an extremely excited Jonathan who looked as if he had slept in his jeans and T-shirt, with his long hair uncombed and streaming over his shoulders. "Look, Charlie!" he had said, grabbing her hand and pulling her over to a workbench clut-tered with radio and TV components, empty boxes of Cocoa Puffs and Fruit Loops.

She looked. "What is it?"

He beamed. "It's the world's first microprocessor-based computer! See? You enter programs in pure binery code here by flicking these switches in the front. Watch. . . ."

She had watched. "What do those flickering lights mean?"

"The program is running! A program I put into it! Two

hundred and fifty-six bytes of memory, Charlie! Think of it! Think of what this means!"

She had seen how he smiled, how proud he was of himself, how beautiful he was in his joy, and she had thought of the secret she had kept from him about her birthday party when she was fifteen, that when she had asked her friends to come, they had said, "As long as you're not inviting that icky Jonathan Sutherland." So she had told her so-called friends to stay away, and her party had just been her and Jonathan, riding the cable cars, picking flowers in Golden Gate Park, and wolfing down steamed wonton and spring rolls in Ross Alley.

He has become such a polite eater, she thought now. Was this the same person who once declared that "eating should be a total-body experience"? He used to do outrageous things, like eat spaghetti or fried eggs with his fingers. Knives and forks remained pristine on his table. Even as recently as ten years ago, he had still used his hand as a plate for buttering a roll — although, by then, the signs of refinement had begun. She wondered if his lovemaking had also changed. Jonathan had known no restraints; sex with him had been a "total-body experience." Which made her wonder now if he had become more polite in bed as well.

Jonathan set aside his bowl and addressed the larger computer, where the database search was running. "Charlotte, do you have a jar of that balm around? The Beautiful Intelligence?"

"Should still be some in here." She opened a desk drawer and brought out a small jar of Beautiful Intelligence Balm, as well as a bottle of Golden Lotus Wine, a packet of Bliss, a box of Keemoon tea.

As Jonathan uncapped the jar and sniffed the fragrant contents, again a polished, refined gesture, Charlotte wondered what else had changed about him in their ten years of estrangement. Suddenly wanting to fill in the blanks, she said, "How is your father, Johnny?"

"He's fine. They're living in Hawaii now."

"They?"

"Ah, that's right. You don't know. He got married."

"You're joking."

"Shocked me, too." Jonathan stood up and brought his wallet out of his hip pocket. He flipped to a color photograph of two smiling people under a palm tree.

"That's Miss O'Rourke!"

"My father's faithful secretary. You remember."

"How could I forget? She was around your house more than your father was! What happened? Did they suddenly fall in love after — how many years?"

"Well, it was sudden for Father. The way he tells it, they had just arrived at the airport in the limousine, as usual, and Father was about to get into the corporate jet to go who-knows-where, leaving everything in Miss O'Rourke's capable hands as he had done for twenty years, when all of a sudden she handed him his briefcase as she always did, and she said in her 'foine' Irish brogue, 'I'll be leaving you when you get back, Mr. Sutherland. I have served you faithfully these past two decades, always at your beck and call, forgoing my own personal life for yours, but I'm not getting any younger and it's time I had a life of my own while there's some years left.' Whereupon, according to my father, she burst into tears, right there in front of the chauffeur and the pilot, sobbing and sobbing until my father couldn't think of anything else to do other than take her in his arms and console her."

"You're joking."

"And do you know what else he said? He said he'd never noticed before what beautiful red hair she had." Jonathan slipped the picture back into his wallet. "They were married a week later and suddenly it was Christmas dinners and hearty slaps on the back and 'Johnny-lad'! Twenty-nine years after his son was born, Robert Sutherland suddenly became a father."

Robert Sutherland, consoling someone! Charlotte thought with a pang of regret: I have missed so much.

Against her will, her mind flew back to the day that had been the beginning of their personal Ice Age, when she had met Jonathan at the Italian restaurant in San Francisco, the two of them politely guarded after six years of little communication. The book of poetry had stood between them — the 1981 *Silver Laurel Wreath Prize Poetry* that he had sent to her six years earlier and that had sliced Charlotte's heart. Why had he suddenly written to her, asking for this meeting? "We must go our separate ways," the poem had said. And Charlotte, who had thought Jonathan loved her and wanted to marry her, had gotten the message. Had he changed his mind? Did he decide he wanted her in his life after all?

They met at Roma Garden on Polk Street, where red-and-white checked tablecloths and candles created a friendly neutral ground for the two who had once been lovers and now were almost strangers. Jonathan's appearance had come as a shock. The last time she had seen him, in Boston, in 1980, he had been long-haired and skinny, in a tattered T-shirt and faded jeans. The man who rose from the table when she entered the Italian restaurant looked like a model for Brooks Brothers. Of course, she had learned through their slim correspondence — mostly in the form of polite Christmas cards — that after he graduated from MIT, he had gotten a job working for the government: "computer specialist," whatever that was. Was this what years of working in an office had done?

They sat down and talked about the weather, the menu, books and movies, making slow inroads to the more personal topics: Charlotte's work in biochemistry research at her grandmother's herbal company, Jonathan's time divided between a residence in London and his work for the United States government. But it was nervous talk, a conversation dotted with cleared throats and tugs at French cuffs. They would both start talking, then stop, then laugh, then say, "No, you first."

They ordered a salad and linguine with clam sauce, and the house Chianti. Charlotte noticed that Jonathan knew which one was the salad fork. He also sniffed and tasted the wine before accepting it.

Halfway through the meal, he surprised her by giving her a gift. She had brought him nothing. And when she saw the beautiful silk scarf and crystal wind chimes, she felt a sudden spike of hope that he *had* come to tell her he wanted her in his life again.

"So, do you still work for the government?" she asked, suddenly having no appetite, suddenly feeling as light as the sky. Such a beautiful gift! And even more wonderful was that as he relaxed he began to seem more like the old Johnny. Memories of their adolescence in San Francisco propelled her along on a magic carpet of high hopes and rekindled love. "I don't remember, is it the FBI? CIA?"

"National Security Agency. We protect our government's communications."

His Scottish accent had long eroded; back at MIT Jonathan had spoken with a very strong English accent, the result of four years at Cambridge. But that accent had softened now, Charlotte noticed, it was more American, the result of years of working for the U.S. government, she supposed. It was an accent that reminded her that Johnny still moved between two worlds. She wondered if he had finally decided to choose one and settle down in it.

"I'm curious, how on earth did you end up working for *them?*" How like Johnny! she thought in sudden happiness. No ordinary office job for him!

"I was recruited." He laughed. "Actually, I got arrested. They rounded a few of us up. A couple of my mates got nabbed for forging degrees and altering grades. With our hacking skills, we could sell anyone a legitimate MIT doctorate for fifty thousand dollars."

"Is that what *you* did?"

He shook his head. "Too easy. What I did was go after the FAA. I figured out a way into their system, managed to hack all the way into the control tower at JFK."

"And?" She leaned forward on her elbows, closing the distance between her and Johnny.

"I didn't interfere, although I could have. I just watched a while — saw a TWA jet make a sharp turn in the path of a Brazilian airliner. It looks like they have some rather close calls up there."

"They caught you snooping?"

"No, I never get caught. I wrote an anonymous letter to the FAA, outlining the security holes in their air traffic control system." He blushed. "I forgot about fingerprints on the stationery."

"And for that you were offered a job?"

"I was given a choice of working for them or going to prison."

This was getting more wonderful by the minute. It suddenly struck Charlotte that they were going to forget the poem and their cold breakup of six years ago. They were going to tour the city and visit their old haunts, and then they were going to go back to her apartment and make wonderful, wonderful love.

"So you're actually a spy. Is that why you're here? I've heard that Silicon Valley really is crawling with KGB operatives."

Jonathan turned his wine glass around, causing the Chianti to glint like a multifaceted ruby. "Well, it's common knowledge that the Soviet consulate here in San Francisco funnels American technology back to Russia. They've even got antennae and other surveillance equipment on their roof to capture classified phone calls in Silicon Valley. They have agents set up dummy companies, acquire advanced computers, and then they quietly fold and go home, taking their hardware with them." He shook his head. "It's sad, really. Their stolen software is a ragtag collection of retooled operating systems and compilers, all transposed into Cyrillic." He raised his eyes and looked right at her. "I don't work for the NSA anymore, Charlie. I left. I'm setting up my own company."

He paused. He seemed to want to say more, so she waited. "Have you heard of the Amsterdam Eight?" he said.

She shook her head. "I'm afraid I've been out of the loop lately. I'm expanding Grandmother's research lab, hiring more chemists, and trying to upgrade our equipment. I've been too busy even to read 'Dear Abby.'"

"Well," he began, and she saw a familiar darkness steal across his face. It meant his thoughts were troubled, and when he averted his eyes and tried to appear interested in passersby on the sidewalk, she wanted to reach for his hand. Johnny was in some kind of deep distress.

"What is it?" she said gently.

He looked at her, seeming to take the measure of her eyes. Charlotte could see the weighing and balancing going on behind his handsome face — Johnny trying to come to a difficult decision. Finally he shook his head. "Never mind. It's a long and rather unpleasant story. Don't want to spoil our reunion with it. But it's the Amsterdam Eight that caused me to turn in my resignation. They were the reason I lost my stomach for the spy game."

"Is that why you asked to meet me today, to tell me you had left the NSA?" she said, knowing full well that it wasn't. There was more, and the anticipation was making her heart race.

Jonathan studied the little glass jar of breadsticks on the table. "Charlotte," he said, his manner alarmingly grave. "I have something to tell you."

She waited. She held her breath, held her heart, and waited.

"I'm getting married."

She looked at him.

He said, "It's someone I met a year ago —"

The little restaurant, its tablecloths and breadsticks, suddenly flew away from her, as if a bomb had gone off.

Jonathan watched her with expectant eyes.

She stared at him as she tried to digest the news along with the undigested linguine.

When it finally began to strike her with full force, Charlotte's mind cried, What happened to, *"I need to go my own way, walk my path alone"?* She wanted to shout: How dare you marry someone else? We're soul mates, Johnny, Siamese twins joined at the heart! We agreed, didn't we, in a contract written in the language of our shared pulse, that we would either be together or be alone?

Where did this third party come from?

She wanted to throw her wine in his face.

"Her name is Adele," he began.

Charlotte stood up, her chair scraping across the wooden floor. "Congratulations."

"Charlie." Beseechingly.

"Thanks for lunch." She grabbed up the box containing the silk scarf and wind chimes and somehow found the entrance, the sidewalk, a sun-blinding escape down the street.

She had not seen him again.

As she watched Jonathan now pick up his cellular phone and dial, asking in a confident, commanding tone for yet another special agent, Charlotte thought: Johnny, you said you read about Grandmother's death. Why didn't you write to me? Or at least send a telegram? Did her passing mean so little to you? Or was it because I walked out on you that day ten years ago?

She felt for the Shang dynasty pendant on her breast, thought of its powerful significance, pictured the contents locked inside. Had putting the necklace on at the last minute, as she hurriedly got dressed after receiving Desmond's call, merely been a coincidence? Charlotte hadn't worn the necklace in months.

It is no coincidence. It is a sign. . . .

Wiping her hands on a napkin as if to wipe away the painful memory, she went to the doorway that led into the museum. Her eyes settled upon a replica of a Chinatown herbal shop, complete with counter and shelves, scales and abacus, and all varieties of ingredients and materials that went into healing compounds: bottles of eels in preservatives; barrels of roots; dried leaves, reeds and flowers; sacks of bark, spice, rice; jars of dried scorpions, snakes, and beetles. A cornucopia of balms, elixirs, curatives, restoratives. And on one of the top shelves, a huge white Persian cat, asleep. . . .

As Charlotte gazed at the antique "shop," the mail alert on the computer sounded. She turned around. "What is it?" she said.

"Oh Christ, it's another video."

She expected to see the interior of her house again, but was surprised to see instead an outside shot filling the screen. The view was of a residential neighborhood at night, with rain coming down. "Is it real or is it —" Charlotte began. "Oh my God."

"What?"

"That's Naomi's house. Jonathan, this is being shot across the street from where Naomi lives!" She grabbed his wrist. "Can you tell if this is fake or live?"

"Hold on." He sat down and began a trace. While they

waited, Charlotte saw a familiar car pull up to the curb. "It's Naomi!"

"Shit," Jonathan whispered as the Internet provider's address appeared in the DOS window. "This could be being rerouted from anywhere."

"But is it live?"

"There's no way of telling."

They watched Naomi get out on the driver's side and, holding a shawl over her head, run up the walk to a pink stucco house surrounded by tree ferns and azaleas.

"Something's going to happen, Jonathan. This time it's real." Charlotte picked up the phone. "I have to warn her."

"How can you be sure?"

"Naomi and I had coffee together this morning before she went to the campus. Those are the clothes she was wearing."

Jonathan retrieved his cellular phone. "What's the number for the police?"

"Better call nine-one-one."

"And if this is another false alarm? You already cried wolf once."

Her eyes met his. "Call the operator. Ask for the Palm Springs Police Department."

Charlotte shook so badly she misdialed her phone. As she tried again, she watched with held breath as Naomi paused at the front door to rummage through her purse and bring out a cluster of keys.

While Jonathan asked to be connected to the police, and Charlotte heard a busy signal at Naomi's end, they watched Naomi slide the key into the lock and turn the knob.

"I don't believe this," Jonathan said incredulously. "I got a recording. I'm on hold."

The front door swung open, but as Naomi was about to go inside, a small dark shape suddenly darted out of the house and flew down the path. Naomi spun around, called out.

"God, I hope this is just a video meant to frighten me," Charlotte said as she dialed again with shaking hands.

"Yes, Officer," Jonathan said quickly when someone at the police station picked up. "I want to report —"

"It's ringing!" Charlotte said.

In the next instant they saw a flash of bright light. The front windows blew out, tongues of flame shot through the open door, and a ball of fire exploded up to the night sky.

22

1925 — San Francisco, California

Did that thief think he had left me with nothing?

He took my emeralds and my American dollar bills, my pearl necklace and jade earrings. But he left the food in my kitchen, the herbs, waxes, and oils I needed for my medicines, a bottle of my mother's tonic wine, a jar of her secret balm, and my two Yixing teapots. Did the foolish man think emeralds more valuable than medicines?

I had carried my papers with me the day I went to the jewelry store, thinking I might need to show proof of who I was, and so although I was penniless, I still had my identity, and the photograph of myself at the mission school, and the letter my father had left my mother.

I told Mrs. Po about the burglary. She asked if I could still pay the rent. I said yes, but wasn't she going to report the burglary? "Who to?" she said.

The thief also left behind my silk dresses and expensive shoes and handbags, which I sold, and with the money I bought more herbs, minerals, compounds, a steamer, a strainer, pots, scales, cheesecloth, a grinding stone, jars, paper, and string. The foolish thief had left behind the most valuable thing of all: the little book in which my mother had recorded all her remedies.

I would make them and sell them to the people of Chinatown.

To save money, I moved into a smaller apartment in Mrs. Po's building, the next floor down, just one room, with an electric hot plate instead of a kitchen. But there was a sink and so I had all I needed to begin my work. She admonished me again, "No men," for she seemed to believe that all girls who lived alone were prostitutes.

I searched for my father.

First I had to know how to spell the name. I had only heard the jeweler speak it. Was it Barklay, Barklie, Barclay? There were so many possibilities. And where did I find them? I could not go back to the jewelry store, I could not inquire with the police. My father seemed as unreachable to me as the moon and the stars.

And so was the love that had sprouted in my heart that day in the jewelry store.

In the days and weeks and months that passed, I could not forget smoky eyes and a curved smile and the way the young man had stared at me when I walked into the shop, as thought he, too, had felt the lightening bolt. My love for him grew — a terrible, forbidden love, for he was my brother. Every night I would fall asleep with the vision of his beautiful face before me, but then the voice of the jeweler would intrude, to mock me and remind me of my sin: "There she is, Mr. Barclay. The girl who stole your father's ring."

So they thought I was a thief. I had to find another way to reach my father.

There was another tenant in Mrs. Po's building, a softspoken young man named Mr. Lee, an artist who made Chinese brush paintings for tourists. When my apartment was burglarized, he offered me assistance. But I would not take his money. When I moved down to a smaller room, he again offered in his shy way. But I could not accept his charity. But one night as I was coming up the stairs with my heavy basket of medicines that I had tried to sell in the streets of Chinatown, Mr. Lee relieved me of my basket and took it the rest of the way. He invited me in for tea. He told me about himself — he was from Hawaii and hoped to bring his family over to California, and I told him about myself, and my search for a certain person.

That was when I learned that people who owned telephones were listed in a city book. Mr. Lee, who owned a telephone in his studio on Stockton, showed me this book, and I read with great excitement the names listed there — no Barklays, no Barklies, but there were Barclays!

I found no Richard, but I wrote down the addresses all the same — perhaps these Barclays were related and would tell me where my father was. And so I ventured once again beyond Chinatown.

The first house I went to see was a rich man's house, a mansion on a hill, and when I saw the bay windows and columns, the lawns and gardens, the view of the Bay, I thought: my father would live in such a house as this.

As I stood on the sidewalk, peering through the wrought-iron fence, a policeman came up to me and demanded to know what I was doing. I didn't tell him the truth — would he have believed me? I said I was just admiring. He told me to "Move along."

I traveled around the city, on the trams and cable cars, but mostly walking miles and miles, going into foreign neighborhoods where housewives gave me suspicious looks. I kept returning to the big house on the hill, my certainty growing that this was my father's house.

And then one day as I stood on the corner wondering how I should go to the door, I saw an automobile emerge from the carriage house behind the mansion; it slowly took the long drive till it reached the street, and there the machine paused and I was allowed a clear view of the driver.

He was the young man from the jewelry store. The young man who had stolen my heart. My brother.

And so this *was* the house of my father. He was one of the richest men in San Francisco.

I could not go up to the door of such a fine house, but there was another way to contact my father. Mr. Lee kindly let me use his telephone, showing me how to speak into it and listen, how to ask the operator for the number in the book.

The first time I heard the lady's voice at the other end say, "Barclay residence," I could not speak. "Who is this please?" she said. I listened in fear. And then I replaced the telephone earpiece on its hook.

I went the next day and Mr. Lee again very kindly allowed me to use his telephone. The same lady answered. Again I had no courage to speak up.

The third time I telephoned, a different lady answered, and when I was silent, she said, "Are you the girl who stole my husband's ring?" Her voice was cold and hard. I replaced the receiver.

Mr. Lee, always quiet and soft-spoken, suggested I try telephoning at another time of the day, when the ladies weren't home alone. So I went back to his shop that evening, and this time a man answered. "Gideon Barclay," he said.

I was silent.

"Hello? Is someone there?" He paused. And then he said in a gentler tone, "Are you the girl from the jewelry store?"

I wanted to speak. My mouth was open but no voice came out. I could think only of the policemen who had harassed me, and maids and housewives who had looked at me with contempt, and all the prejudice I had encountered in this big city. I put my hand to my breast and felt my father's ring there, heavy and reassuring, the only thing I had from him. *They will take it away from me.*

"Did you learn something?" Mr. Lee asked after I hung up without saying anything.

Yes, I had learned something. Gideon. My brother's name was Gideon.

I wrote to the Reverend Peterson and told him I was safe and that I had located my father's family. I asked him if my mother had died, and when, and did she have a respectable funeral, for the fear that she had not died was beginning to haunt me — what daughter abandons her mother when she is so ill?

The letter came back unopened with a note of explanation from one of the ladies at the mission school: the Reverend Peterson had been transferred to a mission in the interior of China. So I did not know whether my mother was dead. Or if she was alive somewhere, alone and sick.

My medicines did not sell.

Every day I went out with my wicker basket and called out, "Good health for sale! Longevity for twenty-five cents! Lucky tea, only a dime!"

But I learned that many of my mother's remedies were already known by Chinese; people made them in their homes and said, "Why pay?"

I also learned that people would not buy something they did not know, when they were used to buying what they did know. I went into herbal shops and saw the red-and-gold packages of Red Dragon Health Company. Everyone in Chinatown bought Red Dragon medicines and teas. There was no room for someone new.

Finally I had to take jobs to earn money — ironing in Mrs. Po's laundry, sweeping Mr. Chin's tea shop, carrying packages for overburdened shoppers. I used the money to buy more ingredients for my remedies, which I toiled over late at night on the single electric burner — pounding, mixing, stirring, boiling, blending. I had such a strong belief in my mother's medicines that I knew my spell of hardship would not last long.

When I could no longer afford the room over the laundry, I moved down into the basement, where I had no window and my living space was five of my feet, heel to toe, in one direction, six in the other. My bed became a straw mat on the floor. As my circumstances sank, so did I sink lower into the earth. Elderly neighbors, also living in cramped basement rooms, said only the grave was next.

But I would not give up hope.

I kept my little stove and managed to obtain the ingredients I needed for my mother's medicines. I would not go to the local church for handouts; I would not beg for money, for my mother had taught me that the coffin was preferable to the begging bowl. There were benevolent societies in Chinatown that helped people in need, but they were made up of clans. Immigrants from Hong Kong and Shanghai, Canton and Peking, and tiny villages in the interior provinces of China found the society that was made up of their clan and they were taken care of. But I was from Singapore, and I was not full Chinese, so I was an outsider even in Chinatown.

When I had no money left over for food, I went to the back of Wong Lo's restaurant, where I had made friends with the cook. He gave me the leavings from what he had prepared that night: chicken bones with gristle attached, fish skin, the chopped-off stems of vegetables, the papery outer skin of an onion, a cabbage core. I boiled these on my little stove and made my nightly soup.

When people in the streets turned deaf ears to my shouts, I wondered if Mrs. Po might be my first customer; her hands were always badly chapped from the laundry bleach. If I could persuade her to try my remedies, I knew she would like them, and then tell her friends and customers. So one day I handed her a small glass jar of my mother's balm. She said, "What it called?" I secretly called it *the medicine that healed the wounds of an American who didn't know who he was.* "It has no name," I said.

"What it good for?" *For soothing the blackened feet of my mother when she could no longer walk on her "golden lilies."* "It heals skin," I said.

"What else?"

"That is all."

"Pah! I spend money on a medicine that does only one thing?" She showed me a jar of Red Dragon Heavenly Ointment. "Read label," she said proudly. I did, and I could not believe all the cures this ointment promised — from sore throat to hemorrhoids.

"Course not work all the time," she added. "Husband still get bad headaches. I tell him, use more ointment, use whole jar, then headache go away."

I offered her the plain bottle in which I kept my mother's tonic wine. "Please try this," I said.

"Hmp! Got better tonic." She brought it out from behind the counter. It was in a fancy red bottle with gold lettering. I tasted it. When she saw my sour expression, she said, "Bitter cures best. You don't know this, then your medicines not good."

But my mother had said, "Please the taste buds and the stomach will follow."

I was becoming dispirited. Mrs. Po was Chinatown — she represented all the people I wanted to sell my medicines to. If I could not convince her, then what hope had I of convincing thousands?

So I used precious money and bought Red Dragon products to try them myself. I found that the teas were bitter, the balms foul-smelling, the herbs of poor quality. It seemed that everyone bought them simply because everyone bought them. I also noticed that Red Dragon products offered more than one cure to a remedy. To the thrifty and pragmatic Chinese mind, the medicine that offered the most cures was the most popular. Why buy six medicines when six cures can be bought for the price of one medicine?

I sat down on the floor to compare. First, I spread out my own remedies that I had made on my stove. I had twelve remedies for twelve ailments. Then I spread out the Red Dragon Ointment that "raises the vigor, expels worms, cools the hot liver, warms the spleen, and dissolves warts." and Red Dragon Tea that "prevents mumps, eases toothache, cures menstrual irregularity, replaces *yin* deficiency."

I wondered how one remedy could work so many wonders. The packets did not say what herbs they contained. But it didn't matter. Chinese thinking: All this in one jar. Very prudent purchase.

I thought of my mother's balm that Mrs. Po had turned down. It was a simple recipe of menthol, wax, eucalyptus, petrolatum, and camphor for healing bruised or wounded or damaged skin. It worked well and fast. But it wasn't enough. Was it possible to add ingredients that would make the balm work on *other* ailments as well?

While I pondered this mystery, I scrubbed floors for Mr. Chin and pots for Wong Lo until my hands were raw and bleeding, I ironed for Mrs. Po and ran errands for shopkeepers until I was exhausted deep in my bones, and with this money I bought more herbs and mixed them into my balm — almond oil for nourishing the skin and powdered cicada for skin allergies; chrysanthemum flowers to reduce abscesses and kudzu root to relieve muscle aches and pains; rhubarb for reducing swelling and gypsum to fight heat rash. I labored nightly over my little hot plate, trying for just the right balance of ingredients — not too much that would make my ointment toxic, not so little that it would do no good. I bought a little clock with a loud alarm so that I could sleep while my gardenia fruit simmered, waking in time to strain the broth, add more water, simmer, and sleep some more.

When I could not afford an herb, I worked at Mr. Huang's Trading Company to earn it. I would stand at his back door at midnight to receive an imported shipment of herbs from China, then I would work all night sorting and inspecting, removing dirt and impurities and nonmedicinal parts from the plants. Then I carefully separated flowers, stems, and roots, washing and drying them, and setting them out for Mr. Huang's inspection in the morning. For this I received a measure of *Yunnan bai yao*, what is called "mountain varnish," a strong drug that stops bleeding and rapidly heals wounds.

Many new ingredients went into my mother's balm. But would they all work together? And how to find out?

I needed a patient. Mrs. Po would not give me her chapped hands, her husband preferred to keep his migraines, Mr. Huang politely declined the chance to cure his eczema, and Mr. Lee had no physical ailments.

In the end, there was only one truly reliable way to test my ointment.

I burned myself. I slept without a pillow so that my neck ached. I went to Golden Gate Park and let the mosquitoes bite me. I applied my balm and determined which worked and which did not, increasing measures of one ingredient, decreasing another. When I broke out in a rash, I made a new pot of balm, leaving out the jimson weed, which is good for topical anesthesia. The next time, I had no rash. Finally, after much experimentation on myself, my new balm soothed the burns, calmed the itching, eased my aches. I had, I believed, made the perfect medicine.

And then Mrs. Po came and told me there was someone who needed my room, someone who had money. She told

eating. I said, "What does it cure? Excessive *yang?*
h heat on the liver?"

sn't cure anything. It just tastes good."

why do we buy it in a drugstore?"

ghed again and shocked me once more by taking
But then I remembered that he was my brother and
he was allowed to touch me. But his touch was dis-
I wore a long-sleeved sweater, yet I could feel the
n his fingers burn into my flesh. I felt the slight
of his hold, a possessive grasp that both pleased
tened me. My feet followed him out of politeness,
eart went of its own accord.

rugstore was like no Chinese herbal shop. Here the
re far apart and the ceiling was high, and the med-
ere all kept under glass or on shelves behind the
I saw no barrels or sacks containing herbs, no
r weighing and measuring, no charts showing
points on the human body. All was scrupulously
clean.

closer to the glass counter because I was curious
stern medicine, and as I puzzled over what I saw
leon said, "While I'm here, might as well pick up
for this tickle in my throat."

ooked over a display of throat lozenges that came
y of flavors and boxes, I moved my eyes over the
hat were displayed under the glass, puzzling over
us names: Anti-Catarrh, Gas-Ex, Dis-Pepso. Very
t-sounding names. Perhaps the bad name drove
illness.

paid for his box of lozenges and then led me to
ll tables were clustered next to a "soda fountain."
ply aware of the stares from other customers, but
her was oblivious or did not mind the disapprov-
I had lived in San Francisco long enough to read
s. They said: white man with Chinese woman.

me to move out. I pleaded with her. I told her I had a new
medicine that I would sell in the streets. "Two day," she
said, holding up two chapped fingers.

I had never known such hunger.

Not even during some of our darkest days in Singapore,
when my mother had no patients and no wine to sell, no
money to buy ingredients to make wine to sell — not even
during those spells had I known hunger such as I knew in
those dark days in Chinatown.

As I made my way through the crowd on Grant Avenue,
carrying my basket and calling out my wares, I tried not to
look at the food in the windows, for my mouth watered at
the sight of succulent Peking duck and whole steamed fish.
I breathed through my mouth so I would not inhale the aromas of stir-fried prawns and crispy chicken stuffed with
rice. I tried not to look as a child sank her teeth into a bright
red wedge of fresh watermelon, as an elderly woman
popped sunflower seeds into her mouth, modestly spitting
out the shells, as a man in a business suit stood at a food stall
delivering steaming noodles into his mouth.

I must not think of food. . . .

I finally had to pause on the corner, for my basket had
grown heavy and my head, light when I suddenly felt a hand
on my arm, I cried out.

And then I turned to look into a pair of gray eyes that had
haunted me for a year.

"Wait," Gideon Barclay said. "Don't run. Please. I'm not
going to hurt you."

I could not have run, even if I had wanted, because I was
under an enchantment. He was dressed in a handsome blue
blazer and white slacks, and when he removed his hat, immediately the sun caught his brown hair, kissing it in places
with hues of chestnut and gold.

"I've been searching for you ever since that day in the

jewelry shop. Are you the one who has been calling our house?"

I nodded.

"Why?"

"I am looking for my father."

"Oh," he said. "Well, that's easily taken care of. What's his name and I can ask among the staff when I get home. Although I don't recall that we employ many Chinese —"

"Richard Barclay," I said as people swept past us like a river going around an island.

Gideon stared at me. "What are you talking about?"

"My father is Richard Barclay. I have his ring to prove it."

"Well, the jeweler did recognize the ring. There would be no mistaking it, since my mother had it made especially for him. But . . . how did you come by it? My father was wearing it when he died."

"Died? Richard Barclay is dead?"

"He died at sea seventeen years ago. He was on his way back from Singapore —"

"*Aii-yah!*" I cried, and Gideon suddenly had to support me and help me off the sidewalk, away from the crowds. "Dead!" I cried in Chinese. "After all these years! My father is dead!"

He took me into a doorway recessed between two shops. From here, a stairway led to offices and apartments on the floors above. The doorway was shelter, dark and quiet. A good place to cry.

"Now what's this all about?" Gideon said after some minutes, watching me dry my eyes with the handkerchief he had given me.

I told him my story, and when I had finished, he shook his head in amazement. "We did lose touch with my father for a while. He had gone to Singapore on business and for several weeks we received no communication from him. And then suddenly my mother got a telegram from him saying he

was sailing that night for San Franci down during a Pacific storm, all crew We thought he had his ring with him. to your mother?"

I searched Gideon's face for traces them there. He did not accept my stor *father's ring. He is going to call a p* the proof that would change his mind had left for my mother. But it was not this letter between two lovers. I had that I would show it only to Richard, was. Not even his son was to see it, then know I spoke the truth.

But there was another reason I cou to Gideon. It was because of what w his father had said to my mother, som Gideon and cause him pain. And that never do.

"What's your name?" he asked ge I told him.

"Perfect Harmony," he said, "fo girl." And suddenly he was offering nary gift. He said he wanted to buy

He laughed at my confusion, thr show even white teeth. "No," he comes before Monday. A sundae is bet you've never had one. A hot fud whipped cream and a cherry on top the next block."

He startled me next by lifting slinging it over his shoulder — a woman's burden. People stared, bu to mind.

I asked what the sundae was g

good for
Too mu
"It d
"Ther
He la
my arm
therefor
turbing.
heat fro
pressure
and frig
but my
The
walls w
icines
counter
scales
meridia
tidy and
I wen
about W
there, G
somethir
As he
in a vari
remedies
their curi
unpleasa
out the b
Gideor
where sm
I was sha
Gideon e
ing looks.
those lool

Gideon held out a chair for me and then seated himself, unslinging my basket from his shoulder and placing it on the floor. The table was small, made of marble with thin metal legs, and the chairs were not very comfortable. Perhaps we were not meant to linger there, but eat our ice cream and make room for the next customers.

He looked at my basket. "How's business?"

"Luck favors me," I replied, tugging self-consciously at my frayed cuffs.

He surveyed my modest wares: plain bottles among packets wrapped in brown paper and string, and the mismatched jam jars I used for my new balm. He smiled and said teasingly, "You need a good ad man."

I did not understand what he said, but he had a funny way of saying it. The way his voice occasionally broke, and the small laugh he added once in a while. I laughed, and then quickly covered my mouth with my hand.

"You have a very nice laugh, Harmony. Don't hide it."

Then I saw how he eyed my dress, the silk threadbare in places, the frog-fasteners repaired with different-colored thread, the mandarin collar frayed. And my long-sleeved sweater with holes at the elbows. "You're very pale," he said. "Are you getting enough to eat?"

"More than I can handle," I said, although I had not eaten since the day before. "I have to give away my leftovers, it is so much."

He waved for the waiter's attention. "Well, wait till you taste the hot chocolate sauce in this place. They add raisins, that's what makes it so special."

My stomach suddenly made a loud noise, and I quickly put my hand there out of embarrassment. Gideon laughed. And then he glanced down at my hand, and his smile died. I, too, looked down and saw to my mortification that the sleeve of my sweater had ridden up, revealing a bandage around my wrist.

"Did you hurt yourself?"

"It is nothing."

He reached out. "Let me see," he said.

I slid my hand toward his, aware of my thumping heart and how my face burned. When his fingers touched mine, I felt the heat enter my blood and race through my veins. He is my brother, I told myself. We have the same father. He pushed my sleeve back and when he saw recent scars from bites and burns, he frowned and said, "What's going on here?"

I told him about my balm and how I found what worked, what did not.

"Good God," he said. "You're *experimenting* on yourself?"

"Who else shall I experiment on?"

"For a blasted ointment?"

I looked into Gideon Barclay's eyes and suddenly I wanted to unburden my heart. "Chinatown is full of medicines. People buy many remedies every day. The ones they pay for are the ones that promise the most. But these remedies make false claims. They do not do what their labels promise. People spend their money and then they go home and are not cured. My mother's medicines will ease many ailments, but how can I persuade people, when they are used to Red Dragon remedies, and I am new to Chinatown, and only a girl?"

I stopped, because even though he was my brother, he was still a stranger to me, and a man, and I was unused to making long speeches to a strange man. "I want," I added more modestly, "to make a medicine that everybody can afford, that everybody will find useful."

"Sounds ambitious!" He looked down at my bandage and frowned. "But there's got to be a better way than experimenting on yourself. How can your family let you do this?"

"I have no family."

He gave me a shocked look. "Good Lord, do you mean to say you live alone? But you can't be older than — well, how old *are* you?"

Did I tell him the truth, that I was seventeen? Or what my papers said, nineteen?

"Sorry," he said before I could respond. "It wasn't right of me to ask that." He fell silent and regarded me for a long moment, first in seriousness, and then his look changed to mild puzzlement. I felt my own face change, from shyness to bafflement. And when Gideon smiled, so did I, as though an unspoken agreement had been reached. It made me think of something my mother had said once about her and my father, when she was taking care of him in the room above Madam Wah's silk shop. "We had between-the-eyes communication," my mother said.

At the time, I didn't know what she meant. But now, my eyes held by Gideon's, I understood.

"Can you tell me about my father?" I said. "I never knew him."

"I hardly knew him either. I was five years old when he went to Singapore."

There was something I needed to know. "In the jewelry store . . ."

"Oh, that! I'm sorry about the policeman. I didn't know he was there!"

"There was a girl with you . . . blond, very pretty."

"Yes, Olivia."

"Is she . . . your sister?" Did *I* have a half sister with yellow hair and white skin?

"Oh no, her family and my family are friends. I've known Olivia since, well, let me see. She came to my thirteenth birthday party. Olivia is six years younger than me, so I would say I've known her for ten years. Of course at that time the difference between a thirteen-year-old and a seven-year-old is a far bigger gap than between a twenty-three-year-old and a seventeen-year-old! We've since become good friends," he said with a smile.

Good friends? I wanted to ask.

"May I see my father's ring?"

When he saw how I hesitated, he said, "Don't worry, I'm not going to take it from you."

I withdrew the chain from beneath my dress and Gideon bent forward to examine the ring. "It's my father's, all right. Exactly as I remember it."

I quickly drew back. As I restored the ring beneath my dress, Gideon gave me a strange look. "You'll pardon my saying so, but you don't exactly seem to be rolling in dough. I mean, you look quite poverty-stricken."

His words hurt me, but I don't think he was aware of it. He spoke with American bluntness in a way a Chinese never would have.

"You could sell that ring for a lot of money," he said.

I gave him a shocked look. "Would *you* sell the only thing you had of your father?" I asked.

And then I saw something in his eyes — an answer to a question that had troubled him. I knew in that moment that Gideon Barclay had sought me out because he thought I was a thief who had stolen his father's ring. He had brought me to this ice-cream shop to find a way to get it back. And I also knew, in that moment, that he believed my story.

"You really are my father's daughter, aren't you?" he said with incredulousness in his voice.

"Why do you believe now and not before?"

"You'll forgive my saying this, but you look like you haven't had a decent meal in weeks. And that dress has seen better days. And these medicines" — he pointed to my humble basket. "I don't think business is exactly booming. And I would wager you aren't living at the Mark Hopkins. Am I right?"

"I cannot ask for more than I have," I said, trying to imagine how my mother would act in this shameful situation.

He leaned forward and touched my arm, the smile returning to his eyes. "If you had stolen that ring, you would have sold it by now. The fact that keeping the ring means more to you than life itself tells me that you are telling the truth."

And a wonderful feeling flooded through me. The son of Richard Barclay, my brother, had accepted me.

"You must come home with me," he said in sudden excitement. "You must come and live with us!"

For an instant I was filled with extreme happiness and joy. Yes yes yes, I wanted to cry. I will go and live with you in my father's house!

But in the next instant I was remembering a cold, hard voice on the telephone saying, "Are you the girl who stole my husband's ring?" — accusing me before I could even defend myself. How could I tell Gideon that I did not think his mother would gladly take in the child of her husband's Chinese concubine?

When he saw the look of confusion, and possibly fear, on my face, he said, "Plenty of time to think about that," as if to put me at ease.

"Do you," I began, "have a picture of my father?"

"As a matter of fact, I do!" He reached into his pocket and pulled out a wallet. As he flipped past small pictures in plastic sleeves, I saw a photograph of the blond girl, Olivia. "Just a friend," he had said. But was it more? Did one carry the picture of "just a friend" in one's pocket?

"Here we are," he said, leaning across the table to show me. "Here's the three of us at the beach."

I leaned forward, closer to Gideon, and gazed in awe at the picture. My father was wearing a hat, his face cast in shadow. Gideon was very small, maybe two years old. But it was the face of the woman that held me: she was not smiling, as if she were saying to me down through the years, "You and your mother cannot have my husband."

Gideon gave me a long, searching look, then he said, "Keep the ring, Harmony. I'll make up a story to tell Mother. I'll tell her I never found you." And then he started to remove dollar bills from his wallet.

"*Aii-yah!*" I cried. I would not accept his charity, not even from my own brother.

"Oh, come *on*," he said, trying to hand me dollar bills.

I was speechless with shame. When he saw this, he put the money away and fell silent to regard me once more. "I've never met anyone like you," he said quietly. "If you're anything like your mother, then I can see why my father —" He reddened and abruptly straightened up.

"Why aren't we getting any service?" He waved to the waiter in the corner. "I am dying for that sundae — ah, here he comes." He turned back to me, giving me the full-attention smile that both gladdened my heart and broke it. How cruel fate could be, to let me fall in love and then forbid it to me. "Perfect Harmony," he said thoughtfully. "What was your mother's name?"

"Mei-ling, which means Beautiful Intelligence."

"The Chinese sure have a way of giving things nice names. The last time I was in Hong Kong — I was working on a bridge, that's what I do, I'm an engineer. Well, . . ." He laughed and blushed. "I'm still learning!"

"On a train?"

"What? Oh God no! I build things — roads, bridges, dams. I go where the big companies have interests, mostly in Southeast Asia — tin mining, rubber plantations, that sort of thing. Anyway, I had dinner at a restaurant called the Pagoda of the Mountain That Flew Away. An American would have called it Harry's Place!"

The waiter finally arrived at our table and I saw at once by the look on his face that something was wrong. The drugstore was not crowded and yet it had taken him a long time to come to our table, and even now he approached reluctantly. I knew why. And so, I sensed, did Gideon.

He said to the waiter, "We would like to order."

When the man didn't say anything, ask us what we wanted, or recommend something, Gideon said, "Is there a problem?"

The waiter looked at me and cleared his throat.

"If there is a problem," Gideon said slowly, "then I would like to know about it." He was still smiling, but I saw that it was a mask to hide the anger that was building behind his gray eyes.

"The management has rules, sir," the man said. "I'm sorry, there's nothing I can —"

"Bring us two chocolate sundaes and two iced lemonades," Gideon said in an even voice.

The waiter cleared his throat again. "Listen, we don't want no trouble —"

"And you won't have any if you just bring us our orders. Two chocolate sundaes and two iced lemonades."

I said, "Please, Gideon, I don't want a sundae."

But he was angry. "Harmony, it's the principle of the thing. These bastards get away with stuff like this because no one does a damn thing about it."

When the waiter shrugged and walked away, Gideon started to go after him. But I put my hand on his arm and said, "It is right that a brother should defend his sister's honor, but I do not belong here."

Before he could respond, I grabbed my basket and fled from that table, with Gideon calling out after me, telling me to wait, to come back. I heard his voice follow me outside, and as far as the alley. But then I ran around a truck that was parked behind Wong Lo's restaurant, and I dashed inside Mrs. Wu's flower shop, and out the front and through the impersonal crowds until Gideon's voice stopped calling me.

*   *   *

I made a vow that night to forget my brother and my forbidden love for him. I would concentrate on improving my
new medicine. I would crowd my mind with recipes and formulas, the names of herbs and minerals; I would fill my
thoughts with auspicious dates and phases of the moon; I
would memorize correct weights and proper temperatures. I
would busy my days with the job of making a medicine, and
cram my nights with desperate sleep. And I would try hard
not to think of him, because I knew he would always be
there, I would always be thinking of him.

The next morning, after a small breakfast of rice cakes
and tea given to me by the compassionate cook at Wong
Lo's restaurant, I took my remedy, which I had decided to
call Cure-All, into the street. But even though my balm now
cured more things: chapped hands, burns and stings and
bites, soothed the stomach, eased the headache, brought
well-being to the skin, dissolved aches and pains in the
joints and muscles, still no one bought it. I added up the
cures: my balm contained two more than Tiger Balm. And
everyone in Chinatown bought Tiger Balm. Why did they
not buy mine?

I realized I had reached the bottom. I was out of medicines. I had no food, no money. My landlady had said I must
leave in the morning, as she had a paying tenant waiting to
come in. My life was shredding, like clouds in a storm.
What was the cause of such bad luck? Was it because the
Reverend Peterson had made a mistake on my papers and
changed me from Dragon to Tiger?

I lay on the floor and wept. I wept because my mother,
who was dead by now, was watching me from Heaven, and
she could see how far her daughter had fallen, how far I had
tumbled to such a disgrace.

In desperation I threw myself upon the mercy of Kwan
Yin. I lit the candles and the joss sticks, and knelt before the

small porcelain statue that had been my companion during the long sea voyage from Singapore. As I kowtowed to the goddess, pressing my forehead to the floor, I prayed so fervently that I did not realize I had ceased praying to the goddess and begun praying to my mother.

Forgive me, my heart cried. I did not want to leave you! I did not want to abandon you so that you died alone! I should never have come! I have no father here! I have no mother!

Suddenly I heard a knock at the door. "You in there?" Mrs. Po shouted. "Open door!" But I did not wish to confront my landlady now. Plenty of time in the morning to face my bleak future.

"*Chow ma!* Disrespectful girl! Whore!"

And I heard her stomp away up the stairs.

I was faint with hunger and fatigue, but I did not cease my vigilance at Kwan Yin's altar. My head grew light, as if my soul were departing through my ears and mouth. I heard a ringing in my ears. Behind my closed eyes I saw visions. And then I heard my mother's voice: *"Listen, Harmony-ah. But do not listen with your ears or your mind. Listen with your heart. The answer is there."*

I gasped, startled. I looked around my humble room. Was she there with me? Why could I not see her ghost? "What answer, Mama?" I said out loud.

"Listen with your senses. Listen with your memories. . . ."

I strained my ears. I heard the sounds from the laundry, and Mrs. Po's angry voice, and shouts from the alley, and jazz music from far away, and the rumble of feet and traffic on the street outside that never seemed to cease. What was I supposed to hear?

I began to weep. I could not hear what my mother wanted me to hear.

"Listen with the senses that please. . . ."

And so I tried, and after a moment I realized that the water trickling through the pipes in the walls sounded like a clear brook in the woods. The smell of damp and decay in my basement room became the smell of rich soil and loam. The sandalwood joss sticks gave off a pungent perfume, like a forest on a hot summer day. And then, all of a sudden, as loud and clear as my mother's voice, as if he were there in the room with me, I heard *another* voice — my brother, Gideon, saying, "The Chinese have a nice way of naming things."

And then, in my mind, I saw him reaching for the box of lozenges at the drugstore, and I saw what I had not seen at the time: that he had examined the entire selection offered, and he had chosen, out of such a variety, the prettiest box with the nicest-sounding name.

Suddenly I was remembering the other remedies offered in the drugstore, the ones with the unpleasant names, and the plain or inharmonious wrappers. Those seemed faded or yellowed or dusty, as if they had sat in the case for a long time. But there had been others, ones with names pleasing to the ear — Ivory Soap, Cashmere Bouquet — and these were on top of the counter and they looked fresh, as if the stock was new because they sold well.

Begging forgiveness of the goddess, I jumped to my feet and went to my medicines, emptying the jars of balm back into the pot on the electric hot plate. I added a pinch of rose oil until the heavenly scent covered the camphor and beeswax, and then the juice of crushed wolfberries to change the color from white to pale pink. When the mixture was cooled, I regarded the jam jars I had used to hold the ointment. They were homely and used, for I had found them in trash barrels.

How could I put my sweet-smelling, pleasing-to-the-eye balm into such jars? I looked around. And then I saw the small ceramic jar Mr. Lee had given to me on my birthday. "I paint these for tourists," he had said in his voice that was as soft as the silk he painted on. "This one did not sell.

Would you like it, Harmony?" And he had offered it to me in such a way that made me realize it was the prettiest of his little pots — decorated with flowers and birds — and that he had saved it from being sold. I had vowed that I would never sell it. It was the perfect receptacle for my new ointment.

Now I had to think of a name. "Something Chinese, something nice," I imagined Gideon saying.

I did not have to search far. I would give it my mother's name, to honor her. Beautiful Intelligence Balm. I did this because I knew now that she was dead, for how else would I have heard her voice if not from Heaven? I prayed that she had not died alone, or in pain.

As I gently scooped my new sweet-smelling balm into my pretty little jar, I was startled by a knock at the door, and I realized from the street sounds coming through my walls that it was morning. I had not slept, and yet I felt refreshed and rejuvenated.

Mrs. Po stood there with a thunderous expression on her face. "You move out today!" she shouted. "That man! He came several times. I send him away. *You* go away! We don't want no whores here. You move out now!"

"This is for you." I held out my hand.

She eyed the jar with suspicion.

"Open it, please," I said.

She unstoppered the jar and peered in. Then she lifted it to her nose. A look of delight passed briefly across her eyes. "What it good for?"

"You rub it on aches and pains, soreness, insect bites, burns, abscesses, chapped skin."

"Oh? What else?"

"Inhale it for stuffy nose, congested lungs, dry throat, headaches."

Her smile widened.

"Massage it into your stomach for better digestion, massage lower down to improve female vigor and fertility."

"Ah?"

"Rub it below your husband's navel, it will improve his virility."

Mrs. Po laughed so hard I saw the rest of her gold teeth. "I start with Mr. Po!" she said, slapping her side. "Get rid of his headache, then make him stand to attention!" She considered the jar. "Hmmm. How much?"

I hadn't thought of the price. Too high and she would turn it down. Too low and she would think the balm worthless. And the jar itself, what price could I put on Mr. Lee's exquisite work of art? "Twenty-five cents."

She pursed her lips.

"And you keep the jar."

She beamed. "You good girl, respectable. I always liked you."

Whether it was from hunger or joy, I was suddenly lightheaded, and more ideas swam into my mind. I would give names to *all* my remedies — the tonic wine I would call Golden Lotus after the lady poet who invented it, and the calming herbs I would call Bliss, for that was what they brought. I would sell them to my neighbors and people in the street, I would earn money and find my self-respect again, and then I would telephone Gideon Barclay and tell him that his sister would be honored to see him again —

"You good girl, respectable, always did like so. So, okay, that man can come visit you."

"What man?" Then I remembered what she had said when I opened the door — about a man coming by, whom she had sent away.

"*Aii-yah!* I forgot. He leave this last night." She dug into the pocket of her cardigan and brought out an envelope. "He come looking for you. I tell him you not home."

I saw the crest on the envelope: GB. "But I *was* home!"

She shrugged. "I didn't want you entertaining customers in my basement."

"I had the devil of a time finding where you live," Gideon had written in the note. "The Happy Laundry. Sounds a pleasant place." I could imagine him smiling as he wrote this. But then he went on to say that he was going away, words that I did not fully understand, about an engineering contract overseas. But what I *did* understand was that his ship was sailing at eight o'clock that morning and that he would be gone for a year. He asked me to come to the dock to say good-bye and said he would wait as long as he could. He wrote, "I know you didn't want me to give you money, but I know you need it, Harmony, so here is something to help you out." In the envelope was a thousand dollars in cash. A fortune.

Mrs. Po's eyes nearly came out of their sockets. "*Aii-yah!*" she cried. "Such good luck comes to my favorite tenant!"

At the end of the note, Gideon had written: "There seems to be some confusion. You referred to yourself as my sister. I am not your brother, Harmony. My mother was a widow and I a baby when Richard Barclay married her. You and I are not related at all. Please come to the dock and see me off. I can't stop thinking about you."

I started to run for the stairs, where sunlight was streaming down through the open door from the alley above. I stopped. "Mrs. Po, please," I said. "What time is it?"

She held up her watch. It was past noon.

Gideon's ship was already far out to sea.

23

10:00 P.M. — Palm Springs, California

She *felt* him.

Even before she turned from the display of Chinese mixing bowls and cooking pots — *"The Making of an Herbal Compound, circa 1925"* — and looked across the softly illuminated museum to see Jonathan standing in the doorway, arms folded, his gaze brooding, she felt his eyes on her, like a moody caress.

She tried to read his look, to discern the emotions underneath, the way she had had to so many times because he couldn't put his feelings into words. Even taking so monumental a step as telling her he needed space, needed to go his own way, Jonathan hadn't been able to say to her face, nor over the phone, not even in a letter. He had sent a book of poetry, 1981 prize winners, with a one-line note on the title page, "This is how I feel. Page 97." He had let someone else's poem speak for his heart. But she couldn't read the message in his dark brown eyes now. He was too far away, in distance and in years.

"Are you all right?" he said.

She nodded woodenly, her body still numb from the shock she had received when they reached Naomi's house.

As soon as they had seen the fireball erupt on the computer screen, they had rushed out into the rainy night to where Jonathan's rental car was parked, and managed to get out of the parking lot unseen. The drive through the storm to Naomi's house in Indian Wells had been torture. Charlotte had prayed the whole way that what she and Jonathan had witnessed was just another video.

But her hopes were squashed when they saw the smoke filling the sky, the arcs of water from fire hoses, the flashing lights from the fire trucks. Despite the rain, the street was crowded with gawkers, and a policeman tried to keep Charlotte away until she convinced him that the burning house belonged to her best friend.

Actually, the house was no longer burning, simply smoldering in the downpour, and as Charlotte searched frantically for Naomi, she realized that the house had not been demolished, although it was badly damaged. She heard on-lookers remarking on the luck of the owner that it was rain-ing.

When she saw her friend sitting on the tailgate of the paramedic ambulance, Charlotte nearly fainted with relief. Naomi sat with a blanket around her shoulders, a fresh ban-dage on her forehead, a dazed expression on her face.

She seemed not to recognize Charlotte at first, and she didn't even glance at Jonathan, who followed Charlotte and then quickly broke off, heading away into the crowd on a search of his own.

"Naomi!" Charlotte cried. "Thank God you're all right!" She saw that her friend was holding a drenched and shiver-ing cat in her arms. The marmalade named Juliette. She sat next to Naomi, putting an arm around her. "Are you all right? Are they taking care of you?"

"Hi, Char, I'm all right," Naomi said, pushing limp red hair away from her face. "I have a headache. Something blew up and pushed me to the ground. I think I cut my fore-head. Did you see my house?"

"Yes, I did. Oh God, Naomi, I am so sorry."

"And I just had the carpets cleaned, too."

Charlotte searched her friend's face for signs of shock or concussion. But when she looked into Naomi's hazel eyes shimmering with tears, she saw that her friend was just mak-ing a joke, as she always did in a bad situation.

Charlotte felt a fist go around her heart. Sweet Naomi, who would never hurt anyone or a living thing in her life, now cradling a soaked and terrified cat, watching men in boots tramp through the little stucco house she so loved. It devastated Charlotte to see Naomi looking so vulnerable — Naomi, who was the strong one, the Valkyrie of the desert, who had actually led the assault that fateful night at Chalk Hill, eight years ago. A lump formed in Charlotte's throat. *This is all my fault. I did this to you.*

"She ran out," Naomi said, stroking the cat's head. "When I opened the door, Juliette dashed out. I went after her. If I hadn't —" She swallowed with difficulty. "Rodeo's dead. He was just a blind old cat, but he didn't deserve to go like a briquette."

"Do you want me to call Mike?"

Naomi ran a sooty arm across her forehead. When she hit the bandage, she winced. "Somebody already has. He should be here."

"Can you stay with him?"

"Sure. *His* house isn't on fire."

One of the firemen approached, his face black with smoke. "We found the origin of the fire, Miss Morgenstern. It started in the kitchen. The gas was on."

Naomi looked at Charlotte, her brows knitting in a frown. "I didn't leave the gas on. I didn't even use the stove this morning. I had coffee with you, remember, Charlotte?"

A BMW arrived, screeching and swerving to a halt, the driver jumping out and running toward Naomi. "The cavalry's here," she murmured with a tremulous smile.

A plumpish man with a long ponytail and Ben Franklin glasses pushed his way through. "My God — Naomi — what?"

"Mike," Charlotte said to Naomi's fiancé, "take her to your house. Don't let her out of your sigh, okay? Keep an eye on her."

"Sure — what — Jesus, Charlotte!"

"It was an accident," she said evenly, having decided not to tell anything more. She knew Naomi would do something rash if she thought the fire had been deliberate. For incinerating old Rodeo, Naomi would want to extract blood from the arsonist at any cost. "The fire inspectors will do a more thorough investigation. For now, Naomi is in mild shock and needs to be looked after."

"Well — yeah — sure. Jesus!"

Jonathan returned and took Charlotte aside. "See that space over there by the curb?" he said quietly, pointing to a small dry spot on the wet street. "My guess is a car was parked there and that's where the filming took place. I'd even wager the bastard hung around to watch, and left only a few minutes ago."

Charlotte saw that Jonathan was right. Even as she watched, the dry spot disappeared in the lightly falling rain. "And no one saw him?"

"In this chaos with all these people coming and going? I looked into every car on this street. No video cameras." And then Jonathan said something that made Charlotte's heart stop in her chest: "Now listen, they say it was caused by gas in the kitchen. But they don't know what ignited it. Well, *I* do."

"What did it?"

"You dialed Naomi's number and as soon as the phone rang, the house blew."

"*What?*"

"It's an old arson trick, rigging an igniter to a phone. When it rings, it creates a spark."

"But how could he count on the phone ringing?"

"Because he knew you would try to call her and warn her."

"Meaning I would have killed her! Jonathan, if it hadn't been for the cat darting out —"

"The smell of gas probably frightened it, made it panic."

They stared at each other, imagining what they would have found if Juliette hadn't run out of the house.

"Then we have to tell the police."

"No. Charlotte, if you're connected to the explosion, they'll take you in for questioning. It could be hours, and in the meantime our friend is free to wreak more havoc. We've got to find him, Charlotte."

"Uh-oh," she said suddenly, looking past Jonathan with a guarded expression.

He turned to see a woman with a microphone heading toward them, a cameraman following. "Mike," Charlotte said urgently, "get Naomi out of here right now. My name has been all over the news tonight —"

"I know," he said bleakly, wringing Naomi's hand between his. "I saw. Jesus — Charlotte — Chalk Hill!"

"If that reporter gets wind that Naomi is my best friend, and then is able to link Naomi to Chalk Hill —"

Charlotte didn't have to twist his arm. Mike was already lifting his dazed fiancée to her feet. "I'll take care of her. Don't worry."

"I'll check in with you later and see how she's doing."

Charlotte and Jonathan had left then, dodging the reporter and driving at top speed back to Harmony Biotech, where Jonathan killed his headlights and guided the car into a space where the federal agents wouldn't see it.

He walked up to her now, to the spot in the museum where she had been standing for the past few minutes, quietly contemplating the past because the present was too much to bear. He took her hands. They were like ice.

"I want you to leave, Jonathan."

He smiled. "That's not an option."

"He's getting to people who are close to me. You could be next."

"Look, no one knows I'm here. We just continue to keep my presence a secret, that's all. And we step up our efforts to find out who he is." He looked down at the smooth, ivory-skinned hands resting in his. Charlotte had cried on the way home, and then she had ranted with fury. Finally she had grown quiet. Within the space of four hours she had escaped an attempt on her life, had witnessed what she thought was her housekeeper's murder, and had nearly lost her best friend in a fire. No way was he going to leave.

"I want to talk to her," a voice suddenly boomed, "and I want to talk to her *now!*"

Jonathan whipped around. "What —"

"It's Agent Knight," Charlotte said, drawing her hands away and turning toward the office.

They arrived at the security monitor as Knight was saying, "Will you please find her and let her know I wish to speak with her?" He stood in the reception area of the corporate offices, hands on hips, chin thrust bulldog-like toward Desmond.

And Desmond, looking nervous and agitated, was saying: "Mr. Knight, I told you, I have no idea where my cousin is."

"Well," said Knight, "she isn't in her office and her secretary has gone home. She seems to have vanished, doesn't she?"

"I'd better go," Charlotte said, reaching for her raincoat.

Jonathan stayed her with a hand. "Are you sure you're all right? You can let Knight simmer for a while."

"There's no time for me to pamper my nerves, Jonathan. We have a job to do." She glanced at the computer, where a horizontal bar was slowly filling up across the screen, indicating how much of the production log data had so far been searched. In a small upper window a number kept changing, noting how many references to the key word had been found.

"You use ephedrine in thirteen products," Jonathan had explained earlier. "And they happen to be very popular products — especially the Golden Lotus Wine. That comes just second to Bliss as your biggest seller. Do you know how much Golden Lotus you produce in a year? It's going to take a while to find the short batch."

Jonathan was certain that the ephedrine had been "borrowed" from one of the other products and somehow written into the formula for Bliss, Ten Thousand Yang, and Beautiful Intelligence Balm. The job was to find which

batches it was borrowed from and compare those logs to the
production logs of the tainted products. From there he would
cross-check user documentation and find out who had access to the production database on those days. Although
Harmony Biotech had nearly a thousand employees on its
payroll, narrowing down those who had the opportunity and
capability of tampering with the products should not be too
difficult. "He would have to have server rights," Jonathan
had said. "Someone who has access to the 'write new formula' function. Or at least someone who has access to those
passwords. The system records user documentation and that
will lead us to the culprit. We'll catch him."

Charlotte was not as confident. Time was running out.
Agent Knight's response team was on the way. And once
they took over, there was no way she and Jonathan could get
into the system.

"I'll make an appearance," she said as she slipped her
raincoat on, "before he decides to come looking for me."
She paused. "I told Des I was going to go back through financial records to see if there was a discrepancy pointing to
a disgruntled employee. I'd better take some proof with me.
Can I access the accounts while that search is running?"

"Just open a new window."

She sat down and, when she had accessed the financial
files, typed in her user name, pass phrase, and password.

Invalid log-in. Please enter password.

"Typed too quickly," she murmured, and reentered her
user ID and password, typing more carefully.

Invalid log-in. Please enter password.

"Why can't I get in?"

"Let me try it. Do you use the same ID and password for these files as you do for the system in general?"

"No. My pass phrase is 'better health.'"

Invalid log-in. Please enter password.

"Let me try something else," Jonathan said as he closed the window and went directly into the operating system.

"Is this the work of our intruder?"

"No," he said as he typed commands on the screen. "Your password is shadowed. See here?" he said, pointing to the data on the monitor. "A cracker will search for the password file. But good security hides the file in another file, and then puts a pointer in the root directory. I'm checking to see if . . . hmmm."

"What?"

"I thought your password had been changed. It hasn't . . . look."

Charlotte leaned forward and peered at the screen. "What does it mean?"

Returning to the financial subdirectory, Jonathan tried opening it again.

Incorrect log-in. Please enter password.

"You've been locked out."

"Locked out! You mean by the intruder?"

"If so," Jonathan said, "we might have a bigger problem on our hands than just corrupted product formulas."

"Why? He can't steal from us. We have security backups on our bookkeeping programs."

"Have you ever heard of salami?"

"Are you trying to be funny?"

"It's a type of attack on the integrity of the data stored in systems. Typically a salami attack is introduced in a Trojan horse — usually an authorized program that has an attack software hidden inside."

"Like what?"

"Well, like for instance," he said, speaking quickly in clipped tones as he opened and closed programs, his fingers flying faster than his words, "you install a new software for evaluating employee-hours efficiency. Right? An innocent enough little program. But what you don't know is that there are instructions written *within* that software that perform unauthorized functions. You've heard of computer viruses? Well, a salami attack is similar, except that instead of corrupting or crashing a system, it removes data, a little slice at a time so that it isn't noticed — hence the name salami. It's usually used to target financial data."

"But we have a security program that alerts us when data have been modified."

"To the tenth of a penny? You're using Dianuba software, Charlotte. It rounds off three-place decimals, and since it's supposed to do that, your security backup isn't going to detect anything unusual. An intruder using a salami attack could funnel those rounded-off tenths of a penny into a specified account. Charlotte, your company's yearly earnings are in the millions. All those pennies going undetected into a private account are going to add up and you would never know it." He swiveled around. "Charlotte, who did you tell you were going to check over the bookkeeping files?"

"Desmond," she said. "Adrian and Margo. Mr. Sung. Everyone knows, Jonathan. It could be anyone in this facility. Over a thousand people."

"And one of them," he said grimly, "is a killer."

24

When she was gone, he turned to the security monitor, which showed Valerius Knight and Desmond Barclay locked in an unfriendly exchange.

Jonathan studied Charlotte's cousin. Physically, Desmond had changed since the last time Jonathan had seen him, twenty years ago. The lush black hair of his youth had thinned considerably, while his body, once athletic and wiry, had thickened. Jonathan wondered about the sunglasses. It was night and raining; why was Desmond wearing dark lenses?

As he watched Desmond pace the reception area in his long black leather coat, which he had been wearing for the past four hours, as though he were perpetually on the verge of going outside, Jonathan decided that although Des had changed physically over the years, his personality appeared to have remained the same. The gold chain and pinky ring, and the way he seemed to be strutting in front of Valerius Knight, completed the picture of an insecure man who felt constantly in need of proving himself.

Jonathan recalled one of the last times he had encountered Desmond — he had been in Charlotte's living room, waiting for her to come downstairs. They were going to drive down to Menlo Park, where the "Homebrew Computer Club" was holding a swapmeet for computer components. Desmond had materialized wearing a Stanford sweatshirt and jogging pants, even though he had only just graduated from high school and hadn't yet started at the university. He had worn that outfit, Jonathan had suspected even then, to cloak a crippling inferiority complex. Desmond had seemed never to miss an opportunity to let Jonathan know that he was "better," even though Jonathan's father was probably wealthier than Desmond's.

"It's because he was adopted," Charlotte had once said in Desmond's defense when Jonathan had nearly taken his fists to the other boy because of a snide remark about the Scots being good only for whiskey and brawling. They were only sixteen and Jonathan had yet to learn to curb his temper; Charlotte had had to intervene more than once. "Desmond is very insecure. He tries to make up for what he thinks of as inadequacies by putting others down. He doesn't mean it."

Jonathan had finally relented, deciding it couldn't be too much fun to have Adrian and Margo Barclay for parents — Adrian being himself something of a bragging bore and Margo being a sexual barracuda in the swimming pool. What would Desmond think, Jonathan had often thought, if he knew his mother had come on to his rival?

For rivals they had been, with Charlotte as the prize.

That day in Charlotte's living room, when Desmond had suddenly appeared the way he and his parents always did, as if they owned the house, he had looked Jonathan up and down, taking in the gangly body, the long, lank hair, the pale countenance of the anti-establishment computer freak, and he had said, "You will never have her."

Ironically, as it turned out, Desmond had been right.

Returning to the desk, Jonathan checked his watch, then sat down at his laptop. He dialed the modem and a moment later a message on the screen informed him that the connection was successful, "awaiting response."

He had tried several times in the past four hours to reach his partner. Apparently Quentin hadn't spent the night in his own bed.

Still no answer. No machine. No call-forwarding. Jonathan frowned. It wasn't like Quentin to be out of touch.

The Messages icon was flashing. Quentin. But when

Jonathan opened the file, it wasn't his partner's boyish face that appeared on the screen, but his wife's aristocratic features. He clicked on Play and the face came to life, Adele's lips moving in perfect synch with her recorded voice: "I couldn't sleep. I need to know when you will be back. Or shall I be making excuses again?"

He froze the face and marveled, as he always did, at Adele's beauty and perfection, even after a night of insomnia. But there was no mistaking the meaning behind the pouting lower lip. They were supposed to go away for the weekend, to the country estate of one of Adele's lord or lady friends, where they would drink champagne for breakfast and then go riding or shooting or punting, depending on which crowd happened to be there, with maybe a black-tie-and-evening-gown picnic in a moonlit meadow, tables on the damp grass, butlers serving on china and crystal.

There had been a time when Adele thrived on making excuses for Jonathan, delighting in informing the group that he couldn't make it because he had been called away on an urgent top-secret assignment. Jonathan's work on classified projects for international corporations and foreign governments had added a certain raciness to Adele's otherwise very proper life.

But now she no longer liked making excuses for his absences.

Picking up his cellular phone, he punched in his home number and listened to the phone ring at the other end. Adele had sent her message at 5:20 A.M., London time. It was now 6:00.

There was no answer.

25

As Charlotte hurried through the rain, putting her hand to her eyes when lightning flashed, she wondered if things could get worse. When she and Jonathan had returned from Naomi's house, they had found a message on the answering machine: a member of the FDA advisory panel in Washington, D.C., someone "friendly" to Harmony Biotech and who was in support of approving GB4204, had called to say, "They have put your case on hold, Charlotte, pending investigation of the three deaths due to Harmony Products. I'm sorry, but if your company is found liable, then you're back to square one and it will be years before the formula is approved. But the news is worse, Charlotte. I shouldn't be telling you this, but I'm a personal supporter of herbal products. I like your company and I like what you've always stood for. You need to know, Charlotte, that Synatech has submitted their own anti-cancer formula. That's all I can tell you, except just to warn you that if your case is held up for too long, Synatech is going to beat you to the punch."

No, she thought as she hurried in out of the rain and placed her hand on her chest to feel the reassuring presence of the Shang dynasty locket. Our formula *must* come out first. I promised . . .

"Charlotte!" Desmond said when she stepped out of the elevator. "Thank God you're still here!"

She removed her raincoat and shook it out. "What's wrong?"

"I thought maybe you had gone home."

"My car is still in the parking lot, Des. And I wouldn't leave without telling you." She turned to Valerius Knight, who was giving her a pensive look. "You have a way of showing up just at the right time," he said. "Do you have a crystal ball?"

She hoped he couldn't see the throbbing pulse at her throat. "Did you need me for something, Agent Knight?"

"I have bad news. There's been a fourth victim, in Chicago."

Charlotte pressed her hand to her mouth. "Oh God, no."

"An elderly man. Not dead, but very sick. Taken to the ER. He had just taken a few shots of your so-called impotence cure —"

"Ten Thousand Yang."

"We don't have the final blood analysis yet, but his symptoms are consistent with those of ephedrine toxicity." He looked at his watch and then glanced up at the wall clock — a man anxious about time, Charlotte thought. Or expecting someone.

"Desmond," she said, turning to her cousin, "see what you can find out about the latest victim, his family. . . ."

"Will do. Uh, Charlotte?"

"Yes?"

"Have you found anything yet? In the financial records?"

She looked into the black lenses of his Ray-Bans and thought of the invalid log-in message she had gotten when she tried to access the financial database. Did Desmond know that the files had been blocked? Had *he* put the block there, as a trap to find out what she was really up to?

She shook her head. "I haven't found anything yet, Des. But I'm working on it. Where's Margo?"

He thrust his hands into his pockets. "Mother is still putting on her lipstick, I expect."

Charlotte gave Desmond a searching look. There was a new tone in his voice, an added layer of bitterness whenever he spoke of his mother. Charlotte had first noticed it last year, when she had returned from her trip to Europe inspecting pharmaceutical plants — the same trip that she had returned from to find a changed Mr. Sung. She had thought at the time that it must be her imagination that Mr. Sung seemed different, because she couldn't put her finger on anything specific. But then Desmond seemed slightly different. He had always been proud of his mother, bragging about Margo's many accomplishments, and how youthful and beautiful she had kept herself. But now Charlotte heard something else in his tone, and something altered in his attitude.

What had happened while she was away?

When you see Margo," Charlotte said, setting aside this new mystery for consideration later, "tell her I want to discuss my televised press announcement."

"Sure. What are you going to announce?"

With luck, the name of a killer.

As she watched her cousin walk away, Charlotte pictured Naomi huddled in a blanket as she clutched a wet cat, and she thought: Could Desmond have done that?

She turned to Agent Knight. "If you have no further need of me . . . ?"

He glanced at his watch again and offered her a polished smile. "I'm just waiting for some . . . information. You will let me know if you leave the premises?"

As she started to leave, he said, "Oh, there is one thing. You said you didn't know the first victim, the woman who died from using Beautiful Intelligence Balm."

Charlotte felt her mouth go dry. She regarded him with a steady gaze. "That's correct."

"And you still stand by that? You never met the woman?"

"To my knowledge, no."

Charlotte made her way down the hall to Adrian's office, where she paused, out of Knight's vision, to draw in deep breaths to steady herself. Did he already know about the interview eight years ago, and that the deceased woman was the one who had conducted it? Or was he just being thorough? Charlotte was afraid that if he asked her one more time she would not be able to maintain her composure.

She found the company's chief financial officer on two cell phones at once. Unlike Margo, who could be counted on to emerge from her office looking fresh and made-up and in control, Adrian was not looking good. He looked for the first time, Charlotte thought, every single day of his sixty-eight years.

"I need to talk to you," she said.

He held up five fingers.

"Now," she said.

He terminated both calls and gave her his full attention. "Okay, what is it?"

As always, Charlotte was struck by Adrian's eyes. She had often wondered if he was aware of the effect they had on people. An arresting combination of smoky gray irises framed by thick black lashes, they seemed to hold both mystery and power. These were the eyes, Charlotte found herself suddenly thinking, that Perfect Harmony fell in love with when she peered through the window of a jewelry store. They were Gideon Barclay's eyes, because Adrian was Gideon Barclay's son.

Charlotte remembered now how those penetrating eyes had watched her that summer when she was fifteen. The Barclays were over at the house on some sort of company business, the adults all gathered in the library — Gideon, Margo, Adrian, Olivia, and Charlotte's grandmother, with Mr. Sung handing around contracts that needed to be approved. Charlotte had sat in the window seat watching the street, picturing Johnny on the sidewalk running toward her, as he would in just a couple of weeks when he returned from Scotland. She had sensed someone watching her and turned to see Adrian's gray eyes on her. She knew the thoughts that lay behind them: Adrian wanted to know, just like everyone

else, where she had disappeared to for three weeks. However, unlike the others, Adrian hadn't asked.

"Did you lock me out of the financial accounts?" she said
now, bluntly.

He sighed and massaged the back of his neck. "Yes, I'm
sorry, I should have told you. I've locked everyone out until
all this had been sorted."

"You had no right to do that without consulting me."

"Yes, I realize that," he said as he rubbed his stubbled
jaw. "But —" One of his phones rang, and when he reached
for it, Charlotte put her hand on it and said, "Adrian, what's
going on? Who have you been talking to for the past three
hours?"

"Who do you think? Our investors, of course."

"Reassuring them that everything will be all right?" Because of the bug Jonathan had planted in Adrian's office,
Charlotte had been able to listen in on some of his conversations, but she had not yet been able to piece together the
whole picture. Adrian seemed to be in some kind of trouble.

"Charlotte, how the hell can I do that when I don't *know*
that everything will be all right! Besides," he said wearily,
"that's my wife's purview — she's the spin doctor. Hell,
Margo could make Exxon look like Greenpeace!"

The phone stopped ringing and instantly the other one
started. "Don't worry about the investors, Adrian," Charlotte said. "If it comes to it, we'll just give them their money
back."

He turned away, raking thick fingers through iron-gray
hair. "We can't do that," he said quietly.

"Why not?"

He went to the window and, parting the drapes, looked
out at the tempest. Normally the view from Adrian's executive office was a breathtaking vista of snow-capped Mount
San Jacinto and emerald golf courses. Now it was a morass

of wind and rain and lightning. "Because we don't have it,"
he said softly.

"We don't have what?"

He turned around and regarded her with a bleak expression, his gray eyes looking like a cold mist. "The investors'
money, Charlotte," he said. "We don't have it."

26

Jonathan kept his eye on the computer screen. The horizontal bar was nearly full — the search was almost done.

Finally: *Search completed. Sixty-eight matches were found.*

Jonathan quickly typed "ephedrine shortage."

He waited impatiently as he watched the little magnifying-
glass icon move in circles next to the word: *Searching . . .*

And then: *0 matches were found.*

He tried again. "Ephedrine batch short."

0 matches were found.

"Damn," he whispered. He tapped his finger on the desktop.

He tried: "ephedrine extra."

0 matches were found.

"Ephedrine overage."

0 matches were found.

He thought again, watching the cursor blink steadily on
the screen. Then he typed "Search by date" and entered the
month and days within which the corrupted formulas had
been manufactured.

Two matches were found.

Calling up the two matches, he compared dates. The two
formulas containing ephedrine had been produced on the

same day as the altered Bliss and Beautiful Intelligence Balm. And there was no shortage of the drug reported.

He then called up the activity records for the whole week and scrolled down the list of products manufactured. When he reached the bottom, he went back to the top and slowly scrolled down again, reading the date and time of each recorded manufacture.

Three dates were missing. The files had been deleted.

Jonathan turned away from the computer and looked at the security monitor. Charlotte was in Adrian's office, a look of fury on her face.

"Stay cool, Charlotte," Jonathan murmured. "We're close. Don't lose it now." And he was suddenly sent back to another night, long ago, when he and Charlotte had run afoul of the law, and he recalled now how cool she had remained under the pressure. That was the night he had shown her his first "blue box" — a gadget that mimicked dial tones, enabling telephone calls to be made for free. It was illegal, which was what had made it so exciting when the two fifteen-year-olds had snuck out during the night and crammed themselves into a phone booth on the corner of Geary and Van Ness, where Jonathan had shown Charlotte how to place the blue box on the handset and then dial and hear the phone ring at the other end without having put a single dime in the phone. It was the middle of the night and Charlotte had been pressed up against him as he held the phone to her ear.

The fun had ended that same night when he had gone rummaging through a Dumpster behind the phone company, handing out old manuals and printouts to Charlotte as she waited, shivering in the dark, a cold but loyal comrade in crime. As they had sat in the police station half an hour later, waiting for Jonathan's father and Charlotte's grandmother to come and get them, Jonathan had admired Charlotte's brave face. They both knew the punishment was going to be severe: they would most likely be forbidden to see each other again.

That was what had frightened him more than anything, he remembered now. More than any police punishment, more than anything his father might do to him — the fact that Charlotte might be taken from him.

27

"You *played* with the investors' money?" Charlotte said, her voice rising.

"I wasn't playing, Charlotte," Adrian said. "It's a sure thing. We can parlay those millions into hundreds of millions."

"Adrian, you had no right! My God, what have you done? This could destroy the company! Do you realize that? And I cannot believe you would be that greedy! Damn it, Adrian!"

He held out his hands. "Look, nothing's lost yet. No one has pulled out. As soon as this tampering business blows over —"

"We've already got devastating publicity, Adrian. Sales are dropping! And now there has been a fourth victim!"

"What!"

"You get on the phone and you tell your investors that you are going to personally give them their money back."

"I can't do that!" he cried. "Where am I going to get that kind of money from?"

"I don't care where you get it," she said evenly. "But you are not touching the employee bonuses! That money is the company's promise to them. If you even try to use that money —"

"You're being unreasonable, Charlotte."

She glared at him, her face blanched with fury. "Do it," she said, and marched out.

Adrian stood for a long moment, staring at the hand-carved, teakwood door Charlotte had swung shut on her way out — a door that let people know this was the office of a very powerful man — then he turned to the large window and, laying his hands flat on the cold glass, looked out at the storm.

He had never felt so old, so helpless, so *useless* in his life.

Did Charlotte really think he had used that money out of greed? That he had a craving for mere dollars?

He put his forehead to the glass and closed his eyes.

It had nothing to do with wanting to be richer than he already was. It had nothing to do with the money at all. It was a simple thing. All Adrian Barclay wanted was to do something totally on his own. He wanted credit for having accomplished something more than just inheriting a name; he wanted something completely of his own creation, without having inherited it, or being handed it.

He released a quick, dry sob. God, what a mess! And he had been so certain he had found his answer at last.

The answer to how you follow a father who comes home from the war with medals, who builds monumental bridges, who seems to march through jungles laughing at tigers. As far back as Adrian could remember, it was always, "Oh, are you Gideon Barclay's son?" And then doors opened for him, the invitations came, the women said yes. Not because of *him*, but because of who had sired him.

The deal he was secretly working with the investors' money would have given him something of his own, a creation that was entirely his, from the first inspired concept all the way to the final result — a model, self-contained, self-sufficient, self-supporting Third World village, the brain-child of Adrian Barclay, conceived in his own mind, drafted on his own computer, funded with his own clever investing, and someday to be running smoothly somewhere in Africa or Latin America, the villagers happy, well fed, living in clean homes, and going to clean, modern schools, churches, and hospitals.

A brilliant idea that would be applauded and recognized around the world, and *he* would get credit.

Adrian raised his head and saw his ghostly reflection in the glass. And behind him, another vision. He turned. Margo stood just inside the teak door, as if she had moved through the wood like a spirit. His beautiful Margo, whom, even after all these years, he still wanted to make proud of him. He hadn't been able to give her a child; maybe fame and recognition were the next-best thing.

Margo regarded her husband against the backdrop of the storm. She had overheard the exchange between him and Charlotte. It made her want to go after Charlotte like a tigress, rip into her, and make an offering to Adrian of the bitch's bones.

She would kill for him.

Adrian, her savior — Adrian, who took care of her and protected her from having to live a life of men and sex — Adrian, who understood the meaning behind her sexual come-ons, who knew why she flirted and seduced, the way she had with Agent Knight, pretending she found him desirable, sending signals that she was interested.

It was because it always drove them away. Come on strong enough, with sharpened teeth and claws, and they ran, as Valerius Knight did, warming to her and then stiffening, clearing his throat and being very obvious about making sure she saw the wedding band on his left hand. Thus rejected, Margo was free from having to worry about a man coming on to *her*, she was free from the politics of sex, free from sex period.

It had been raining then, too, that night long ago when seven-year-old Margo had woken from a nightmare. She

had made her way down the long frightening hall, past
"Uncle" Gideon's room to Adrian's. She had tugged on his
pajama sleeve and said, "I'm scared." The two children
didn't know each other well; Margo had only just come to
stay with the Barclays — with Gideon, whom she was to
call "Uncle," and the older lady, Fiona, whom she called
"Auntie." It was only to be for a little while, until her mother
came for her. But she was having the nightmares, even here,
miles and miles away from home, and she was afraid to
sleep alone.

If she slept alone, the alcohol might come . . . and the
pain.

Without a word seven-year-old Adrian had lifted up his
blanket and Margo had crawled in next to him. She had slept
soundlessly, and without dreams.

Margo recalled very little of her childhood in Philadelphia — she remembered fine furniture in a big house, chan-
deliers, elegant women in white gowns. But the memory
blurred at the edges — there was the smell of alcohol followed by pain. And at the train station, Mommy saying,
"Hurry, Margo. Don't look back. Whatever you do, don't
look back."

And Margo hadn't. In sixty-two years, she had never
looked back.

Until tonight.

Now the memories were rushing back — not memories
from before, when she would lie in bed and wonder if she
was going to smell the alcohol and feel the pain — but memories of the big house in San Francisco, where she had
grown up discovering that other people's envy — of your
house, your clothes, your success — helped you forget the
dirty feel of men's hands on your body and the sight of dollars going from a strange man's hand into your father's.

"The Depression had caused us to come down in circum-
stance," Margo remembered hearing her mother say long

ago to Gideon's mother, Fiona, to explain why she would like her daughter to stay with the Barclays for "just a while longer, to give my daughter every advantage." Margo's mother, an old school friend of Fiona's, was supposed to come and collect her after a while. But she never came. A few months after Margo's father had died under a subway train —"Lost his footing somehow," witnesses said — Margo's mother exited the world on gin and sleeping pills. There was no question of Margo leaving the Barclays after that, no question of leaving Adrian's bed.

Just as there had been no question about marrying Adrian. He was the only one who knew her secret, that her father had sold her to other men for sex. Adrian was the only one who had seen her weep in her sleep, he was the only person who knew that for Margo sex was going to be impossible, and that he loved her and wanted to marry her anyway. That was because she understood *his* secret: the secret pain of believing he was inferior.

He had been good to her all these years, loving her and respecting her, being careful to keep his affairs discreet and brief. And she had been good to *him*, building him up as he had gradually weakened in his great father's shadow, worshipping Adrian while everyone else had worshipped Gideon.

As she watched him now, standing there looking more helpless than she had ever seen him, Margo found herself thinking back to another night, thirty-eight years ago, when the midnight fog had produced Charlotte's grandmother, Perfect Harmony, on her doorstep with a baby in her arms. The sight of those miniature fists, the puckered pink face — A baby! A gift from God!

"I will take him," Margo had said, not asking where the child came from or why Harmony had brought him in secret, and not giving a damn what the others were going to say.

She and Adrian named him Desmond, out of a romantic novel.

"You heard?" Adrian said now. "You heard Charlotte and me?"

There was such fear in his voice that he sounded like a little boy again. He looked smaller, too, as if he were regressing to the youngster who knew he could never measure up to his father. Margo wasn't frightened by what was going on, she wasn't afraid of Charlotte or anyone. But she knew Adrian would be, and so she had come to him to reassure him, to take him into her arms and say, "Don't be scared, everything's going to be all right."

"Adrian, I'm scared," she said instead.

He opened his arms and she slipped into them. And as he drew her into a comforting embrace, she felt his arms increase in strength, she heard his voice grow in power, the voice of a man regaining control. "Don't worry, bunny," he said. "Everything is going to be all right."

28

When Charlotte flew into the museum, securing the door and locking it, she hurried across to the office where Jonathan was tearing a sheet from the printer. "I think I was followed," she said, going straight to the security monitor and hitting keys, bringing up different locations in rapid-fire sequence.

"By whom?"

"I don't know," she said as scene after scene came up on the monitor. But all areas of the plant and grounds seemed to be deserted, the buildings appearing almost abandoned in the relentless rain.

"I heard the exchange between you and Adrian."

"I could strangle him!" she said, punching the keys on the console, tears in her eyes. "And Desmond!" She whipped around, her body a pillar of fury. "Do you know what he said to me? He wants me to sell the company. Can you believe it? We've been getting offers. Desmond says if we accept an offer now, we can bail and still have a profit. My God! Des has been having private talks with Synatech for weeks! I asked him outright if he had discussed our GB4204 formula with them. He swears he hasn't. But I don't believe him! That family!" she said. She turned and stood with her hands on her hips, glaring at Jonathan as if he were the three Barclays. "They resent me for inheriting the house. Did you know that Grandmother left it to me? Margo thought she and Adrian were going to get it. I offered to sell it at a very reasonable price. Margo was outraged. She said the house belonged to her and she wasn't about to buy what was already hers. So I told Mr. Sung to find a buyer, and he did!"

Through tears that she was helpless to stop, Charlotte shot her gaze from the big computer to the smaller one to the printer, finally settling her eyes again on Jonathan. "I don't know what I would have done if anything had happened to Naomi. I wouldn't have been able to live with myself."

He put his hands on her arms, looked into her eyes. "It wasn't your fault, Charlotte. You're as much a victim as Naomi was."

"Tell me you have good news. Tell me this nightmare is going to end."

He retrieved the printout from the desk. "Three lots of Golden Lotus didn't get ephedrine."

"Are you sure?"

"There's a gap in the recorded dates. Someone had deleted three production logs."

"How did you find them?"

"When I first couldn't find files recording an ephedrine

shortage, I realized they wouldn't have been left in the system — the culprit would not have been that stupid. I figured he deleted them. And apparently he had."

"But you were still able to retrieve them?"

"Not only retrieve them, but it has taught me something about our saboteur," Jonathan explained. "Most people think that deleting a file actually erases it, leaving a space on the hard drive. It doesn't. When you erase a file, a flag goes up, alerting the system that that space is available for new data. The deleted file is still there, and remains there until new data is written over it. All I had to do was run a utility and there they were, still recoverable."

Charlotte frowned. "What did you mean when you said it taught you something about the saboteur?"

"It tells me that whoever we are dealing with isn't a complete computer whiz."

She scanned the printout. "Three batches of Golden Lotus didn't get ephedrine. Which means three lots of another product, or one lot each of three other products, did." She threw the sheet down. "I've dedicated my life to GB4204. I can't lose it all now. That's why I persuaded Grandmother to purchase a biotech company in the first place — so we could get into biochemical assays of our herbal extracts. I just knew that somewhere in my great-grandmother's remedies I would find a cure for cancer."

Charlotte didn't have to convince Jonathan how devoted she was to Formula GB4204. It was a personal monument to the memory of a man she had adored. Jonathan knew the story of her mother's tragic death from a fall down the stairs, a young widow whose husband had died in a scuba-diving accident before their baby was born, leaving Charlotte to be raised by her grandmother in a big house filled with dark furniture and silent servants. Gideon Barclay had been more than an uncle to Charlotte.

Jonathan recalled how Gideon had come to the police station that night instead of Charlotte's grandmother, how he had smiled and teased the two miscreants while they waited for the butler to come and get Jonathan because Robert Sutherland was out of town. The two kids ended up not being punished for their assault on the phone company's Dumpster; instead Charlotte's uncle had taken them out for Zimburgers on Powell and listened with interest to Jonathan's passionate discourse on electronics and communications. Gideon had even promised not to tell her grandmother about the incident, and as far as Jonathan knew, he had kept his word.

The mail alert suddenly sounded. *Tell me your plans, Charlotte. You have less than eight hours. Write to me at RB@outlaw.com. P.S. Did you like the weenie roast?*

Jonathan immediately sat down, closed the database search window, and went to the Netscape icon.

"What are you doing?" Charlotte said.

"Running an ID on this place. Hold on . . ."

"RB," she mused. "Is that supposed to be an inside joke?"

"What do you mean?"

"RB, for Richard Barclay?"

A moment later, Internic produced the street address of Outlaw.com. "It's a cybercafé in West Hollywood."

"Then that's where he is! We can have him picked up!"

"He could be there, or maybe he isn't that stupid. He might just be remote-accessing his mail from that account." Jonathan typed again, cutting and pasting the mail administrator's address from the header, and then writing, *We are being threatened and harassed by this individual. Can you provide his identity?*

"Jonathan, the weenie roast remark —"

"He either booby-trapped Naomi's house, or he knows who did." He was thoughtful for a moment. "Charlotte?"

"Yes?"

"Your grandmother's death."

"What about it?"

"Are you sure it was an accident?"

Before she could respond, they heard a sudden clatter fill the air. Agent Knight was typing on his laptop, the keystrokes being broadcast to Jonathan's machine. They stood before the monitor watching the letters appear.

"My God," Charlotte whispered when she realized what Knight was writing.

"Oh Christ, Charlotte."

"I didn't know," she said. "I swear to you, I didn't know!"

They stared in disbelief as the full text of Knight's report wound down to its conclusion: that, through intelligence recently made known to the FDA, not only did Charlotte Lee have a negative encounter with the first victim, but that Ms. Lee was named co-respondent in a divorce suit, eight years ago, filed by a Dr. Laura Phillips, who claimed Ms. Lee had engaged in an adulterous affair with her husband. Dr. Phillips was director of the Chalk Hill Research Lab at the time.

She was also the second victim, having died from using Harmony House's Ten Thousand Yang.

29

1927 — San Francisco, California

"You need a name, Harmony," Mr. Lee announced unexpectedly one sultry afternoon as he labored over one of his brush paintings.

His words startled me because I thought he meant *another* name, the name that I, too, had been thinking about. And then I realized I had misunderstood, because I had never revealed my secret quest to Mr. Lee.

When I said that the thief who robbed my apartment had left me with my identity, that was not completely true. I had only half an identity. I was Perfect Harmony. But I had no last name.

"When you find your father," my mother said to me on my last day in Singapore, "he will acknowledge you as his daughter. He will give you a proper birth certificate and then you will have his name."

I did not have the name of my mother's family because she had dishonored them and made herself an outcast. She had removed her father's name from her own, so that she was simply Mei-ling. I had come to America to claim my name, but instead found that my father had perished at sea, and all I had to connect me to him was his ring, and the letter he left for my mother.

Small evidence to take to a court. This is what the lawyers told me, each one that I went to, first Chinese, then American. They said, "You don't have a leg to stand on."

I would ride the cable car up California Street and look at the big house behind the tall fence — the Barclay mansion. It was my father's. It should have been mine. Because this is what a lawyer found out: that Richard Barclay had left no blood heirs, only an adopted son. Therefore I was his only child. The lawyer said I could make a claim on that house, and even though it might take a lot of money and a lot of time, I could possibly win.

But I did not want that big house with many rooms and windows. I was content to live above the Happy Laundry, for now I had moved back up to the third floor, to the spacious apartment with the good-flowing *chi* and lucky east-west orientation, now that my medicines were selling well.

All I wanted was a name.

"You can't prove the letter was given to *your* mother,"

one lawyer said. "You can't prove Richard Barclay *gave* her the ring," said another. The third said, "Fiona Barclay is a very rich and powerful woman. You would never win, she would never let you have her name." And the fourth took my money and said, "Want my advice? Go back to China."

I was nineteen years old, but my papers said twenty-one. It was time I had a name.

I never actually showed the lawyers my mother's letter, because of the promise I had made to her to show it only to my father. But it was the only proof I had that he was my father, and now he was dead. What was I to do?

I had thought of taking the letter to Gideon. I sensed that I could trust him. But I also could not trust my feelings toward him. It was easier when I was confused, when I thought I was in love with my own brother. But when I learned that we were not related, that I was simply in love with a man, it became a burden of unbearable weight. For that raised the question, Could we ever be together?

Gideon returned to San Francisco exactly one year after the day he sailed away at eight o'clock in the morning, taking my heart with him. In that twelve months I devoted myself to my medicines, to making my remedies known in Chinatown, to improving them and dispensing them as far and wide as I could. I even began seeing patients — mostly the elderly who could not afford a more experienced practitioner, or those who could not pay at all. It was a humble start, and I was regarded with caution as I was very young, but word began to spread and my reputation started to grow. So I did not miss my heart very much in that time; busy days and sleep-filled nights leave no room for yearning. But when I read in the newspaper about the docking of the big ocean liner, and saw the names of the notables on the passenger list, and then saw a photograph of Gideon at a welcome-home party at the Barclay mansion to which even the mayor of San Francisco and several film stars and politicians had been invited, I felt my heart land back in my chest and give me sweet grief once more.

The blonde girl Olivia was in the picture with Gideon, her arm threaded through his, and the way she looked up at him, her smile so radiant, as he beamed straight at the camera — this "friend of the family" whose photo he carried in his wallet — I knew that my secret love was futile.

So when he sent me a note by messenger, asking if he could come and see me, I did not respond. When I received another a week later, I sent the messenger back. The third note was delivered by Gideon himself.

I was by then renting a small room at the back of Mr. Huang's Trading Company, so that the herbs and minerals I purchased from him did not leave the premises but went straight to workbenches and sinks and stoves, where my small staff of four girls helped me make, package, and deliver my remedies.

We were a humble operation. Each tiny packet, each slender bottle, each ceramic jar, was hand-filled, labeled, wrapped, and packed into boxes. One of my girls sat at a cramped desk and painstakingly wrote out the labels in Chinese and English, the date of manufacture, the herbs contained inside. Most herbalists did not list ingredients for fear others might replicate the compound. But some people are allergic to certain herbs, as I am to jimson weed, and could have serious reactions.

At first the local herbalists were reluctant to stock my remedies; they said, "We got plenty of Red Dragon. Why stock yours?" So I went around and gave each three bottles of Golden Lotus, three packets of Bliss, three jars of Beautiful Intelligence Balm, and I said, "Keep all the money you make on these. The next lot you order from me, you can sell on consignment." I had that much faith in my own products. The herbalists sold those nine and called me for more. That was when the profits began.

When I sold something to a friend or neighbor, I said, "If this does not cure you, I will return your money." With the exception of Mrs. Po, all were too embarrassed to bring the remedy back; I think perhaps they were shamed into healing themselves.

And so it was on the anniversary of my prayers being answered, when Kwan Yin spoke with my mother's voice and taught me to listen with my eyes and memories instead of with my ears, that Gideon Barclay walked back into my life.

I was wearing a butcher's apron, my long hair caught up in a white surgical bonnet, as I stirred the delicate balm on the stove, melting the solid wax to just the right consistency before adding the petrolatum and the first of the herbs, when I realized my girls had stopped gossiping — my little factory was never silent. I turned to see what was wrong and a tall American filled the doorway, his face more tanned than I last recalled, his hair a little longer. And he was smiling, although not as boyishly as that day in the drugstore.

"Hello, Harmony," he said.

My girls giggled and went back to work. I put Judy Wong in charge of stirring the balm while I went outside with Gideon, not even removing my apron and hat. It was a brief exchange. He had come to tell me he wasn't home for long, that he already had another assignment in Panama. But he had his degree now, in engineering, he could build bridges, dams, roads anywhere in the world. And there was a lot of demand.

Was that what he had really come to tell me? That he could never be a constant in my life? That we were destined for stolen encounters between contracts in faraway places?

He glanced in at my girls working and said, "You seem to be doing well since the last time we met. Are you happy, Harmony?"

"I am very busy, my hours are full."

He had stepped closer, that afternoon over a year ago, so

close that I could see a small flaw in his right eye, a gold fleck floating in the smoky gray iris. "Are you happy?" he repeated more softly. If Gideon had kissed me then, I would have surrendered to him. I would have left Chinatown and my medicines, and followed him to the farthest edges of the earth.

But he suddenly leaned away, his face darkening. "You aren't going to tell me, are you? Why are you such a mystery, Harmony? Why can't I stop thinking about you?"

"You mustn't think about me," I said.

"Why not?"

Because I want your father's name. I want to be acknowledged as his offspring, his only child. I would depose you, Gideon. We would become rivals. "Because I am Chinese and you are American," was all I said.

"Damn it, Harmony, you're still thinking about that blasted waiter at the drugstore!"

How could I not? To be treated worse than a dog because of the shape of my eyes?

"I want to talk to you. Okay, if my being personal bothers you, then call it a business meeting. I'm interested in investing in your medicines. You don't have to work in a back room with four girls. You could buy a factory and distribute all over the United States. Would you like that?"

Yes, I would like that, but with what money? And then I realized: he wanted to give me the money.

I shook my head. It was one thing when I thought he was my *brother*, giving me money. But now that we weren't even related, it was unthinkable.

I told him I had to get back to my balm. He would not leave until I agreed to meet him for dinner the next night. I agreed. I did not show up. And I did not hear from him after that.

So now it was a sultry afternoon a year later, and Mr. Lee

was laboring over a brush painting and announcing suddenly and unexpectedly that I needed a name.

I loved watching him at his art, for he used his paintings to convey the Taoist admiration for the beauty of nature. Mr. Lee executed each stroke in a precise, traditional manner, the brush of his pen kissing the rice paper and leaving color behind — the image of his inner vision. He painted tigers that leapt off the paper, and stunning landscapes suspended between heaven and earth. People exclaimed over his gift, for his paintings were the most lifelike of any artist's in Chinatown. I believe the secret of his skill came from the fact that each morning, when he prepared his ink stones and lamb's wool brushes, Mr. Lee would silently pray for inner illumination.

On this sultry afternoon, one year after Gideon walked into my life and then out again, Mr. Lee drew his gaze up from his painting and looked at me with his curious pale eyes. To see a Chinese with such eyes was unusual. But everything about Mr. Lee was unusual. He had told me he was not yet thirty, but he looked older. His hair was receding from his forehead, and he wore very thick spectacles. His shoulders bowed with a slight stoop from so many years laboring over his paints, and also from being self-consciously tall. Painfully shy, modest and private, Mr. Lee belonged in another age, I often thought, a distant era of cloistered scholars who wore whispering silk robes and contemplated the nature of angels.

He had literally come down in the world these past two years, for now he lived below me in the small room I had once briefly occupied. Although he was an excellent artist, the best in Chinatown, he was painstakingly slow, too slow for the tourists who wanted hurry-up pictures of lesser quality. As other artists moved in and prospered, Mr. Lee slowly lost ground. He sold few paintings now, and he feared he would have to return to his family with great loss of face. As

I had once declined his generous charity, so now did he decline mine. If he could not be a success in California on his own merit, then he would swallow his pride and go back to Hawaii.

"You need a name," he said softly, laying aside his brush.

He was not referring to Barclay, for I had not discussed so personal a problem with Mr. Lee. He was talking about my remedies.

I knew that he was right. As my modest reputation began to spread, people would go into an herbal shop and say to the owner, "I need some of that pink balm made by the girl who lives over the Happy Laundry." So awkward, and so inconvenient. It was easier for the customer to say, "I need Red Dragon balm."

But what name should I give to my medicines? What symbol should I choose? Red Dragon Health Company used red and gold, the colors of good luck, and of course, the dragon symbol, which is recognized by all Chinese as a powerful symbol of good luck. And while my remedies looked nice in their pretty bottles and wrappers, they did not stand out on the shelves as Red Dragon's did.

I had never met the man who owned Red Dragon Health Company, but I knew of his reputation. I even believe some shopkeepers feared not to carry his products, that they were bullied into stocking his wares. For how else could it be explained that medicines of such inferior quality — indeed some I believed to be dangerous — were steadily stocked on the shelves of reputable herbal shops?

"You need a symbol, Harmony," Mr. Lee said. "To make your remedies stand out, and so that people will remember them."

But what? I wondered. How could I compete with a dragon?

*   *   *

The big house on the hill was filled with heavy Victorian furniture, and as I sat among the stately furnishings, the potted plants, the softly ticking clocks, and the delightful scent of lemon oil on wood, I could not help but wonder: if my father had lived, would he have brought my mother and me back here to live? For surely the course of our lives would have gone very differently within this house.

I had come to talk to Fiona Barclay. I had come to ask her for my father's name.

When she entered the room, I respectfully rose to my feet. I had never been in a Western home, and except for the ladies at the mission school in Singapore, where I had gone to learn English, I had never met a Western woman. She said, "I understand you wish to —" And then she stopped and stared at me.

I did not know what was considered beautiful among American women, but I thought Fiona Barclay was pretty. She was artful with cosmetics and her hair was done in a fashion I had seen in a magazine; her clothes were silk and well tailored. And she carried herself with the poise and dignity that befitted the mistress of such a magnificent house. I placed her in her mid-forties, yet I detected a puzzling breathiness in the way she talked, the way Mrs. Po's mother-in-law, a woman of advanced age, sounded after spending a day smoking her pipe.

"Are you the girl who has my husband's ring?" she said after she stopped staring.

"I honor you, First Wife."

"I am not First Wife. I am *the* wife, and that ring belongs to me."

"Forgive me, but this ring is all I have of my father."

She did not invite me to sit, she did not offer tea. Perhaps Americans had different ways of honoring guests. "Your father?" she said.

Another person came into the room then — I recognized

her from the photograph Gideon carried in his wallet. Olivia, who Gideon had said was his friend. I saw her more closely now, how pretty she was, how her blond hair shone like a film star's. I remembered, two years ago in the drugstore, Gideon had said Olivia was seventeen, which meant she was nineteen now, the same age as me. She smiled and asked if I would like some tea.

But Mrs. Barclay said, "No tea, Olivia. This person is not staying long." She aimed cold eyes upon me. "You claim Richard was your father. Have you proof? Do you have a marriage license?"

The license was a fake — it said Richard Smith so I could get into the United States.

"A birth certificate?"

That, too, had been falsified.

"Young lady, I don't know what your scheme is, and I don't care. But that ring is mine and I want it back."

"I have no scheme —"

"What is it? You want part of his inheritance? Money? You want to live in this house, perhaps?"

I shook my head. "I want none of these things."

"You must want something."

"I want his name."

She stared at me while Olivia watched us, a puzzled look on her face. "You can't be serious."

"It is my name. You are the only one who can legally restore it to me."

Richard Barclay's widow regarded me for a long moment while we listened to an afternoon filled with the sounds of cable car bells and, in the distance, foghorns warning of fog rolling into the Bay. "I should not give you one more minute of my time," Mrs. Barclay finally said, "but I confess to being curious as to the outrageous tale you clearly have concocted. How did my husband ostensibly meet your mother?"

I told her how Richard had been beaten and my mother

had taken care of him. I told her about his amnesia and deep wounds. I did not tell her that all this took place in secret above Madam Wah's silk shop, or that my mother and Richard were not in fact married when they first made love.

"Amnesia? Then how do you know who he was?"

I explained about the ring and the jewelry store and hearing the jeweler address the young man as Mr. Barclay — I did not tell her that Gideon took me to a drugstore and tried to buy me a hot fudge sundae. I believe Gideon kept his word when he had assured me he would tell his mother he never found me. "But there is more," I added with hope. "While my father could not remember things about himself, he remembered San Francisco, and he told my mother stories —"

Fiona held up her hand. "Enough. Nothing you have told me is proof."

But I did have proof: the letter Richard Barclay left to my mother. Mrs. Barclay would recognize his handwriting, his signature. I had it in my purse, and as I started to reach for it, Mrs. Barclay said, "This is too painful for me. I should not have agreed to see you." She drew in a labored breath. "Give me my husband's ring and I shan't call the police."

"But I have proof," I said as I brought out the letter. Mrs. Barclay needed only read one part of it, and she would know I was Richard's daughter.

"I am not interested in your so-called proof," she said, her breathing becoming more labored.

"Fiona —" Olivia began, a look of worry on her face.

Mrs. Barclay waved her back. As she laid a hand on her chest, she said in a tight voice, "I should not have to explain myself to you. But just in case you think this is a frivolous matter, Richard Barclay was my beloved husband. He loved me very much, we were devoted to one another, and for you to come in here with your filthy stories —" She suddenly started gasping.

Olivia rushed to help her into a chair.

"The ring —" Mrs. Barclay whispered hoarsely. "I must have —"

Olivia ran into the hallway and cried, "Call Dr. Hafner! Mrs. Barclay is having an attack! Hurry!"

When she came back in, rushing to Mrs. Barclay's side, Olivia fumbled at Fiona's collar, trying to loosen the buttons. But Mrs. Barclay was now fighting for breath; she pushed Olivia out of the way and stretched her mouth wide, trying to take big gulps of air.

"Fiona, don't fight it!" Olivia said. "Oh my God —"

Dropping my purse onto a polished table, I stuffed the letter back in and brought out a small bottle of Golden Lotus Wine, which I always carried with me for first aid. I held it out to Olivia. "Give this to her."

"Can't you see she can't breathe? She's choking!"

I went to Fiona's side and put my arm around her shoulders, pressing the opened bottle to her lips. "Do not fight it," I said to her. "Do not struggle. You have breath in your lungs, it is enough. Take this in your throat. Swallow. It will ease the spasm."

The first swallow made Fiona cough and spit and gasp even more. But I persisted. "Try to get this down your throat." I poured a little more, but it only ended up running down her chin.

"What are you doing?" Olivia cried.

Mrs. Barclay's eyes were wide with terror. I saw a blue tinge in her lips. I held her shoulders tight and tilted the bottle into her gasping mouth. She coughed again, spraying the wine everywhere.

"You'll drown her!" Olivia shouted as she tried to pull me away.

Others rushed into the room now. Someone said, "Open the windows, get some air in here!" Someone else said, "Dr. Hafner is on his way!"

I ignored them and tried again to get the Golden Lotus down Fiona's throat. I did not persist so out of love for Mrs. Barclay; I did not like the woman. I was doing it for Gideon.

The fourth time, the wine stayed down. Mrs. Barclay coughed less and her labored wheezing began to subside. As she filled her lungs, she collapsed in my arms. I let her sink into the thickly upholstered chair and then stepped back so the others could take care of her. A big man in a gardener's apron lifted the half-unconscious woman into his arms and carried her out of the room.

Within minutes I was left alone. No one said anything to me, no one even looked at me.

While I waited in that big silent parlor, I took out my father's letter and read it, even though I had read it so many times that I had it memorized:

I leave you reluctantly, my precious Mei-ling. But before you and I can be wed, there is something I must take care of at home, and I must do it personally. I am locked in a loveless marriage, my darling. I married a woman out of pity because she had been abandoned by a cad. I have no wish to continue living with Fiona. I will have my attorneys draft an arrangement that will take care of her, and then I shall return to you, my love, and we shall truly live happily ever after.

Carefully folding the letter back into my purse, I looked up at the ceiling, as if I could see through it and learn what was going on in the rooms above.

"Richard Barclay was my beloved husband. We were devoted to each other."

This letter was proof that the ring was mine and that I had a right to the name of Barclay. But if I showed it to Fiona, then I would be shattering her precious memories of

Richard, and the illusion of a love she thought they had. Keeping the letter a secret meant I would have no evidence of legal claim to the ring and she could have me arrested.

Which, then, was I to give her?

Olivia entered the parlor. "Fiona is asking to see you," she said. "Will you come this way?"

At the foot of the stairway, Olivia turned to me and said, "That was very brave and very kind of you. Especially after how she treated you. I don't know what business you have with Mrs. Barclay, what you are to each other, but I think she was harsh. Anyway, thank you for what you did."

As I followed Olivia up the grand staircase, I saw how big the house really was, how filled with riches and the mementos of a glorious past. Paintings hung everywhere, of ancestors in antique costumes, a house filled with generations of spirits, much like my mother's house in Singapore, which we had been forced to leave. Fiona Barclay had everything, while I had nothing.

I made my decision. I would give her the letter and claim my name.

As I entered the bedroom, however, and looked around, I saw pictures everywhere — painted portraits, small snapshots, photos clipped from newspapers — a veritable shrine to my father. Fiona had kept her husband and her love for him alive in this room. And then I saw other pictures — of a baby, a toddler, a little boy in short pants, an older boy in tennis whites, and a young man in a blazer and slacks — her son, my darling Gideon.

"My mother was a widow and I a baby when she married Richard Barclay," Gideon had told me in his note. And yet Richard had written in his letter that he had married Fiona out of pity, because she had been abandoned by a cad.

Gideon did not know this! Fiona must have told him a story, perhaps a noble one, perhaps telling young Gideon that his father had died in a war as a hero, the same way my mother had had her servant tell her own father that she had died in the bay while trying to save a drowning child.

How narrow my sight had been! I had been thinking only of myself and Fiona Barclay. I had not weighed the heart of another in the equation, my beloved Gideon, who would be hurt by what I had brought with me today.

"I am breathing better than I have in years," Mrs. Barclay said from her grand four-poster bed. She was dressed now in satin and lace, and propped against plump white pillows. "Olivia tells me you gave me some of your own medicine."

I took out the bottle of Golden Lotus and handed it to her. She inspected the label. "I shall have my own chemist analyze it, of course. Perhaps he can make some up for me." She set the bottle aside. "Now, may I please have my husband's ring?"

I regarded the outstretched hand. I considered why I had come here, I thought about what I had in my purse. I looked at the woman who was Gideon's mother, and then I looked at the small photograph in a silver frame beside the bed: Gideon as a little boy.

Finally I lifted the chain from around my neck and, for the first time since my mother gave it to me, parted with my father's ring.

As her fingers curled around it, Fiona Barclay closed her eyes and brought her fist to her breast. In that moment, I knew she was embracing her beloved Richard again.

Finally, with eyes glistening, she said, "I am tired now. Olivia will see you out."

"I am Richard Barclay's daughter," I said softly. I wanted her to say yes, in front of Olivia, in front of a witness who would tell Gideon. I asked for nothing more. Just "Yes."

Fiona shook her head. "You are not my husband's daughter." She summoned the houseboy to bring her lunch, and then she asked Olivia to rearrange her pillows and open the drapes and bring her a magazine. And while the Chinese houseboy, whom I had seen standing outside, handed the lunch tray to Olivia, who then placed it on Fiona's lap, I stood rooted to the spot. What more was I expecting? I did not know.

Fiona Barclay started to eat her lunch, making a comment that the soup needed more salt, which she proceeded to add. "Mrs. Barclay," I said. "When you entered the living room earlier, you stopped and stared at me. My appearance had startled you. Why? What was it you saw? My resemblance to your late husband?"

Without raising her eyes from her soup, she said, "When the maid told me I had a visitor, I was not expecting a Chinese. Thank you for returning my ring. You may go now."

I continued to wait, but finally Olivia came up to me and said in a kindly tone, "Please, let me show you out."

But I still had my dignity. I could show myself out. I turned to Fiona and said, "It has been an honor meeting you, First Wife."

I found my way back downstairs, nearly blind with pain and disappointment. And when I reached the front door, I thought I heard someone calling softly to me. I saw the Chinese houseboy step out from behind a drape and beckon me toward him. I stepped closer. "It okay," he said in English, grinning. "All okay."

"What is okay?"

"Lady not nice to you. But it okay." His grin widened. "I piss in her soup."

When I returned to my apartment, I found Mr. Lee waiting patiently. "I have something for you, Harmony," he said, and he shyly handed me a small piece of paper. It was the most beautiful miniature brush painting I had ever seen — a weeping willow reflected in a lake. Cleverly intertwined with the leaves and branches were Chinese characters and

English letters, spelling out: "Perfect Harmony's Chinese Remedies."

"I thought," he said shyly, "about what symbol you should use. Red Dragon is red and aggressive, too much heat, too much *yang*. Your remedies are gentle, more *yin*. This image came to me. We can put it on all your remedies."

"Can you duplicate this, Mr. Lee?" I asked. Even though we had been acquainted for two years, I still did not address him by his first name.

"I can take it to a man who will do it. And I can make others — labels for your teas, for your pills." I realized that he was seeing the same vision that I suddenly saw: my whole line of remedies sitting on shelves, with their pleasing new blue-and-silver labels for people to recognize.

He smiled and said, "Now you have a name." And when he saw my tears, he mistook them for tears of joy.

30

11:00 P.M. — Palm Springs, California

The news was bad and somehow Jonathan had to find a way to break it gently to Charlotte.

Going to the doorway that led into the museum, he saw her standing before a display case filled with boxes, bottles, and jars wrapped in blue-and-silver labels. The sign on the glass read: *"Harmony Products, circa 1927."* After reading Knight's report about her connection to the second victim, she had returned to the museum to go in frantic search of clues as to who might be doing this to her. "I swear to you, Jonathan," she had said, "that not a word of those adultery charges was true. Dr. Phillips's marriage fell apart during the Chalk Hill incident. And because she was so certain I had targeted her lab for my nefarious ends — all imagined by Laura Phillips — she came to some strange conclusion that I was having an affair with her husband as well. The husband and I both refuted it, and Dr. Phillips eventually dropped the suit. But the reason I didn't make the connection when I read about the second victim was that the Phillipses did get a divorce and Laura remarried. I didn't know her new name, and she left the lab five years ago."

Jonathan would never forget the shock he had received when he had turned on the TV, one foggy night eight years ago, and seen a startling film clip from an American news service reporting on an animal massacre at a research facility in northern California: at first he hadn't even recognized Charlotte, her face was so distorted with rage and pain. But as her hands had come down again and again on the head of a defenseless German shepherd, bashing his skull in with a big rock, Jonathan had realized that the Charlotte Lee the commentator was identifying in the scene was *his* Charlotte — on her knees, bloody, savage, saying in a voice-over, "If this is the only way we can get ourselves heard, then this is what we will do."

He had wished then as he wished now that he could take her into his arms and comfort her, because he knew why she had done it, even if the rest of the world didn't. But her invisible barriers were not to be scaled. Each time he tried to reach out, he met a wall.

But, he had to admit, he had walls, too. During the drive back from Naomi's, they had stopped for a red light. In the silence, Charlotte had suddenly asked, "What happened in Amsterdam?" She was referring to the Amsterdam Eight, the hacker gang that had ultimately led Jonathan to leave his position with the National Security Agency. Jonathan had found himself unable to respond, and she had not asked again.

"Charlotte," he said now. "Knight's people have just arrived."

She looked at him. There was no surprise in her expression. Following him into the office, she saw on the security monitor the two cars and van that had just pulled up, the drivers and passengers jumping out into the rain.

"They're going to take the network server first. We need to stall them." He went to the computer and typed in a command to call up the file directory. "I've been copying your database, but I still need more time."

Their eyes connected for a heartbeat. They both knew what he was referring to: Charlotte had to find a way to stall Knight and his men. Which also meant risking having Knight interrogate her about the two victims that she claimed never to have met.

"How much time?" she said.

"It's nine gigabytes. I've had to download it directory by directory. I need another thirty minutes at least. Wear your earplug and wait for my signal before you let them near the server."

She looked back at the security monitor. The federal agents were hurrying into the main building, and they looked as though they meant business. "I'll think of something." She searched around, felt in her pockets. "I think I've lost the earplug. I must have dropped it."

"I don't have another. Do you have a pager?"

As she hooked the pager to the waistband of her skirt, telling Jonathan the number, she said, "I have it set on vibrate. As soon as you're finished with the download, page me. That way I'll know it's okay to let Knight's men take the machines."

"Yes, but be *sure* you wait for my page. If they get into the system while I am still downloading, they'll detect me and find me. They'll accuse me of tampering with evidence and that will mean my arrest. Charlotte,'" he added, "I cannot be arrested, do you understand? Not on a computer crimes charge."

"I understand. Don't worry. I won't let them catch you."

He smiled. "And try to keep out of Knight's way if you can. He would have sufficient grounds to detain you for questioning."

"I can handle Knight."

"Above all, keep them away from the server."

31

"We'll take the server first," one of the agents was saying to his men as Charlotte stepped out of the elevator a few minutes later. "That's priority."

"Excuse me," Charlotte said. "But who are you?"

He produced an ID wallet and said, "We have a warrant, ma'am."

"I'm sure you do." She looked around the reception area that, except for the newly arrived team, was deserted. She saw offices standing open, also deserted. She wondered if the Barclays had gone home. "I would like to read the warrant," she said, holding her hand out.

He fished papers out of the inside of his loose jacket, giving her a glimpse of a shoulder holster and gun, and said, "We're going to proceed with taking your system, ma'am."

"I have a right to read this warrant first."

"You have that right, ma'am," he said, and then he turned to the other agents, deploying them throughout the floor with instructions to target first those offices with occupants, reminding his men just to tag and photograph the equipment and to wait for the technical adviser before shutting down any machine.

As she saw them move swiftly and with purpose toward the offices, oblivious of her insistence upon reading the warrant first, Charlotte slapped the papers onto the reception desk and hurried off after the agents, peering into offices along the way to see who was still here and to find a way to stall them.

She ran into Valerius Knight outside the photocopying room, showing the team leader a map of the Biotech grounds, pointing out buildings, the locations of various departments. She came to a halt. If she turned back now, she could avoid his questions.

"Ah, Ms. Lee, I see you have conveniently materialized again."

The best defense, she decided, was an offense. "I know my rights, Agent Knight," she said, walking up to him. "Your officers are required to announce their identity and purpose before entering the premises."

He snapped a quick smile. "Except of course in cases where the announcement might result in the destruction of evidence."

"Oh come now. Do you see anyone here madly erasing files?"

"That is precisely what my team is here to prevent."

When she glanced at the map in his hands, indicating the location of every computer terminal at Harmony Biotech, she realized Valerius Knight had not been idle for the past four hours. She also noticed that the museum was not on his map. "You're taking *all* the computers?" she said.

"The entire system and every last floppy disk," he said. "Starting with the network server. By the way, I will need you to open the wiring closet, if you don't mind."

She tipped her chin. "I insist that your men put together a complete inventory of everything they take."

"Certainly. It's standard procedure."

"And I want my system administrator on hand while they do it."

"I've already spoken with him. Unfortunately he lives on the other side of Saguaro Canyon, which is currently a raging flood. Now, shall we open the network closet?"

Because Harmony was a pharmaceutical company with classified drug formulas in their database, the air-conditioned closet where the network server was housed was kept under extreme security. As Charlotte reluctantly escorted Agent Knight down the corridor, trying to think of how she was going to stall him, she explained that security was such that no single person could gain access to the network hub — it required two people to unlock the door. "Usually it's myself and my system administrator."

"I am sure we can find someone who has a key card besides yourself."

"I'm not so sure. Everyone seems to have gone."

"By the way, Ms. Lee, when you have a moment, I would like to discuss the three victims with you again."

Her guard went up. "I thought we had already covered that ground."

His eyes were two black probes on her face. "Some new information has come to light that I would like to explore with you. Especially as you say you did not know the three women. You might find what I have to say enlightening."

"What the *hell* is going on?" Adrian boomed as he came out of his office. "Some bastard just barged in and told me I couldn't use my computer! And now the son of a bitch is videoing it!"

Margo appeared, too. "What exactly is it you are going to be looking for in our computers?"

"Digital fingerprints, Mrs. Barclay. I believe those products were altered by someone here at Harmony Biotech. I also believe I will find out *who* by searching for evidence in your files."

"Are you suggesting sabotage? A disgruntled employee perhaps?"

"Oh, the motive could be anything." He smiled. "Could even be something like covering up embezzlement at the corporate level."

Margo met his gaze with a hardness that even Knight found difficult to hold up under. "Are you suggesting that *we* are suspects?"

"At this point, ma'am, I suspect everyone."

"We are Barclays," she said coolly. "We do not embezzle or cheat or commit other crimes."

"You'll pardon me, ma'am, but I've heard that one before."

Ignoring him, Margo turned to Charlotte. "I have arranged for that press conference. Nine o'clock. Local stations as well as CNN will be here."

Agent Knight looked at Charlotte. "And what might this press conference be about?"

"It's about preserving the good reputation of my company," she said, tugging at the cuffs of her white blouse and taking a surreptitious look at her watch. Only five minutes had gone by. How to stall for another twenty-five?

"Agent Knight, I have been going back through the records," she said, "and I feel confident that I can find the source of the tampering if you would just give me more time."

His eyebrows rose. "May I ask where you have been conducting this search? I don't recall seeing you in your office."

"This is a large plant, Agent Knight. We have terminals everywhere."

He kept his eyes on her as he nodded slowly. "I'm sure you do." He looked at her for a moment longer, then said, "Open this closet, please."

"How long is this going to take?" Adrian said impatiently as he scowled at the open door to his office, where he could

see the agent inside, down under the desk, labeling cords
and cables. "I need to get to my files."

Charlotte thought Adrian Barclay was looking better than
he had a while ago. His color had improved, he even seemed
to stand a little taller. She glanced at Margo, who had followed her husband out of his office. She, too, was looking
more confident.

"We are taking the system to the computer crimes lab,
Mr. Barclay," Knight explained patiently. "As of this moment, no one will be allowed access to those files."

"But you can't do that!" Adrian blustered.

Knight put his hands on his hips and said wearily, "Now,
who else has a card key to this room?"

"I have no idea where mine is," Margo said, also watching her own office, which an agent had just entered. Sounds
came through other open doors as well — the system being
swiftly and methodically taken over. Soon the agents were
going to shut it down completely and cart the equipment
away. Charlotte felt the pager under her jacket and prayed
she could stall long enough for Jonathan to finish the download. There was still twenty minutes to go.

"I never have any need to unlock that thing," Margo said,
pointing to the network closet, and when Charlotte heard the
note of disdain in the older woman's voice, she recalled that,
other than for e-mail, Margo had never relied much on computers. Would she know that deleted files would remain on
the hard drive?

"I'll go get my card," Charlotte said. "And I think
Desmond has one, if he's still around." As she hurried off
down the hall, she glanced back and saw that Adrian had retreated to the privacy of a corner, the cell phone to his ear.
Margo was standing close to Agent Knight again, and they
seemed to be sharing a joke. The federal agents were working quietly and efficiently, tagging, photographing, unplug-
ging machines that were already turned off and wrapping

them in plastic, seizing floppy disks, sliding them into protective wrappers. Where, she wondered, were Desmond and Mr. Sung while all this was going on?

When she neared her own office, she saw that the door was ajar. She distinctly remembered closing it and locking it when she had left earlier. Had an agent gained access? She saw no one inside. And her computer was on. As she neared the desk, realizing that there was a new message on the screen, she noticed a fragrance in the air — familiar but not quite identifiable.

Smart girl, Charlotte, the e-mail said. *You haven't told the Feds about me. Ha ha. They can search the system all they want. They'll never find me in there. You only have seven hours.*

There was no mention of the press conference. He had told her to write to him and tell him when it was scheduled, but she hadn't had a chance because she hadn't known when Margo had scheduled it. And yet, strangely he wasn't asking her about it.

As if he already knew.

He also knew about the FDA agents. How? But for some reason he didn't seem to know about Jonathan.

She glared at the computer screen, barely keeping her anger under control. I swear, she said silently to her anonymous tormentor, that I will make you pay for what you did to Naomi.

Unlocking a drawer in her desk, Charlotte brought out her security card and slipped it into her pocket. She looked at her watch. Fifteen minutes to go. She briefly considered telling Knight she couldn't find her card, but she had a feeling he wouldn't believe her. And anyway, she decided, the best way to stall was to appear cooperative.

As she left her office, it came to her what the lingering scent in the air was: Tuscany, by Estée Lauder.

Margo's current favorite.

Before joining Knight and the others, Charlotte slipped
into the employees' lounge, where the refrigerator was covered with notes and memos held in place with fridge mag-
nets. Choosing the largest magnet, she ran it over her
security card, then replaced the magnet and hurried back to
join the others.

Mr. Sung was there now, still in the gray suit he had been
wearing when she first got to the office, hours ago. Unlike
Agent Knight, who by now was in shirtsleeves, with a loosened tie and unbuttoned collar, a shadow on his jaw, Mr.
Sung was as neatly groomed and attired as if the day had
only just begun.

Charlotte heard him saying to Knight, "It would be most
helpful if you could leave our system intact. We have formula models to run and the employee bonus checks to
process. Perhaps you could have your men examine the system on the premises?"

Knight spoke as if he were orating from a pulpit. "Proto-
col, Mr. Sung, requires us to take the system *off* the premises
and examine it at the FBI lab. That way we are assured that
it is not tampered with during our investigation." Knight
flashed a smile. "As a lawyer, sir, you will appreciate the
fact that we have to be very careful in preserving the evidence. If we were to examine the system on site, we leave it
open for possible tampering, such as deletion or alteration of
files."

"What the hell kind of evidence is a damn computer!"
Adrian blustered as he rejoined them, angrily snapping the
flip phone shut.

"Not just evidence, Mr. Barclay," Knight said with equanimity. "I believe the formulas were altered here at Harmony Biotech, on your system. Therefore your computer is
also the instrument of crime. Think of it," he said, his smile
widening, "as a smoking gun." He turned to Charlotte. "You
have your card key? Mr. Sung has offered his."

Charlotte pulled out her card and hesitated. If the magnet trick didn't work, they were going to catch Jonathan doing the download.

Mr. Sung went first, sliding his card through the metal slot embedded in the door jamb. A digital display confirmed sequence number one, followed by: Please insert second card.

Charlotte felt her pulse race as she stepped forward. What would they do to Jonathan if they caught him? He was tampering with evidence in a federal crime.

He is putting his career on the line to save my company.

The card slipped from her fingers and dropped softly to the carpet.

"Sorry," she mumbled, retrieving it.

Come on, Jonathan! Page me!

She drew in a breath and held it as she ran her card through the slot. When nothing happened, Agent Knight said dryly, "I believe you put it in upside down."

She turned the card around and ran it through again. There was a split second before the display read: Card invalid. Please insert second card.

"If I may?" Knight said, holding out his hand.

She gave it to him and he tried it, sliding the card through more than once, upside down, and backward. Nothing.

"That's never happened before," Charlotte said, looking at Knight and calmly meeting his probing gaze. "Do you think maybe the lock has been tampered with?"

She glanced at the wall clock. Twenty minutes had gone by — ten to go.

"Don't worry," Knight said. "We come prepared. Randall?" he called out. "We need the blowtorch here." His smile had now turned to a scowl. "It'll take an hour, but we'll get it open, you can be assured of that."

Charlotte felt herself relax. An hour was more than enough time.

"Oh for heaven's sake!" Margo suddenly said. "Such

brute methods!" She turned on her heel and marched back into her office, reappearing a moment later with a card key. "Here. I don't know if it works, I've never had to use it."

Before Charlotte could react, Knight slid the card through the slot, a green light appeared on the digital display, and the door swung open.

She looked at her watch. Jonathan still needed another eight minutes.

"Agent Knight, couldn't your men just wait until morning?" she said. "The data processors in accounting will be arriving in a few minutes to start their shift and run the bonus checks —"

"Ms. Lee, we are dealing with three homicides and a possible fourth. We can't waste any time. There might be more lives in jeopardy. I think the checks can be held up a day or two, don't you?" He turned away and called out, "Where's O'Banyon? Tell him we've got the server."

As she waited, hoping that his O'Banyon person would be late arriving, Charlotte looked at Margo, Adrian, and Mr. Sung, and wondered if one of them could be the culprit. Did Adrian have what it took to rig an explosion with a stove and a telephone? Would he really want to kill her with a garage door? Did Margo have the technical know-how to fake the video of Yolanda's murder? And what could their motives possibly be? Any one of them might be capable of embezzling, as Knight had insinuated. But murder?

"Our friend knows enough about computers to tamper with a formula," Jonathan had said, "but he or she doesn't know that deleting a file doesn't destroy it."

All three of them, Charlotte knew, had some computer expertise, but not to a great extent. Mr. Sung used his computer for word processing and running legal searches on the Web; Adrian used his computer for the stock market and to read the *Wall Street Journal*; Margo probably rarely used hers at all.

Charlotte thought of Desmond, who was conspicuously absent at the moment. He disdained computers. Charlotte remembered how, when they were teenagers, he had made fun of Jonathan and his electronics. When Jonathan had said, "Someday computers are going to run everything," Desmond had archly responded, "Well, they aren't going to run *me*."

Ironically, Charlotte realized now, they did. Desmond was the most computerized, high tech–focused person she knew, surrounding himself with the latest, most expensive, state-of-the-art electronic gadgetry. "I'm what's known as a heat-seeker," he had pretentiously declared one day when he was showing off a new computerized pinball machine in his home. Charlotte's grandmother had once observed that the game room in Desmond's hillside house was like a spaceship, it was so full of flashing lights and digital displays. Even the home itself was operated by a central computer that regulated temperature, light, music, security. However, beyond the occasional hour or two of Myst he engaged in on his home computer, Desmond had not demonstrated any passion or skill for computers.

Could the Barclays be suspects, as Knight thought, as Jonathan also seemed to think? All three of them had password privileges into the classified files, and enough expertise to change the formulas. And yet none was expert enough to know that deleted files were still on the hard drive.

But what would their motives be? Charlotte asked herself as she looked around and saw the monitors starting to pile up on the receptionist's desk, their cords dangling, modems sitting on top. Knight's men worked incredibly fast.

She looked at the wall clock. Only five minutes to go. She should be getting Jonathan's page any minute. *Hurry, Jonathan*, she mentally urged. *Hurry, hurry. . . .*

Charlotte regarded the two people with whom she was in

some strange way inextricably bound. She had stopped calling them "Aunt" Margo and "Uncle" Adrian long ago, when she had learned from her grandmother that she was related to the Barclays only by marriage. That was also when she had learned why Adrian's mother, Olivia, and then Adrian's wife, Margo, had resented Harmony for so many years. The fact was that they, who considered the name Barclay to be tantamount to American aristocracy, possessed only the name, while Harmony and Charlotte, although not possessing the name, possessed the blood.

But was this reason enough, Charlotte wondered, to destroy the company? And why now, after all these years?

She stepped back a little from the group and moved her jacket to the side in order to read the digital display on her pager. Had Jonathan already paged her and she somehow missed it?

She froze.

A message was flashing. *Low Battery.*

The pager wasn't working! There was no way Jonathan could alert her when it was clear!

"What's going on!"

Charlotte whipped around to see Desmond marching down the hall toward them, a nervous man in black, his eyes hidden by black Ray-Bans. As she watched him approach, demanding again to know what was gong on, Charlotte thought: He didn't used to be this aggressive.

There was that strange feeling again — that Desmond had somehow changed. Both he and Mr. Sung. But Adrian and Margo . . . She did not get that feeling from them. What happened last year, she wondered, while I was away in Europe? Did something happen between Desmond and Mr. Sung?

"Are you sure your grandmother's death was an accident?" Until Jonathan had uttered those words, it had not occurred to Charlotte to think it had been anything other than that. And then he had asked further, more troubling

questions: Was there a police investigation? Who was it her grandmother was supposed to meet on that outer island? How did Mr. Sung manage to survive?

When she had responded, "He wasn't on the boat; he witnessed the accident from shore," and Jonathan had said, "Why didn't he go with her?" a whole floodgate of doubts and questions had opened up.

First, she had gone to Europe a year ago, and when she had returned, Desmond and Mr. Sung seemed to have undergone a change. And then suddenly, six months ago, her grandmother had died in a freak boating accident. As Charlotte had watched the casket being lowered into the ground, all she had been able to think of was that she had lost the only family she had in the whole world. It hadn't occurred to her to ask why.

But now she did.

"They're taking the system, darling," Margo said to Desmond. She reached out to push a lock of hair from his forehead, but Desmond shrank back.

And Charlotte thought: Desmond has changed toward his mother.

When they were kids, Charlotte had rarely seen Desmond and his mother apart; they had come as a set, it seemed, a mutual adoration society with Desmond bragging about his mother, Margo singing her son's praises. But Charlotte saw now that Desmond's curious new attitude toward his mother was almost one of disdain.

O'Banyon, the technician, finally arrived, flinging off a wet raincoat and making a comment about the storm. He immediately went into the computer room and made a quick survey of the equipment.

Charlotte looked around the office area, at the cubicles where the secretaries worked. Could she use one of the phones to call over to the museum, to warn Jonathan? But would he pick up?

"Ms. Lee?"

She spun around. Agent Knight was giving her a quizzical look. "You said you wanted to be on hand for the shutdown. O'Banyon, here, is our technical adviser. He knows computers," Knight added with a grin.

"Well, before I shut down," O'Banyon drawled as he contemplated the hardware and wiring, "I have to make sure no one is usin' the system. If I don't, they'll lose any data they were workin' on."

"But we also have to interrupt any tampering with the evidence, Mr. O'Banyon," Knight pointed out.

"True . . . true," the technician said as he checked the connections between the monitor, keyboard, and master console. "Got three servers," he murmured. "Okay, that's the server cluster there. . . . Let's see which one the monitor is connected to at the moment. . . ."

Charlotte looked at the clock. Thirty-five minutes. Was Jonathan done? Had he already tried paging her?

Having familiarized himself with the setup, O'Banyon sat at the keyboard and hit the space bar; the screensaver disappeared, exposing the command to enter account name. He typed in the system administrator's name, as it had been given to him by Knight, and when the request for password came up, he entered the password Knight had also provided.

But instead of getting instantly into the system, he saw a new message appear on the screen:

Incorrect log-in. Please enter password.

With a frown, O'Banyon ran his hand back and forth over his crew cut, and then entered the information again.

Incorrect log-in. Please enter password.

As he was about to try one more time, another message flashed on the screen:

Warning! Three incorrect log-in attempts will result in system shutdown and deletion of all files!

"What the hell?" Knight barked.

"Heck of a security program," O'Banyon said, sounding impressed.

"But what does it mean?"

"It's an extra safeguard against intruders who keep guessin' at passwords until they hit on the right one. What's called a poison pill."

"But will it really delete the files?"

O'Banyon shrugged. "Sure, why not? The company's no doubt got everything on backup tapes." He looked up at Charlotte, admiration in his smile. "You were right smart to install this, ma'am. I've only ever seen security like this in classified military installations. Ain't no one gonna steal or tamper with *your* drug formulas, that's for sure."

Knight turned to one of his men. "Get that system administrator on the phone," he growled. "His number's by my laptop. Ask him for his account name and password again. Maybe he misspoke himself the first time. And if that doesn't work, then we'll just disconnect the whole damn thing anyway and take it with us."

"Well, that might not be a good idea, sir," O'Banyon said.

"Why not?" Knight snapped.

The technician tapped the lower screen, where a small icon was flashing red. "Means the server has an uninterruptable power supply."

"Yeah, so? We're in the middle of a storm. The lights have been flickering, O'Banyon, or didn't you notice? The server is protected by that UPS contraption."

The technician looked at Charlotte. "I saw a generator shed behind your processing plant, ma'am. I assume it runs this whole facility in the event of a power failure?"

"Yes."

He turned to Knight. "Then in this case, sir, the UPS isn't a power backup, it's an alarm. It alerts the computer to a *local* power failure, not a general one."

Knight frowned. "You mean, if the power has been shut off right here at the machine?"

"Correct. Power failure to this machine would mean it was local, which means it's an intruder. Machine then protects itself by deleting data. Very impressive. The company don't lose anything as long as they've got backup tapes, but your cracker sure doesn't get very far!"

"Then how," Knight said slowly, visibly controlling his patience, "do we get into the system?"

"I reckon that would be the job of the company's sysadmin. He'll be the only man who can get into this beast."

Knight was pondering this when the other agent returned to say there was no answer at the system administrator's residence.

"All right," Knight barked, "seal off this room and put a twenty-four-hour watch on it until the system administrator can get here. I don't want anyone having access to the files, and I want your men to disconnect every single machine in the facility, including the goddamn Nintendo in the goddamn employees' lounge. I don't want anything hooked up to this network hub until we have control of it, you understand?"

"Hullo, everybody."

All heads turned.

"Who the hell are you?" barked Adrian.

Charlotte turned to see Jonathan standing there, smiling.

"Jonathan!" Desmond said in disbelief.

Knight pushed his way through. "And may I know who you are?"

Jonathan held out his hand and said amiably, "Jonathan Sutherland, security technical consultant."

Knight's eyes narrowed. "Security tech? You the same

Sutherland who tracked down and caught the Amsterdam Eight?"

Jonathan's eyes flickered.

Knight nodded. "I've heard of you."

"And you are?"

He flashed his badge. "Valerius Knight, Food and Drug Administration."

Jonathan turned to Charlotte and held out a sheet of paper. "I found what you were looking for."

"What's that?" Knight said.

"Your culprit," Jonathan said with a smile. "The person who tampered with the three products, murdering three women."

32

1928 — San Francisco, California

I awoke to screams and shouts of "Fire!"

Running to my window, I saw flames against the night sky and smoke billowing up in menacing clouds. I quickly drew on my dressing gown and flew downstairs, running into Mr. Lee on the way as he, too, was fumbling into a bathrobe. Other neighbors came pouring out of buildings, clogging the street. We heard the fire engine bells drawing near, but how were they going to reach the fire?

And then I realized what was burning. Mr. Huang's warehouse.

Someone had already started a bucket brigade. Mr. Lee and I threw ourselves into the line and began frantically passing the buckets along, sloshing so much water that the buckets arrived at the fire half empty. People were shouting, "Let the fire truck through! Let the fire truck through!"

And then we heard a woman crying, "Where is my husband? Where is Mr. Huang! *Aii-yah!*"

Without a thought, Mr. Lee ran inside. I saw the flames and smoke swallow him whole. I ran after him, but I was shoved out of the way as firemen ran up with hoses. "You have to get him out of there!" I shouted. "Mr. Lee is in there!"

The pavement was wet and slippery. I lost my balance and flew off my feet but was quickly caught in someone's arms. I turned to look right into a pair of worried eyes.

"Thank God you're all right," Gideon said.

"Mr. Lee is in there!" I cried.

Gideon immediately pulled off his jacket and plunged in, arms protecting his face. I covered my mouth with my hands when I realized what was happening: three men were in that inferno now, three men who were dear to me as friends, one as my love. "Help!" I shouted, running from fireman to fireman. "You have to save them! Bring them out!"

But everyone was screaming, and more trucks and hoses arrived, and there was such confusion in the smoke and heat that I could not tell the firemen *where* Mr. Lee and Gideon had gone, which entrance they had run through.

Firemen went in with axes but soon were driven out by flames. I tried to run into the building myself, but hands grabbed me and pulled me back. "Gideon!" I screamed. *"Gideon!"*

And then I saw Mr. Huang, sitting on the curb, cradling his scorched head. I ran to him. Had he seen Mr. Lee? Did he know where Gideon was?

He shook his head, numb with shock, while his wife embraced him and cried his name over and over.

I stared in horror as flames shot out the windows, licking the black sky, and smoke rose up like evil ghosts, expanding and spreading to block out the stars. "Gideon," I sobbed.

And then Mrs. Po was standing next to me, her short hair standing out in all directions. She was saying, "You come, you come!"

She had to pull me away from the burning building, down the street and down an alley, as I stumbled and looked back through tears. Gideon . . .

But when I rounded the corner, where there were more fire engines and long hoses and more people and cars, I saw only one man — Gideon, leaning against a lamp post and wiping his forehead.

I flew to him. He caught me in his arms.

His mouth on mine tasted of fire and heat.

And then I said, "Where is Mr. Lee?"

"He's all right. We both managed to stumble out the back way. He's gone back to help that other gentleman — Christ, it was an inferno in there."

Then I saw that they had come out through the rear entrance, at the place where trucks deliver herbs, and where I had my small factory. The fire had not reached this far.

I sobbed and Gideon took my face between his hands. "I thought I had lost you!" I cried. Or was it Gideon who said it? And his lips sought mine again, right there in the middle of that busy street, with the crowd swimming around us as I stood in my dressing gown, my hair down past my waist, Gideon in a fancy tuxedo, his face black with soot, our arms around each other's bodies, hanging on as we drowned in the noise and the smoke and the heat.

When my eyes were no longer blinded by tears, I was able to search Gideon's face for wounds, but he seemed to be suffering from little more than smudged cheeks and singed hair. I took him by the hand upstairs to my apartment, where I insisted that he drink an herbal tea that he insisted he didn't want.

The fire was under control and finally doused. Neighbors returned to their beds while others stood surveying the damage, shaking their heads. Most of the residents remembered the big fire of 1906, when all of Chinatown had been destroyed.

I got dressed in the bedroom while Gideon drank his tea in the living room. He had been home for six weeks. I had not heard from him but I had seen his photograph on the society page.

When I returned to the living room, he stared at me. "How is it," he said after a moment in which we filled in the silence with our eyes, and filled in this past year of separation with a palpable longing, "that every time I come back, you are more beautiful? I was at a party on the hill. When I saw the fire, all I could think of was you. I ran out of there without saying anything to anyone."

"You have been home for six weeks." Why did I say this? It sounded like an accusation. It sounded as if he had an obligation to see me, which he did not.

"I know. I wanted to see you, Harmony. But the last time I tried, you stood me up, remember? I waited for you that day. I waited all day, Harmony, and you never even telephoned. I wasn't going to go through that again. But damn it, Harmony, I've spent this past year in a stinking jungle thinking about you. Why can't I get you out of my mind?"

We fell silent and the noise from the street drifted between us. The firemen were leaving, neighbors were shouting out to one another. Someone was playing a phonograph record.

I could not take his eyes on me anymore, so I went to the window and regarded the blackened windows above Mr. Huang's warehouse. "Gideon, I feel so awful about this," I said, not certain which I meant, the fire or his suddenly showing up.

"Why?" he said joining me at the window and offering me a conciliatory smile. "Did *you* start the fire?"

"I was the target."

"You! Why?"

"Because I had decided to rent that space for my new factory. But Gideon, it was a secret. No one knew."

He rubbed his chin, which was still smudged with charcoal, then he said, "Come on, let's go for a ride."

"A ride! At this hour?"

"We need to get away from that smoke. And you can tell me what this is all about."

We headed down Columbus Avenue toward Fisherman's Wharf. It felt strange to be in an automobile, I had had so little opportunity to ride in one. It felt even stranger to be sitting next to Gideon, so close, as if we were on a small sofa, and yet so lacking in intimacy as cold wind blew through the open windows and we were jolted when the tires bumped over cable car slots in the street.

"So you think that fire was set to prevent you from putting your factory there? Why?"

As I watched the sleeping city fly past and the Bay loom ahead, drawing closer like a black wall, I filled Gideon in on what had happened in the past year.

My company was growing. My new trademark — a weeping willow beside a pond — had become familiar. People who could not read knew that when they saw this picture, they could trust the remedy inside. But although I was making a profit, my few items in their blue-and-silver packages still stood on shelves beside mountains of red-and-gold Red Dragon products, many of which were useless, some even dangerous. How were people to choose? My dream was to expand my little factory and get my remedies to as many people as possible.

I had talked with Mr. Lee late one night, while I and my workers were having tea after a day of bottling, labeling, and wrapping. Mr. Lee suggested I lower all my prices by a penny, for the Chinese cannot pass up a bargain. But when I went around the shops the next day, I discovered that all Red Dragon prices had just been lowered by a penny.

And so I came up with the unique idea of stocking my products in non-herbal shops, such as groceries, cigarette vendors, even bicycle repair shops. And only days after I discussed this idea with Mr. Lee, suddenly Red Dragon products were appearing in the groceries, cigarette vendors, and bicycle repair shops.

The coincidence of this puzzled me until I invented a new kind of breath sweetener, a square tablet, flat and hard, consisting mainly of licorice and menthol, and before I had even delivered it to the shops, Red Dragon already had a brand-new product that was similar, except that it claimed to both sweeten the breath *and* cure sore throat.

Finally, when I decided to add red dye to my Golden Lotus Wine, to remind people that it was a blood tonic, and also because I thought it a more suitable color than the original amber, Red Dragon added red dye to their popular skin balm, adding the claim that it "strengthened the blood."

So I knew someone was giving my secrets to Red Dragon Health Company.

Gideon said, "I'd definitely say you have a spy among your ranks, Harmony. Someone who is reporting to Red Dragon what's going on in your operation."

"Mr. Huang said the fire was not accidental. A fireman found an empty petrol can and rags. I am such a small company, Gideon," I said, "and Red Dragon is so big. Why would they do this?"

The wind whipped my beautiful Gideon's beautiful hair as he talked over the roar of his automobile engine. "I know how big they are, Harmony. Every job I've been on, I've seen the workers using Red Dragon products. I personally think it's inferior stuff." He flashed me a smile. "Not excellent quality like yours. Unfortunately, Red Dragon has contracts with all the big foreign companies. Like Titan Mining, the people *I'm* contracted with. The company provides its workers with shelter, food, and medicine as extra benefits."

We stopped at a signal light and watched a truck roll by. The light turned and we sped on.

"Red Dragon moved into Southeast Asia about twenty years ago," Gideon said, "and pretty much tied up all the foreign companies. The native workers get Red Dragon stuff on the job, they take it home, their wives use it, so when they go into the village to buy more medicines, they see the familiar red-and-gold label, and there you are. Everyone buys Red Dragon simply because it's there, not because it's good."

I put my hand on the dashboard, wondering how people could travel this way, with the road speeding so quickly underfoot. "Red Dragon is so big, why do they go after a small company like me?"

"You must be offering some good competition for them to go to the trouble of planting a spy. Have you ever met the fellow who owns Red Dragon?"

I had seen his picture in the papers. He was a Chinese who liked jazz and went to speakeasies with white women, a man who did not care that his medicines were inferior, or that they even harmed people, or that they made false claims.

I fell silent as we rushed along the highway that curved with the Bay, racing with the moon as it, too, sped along the black water. We had left Chinatown and Fisherman's Wharf and the Marina far behind. Up ahead was Fort Point, and beyond that, the Golden Gate.

Finally Gideon guided his car off the main road and onto a small dirt track until we came to a grassy cliff, and I released a sigh of relief. He stopped the car and got out, and then he came around, opened my door, and took me by the hand to lift me into the bracing night air.

He led me to the edge of the cliff, where the wind plucked at our clothes and snatched greedily at our hair. "Look out there, Harmony," Gideon said, waving his arm. "What do you see?"

I saw night sky and a black star-splashed ocean and eternity.

We walked along the grass, inhaling the salty smell of the sea. We were the only ones on that green promontory; it made me feel we were the only two people on earth. "A bridge is going to be built right there, Harmony, across those two points, lining San Francisco with Marin."

"*Aii-yah*," I whispered. "It's too far! The water is too deep. The bridge would fall!"

He laughed. "It won't be a normal bridge, Harmony, but a *suspension* bridge. It will be held up. Look!" He reached into his jacket and brought out a small notebook. He flipped past pages filled with diagrams and numbers until he found a fresh page. He spoke as he sketched by moonlight: "This idea came to me one night in a dream. What we have to do is create three separately poured massive concrete base blocks that are keyed into one another by a stair-step configuration. See?" I looked but I did not see. My eyes were on the hand of the writer, not on what was being written. Gideon had beautiful hands, slender, expressive, the hands of a poet, I thought, not a builder.

"The object of this anchorage. . . ," he said, drawing lines this way and that, arches and arrows, rapidly filling in spaces with ink, forming a picture that meant nothing to me but that clearly was the vision in his mind, "is to resist the cables' pull due to their own weight as well as to bridge load, you see."

"The cables hold up the bridge?"

He beamed at me. "Precisely! There's a lot of opposition to building a bridge across the Golden Gate. People are saying it will disfigure the landscape. But it won't! It will be a beautiful monument to how man and nature can work together. In harmony!" he added with that funny laugh I so loved.

He started to put the notebook away, but I shyly laid my

hand on his wrist and reached for the page he had scribbled on. Still laughing, he tore it out and gave it to me. While I carefully folded the sketch into the pocket of my dress, Gideon looked out over the Bay and said, "Everyone is saying it can't be done. That winds and fogs and tides will fight us every step of the way. But it can be done, Harmony. And I am going to be the man to do it."

"Yes, you are. I know you can do it."

He turned to me, his eyes boring into mine as he put his hands on my arms. "You do believe in me, don't you? I can see it in your eyes. Did you know that you look at me the way no woman ever has? And then when I look at you, I feel in a way I never have."

I felt it, too. And I knew what it was. We had between-the-eyes communication.

Suddenly his lips were on mine. And my arms were around his neck and this time it was not the frantic kiss of panic and fear and burning buildings; I was kissing my beloved Gideon in the way I had dreamed about, tenderly, with love.

He drew back and gazed at me with gray eyes filled with amazement. "Marry me, Harmony," he blurted. And then he gave me a surprised look. "Yes!" he said, laughing. "That's it! We'll get married!"

I was too taken aback to respond.

He mistook my hesitation. "I can take care of you, Harmony. I'm twenty-six years old and I'm finally making a name for myself in my profession. With you as my wife —"

"Oh Gideon," I cried, seeing that he was truly serious. "We cannot marry! Have you forgotten what happened that day in the drugstore?"

"You can't still be thinking about that! Harmony, that was one small shop owned by one ignorant bigot."

"Gideon, I am considered a 'woman of color.' The law says I cannot marry a white man."

"That law doesn't apply to us. Harmony, you're American."

"But I am also Chinese."

"And I happen to be in love with both of you."

"With you dropping in and out of my life,'" I cried. "Like rain — never knowing when it comes, when it will leave, if it will be a sweet rain or a storm! I want stability, Gideon. I want a home —"

"But that's what I am saying. I won't go away anymore. After this last contract is completed, I'll stay here in San Francisco. I have already put in a bid to work on the project. I've been told I have a good chance of getting it. Say you'll marry me, Harmony, say that you will make my life complete."

But the scene in the drugstore continued to haunt me — the waiter, the patrons who stared and said nothing, Gideon's anger and helplessness.

"What about Olivia?" I said.

"Olivia?" He frowned. "What about her? She and I are just friends."

But I had seen in the newspaper photos the way she looked at Gideon. It was not a "just friends" look.

"And your mother?" I said.

"Mother will understand when I tell her how much I love you. She might seem a cold and heartless woman, Harmony, but she does understand love. She and Richard Barclay shared a passion that few are lucky enough to know. And maybe that's what made her the way she is today — she met Richard when she was a widow, struggling on her own with a child. Theirs was a romance out of a storybook, and then she lost him. She understands love, Harmony. She'll understand ours."

I held back my tears. Richard Barclay's letter to my

mother — "*Loveless marriage. . . . I married Fiona out of pity. . . . She had been abandoned. . . .*" Gideon must never know.

He took my hands. "Harmony, you went to my mother that day in the hope that she would acknowledge you as her husband's daughter. You wanted your father's name. It was only right. She shouldn't have treated you the way she did, she shouldn't have taken his ring from you. But if you marry me, Harmony, I will give you your father's name. And I will restore the ring to you."

I shook my head, at first unable to speak, my heart was so full. Then I said, "I will not marry you for those reasons, Gideon. Everything that has gone on before — the past, my father, our two mothers — these things mean nothing to me now because my life begins now, at this moment, with you. Yes, my darling Gideon, I will marry you."

He drew me to him and murmured, "You have made me the happiest man in the world." And then he kissed me again.

We made love there, beneath the stars over the Golden Gate, on the place where Gideon's dream, and mine, was about to begin.

I faced the eight girls who worked for me. "One of you is giving my secrets to Red Dragon Company. Which of you is it?"

From the way they looked at each other, and then cast their eyes down and protested feebly that they didn't know what I was talking about, I knew that the others were shielding the guilty one.

How to solve the problem? What would Gideon advise?

Despite the unpleasant situation I found myself in, I smiled. How could I not smile each time I thought of my beloved Gideon? He had been gone for only five weeks and already I was counting the days till his return. Ten months seemed an eternity. But once he was home, he would stay home and never go away again.

"I have been good to you," I said to the girls. "I would expect some loyalty in return. What one of you has been doing is hurting this company, and therefore hurting her fellow workers. Is this what you want?"

They looked ashamed and would not meet my eyes. What could I do? I certainly could not dismiss all eight because of the treachery of one.

I thought of seeking Mr. Lee's advice, but he had his own troubles burdening him now. His family's financial woes were continuing to bow his shoulders so that at thirty he looked sixty. I offered him a loan but he would not take it. And because he was troubled, he could not concentrate on what little work came his way. Now that my labels had been designed and were being printed by a firm in Oakland, I had no more work for Mr. Lee. Occasionally, I would tell him someone had come into my factory and inquired about the man who painted my labels, and inquire if he would consider doing a larger painting for a private party. Mr. Lee would cheer up for a while, and get busy with his inks and brushes, but then he would soon lose enthusiasm and berate himself for being a failure and the painting would not get finished and I would have to assure him the customer — who did not exist except in my imagination — would understand and wait for the painting to be done.

Finally, looking at the eight girls, I decided there was nothing I could do. Before he left, Gideon had made me promise I would do nothing to spark the attention of Red Dragon Company. I was to put my plans on hold, not even try to expand a little, not to experiment with any new remedies . . . just suspend my life until he returned. "The next fire might be your place," he had said when dawn broke over the Bay and we walked back to the car. Gideon had only three hours to pack and get to the dock.

He had taken my face again between his hands and said, "Promise me, my love. You will do nothing. No changes, no hiring or firing. I don't trust that Red Dragon bastard. Let him think for now that he's succeeded in frightening you."

So I dismissed the girls and let them go back to work, and as I turned, I saw a man in a uniform in the doorway. For an instant I thought he was a policeman. Then I saw his dark skin. Africans did not wear San Francisco police uniforms, any more than Chinese did. He asked me if I was Perfect Harmony, and then he told me that Mrs. Barclay wished to have a word with me.

I had been expecting this. Gideon had promised me he would tell his mother about our engagement before he left. I wondered what her reaction would be. Now I was about to find out.

I had anticipated many reactions — from money to threats. What I had not expected was to find a smiling and gracious Fiona Barclay seated in the back of a long, shiny motor car — the uniformed man was her chauffeur — inviting me to have luncheon with her at her club. "We have to put the past behind us," she said with warmth in her voice. "I respect my son's wishes. You are going to be a member of the family. It is time you and I got acquainted."

We set a date for a week from then, when she would pick me up in that long, shiny car.

I worried over my clothes, trying to choose the perfect *cheongsam*.

But as I held each dress up to myself in the full-length mirror, I realized what a terrible mistake that would be. Mrs. Barclay would not want to go to luncheon with her Chinese daughter-in-law! For this I must be American.

I left Chinatown and went to a beauty salon on Clay Street, where I had my waist-length hair cut off and then a painful razor cut to bob it, finally getting it curled to match

Clara Bow's look on the cover of *Photoplay*. I bought the latest cosmetics — Elizabeth Arden "oxblood" lipstick and nail polish. Finally I purchased the very latest style dress — sapphire chiffon with deep blue floating panels, elaborately trimmed with beads and tassels and bows. The saleslady told me that in Paris it was called "le cocktail dress."

When Mrs. Barclay's long car arrived, my Chinatown neighbors all stood on the sidewalk to admire and comment, and to wave me off. Mrs. Barclay smiled and told me how lovely I looked, and that she was looking forward to introducing me to her friends.

The club was near the Palace of Fine Arts, and it had once been a private residence, Mrs. Barclay explained, but was now converted to a ladies' social club where they played tennis and held fund-raising benefits. I was so excited and my heart was thundering so in my ears that I didn't hear anything of what she said. And then my eyes grew wide as our car pulled between magnificent wrought-iron gates, and a man in a uniform opened the door for us and escorted us up the steps to a stately entrance.

Inside, we found ourselves standing in a magnificent foyer, where ladies in fine clothes chatted leisurely and sipped tea among small palm trees in wicker pots. The club was like a grand hotel, and I was overwhelmed by it.

The dining room, called the Garden Court, had a high glass ceiling that admitted defused sunlight; the room was filled with plants and flowers, and musicians played violins and harps, filling the air with delightful music. As we followed the maître d' to a table, I was filled with so much joy to be in such a place, and to be treated so kindly by Gideon's mother, that I thought I was in a dream.

And then I overheard a whisper: "I thought this club had a policy."

And I saw how all the women were staring at me.

But Gideon's mother seemed unaware of the stares and

whispers, and we finally arrived at our table. Olivia was there. I had not expected Mrs. Barclay to invite her as well. Olivia's mouth smiled but her eyes said, *I will never forgive you*.

And that was when I began to realize I had made a terrible mistake.

And when I saw how Fiona and Olivia and the rest of the ladies were dressed, in expensive-looking jumpers with pleated skirts in beiges, whites, and pastels, I realized how outrageous I must look with my frizzed hair and scarlet lips and nails and Parisian cocktail dress.

Gideon's tasteless half-breed fiancée.

The food was foreign to me. We began with fish eggs — caviar Mrs. Barclay said — and I made the mistake of taking several huge spoonfuls, which would be complimentary to the hostess at a Chinese meal but which I later learned was the wrong thing to do. Next came the artichoke, which I had no idea how to eat.

The lady on my right turned to me with a smile and said, "So tell me, Miss, um . . ."

"My name is Harmony."

"Do you play bridge?"

I did not know how to respond. What kind of bridge was she referring to?

"Do you play tennis?" she asked.

I shook my head.

So they talked across the table, they talked in front of me and around me, about other members, vacations, recent films and books, subjects I could not possibly join in.

The lady on my left said, "Where did you say you live, my dear?"

How could I say, "Above the Happy Laundry"? I could not even say "Chinatown." "Jackson Street," I said.

"Oh! Are you near the Lovecrafts? They're on Jackson near Broderick."

And I realized she meant Jackson Street *up* on the hill while I had meant Jackson Street *down* in Chinatown. "I do not know them," I said.

Another lady said, "You have a delightful accent, my dear. Where are you from, may I ask?"

"Singapore."

"Ah, my husband and I visited there three years ago. We had the delightful experience of meeting Mr. Somerset Maugham at Raffles Hotel. Have you ever met him?"

I had no idea who he was.

And then a moment that I had known all along was going to come finally arrived.

It was the maître d' this time instead of a soda shop waiter. That waiter had been young, this man was elderly. But in that moment they looked exactly the same. "I'm sorry, Mrs. Barclay, the other members have asked me . . ." and he murmured the rest privately, out of our hearing.

But we all knew what he was saying. The other ladies at our table suddenly had other things to look at, they folded and refolded their napkins, they turned crystal glasses on their delicate stems. Only Olivia kept her eyes on me, as if waiting to see my reaction.

"You can tell the other members, Steven," Mrs. Barclay said quietly, "that this young lady is engaged to my son and will soon be my daughter-in-law. And so you see she has every bit as much right to be here as I do."

The man turned so scarlet that I felt sorry for him.

And that was when I saw how my life with Gideon would be: filled with food I did not know how to eat, gossip I could not understand, games called "bridge" and "polo," and people staring, coughing uncomfortably, always finding ways to invite us to leave.

I rose from my chair and said, "Thank you so much for inviting me to luncheon, Mrs. Barclay." I looked at the other ladies. "It has been a pleasure to meet you all."

From the club I went straight back to Chinatown, where I washed out my curly hair, scrubbed Elizabeth Arden from my face and nails, folded my Paris clothes, and put my *cheongsam* back on. I went across to my small factory behind Mr. Huang's Trading Company and I fired the eight girls, dismissing them at once and locking the premises. Then I went to Mr. Lee's apartment, where I told him: "I am going to find another space to rent and expand my factory. I want you to design an advertising campaign for me, complete with posters, magazine ads, and billboards. I am going to give the Red Dragon a fight he won't forget." Then I said, "I will also give you the money to bring your family over from Hawaii, and I will give them all jobs in my factory. This is not charity or a loan. I will give you the money in return for a favor I will ask."

Finally I returned to my own apartment, where I sat down and wrote a letter to Gideon.

When I heard a knock at my door, I thought: Ah, a late guest. But when I started to open it and saw Gideon standing there, I froze, the door open only a few inches.

"I know I should have warned you," he said quickly. "But I wanted to come straight here." He stopped and stared. "Harmony, you've cut off all your hair."

I put my hand up to the straight Chinese bob that came just below my ears. "You are not due back for another eight months," I said. I was numb with shock. I thought I was looking at a ghost.

"I canceled my contract. When I got your letter —"

I saw the pain and confusion in his eyes. I saw my letter in his hand, the one I had written telling him I could not marry him.

"Harmony, what happened? What made you change your mind? My mother said something, didn't she? What was it? Did she tell you that she would dissuade me from marrying you? My God, Harmony, you don't think I'd let anything stop me from marrying you?"

"Your mother was very kind to me. She invited me to lunch."

He put his hand on the door. "Please let me come in. We need to talk."

But I wouldn't let him in. "I would never fit in your world, Gideon," I said, my voice almost a plea. "And you would never fit in mine."

"Then we'll make our own world, Harmony. Here," he said, smiling as he held out an envelope. "This is for you. It's my wedding gift to you. I was going to wait till our wedding day, but this seems a better time."

"What is it?"

He opened the envelope and unfolded several sheets bound together. "It's a contract between Titan Mining Company and Perfect Harmony's Chinese Remedies, stating that Harmony has exclusive rights to the distribution and supplying of their products to the staff and workers of Titan Mining."

I looked at him in confusion. His smile widened. "It took some doing, Harmony, but I got them to agree to use only *your* products. It means thousands of workers all over Asia, Harmony, all using your tonics and ointments. That's your inroad to the export market! Those workers will take your Golden Lotus Wine home to the wife and kids and that's all they'll buy after that! Red Dragon will no longer dominate the market. Well? Aren't you going to say something?"

"I did not know you were going to do this."

"I wanted it to be a surprise. I had all kinds of plans for when I got back, but my God, when I got your letter, saying you had changed your mind, I nearly went insane. That's why I left early. I told them I had an emergency at home. But you'll notice that my name is on that contract, too," he added with a grin. "You didn't say in your letter why you had changed your mind, so I added a clause that would make you change it back. We're business partners, Harmony. This contract is between Titan Mining and you and me."

I took the papers and stared at them.

"You're my life, Harmony, my soul," he continued with passion. "I can't live without you. I don't care what my mother thinks. If it means choosing between you and her, I choose you. I'm begging you, Harmony. Say you'll marry me."

I gazed down at the contract in my hand, barely able to read through my tears the terms laid out guaranteeing that I would be the sole supplier of herbal and medicinal products to the staff and workers of Titan Mining, which had holdings in countries I recognized as once being the sole territory of Red Dragon Health Company. I felt my heart rise in my throat as I realized the terrible, terrible mistake I had made.

I could not look at Gideon's confused expression as I stepped back, opening the door wider so that he could see the people inside my apartment, the sliced wedding cake, Mr. Lee wearing a groom's tuxedo.

"Who just got married?" Gideon said.

With his wedding gift in my hand, and my two-month-old secret stirring in my womb, I replied, "*I* did."

33

Midnight — Palm Springs, California

"It's over," Jonathan said as he came into the museum. "Riverside County sheriffs have arrested Rusty Brown."

Charlotte looked up from the photograph she had been

studying. She saw the plastic bag in Jonathan's hand — he
had been to the greenhouse to unearth his gun. And then she
saw his face, dark and unreadable, as though he were
wrestling inner demons.

She, too, was caught in a maelstrom of conflicting emotions: overwhelming relief that he had found the perpetrator
so quickly, but despair also that Jonathan found the man so
quickly, because that meant he would go home.

"They said Brown confessed to the tampering. The police
found floppies at his house that are backups of the logs he
tampered with. Apparently he was planning on using them
somehow to make the company appear at fault."

There was further damning evidence as well. While the
police had gone to Brown's house to arrest him, the federal
agents were going through his locker at the plant and found
old newspapers with Chalk Hill headlines, a map to Naomi's
house with a floor plan indicating the stove and a telephone,
and a camcorder with the video of Yolanda. After Charlotte
made her statement to Valerius Knight regarding her own
connection to the first two victims, explaining how she had
not realized she knew them, Knight speculated that Brown
had selected those women on purpose, so that the connection would make Charlotte appear to be the guilty party.

"Did he say why he did it?" she asked softly, voicing
words that had nothing to do with what she really wanted to
say.

"He said the company had broken a promise to him."

"Rusty Brown," she murmured — the man who had
signed off on three lots of Golden Lotus Wine that were
made without ephedrine, and then one lot each of Beautiful
Intelligence Balm, Ten Thousand Yang, and Bliss that were
compounded *with* the ephedrine. Brown had passed all six
lots as approved and then had deleted the system files, thinking they would never be found. "RB," she said.

"RB?"

She regarded the dark look beneath thick brows. She and Jonathan were talking about Rusty Brown because they had to, she realized, because neither knew how to voice the deeper, more turbulent thoughts they both shared. "The RB in the e-mail address at the cybercafé," she said, feeling the pain start to approach, like an ocean wave that begins far out, rolling relentlessly to shore, massive and unstoppable. Charlotte knew that the pain of Jonathan's leaving this time was one she might never recover from. "I thought it was like an inside joke — Richard Barclay. I thought it was someone close to me. I've never even met Rusty Brown."

"According to Knight, Brown has a personal grudge against drug manufacturers, something to do with his past. He was arrested for something at his last job. They almost got a conviction on him but he had a good lawyer."

"So he was working alone? Brown wasn't being paid by someone here?"

"He said he was due a promotion and didn't get it."

"He went to an awful lot of trouble over a promotion."

Jonathan looked at the plastic bag in his hands. He brushed off invisible dirt. "Did you get hold of Naomi?"

"She's sounding better. She said that, all things considered, she'd rather be in Philadelphia. I told her what happened, why her house blew up. She doesn't blame me. She said the same thing you did, that I was a victim, too. Still, I feel responsible. Rusty Brown was one of my employees and I take responsibility for everything that happens within this company's walls."

They fell silent then, as thunder rumbled softly and the glass display cases trembled and tinkled. Charlotte saw shadows pass over Jonathan's face, and a tempest rise in his eyes. He looked at the photograph in her hand.

She held it out to him. "This was taken in 1930, when my mother was one year old." She handed it to him, watching Jonathan's hand reach toward her, take the photo, retreat.

She studied his face as he contemplated the black-and-white snapshot of two people standing in front of a doorway with a sign over it that read *Harmony-Barclay Hong Kong Ltd.* She filled her eyes and mind with every detail of him — the long straight nose, the shadow on his jaw, the lower lip, moist and inviting — capturing him like the two captured in the photograph, as a way of keeping him because he was about to vanish, and this time she knew it would be for good.

As she watched his mouth, she recalled the first time they had kissed, when they were sixteen and in Johnny's basement hideaway. He had been wiring something when all of a sudden he had looked up and said, "I heard a strange sound last night. It was coming from my father's room."

Charlotte, sitting on the bed: "What sort of sound?"

"My father was crying. I listened at his door. It was terrible . . . like anguished weeping."

"Why was he crying?"

"I knocked. He didn't say come in, he didn't say go away. So I tried the knob. It wasn't locked. I swung the door open and I saw him at the window in his pajamas, just standing there sobbing. I said, 'Dad? Something wrong, Dad?' He turned and looked at me, still crying, tears streaming down his cheeks."

"And?"

"That was it. He just . . . looked at me."

Seeing the incipient tears in Johnny's eyes, she had slipped from the bed and sat next to him on the floor. "What could it be? What made him cry?"

"I think I know."

"What?"

"I think he wanted to tell me he was lonely but he didn't know how."

"What did you do?"

"I left. I closed the door and left. Oh Charlie, why couldn't he say it? You could feel it in the air thick as smoke. My

rich, influential father, standing in his pajamas crying because he was lonely. Why couldn't he have said how he felt?
Maybe I could have helped."

Why can't *you* say how you feel? she had wanted to
counter. But that would have been cruel, to tell Johnny that
he had been looking in a mirror. So she had consoled him instead, taking him in her arms, the lonely boy who was crying for his lonely father, and then she comforted him with
her lips.

They had kissed a lot after that, in the months that followed, and explored and experimented, delighting in the
pleasure they could give each other. But, by unspoken
agreement, they never went all the way. They both wanted
the first time to be special, and they both knew that when
that moment came, it would be the exact right moment.

It came a year later, when it was Johnny's turn to comfort
her, gathering her into his arms and pressing her head to his
chest while he crooned something Scottish and grieving.
She had buried her face in the roughness of his shirt and finally began to give up the sobs, releasing them in great rack-
ing shudders as Johnny had tightened his arms around her
and rocked her back and forth, because he understood losing
a loved one — a mother, or an uncle who was like a father.
But this time, the comforting hadn't stopped with a kiss.

She brought herself back to the present. "I always knew
Uncle Gideon and I weren't really related, that he was the
adopted son of my great-grandfather. But now . . . ."

"What?"

"Look at that picture. The woman is my grandmother,
Perfect Harmony. She was twenty-two when that was
taken."

"She was very beautiful," Jonathan murmured.

"Now look at the man. That's Uncle Gideon."

"I know. I recognize him."

"But *look* at him, Jonathan, notice the way he's gazing at

my grandmother while she's facing the camera. That's a look of love. And see the expression on my grandmother's face? There is such sadness there. Jonathan, this picture was taken when they opened their first office in Hong Kong, when they began supplying herbal remedies to Titan Mining. It's supposed to be a happy event. But my grandmother looks so forlorn. Why?"

"Why do *you* think, Charlotte?"

"The way Gideon is watching her, the love in his eyes, and the unhappiness in hers. . . . Jonathan, my mother was born seven months after my grandmother married Mr. Lee. I was told she had been two months premature. But I don't think so now. I think my grandmother was already pregnant when she got married. And I think that Mr. Lee was not my mother's father. Gideon Barclay was. Uncle Gideon was really my grandfather.

"You're probably right," Jonathan said as he handed the picture back. "He was a good man. You know how much I admired him."

"Jonathan, Agent Knight insists that Harmony Biotech is responsible for those deaths. He's going to go after us with everything he's got. I can weather that storm, Jonathan. Harmony Biotech will survive the fight ahead. But what is going to become of GB4204?"

Jonathan knew that Charlotte had named her formula GB4204 in memory of Gideon Barclay. He had been genuinely sorry when Gideon Barclay died, but his sorrow had not so much been for the man himself but for Charlotte, who had been devastated. They were seventeen, and Jonathan had gone with her every day to the hospital, where she had sat at her uncle's bedside in the intensive care unit, holding his hand, talking softly to him even though he was comatose and the nurses said he couldn't hear. Jonathan would never forget the night of Gideon's death, because it had also marked the beginning of a new *life*.

Charlotte was supposed to come over. They had planned to see a movie. When she didn't show up, he called the house. No answer. Not even the maid had picked up. With a terrible foreboding, he had grabbed his jacket and run through the dark streets.

Lights were on in the house, but no one answered the door. He peered into windows; it was like looking into a museum — all those furnished rooms with no people in them. He made his way around to the back, where a terraced garden dropped away toward the Bay. The fog was devouring the city, white tendrils of vapor snaking over the glittering grass, between hedgerows, causing citrus trees to drip with moisture and flowers to bow their dewy heads.

"Charlotte?" he had called softly.

He traipsed over a lawn sodden with fallen leaves. "Charlie?" She was in the mist somewhere, he could feel her.

Then he found her, a spectral shape leaning toward the Bay, her eyes peering into the thick fog. He hadn't said another word. As he neared, she had turned, and they had slipped into a mutual embrace that was more eloquent than any words they could speak. He had removed his jacket and laid it on the grass and then he had covered her body with his. She had held in the sobs until finally Johnny's gentle lovemaking had released them, and she held on to him as she wept until her heart broke right in two.

"I know that GB4204 can't bring my uncle back," she said softly now, unable to take her eyes off the photograph, thinking of Gideon and the night he died and the feel of Jonathan for the first time. "But he suffered so at the end that I vowed to him I would find a way to prevent other people from having to suffer the same way. I know he heard me, Jonathan. He was in a coma, but I know he heard me. And now, I feel somehow that I have let him down —" She raised moist eyes. "I understand other things now. The original contract between Harmony-Barclay and Titan Mining i̇ on display in the museum. The placard says that it was a wedding gift from Gideon Barclay to Perfect Harmony Lee. It's possible I already knew that, but I had forgotten. Now I know why my grandmother was tied up with a family that treated her so badly."

He smiled, gently, a smile reminiscent of the one she had seen in the mist, when he had looked at her with such love and tenderness. "You might not have found a saboteur here," Jonathan said, meaning the museum. "But at least you have found the answers to some questions."

The moment stretched, his look turned dark and brooding again, and she was fearful for an instant that he was going to kiss her.

Instead, he said, "Charlotte, I'm staying."

She stared at him. "What? No! You can't. There's no reason for you to stay! Jonathan," she cried suddenly, stepping away from him, "you have to go home. And you have to promise me that you will never come back."

He gave her an astonished look. "Why?"

"Jonathan, too much has happened since that day in the Italian restaurant when I walked out on you. I have built a life, and you have, too. We belong in two different worlds."

"I'm not leaving until we have worked things out, Charlotte," he said angrily. "I'm not leaving with things the way they are between us."

"Things are between us because that's the way they have to be, Jonathan. We can't go back. And we can't go forward. We're like broken wind chimes that can't be mended. Jonathan," she said, "you had two calls while you were gone. They came in on your computer. I heard them, I couldn't help it."

He regarded her in silence.

"One was your partner," she said more quietly. "The other was your wife."

Charlotte invented an excuse to visit the cafeteria, leaving him alone. When she returned with hot water for tea, he was in the middle of a conversation with Quentin. She didn't mean to eavesdrop, but once she heard part of it, she felt a compulsion to hear the rest.

It was a curious exchange, Jonathan's British accent and Quentin's American one, but Jonathan in America and Quentin in London. "Well, I'm telling you, John, they won't accept anyone else," his partner was saying in a Midwestern twang. "They are insisting on you. I'm just not enough. *You're* the glamour boy."

"God, Quentin," Jonathan said. "Not that again."

A laugh came from the computer, but it sounded bitter. "John, you know that *I* don't give a shit. Hell, that was all a media blowup anyway. But the problem is, these people don't know that. And we need this account. The competition is growing like mad in this field. You know that if we sew up this sweet deal, then we'll rule the heap. But damn it, John, they won't settle for just me! They're insisting that you sit in on the meeting or they won't *take* the goddamn meeting. Now, I've taken the liberty of booking a seat for you on a flight out of LAX. You've gotta be on it, my friend, or we can kiss this deal good-bye."

"You see?" Charlotte said softly as she came into the office. Jonathan had disconnected from Quentin and was closing up his laptop. "Two different worlds."

"Not so different," he murmured as he unplugged the peripherals and began packing everything into the many compartments of his black bag.

She watched him, recognizing familiar movements, the quick, snappish motions that always signaled when Jonathan was angry or frustrated. "What did he mean by saying you're the glamour boy?"

"It has to do with the Amsterdam Eight, a team of crackers that was wreaking havoc all over Europe. Quentin and I were part of an international team tracking them down. We finally caught them and somehow *I* wound up in the limelight and Quentin was barely mentioned. So these new clients think that if they deal only with Quentin, they aren't getting the full treatment."

"How did you end up in a partnership with Quentin?"

"We worked together for the NSA," he said in an even tone, not looking at her, his hands moving quickly, picking up wires and clips and little black boxes, shoving them into pockets and yanking zippers closed. "I didn't leave the Agency on friendly terms, Charlie, like I told you; it was in fact a very nasty break."

Charlotte stared at him, hearing again the curious strain of bitterness that seemed to creep into his voice each time the subject came up. "What happened?" she said. "You never did tell me."

He finally turned around, looking at her with an open expression. "No," he said, keeping his eyes on her, "you left the restaurant before we could finish our conversation."

That's not fair, she wanted to shout. You changed the subject.

Jonathan returned to collecting his gear and packing it into his kit. "When I quit, Quentin left with me and we decided to go into business together. Quentin likes London, and I already had a residence there, so London it was."

And to London you must return. . . .

"Quentin's my best friend," Jonathan continued as he buttoned his vest and shrugged into his suit jacket. "He gave up a sterling career with the NSA because of me. I was the best man at his wedding. I'm his daughter's godfather. Quent's more like a brother than a friend."

"And that is why you've decided to leave after all, when only a few minutes ago you said you were staying?"

He looked at his watch. "I'm booked on the three o'clock flight. I should be able to make it." He reached into the pocket of his raincoat and produced car keys with an Alpha Rents key fob.

He stopped and regarded Charlotte. She had made herself a cup of tea, painstakingly tearing open the foil packet, removing the tea bag, dunking it in the hot water, up and down, up and down, to keep her hands busy, to keep her mind closed, lifting the soggy bag out and placing it in the sink, to watch the residual tea dribble away down the aluminum drain.

"No, I'm not leaving because of Quentin," he said, finally answering her question. "I've decided to leave because you're right. We can't go back and we can't go forward. We said our good-byes long ago, on many occasions. We can't build a life on farewells." But that wasn't the real reason. Jonathan realized now that he could never stay with Charlotte — Quentin's phone call had reminded him of that. Or rather, the call had reminded him of the Amsterdam Eight and his nightmares. If he were to stay with her, he would eventually have to tell her what really happened. And he could never introduce such a horror into her life.

Charlotte said nothing as she watched the dark undercurrents in his brown eyes, and the tension in his jaw. Johnny's feelings, trying to come out.

He stepped close to her. When he put a finger under her chin, she allowed him to raise her face to his. Even if she wanted to draw away she couldn't. She was caught in the magnetism of his gaze. "I'll always think of you, Charlie," he murmured. Then he kissed her softly on the cheek and stepped back.

She watched him pick up his raincoat and sling it over one shoulder, then seize his black bag and head out of the office, across the museum, and, just like that, through the entrance, letting the door whisper shut behind him, leaving Charlotte to stand and stare at the closed door, bewildered, wondering what had happened, expecting the door to suddenly open and Jonathan walk through, saying he hadn't meant it, that he *was* staying. But when the door remained closed, she turned to the security monitor and saw him walking through the rain, a man with resolution and purpose in his gait. He didn't look back, and when he reached his car, he got right in, started up the motor, and drove away.

What had happened? One minute he was insisting on staying, and the next he packed up and left. *Was* it the phone call with Quentin that had changed his mind, the urgent meeting that was so vital to their company? Or had something taken place during the other call, the one he had made to his wife while Charlotte was out of the office?

The sob that had been building behind her throat, like the sobs on the misty night Uncle Gideon died, finally escaped. She pressed her fingers to her eyes and leaned against the kitchenette counter as more sobs came, and tears streamed down her cheeks until she felt the oceanic wave of pain hit her like a tsunami.

She could not get an image out of her mind.

While Jonathan was in the greenhouse, exhuming his gun, Charlotte had been here, staring at his computer screen as the video call came through from London, a face suddenly appearing on the monitor, startling her and freezing her to the spot: Adele Sutherland, looking straight at Charlotte — or so it seemed — and saying, "We have received an invitation for the opening of the opera season, Jonathan. The Royal Box. Please tell me you'll be here for it. It means so much to me."

Charlotte had been rooted to the spot. She was actually seeing and hearing for the first time the woman who had managed to get Jonathan after he had told Charlotte, by way of a poem, that he needed to walk his road alone. She had studied the face, searching for evidence of the evil enchantress she had pictured all these years. Charlotte knew that Adele was the daughter of a lord, that she herself pos-

sessed a title: "Honerable." And so Charlotte had imagined
chiseled features — an aristocratic nose and arched eyebrows. Instead she had looked into a pretty face, round and
warm, framed by a cloud of soft brown hair. Adele's manner was soft as well, as she had said, "Hullo, Johnny. I'm
wondering where you are."

That was the worst part, that he had married someone
nice.

And then she thought: An invitation to the opera. The
Royal Box. *Jonathan went to the opera with royalty.*

We *do* live in two different worlds. . . .

She blindly reached for the cup of tea, forcing herself to
inhale the calming fragrance as she struggled to restore balance and harmony while she fought back the tears, her chest
growing tight with suppressed sobs. She laid her hand on her
breast and felt the amber-and-silver drop pendant against
her silk blouse. It made her think of the day she and Johnny
had gone to Walgreen's on Powell and sat in the photo booth
taking strips of little black-and-white pictures of themselves, Charlotte on Johnny's lap while he had his arms
around her waist. Later, while she had lain on her bed reliving the feel of his body beneath her as she had squirmed in
his lap until she had felt a hardness that had made her gig-
gle and Johnny turn red, she had chosen the best picture, cut
out the two faces, and placed them in the two halves of the
locket, facing each other, so that when she closed it, she and
Johnny would be kissing for eternity.

Oh Jonathan, her broken heart cried. Does Adele know
about your days of computer hacking? Does she know about
the arrests for making thousands of dollars in illegal phone
calls? Have you told her about our nights and days together,
when we pledged eternal devotion? Jonathan! she wanted to
shout. It isn't fair! Adele doesn't have the history with you
that I have.

Why did you choose her and not me?

The steam from her tea continued to drift up into her head, slowly working its healing magic. Charlotte felt wrung out. She needed sleep. Tomorrow she would sort out her emotions and start the painful process of reconstructing the barriers around her heart and return Jonathan to the small chamber where she had kept him these past ten years, pack him and all her memories away, and get on with the business of making a life for herself.

She brought the fragile china cup to her lips.

Tomorrow she would look for a new house for Naomi, and she would begin the process of healing her company. She would sit down with Adrian and Margo and Desmond —

"Do not drink the tea."

Charlotte gasped. The cup slipped from her fingers and shattered on the countertop.

She spun around. "Who's there!" She listened but heard only the muffled roar of rain beyond the walls.

"The tea is poisoned."

She looked up at the security monitor and saw only the rain-swept parking lot. Running into the museum, she turned on all the lights, but all she saw were silent glass cases housing their dusty mementos.

Who had spoken?

She hurried back into the office and, retrieving the box of tea, sat down at the computer and accessed the production logs for the lot number stamped on the wrapper. Sixty seconds later she had her answer: Rusty Brown had signed off on this batch.

"Oh God," she whispered. The tea was toxic! How many other products had he contaminated? How had he been able to get away with so much?

As she stared at the computer screen, trying to understand how this calamity could possibly have occurred, Charlotte began to realize that something had been nagging at the back of her mind. She had avoided facing it; she had had no energy left. But now, as she rested her fingers on the keyboard, she tried to figure out what it was that was bothering her.

She looked up at the security monitor again, this time to see Agent Knight, wearing a raincoat, make his way toward the unmarked van his team had arrived in.

It was something Jonathan had said about Knight. . . .

It had struck her at the time as odd, but she had pushed it away; there was too much else to think about. But now she made room for it, opened up her mind and let it come in.

"Knight said Brown has a personal grudge against drug manufacturers, something to do with his past. He was arrested for something at his last job. They almost got a conviction on him but he had a good lawyer."

Charlotte frowned. Harmony Biotech had strict hiring practices that involved careful screening of a person's past. How had a man like that managed to get hired?

Quickly accessing the personnel directory, she brought up Rusty Brown's file. His personal history was listed, place and date of birth, work experience. No mention of an arrest record. He had been hired six months ago, the day after her grandmother's funeral.

Charlotte was startled by the sudden sounding of the mail alert. Before she even clicked on Read New Mail she knew what she was going to find.

Don't cancel that press conference, Charlotte. They got Rusty Brown but they didn't get me. He wasn't your man. Do as I say or thousands will die. . . .

"Oh my God," she murmured, her eyes growing wide.

. . . and I will start with that limey boyfriend of yours.

Making sure she locked the museum entrance behind herself, Charlotte dashed through the rain back to the main office building, where she took the emergency stairs instead of the elevator. When she reached the third floor, she opened the door and peeked out. The hall was deserted. But as she stole carefully toward the main reception area, she heard voices.

Rounding the corner she saw Mr. Sung and Margo talking with one of the federal agents. Adrian could be heard in his office, shouting into a phone. Desmond was nowhere in sight.

Charlotte managed to make it to her office without being seen; she quickly grabbed her purse and car keys and ran silently back down the carpeted hall, down the stairs, and out into the rain. Jumping behind the wheel of her Corvette, she started it up and squealed out of the parking lot.

The rain was blinding. She turned the windshield wipers up as fast as they would go and still she could barely see the road ahead. As she leaned forward, trying to get her bearings, she thought: Which way would he have gone? Palm Canyon Road or the freeway? She had to catch Jonathan before he entered the complex L.A. freeway system or she would never find him.

The freeway, she decided, and drove as fast as she dared on the rain-slicked desert road. When she neared Interstate 10, she aimed her headlights up the on-ramp and headed west, following the signs for Los Angeles. There was almost no traffic at this hour. She only occasionally saw headlights speed past. Up ahead there were no red taillights.

The freeway was only sparsely lit along this section through a mostly sand-dune region, with occasional breaks in the black rain when billboards whizzed past: advertisements for motels, turn-offs for Joshua Tree National Monument and Painted Hills, enticements to play bingo at the Morongo Indian Reservation.

How far ahead would he have gotten? He had had a fifteen-minute head start. And she knew Jonathan was not a slow driver.

As she sped past the off-ramp for San Gorgonio, she

glanced at her gas gauge and received a shock. Her gas tank was almost on empty.

A few miles ahead lay the town of Banning, and beyond that, a stretch known as the Badlands — a treacherous, winding road notorious for fatal car accidents. Once in the Badlands there were no emergency telephones, no off-ramps, no shoulders to pull over to. She would be trapped.

Should she stop and get gas?

It would take too long. She looked at her watch. Jonathan's flight left in two and a half hours. If he got to the airport before she could catch him, he would board straightaway.

She gripped the steering wheel with damp palms. She had just enough gas to get back to Harmony Biotech. This was the point of no return.

Taking a big gulp of air, she pressed her foot down and sped up.

When she finally saw taillights up ahead, she cried silently, Please! Let it be Jonathan. But as she drew near, she saw a red pickup truck loaded with palm trees.

Pulling around it, she tried to go faster. But the road surface was slick. The first rains in California always brought up the oil dripped from millions of cars; there hadn't yet been enough rain to wash it away.

When she felt the rear of her Corvette fishtail slightly, she gripped the steering wheel harder and fixed her eyes through the storm.

Another set of taillights.

Her headlights flooded the car ahead as she zoomed up behind them. But it was a white Honda with four people in it.

She zipped out in the next lane, and kept going.

The town of Banning came and went. Next was the Badlands. Her gas gauge read Empty.

Another pair of taillights. "Please," she whispered. "Please!"

But it was a Ferrari with two heads silhouetted in the front seats.

Charlotte was concentrating so hard on looking forward that she did not at first notice the lights drawing up behind her — not just headlights, but red lights flashing as well.

A police cruiser.

"Oh God!" she cried. "No! Don't pull me over now!"

The cop flashed his headlights and Charlotte experienced a brief, mad impulse to floor it and speed on ahead. Instead, she eased up on the pedal and braced herself for the worst.

To her surprise, however, the police car pulled out around her and sped on past, apparently satisfied with his warning to her to slow down.

Drawing in steadying breaths, gripping the wheel and trying to hold back as long as she could, she waited until the cruiser had vanished far ahead before she pressed on the gas again and sped up.

More off-ramps zipped by, more opportunities to stop and get gas. But she had to keep going, she had to catch Jonathan. . . .

Finally, another pair of red taillights appeared up ahead. It looked like a fairly large vehicle, not going too fast. She kept her eye on her gas gauge as she shortened the distance between herself and the other car. The red light on her gas gauge had come on.

Her headlight beams spotlighted the rear bumper and a sticker that said *Alpha Rents*.

Jonathan!

She flashed her lights.

He sped up!

"No!" she shouted, speeding up with him.

She swung out into the next lane and tried to pull up alongside. She pounded her horn. She felt her car begin to hydroplane. "Jonathan!" she screamed, trying to keep up with him, honking her horn, flashing her lights.

By his tight profile she knew he was deep in thought, with his windows rolled up, eyes fixed on the road ahead.

She pressed the pedal and sped up, feeling her rear tires spin sickeningly. With a final desperate surge, she sped forward, cleared his car by a few inches and then, bracing herself, swung the wheel to the right to cut him off. She saw his headlights dip as he slammed on his brakes.

She flew off the freeway, steering her car into a soft shoulder, the motor dying as the gas finally ran out.

Charlotte thought she was going to be sick. She shook so badly that her teeth rattled. Realizing she was about to pass out, she rested her head on the steering wheel.

"You in there!" Jonathan was shouting, pounding on her window, trying to see inside. "Are you all right?"

He flung the door open. "Jesus! Charlotte!"

She reached for him and he pulled her trembling body into his arms.

"My God!" he said, as they stood in the downpour, his hands cradling her face. "You nearly got us killed!"

"It isn't over, Johnny," she said breathlessly. "You have to come back."

34

They left her car locked and secure beside the road and drove back to Harmony Biotech at top speed, Jonathan easing up on the pedal as they neared the entrance and killing his headlights as he quietly guided the Lincoln into a space that wasn't illuminated by the lamps in the parking lot. Making sure they weren't seen, they made a dash to the museum, shaking off the rain as they ran inside, and locking the door behind themselves, in time to hear the mail alert sound on the computer.

Jonathan clicked on Read New Mail and Charlotte held her breath as the new message came up:

It's almost one o'clock, Charlotte. Only five hours left.

Without removing his raincoat, Jonathan immediately brought out his laptop computer and had it set up and plugged in within two minutes. He hit a hot key and the sound of telephone dialing tones came through the speaker. A moment later, a message appeared on the screen: *Destination number reached . . . call-forwarding in progress . . . please wait . . .*

Suddenly a window on the screen opened up and Quentin's face appeared. "Hello?" he said. And then, "John! You're supposed to be on a plane back to London! What gives?"

"I can't leave yet. Something has come up."

"What? Now look here —"

"I want you to set up a conference call, Quent. Tell them our current client is in crisis and I won't leave, but I can take the meeting by way of videophone. If anything, it might put a positive spin — Quentin, what's that noise?"

In the background, there was a steady *ka-chunk, ka-chunk, ka-chunk.*

Quentin put a hand to his ear. "Awful, ain't it? They're excavating for a new underground station, and it's right under my window."

"Where are you?"

"I thought I told you. I'm staying at the Four Seasons while my flat is being renovated. I'm sure I told you."

Jonathan frowned. "As of twenty hours ago you were

still in your flat. I don't recall you mentioning anything
about —"

"Sorry! Impossible to hear! But hey, the conference call
is a stroke of genius. It'll show the new guys how dedicated
we are to our clients, give them a taste of the loyalty they
can expect when we troubleshoot for *them*. I like it, John-
boy!" *Ka-chunk, ka-chunk.* "Just listen to that! I think I'll
move to the Dorchester before I lose my mind! Okay, I'll set
up that call. Dazzle them with a little high tech! I'll get back
to you in a couple of hours then."

After they signed off, Jonathan continued to stare at the
screen.

"What's the matter?" Charlotte said.

"Something is wrong. I know Quent, and I know when he
isn't telling me something. He's nervous about something."

"Jonathan, go home. I shouldn't have brought you back.
You're needed there."

He continued to frown at the screen, and was about to say
something when the mail alert sounded again. The new message came up:

LOLOLOLOL

"What does *that* mean?" Charlotte said.

"Ell oh ell," Jonathan said, suddenly standing up and
whipping off his raincoat. It's Internet slang for 'laughing
out loud.' " He sat back down and, rolling up his sleeves
with sharp, decisive movements, said, "The bastard is laughing at you. By God, he's going to be sorry he did."

PART
TWO

PART

TWO

35

"Why didn't you wait for me, Harmony?" Gideon cried when he saw the wedding cake, the guests, Mr. Lee in a groom's tuxedo.

But how could I? Harmony replied silently, with her heart, so that no one, not even Gideon, could hear: *How could I wait when you were going to be gone for ten months and our baby was gong to be born in nine?*

"I shall never love another as I have loved you, Charlotte," Gideon declared with passion, except that he was no longer Gideon but Jonathan, and he was reaching for her, his hands on her shoulders. . . .

Charlotte cried out.

"Hey," Jonathan said softly, shaking her shoulder. "Are you okay?"

She blinked up at him.

"You were having a bad dream," he said.

Charlotte sat up and rubbed her eyes. She had decided to lie down on the couch in her grandmother's office and take a brief nap. She looked at her watch. She had been asleep for an hour.

"That must have been some dream," he said.

"Yes. . . ." she said. "A strange dream." She looked up at him. Jonathan's dark brown hair had fallen forward onto his forehead, and his jaw was unshaven. But his eyes showed no signs of fatigue.

"I found something," he said. He smelled of the rain. Had he been outside? "Our culprit is after something and I think I know what it is."

Swinging her feet to the floor, Charlotte waited a moment, her head cradled in her hands. The dream was still crowding her mind, filling her brain with swirling images that made little sense: her mother, whom she had never known, sitting with her in the rooftop gazebo saying, *"It was the tea, Charlotte, the tea. . . ."* Mr. Sung turning a puzzle box around and around in his hands. Her grandmother turning her face away from an artichoke that Charlotte had just steamed for dinner.

The nap had not refreshed her. She felt, in fact, wearier, the memories dogging her, weighing her down.

She got up and went to the kitchenette, where she turned on the faucet and splashed water on her face until the dream began to shred, the faces and voices receding. By the time she patted her face dry with a towel, the disturbing images were gone.

She turned and looked at Jonathan, sitting at his laptop. He had been working while she was asleep. "What did you find?" she said.

"I've been going through the files I downloaded onto backups. And I found something very interesting in the directory where you keep your ultra-sensitive classified formulas. Look." He tapped the screen.

Charlotte leaned close. "They've been *copied?*"

"Our intruder doesn't seem to be aware of the fact that your system automatically records when files are accessed and copied. And look at this," he said. "Look at the times and dates on these accesses."

"It's been going on all evening!"

"Can you believe it? The bastard's been popping in and out for the past twelve hours, copying one file at a time so he won't get caught. But this is the vital one, Charlie. His most recent access."

She looked to where he was pointing. "This formula was copied *after* Knight disconnected every terminal from the hub."

"Which means there's a hidden modem somewhere."

She frowned. "Can you find it?"

"Oh, I'll find it all right. I'm already running the search." He left the computer and went to stand over the facility blueprints, still spread out on the desk. "One way to get into a system," he said, his eyes scanning the plans, "is to disable the dial-back at one of the modems. However, your system would have recorded any dial-back modem being disabled. Since there aren't any, we know there's a *hidden* modem, one that got hooked to the network and set on auto-answer."

"How are we going to find it?"

"I installed a war dialer in my computer," he murmured as he traced a line with his fingertip. "Did you ever see the movie *War Games*? A war dialer is a software that dials hundreds of numbers, searching for a modem to connect to. While you were asleep, I inputted the parameters of the phone numbers in this region. It will keep dialing until it finds an active modem at this facility. I've tied it into my pager to alert me when the dialer finds something."

She watched him study the blueprints, his eyebrows coming together to form a deep vertical furrow as he studied lines, arcs, and squares, concentrating as intensely as if he were solving a Chinese puzzle box. It was the same look he had had on his face after he hung up from talking to his partner, when he had said something was wrong with Quentin. That same furrow had appeared then, as he had weighed the situation, deciding what to do, and Charlotte had tried to tip the balance and help him by saying, "Go home." But then the *LOLOLOL* had appeared and he had made up his mind.

Just an hour before that, Charlotte had insisted he leave. Now she was glad he had stayed.

"Jonathan," she said as she rummaged through her leather tote bag, retrieving a gold-handled comb buried beneath the broken wind chimes. "We need to find the connection between this intruder and Rusty Brown. Maybe it was someone who was working with Brown, or someone who found out about Brown's sabotage and decided to take advantage of it. Brown insisted he was working alone. And that *is* his modus operandi, according to his criminal record."

"I did a bit of investigating while you were asleep. I took a look at Rusty's locker. There was nothing in it, of course, Knight's men had cleared it out. But I ran into an old janitor who told me two very interesting things. First was that he and Brown used to go drinking at a place on highway one eleven."

"The Coyote Bar and Grill," she said. "A lot of the employees go there."

"He said Brown was a secretive sort of fellow, and never bragged about tampering with the products. Brown didn't seem to have any friends, except for one 'dude,' as the janitor put it. Apparently this bloke joined them a few times, buying expensive drinks. He was being sympathetic with Brown about something. Rusty was upset about his performance evaluation; he didn't get the promotion he expected. So this stranger buying the expensive drinks started telling Rusty he shouldn't put up with being treated like that, he should show this company just who they were dealing with."

"When was this?"

"Five months ago."

Charlotte stared at Jonathan. The product formulas had been altered *four* months ago. "Rusty said he had been *promised* a raise?"

"And a promotion, too. Rather big promises for a brand-new employee."

"Was the janitor able to describe the stranger?"

"He said he had a beard and wore his long hair in a pony-tail. He also wore a baseball cap. But that's not the strange part, Charlie. It's the way Rusty was hired. He claimed he was *recruited* for the job. He said Harmony Biotech called *him*, saying they were sympathetic to him losing his last job, said how they needed someone with his skills and talent."

"So someone heard or read about his previous arrest and trial and decided to use Brown to destroy this company while staying completely behind the scenes!" That suspicion had already crept into Charlotte's mind. "You said you learned two things."

"The second thing confirms our suspicion. The janitor said he caught someone about two hours ago at Brown's locker. He said they got away before he could get a good look at them, he couldn't even tell if it had been a man or a woman — apparently he or she was wearing a long coat and a hat. The thing was, whoever it was was doing something *inside* Brown's locker."

"Planting the evidence."

Jonathan nodded. "Precisely. And Brown is probably just about telling the police that right now. He confessed to tampering with the products but when they question him about diddling with your garage door and rigging Naomi's house to explode, they're going to draw a blank."

"And Knight is going to arrive at the same conclusion we did — that someone used Rusty without his knowing it."

Jonathan extended the fingers of his right hand, then curled them into a tight fist. "I'm afraid we haven't seen the last of Federal Agent Valerius Knight."

"Rusty's criminal record," Charlotte murmured, as she reached back to undo her hair clip. "How did he manage to get past our screening process? There's no mention in his personnel file of an arrest record. I called Mrs. Ferguson, the personnel director, at her home but all I got was an answering machine. I left a message telling her it was urgent. Unfortunately she lives on the other side of an arroyo that is currently a raging flash flood. We can't reach her by car." Charlotte looked up at the security monitor, which was displaying a deserted reception area. "Where *is* everyone?"

"Knight and his men left a while ago," Jonathan said, contemplating the blueprints. "I gave him a copy of the download. That made him happy for now. He's taken it to the lab, where they'll examine it for evidence of Rusty Brown's crime. They left a man to guard the computer room, but it doesn't matter. We can still get into the system. We'll just have to be cautious, as I have a feeling Knight will be back."

"What still puzzles me," Charlotte said, turning away from the security monitor, "is how is he going to do it? I mean, this madman who has tried to kill me and Naomi and who knows who else — he said he will kill thousands. But how? If it's using our tainted products, how can he force people to ingest something they've been warned against?"

Jonathan looked up from the blueprints. When he saw the long black hair streaming wild and free over her shoulders, he stopped. A vision of that same hair, long ago, flashed in his mind: silken tresses fanning out on dewy grass, Charlotte's eyes closed, a sublime smile on her lips.

He looked away. "We'll find that out when we examine your system. I'll need to log in."

"All right," she said, pulling the chair out.

"No, I mean *me*."

"But you don't know my password. You even told me when you first got here that you didn't *want* to know it."

"It's part of my customized penetration test," he said as he took a seat, "when *I* pretend to be the intruder. This is how I find holes in security that can't be determined by any

other means. It begins right at the log-in. I purposely didn't
want you to tell me your password. Now watch this."

"You mean you're going to guess?"

"Bet I get in in three tries."

"Wait," she said, putting her hand on his arm. "Knight's
technician discovered a security program that I didn't even
know about. If you try two invalid log-ins, the third will
cause the system to delete all the data."

He shook his head, his eyes dark and intense. "I did that,
Charlotte. I figured that even after I had downloaded all the
files, I didn't want the feds taking the network, we might
still need it. So I went in and changed the passwords, and
then I planted a fake message about deleting the files."

At the command *User Name* Jonathan typed "Charlotte
Lee" and hit Enter.

The next command was *Password*. As he typed, asterisks
appeared on the screen. He hit Enter and a new message appeared:

Welcome to Harmony Biotech

Charlotte stared in amazement. "How did you do that?"

"Simple shoulder surfing," he said, typing rapidly. "It's
how criminals steal bank account numbers. A fellow
watches over your shoulder as you enter information at an
ATM."

"But when I typed my password, there were only asterisks
on the screen, just like now. Even if you were looking —"

"I was listening, too. Nine keystrokes, and you didn't hit
the space bar or the shift key. Of course," he added, his eyes
sweeping over the data on the screen, "it helps that I already
know something about you. The number one password people like to use is either their own name or their dog's name.
They also use their birthdate or license plate number or
place of birth. Words like 'wizard' and 'gandalf' are very

popular. You'd be surprised how many people just use all the same letter or number, like seven sevens."

"That's still a lot of guessing," Charlotte said as she ran the comb through her hair, fastening it all in the clip, and tossed the comb into her leather bag.

"Most intruders manage to guess the password within ten tries, and if they're breaking into a system that doesn't have safeguards against multiple failed log-ins, then they're in. But, like I said, in this case I already know something about you, I had a base to start with. When I heard those nine letters, I had a pretty good idea what the password was."

Charlotte had chosen it because no one else knew that word: her real name.

Jonathan suddenly stretched his arms forward, cracking his knuckles. Rising from the desk, he went to the kitchenette, where he filled the kettle and put it on the stove. We've got less than four hours and I'm going to need some rocket fuel."

Unzipping a side compartment in his computer bag, Jonathan withdrew a packet of coffee, filters, and a box of Scottish shortbread biscuits.

As soon as she saw the familiar package with the red-and-yellow tartan, Charlotte felt the simultaneous shock waves of joy and pain.

They were seventeen again, with Charlotte sitting on the bed in Jonathan's basement hideaway. They were munching on shortbread biscuits as he showed her his latest gadget, a computer game called "Pong," currently only available in arcades and bars. But Johnny had one because he had just come back from his summer in Scotland, and his father, who had to leave right away for an international conference in Peru, had consoled his son with an expensive toy. Jonathan was eating and laughing and talking at the same time, explaining how it was originally called Ping-Pong but Atari had had to change it because of copyright infringement.

tening to him as he had talked about becoming an MIT hacker, laughing at his tales of computer invasion while he was at Cambridge, and then launching into her own dream with unharnessed enthusiasm. "Biotechnology, Johnny!" she had said with her green eyes afire with visions. "It's the future! And I'm trying to convince Grandmother of the potential she has right at her fingertips. Harmony's warehouse is a treasure chest of healing herbs! But Grandmother just continues to bottle them the way she has for years. I'm trying to make her see that those herbs can be analyzed at the *molecular* level and taken to their most extreme healing limits. Look at the willow tree! Herbal extracts made from its bark have cured headaches and pain and fever for thousands of years! Once chemists discovered the molecular construction of the willow's healing power, they were able to synthesize the medicine. And now we call it aspirin! Harmony House is sitting on a veritable Aladdin's cave of cures! I am determined to find them, Johnny! Every last one of them!"

They had made love that night in Johnny's apartment, all night long, to celebrate their togetherness in America, to spin their separate dreams into one tapestry. And then a year later had sent her the *1981 Silver Laurel Wreath Prize* and she made a phone call that caused the warp and their interwoven dreams to come unraveled until the y tangled and unsalvageable.

he hadn't taken the chance and bared his feelings — would he and Charlotte have continued as had kept the book to himself, would she still say she needed her space, her freedom? And later, would she still have met him in San d they have made love instead of Charlotte m?

aid now, suddenly curious, "how did you dmother to relocate the factory down ould never leave San Francisco."

That was the joyous memory. The painful one was six years later, a rainy night in Boston when Jonathan had announced he was going to be an MIT hacker. They had celebrated with red wine and Scottish shortbread, and then they had made slow and wonderful love on the madras bedspread in his apartment. They had snuggled all night beneath the blankets, twenty-three years old and sketching their future together, each filling in the other's outlines: *she* was going to find a cure for cancer, *he* was going to build the world's fastest supercomputer. They were going to be *hot*, two young missiles zooming into the future. And they were going to travel, see the world. "We'll stand by the Bosporus," Charlotte had said, "and watch the sun set behind the domes and spires of Istanbul." "In Venice," Johnny had said, "we will sip cappuccino in the Piazza San Marco and watch the tide come in." They were going to do everything, taste everything, experience all that life had to offer. When Charlotte had left the next day for San Francisco, Jonathan had seen her off at the airport and she had never seen him look so radiant and happy.

And then, twelve months later, the book of poetry had arrived, shattering her world, ending their dreams forever.

Switching off the boiling water, Jonathan produced a hinged metal cone from his black bag. Folded flat, when it was snapped open the cone fit over a mug and accommodated a small paper filter and two heaping teaspoons of rich ground coffee. "Never travel anywhere without my coffee," he said as he prepared two mugs. "Do you still take it black? I have powdered cream if you like."

"Black," she said. Then she said, suddenly, startling herself, "Jonathan, are you happy?"

He turned around, a surprised look on his face. And then the look turned somber. "As much as the next man, I suppose."

She couldn't help herself. She had been wanting to ask

the question for the past eight hours: "Do you have a good marriage?"

"I can't explain," he said with a cryptic expression, his eyes roaming her hair, which was now tamed and tied back. "Life with Adele is comfortable. Predictable."

Charlotte turned away. For Jonathan, comfortable and predictable sounded sad.

Jonathan regarded the back of her head, where her shiny black hair was still mussed from her nap, a spot she had missed with the comb. He longed to reach out and smooth it down, but Adele came back to his mind, and their conversation by videophone just after midnight, while Charlotte was in the cafeteria. Adele's eyes had sparkled with tears as she said, "You're with *her*, aren't you? Quentin would only say you're on a case. But it's her you've gone to rescue, isn't it?"

Jonathan could never understand how a subject that he was so careful never to bring up always seemed to be there nonetheless, substantial, standing between them. The pain in Adele's voice . . . what could he do except reply, "Yes. I'm helping her." Adele deserved honesty, she deserved that, at least.

As Jonathan set the kettle down next to the box of tea, Charlotte's eyes followed it, and rested on the box. "I still can't shake the dream I had," she said. "There is something about that tea that I am supposed to know."

"You already found out. It's from a tainted batch."

She frowned. "There's more to it. But I can't . . ." She looked at him. "My grandmother believed in all kinds of superstitions and what I thought of as old-fashioned hocus-pocus nonsense. She told me that because we come from a long line of motherless daughters, in our time of need we hear our mothers' voices. I never really believed her. But my grandmother said she heard *her* mother many years ago, when she was reduced to living in a basement and she was

starving and couldn't sell her medicines. She said her mother spoke to her from Heaven, telling her how to make her medicines pleasing so that people would buy them. And then tonight, as I was about to drink the tea . . . Jonathan, I heard that voice as loud and clear as if were *you* talking."

"And was it your mother?"

"How would I know? I never heard her voice. But in my dream just now, she spoke to me again, telling me about the tea. . . . I am supposed to figure something out about it."

He regarded her with a probing gaze, as if trying to delve into her mind and see with his own two eyes the dream and its mysterious message. "Call it back, Charlotte," he said. "Bring the dream back and go through it step by step. If you're receiving a message, then you've got to hear it."

As she accepted the coffee, she thought: He's still superstitious, just like in the old days, when he would return from the Highlands with tales of haunted battlegrounds a women who turned into seals.

As Jonathan watched her dip the shortbread into her fee and raise it to her moist, pink lips, her small tongue ing out of her mouth, he thought of times in the pa he had watched Charlotte eat — always with a gust brought to everything she did. Like the time Boston, when she had asked for extra then had forked the lettuce into h of buttered breadstick, talkin "It is the one thing my g that Western medicine gether. She used t icine is new an balance, like *yin* med school, Johnn that doctors can't help don't have the proper m

She had been so lively

"When I did some research and found that southern California conducts more biomed research and development than anywhere else in the world, I knew this was where Harmony should be. Adrian thought it was a good idea, and tried to convince her, using spreadsheets and pointing out profit margins and calling this area a 'community of science.' She turned a deaf ear. *I* simply said that we would be joining a family of pharmaceutical companies, and that opened her up. Grandmother had always been fond of the word 'family.' "

"No wonder she made you her successor," he murmured. "You shared her vision."

"There was a time," she said softly, "when you and I shared a vision."

His eyes met hers, and in the space of three heartbeats they were joined in mutual memories of a shared past.

"We don't have much time," he said, the first to break the dangerous moment. Setting his coffee aside and brushing off his hands, he said, "First I'll check these classified formulas and see if our intruder left an audit trail. Then I have to get back to the main building."

"Audit trail?"

"It's a chronological record of system activities. Audit trails check for failed log-ins to a particular user ID, strange log-in times, deletions, changes, that sort of thing. Our friend here did his dirty work during business hours. The intruders that get caught are the ones who make stupid mistakes like invading a system during the middle of the night, or using the ID of an employee who's on vacation."

"How did this one get into the system?"

"Possibly through a back door — such as a master password installed by the software manufacturer — or a hole in your firewall. The front end is all security, while your database sits behind it, basically insecure."

While Jonathan ran a search, Charlotte's eye fell once

again on the box of tea, and suddenly the troubling dream came back, and the strange warning that had sounded so real, that had made her drop and shatter her teacup. *Had* she really heard her mother's voice? Or had it only been her imagination?

She picked up the box and examined it, searching the blue-and-silver lettering and miniature painting of a weeping willow on a lake for clues. She pulled out a teabag and held it in her palm. And then she noticed . . .

"This is it!" She said suddenly. "This is what I was supposed to figure out! Jonathan, look! These teabags have been tampered with! This batch wasn't tainted in the plant but *afterward!*"

"What? That means this isn't Rusty Brown's work."

"No! It's someone wanting it to *look* like it was part of Rusty Brown's sabotage. I'll bet if we analyzed the rest of the tea in that batch we would find it uncontaminated!"

"Christ!" Jonathan shot to his feet. "It was done deliberately to your *personal* box of tea. Charlotte, *you* were the target."

36

"The killer is no stranger," Charlotte said grimly as she regarded the adulterated teabag in her palm. "This is someone who knows me so well he knows that I always drive my Corvette, that I always drink this particular tea, that I am fond of my housekeeper, that Naomi's death would devastate me. A stranger wouldn't know these things, Jonathan, he wouldn't know enough to use these facts as weapons against me."

Charlotte turned and went into the museum, coming to a

standstill in the center, as if she were about to call out for the culprit to reveal himself. "Are you in here?" she said softly. "Have I already looked upon your face and seen what I thought was a friend?" She was standing next to a display case titled *New Factory, 1936*. It contained a diorama of a manufacturing-and-bottling plant, complete with miniature people standing at a miniature conveyor belt, and above it was a photograph of a group of people under a huge sign: Perfect Harmony Chinese Herbal Co.

Charlotte leaned close to scrutinize the picture, focusing on the central figure in the group, her grandmother, except that it was difficult to imagine this beautiful young woman as her grandmother. Harmony had been only twenty-eight when the picture was taken, although officially she was supposedly thirty. She was dressed all in white because she was in mourning.

In the front row, standing side by side, were Margo and Adrian, seven years old and already a couple, Margo taller than her future husband, Adrian's face already showing the pugnacity that would increase over the years.

Of course Charlotte wasn't in the picture, nor were Desmond or Jonathan. They wouldn't come along for another generation. But there were others in the photograph whom Charlotte recognized, wearing smiles that made her wonder if there were secrets hidden behind them, the secrets of a killer who was out to murder her. . . .

"Charlotte?"

She turned. Jonathan's face wore a troubled expression.

"It's possible the person we're looking for isn't in here."

"What do you mean?"

He hesitated, weighing his words. "While you were asleep, I looked into the finances of some of your competitors, thinking that maybe industrial sabotage is still the key."

She could tell by his tone that he had found something — and that it was unpleasant.

"Charlotte, which company would you say would benefit the most from Harmony going bankrupt?"

There were several. "Moonstone, I suppose. They are our closest competitor."

"I obtained a list of their investors." He handed her the printout. "It's a long list, but it's alphabetical, so it's easy to scan for familiar names."

She was almost afraid to look at it. "Don't tell me you found one of the Barclays on here."

"No, but I found another familiar name."

Charlotte's eyes moved down the list, looking for a name to jump out. One did. "Naomi Morgenstern!"

"Twenty thousand shares. Notice the date."

"She bought these four days ago!"

"Did she ever mention it?"

Charlotte mutely shook her head. She couldn't think of any reason why Naomi would buy shares in a rival company. Unless — "Mike," she said suddenly. "Naomi's fiancé is an investment broker. He must have talked her into buying these shares. Naomi wouldn't do it otherwise."

"How well do you trust Mike?"

"As well as I trust Naomi," she said, but at the same time she suddenly remembered something Jonathan had said: the stranger at the Coyote Bar and Grill, who had goaded Rusty Brown into taking revenge upon the company, had had a long ponytail.

Naomi's fiancé wore his long hair in a ponytail.

She resolutely shook her head. "No. It's too ridiculous. The idea of Mike being the killer is about as feasible as Bozo the Clown."

Jonathan spread out his right hand and stared intently at his palm as if measuring his life line. "Charlotte, where did you meet Naomi? Did you say it was at Chalk Hill?"

"Yes, Naomi was a member of a group called Bless the Beasts."

"The animal rights group?"

"You've heard of them?"

"There's a chapter in London. What happened exactly?"

Chalk Hill was the last thing she wanted to talk about, but Jonathan deserved to know. "Bless the Beasts had launched a major campaign against animal test labs. Their method was to break in, set the animals loose, and then torch the lab." She looked at the Moonstone printout in her hand, as if surprised to see it there. "The authorities received a tip-off. Police, and the media, arrived before we could all get away. Naomi and I were arrested."

"But you were never convicted."

"The charges against me were dropped."

"And Naomi?"

Charlotte bit her lower lip. "Naomi was fined and received six months probation."

"You were both arrested for the same thing, both had the same charges brought against you. Your charges were dropped, you were set free, whereas Naomi had to pay a fine and serve probation. Did she ever resent that?"

Charlotte snapped her head up. "Of course not!"

"You don't think she might have carried a grudge?"

"Even if she did, it wouldn't drive her to try and kill me or destroy my company or blow up her own house, for God's sake!"

"Her house is insured for a lot of money."

Charlotte gave him a shocked look. "Why have you been prying into Naomi's private business?"

"I'm prying into everyone's business, Charlotte, anyone who might be a suspect."

"Well, Naomi is not a suspect, so you can forget that! My God, she joined Bless the Beasts because she holds life sacred above all else! And furthermore —"

Jonathan was frowning suddenly.

"What?" she said impatiently.

"That name, Bless the Beasts. I'd swear I came across it recently."

Charlotte followed him back into the office, where he quickly sifted through the stack of printouts on the desk. "I've been trying to find some clue, some connection between the victims and you and Harmony Biotech. I searched the National News Files Service and I found something . . . yes, here it is." He held up a sheet of paper. "Right, Bless the Beasts. It's about — oh, Christ."

"What is it?"

"I ran a search on Chalk Hill. I came across this item about the president of Bless the Beasts. But when I saw that it wasn't dated eight years ago, I dismissed it as not being germane."

"And now?"

"Charlotte, this article is an obituary!" He handed it to her. "This woman, who was the president of Bless the Beasts eight years ago — Charlotte, she's the third victim. The one who died from Bliss."

Charlotte's eyes flew over the text. "Oh God. Now I remember her. She and I had an ugly confrontation in which we called each other names on nationwide television. I didn't remember her name, Jonathan! I honestly didn't. There were so many people involved! When Desmond told me about the third victim — Oh God!" Her hand flew to her mouth. "Knight!"

"Yes, Knight," Jonathan said as he quickly opened a compartment in his bag and began lifting out tools. "If he doesn't already have this information, he soon will, just as soon as he learns that Rusty isn't our man. And then" — Jonathan looked at her — "Knight is going to go fishing for another suspect."

Charlotte didn't need to ask who.

When she saw the things that he was laying out, filling the

pockets of his black windbreaker, hooking tools to his belt, she said, "What are you doing?"

"We have to get out of here, Charlotte. It isn't safe here for you anymore. Neither from the killer nor from Valerius Knight, who could show up any minute with a warrant for your arrest. I'm going to set up remote access so we can continue working from another location, and then we are going to find a place to hide."

She reached for her leather tote. "I'll grab some things to take." She paused. "Jonathan, you didn't really suspect Naomi, did you?"

"Yes, I did." He faced her squarely. "And I still do."

37

1936 — San Francisco, California

The day the Dragon finally came for me was a day of cold winds and hot sun, with a sky the color of blue porcelain, and clouds so white they blinded — a good luck day. I dressed with care, trying not to rush in my excitement and accidentally break something, for then I would have to reschedule my meeting for another day. Mr. Lee went with me, of course, and we took our daughter. We never went anywhere without Iris.

As we drove to Daly City, I kept a careful watch for omens — at the first sign of bad luck we would turn around and go home. Today of all days required the most luck, because today I was to see the final realization of my dream.

When I had left Mrs. Barclay's club in humiliation, eight years ago, I had gone straight to Mr. Lee and told him I would pay for his family's passage to California. I would also give them jobs, if he would do me a favor in return. I asked him to marry me.

For a Chinese woman this is a shameful thing to do. But Mr. Lee did not treat it as a shameful act. He responded to me with honor and dignity. He knew I was pregnant, he said it did not matter. We did not mention love, but I believe he loved me. I believe now that Mr. Lee had loved me all those years in Chinatown when I used his telephone, when our apartments went up and down as our circumstances changed, when I watched him paint his inner visions, and he listened to me spin my dreams. He expressed this quiet love by accepting another man's child as his own. Everyone believed us when we said Iris was born two months too soon, because as it happened she was a small, frail thing who nearly did not survive her first weeks of life.

Gideon was not fooled. That night, eight years ago, when he had stood outside my door looking in at my wedding reception, he had said, "Why, Harmony? Why didn't you wait?" Seven months later he had his answer.

Iris became the center of my universe. How could she not? In her veins flowed the blood of my honored father, Richard Barclay, and that of the caretaker of my heart, my beloved Gideon. Sweet, enchanted child, the moment she was laid in my arms my new dream was born — for Iris I would build my small company into an empire.

I went back to being Chinese. After that day at the club, I never tried to be white again. I saw Fiona Barclay only once — when Gideon and Olivia were married, and Mr. Lee and I attended the wedding. Their son was born six months after Iris. They named him Adrian, for Olivia's grandfather. That should have been the parting of our ways for me and my darling Gideon, but we were bound together, both by our knowledge that Iris was ours — although we never spoke of it — and by the contract Gideon had obtained from Titan

Mining Company. We were business partners, and that was how we kept it.

Mr. Lee was a good father to Iris and a respectful husband to me. Because Perfect Harmony Chinese Herbal Company was flourishing, our profits steadily rising, my scholarly husband was able to quietly pursue his art with full-time devotion, creating paintings so inspired and magnificent that they began to be very much in demand. I did not know it at the time, but the day the Dragon came back into my life, Mr. Lee had just begun what was to be the masterpiece of his life.

When we reached Daly City, Mr. Lee pulled the car off the main highway and took us through orchards and groves green with life and good luck, and when we came at last to a high fence and a sign that read Taft and Sons Cider, I said to Iris, "Look, do you see? All the buildings?" But of course she didn't see. Iris didn't understand what I was saying. She didn't look where I was pointing. She didn't look at me as I spoke. Her eyes were everywhere, up on the sky, down on the grass, this way and that, always fluttering like a pair of trapped butterflies in an invisible cage.

"Retarded," the specialists said. "There is nothing wrong with her hearing or her eyesight, Mrs. Lee. The problem lies in your daughter's brain. She will never speak, she will never understand what you say."

Still, I took Iris by the hand and led her toward the large factory building where I was going to show her the machinery and conveyor belts, and storage sheds and offices, and I was going to describe to her the many workers who would be here, manufacturing and labeling and packaging all the wonderful medicines made by Perfect Harmony Chinese Herbal Company. I was always going to treat my daughter as a normal child, because who knew for certain that her brain was not understanding my words? And who knew that maybe someday she wouldn't suddenly look at me and say, "Yes, I see."

The caretaker at the factory, a kindly old gentleman in blue coveralls, waved to us and came over with his broom. He said hello to Iris, but she didn't acknowledge him, even though she had met him several times. Reaching into his pocket he brought out a piece of candy. But when he held it out, Iris didn't take it. She squinted up at the sun and then down at her shoes, and then back over her shoulder and then up at the sky again.

I thanked the caretaker, taking the candy from him. I didn't give it to Iris, because she did not understand giving and receiving. I put the candy to her lips and she immediately sucked it in, crunching on it as her eyes kept moving, searching, looking for a place to rest.

"Beautiful little girl," the caretaker murmured.

And she was. Although, like me, Iris's father was American, my daughter possessed the almond-shaped eyes and high cheekbones of her Chinese ancestors. I remembered once seeing a photograph of my mother, Mei-ling, when she was a child. Iris resembled her.

Finally the real estate agent drove up in his car, but when I saw the look on his face as he got out, I knew at once that something was wrong.

"I'm sorry, Mrs. Lee," he said as the wind turned sharp and a cloud blocked the sun. "The owner has backed out of the deal."

"But that is not possible," I said, already knowing what he was going to say, and wondering why I had not seen it coming.

Mr. Osgood sniffed, glanced at the old caretaker, who was leaning on a broom, and said, "Well, I'm sorry, but he got a higher bid and he accepted it."

"But that is not legal. I gave you a deposit. That check is binding, Mr. Osgood."

"Yeah, well" — he reached into his jacket and brought

out the check, uncashed — "I'm giving it back. The owner got a better offer."

I had heard those same words before.

The first time involved a large shipment of herbs from Shanghai. Due to growing strife in China, with Chiang Kai-shek and Mao Tse-tung competing for power, and Japan mounting raids on coastal towns, imports from China were becoming scarce. But I had a standing contract with East-winds Trading Company, and those herbs that disappeared from the docks had been mine. A secret deal had been struck, I later found out, and the entire shipment of rare herbs, minerals, and spices went to Red Dragon Health Company. The second incident involved an antiques dealer who specialized in Oriental rarities. He had excitedly informed me of a book that had been recently discovered, over four hundred years old, believed to have been written by Dr. Li Shizhen, the great physician of the Ming dynasty. Supposedly it contained many medicinal recipes not previously known. The book was promised to me; it ended up in the possession of Red Dragon.

And now my factory, my dream, was his, too.

"Who is the higher bidder?" I asked, my hand still holding my daughter's as she tugged this way and that, like the wind, wanting to follow it away from this bad luck place. I already knew the answer, but I wanted to hear it, I wanted this man to say the words to my face.

He cleared his throat and didn't look me in the eye. "Red Dragon Health Company."

I felt the day fall away from me, like pebbles tumbling down a cliff. I put my hand on my husband's arm to steady myself. "Mr. Osgood," I said, "the man who owns Red Dragon Health Company is an unscrupulous person who has no honor."

"Look, I know you're upset —"

"He tried to burn down Mr. Huang's warehouse. He paid

a spy to tell him my secrets. He stole from me. And he knowingly makes poisons that hurt innocent people."

"Well, look, I don't know about those things, I only just —"

"And you have dishonored yourself, Mr. Osgood."

"Me! Now wait a minute!"

"How much did he pay you to give me back my deposit, Mr. Osgood?"

When the legal papers were served a week later, I was in my office in Chinatown, a small room above Huang Trading Company. The owner of Red Dragon Health Company was suing me for defamation of character and intentional infliction of emotional distress.

I immediately telephoned Gideon. I told myself it was because he was my business partner and that he should know about this. I told myself that it was because this matter would go to the courts and I knew Gideon was connected with the best attorneys in the city. I told myself many reasons why I called him and not my own husband or my own attorney or Mr. Huang or any other person who might help. I knew the real reason. I was frightened, and I needed Gideon.

It was the first time I had set foot in the Barclay mansion since the day I gave Fiona Barclay my father's ring.

The interior of the house seemed unchanged in nine years — still the same heavy Victorian furniture, the velvet and tassels and needlepoint pillows, and a vast collection of bric-a-brac taking up every inch of surface space. Gideon had told me that Olivia was running a subtle campaign to convince his mother to redecorate. Gideon and Olivia and their seven-year-old son, Adrian, occupied one wing of the house, and while they were welcome to refurbish their own rooms in any way they wished — which they did, Gideon told me, with Olivia's passion for the new interior design coming from Europe, Bauhaus, tubular steel, and Scandinavian molded wood — Fiona forbade them to change one ashtray, one tiny picture in the rest of the palatial mansion.

The study where I met with Gideon and his attorney was claustrophobic with Victorian clutter, busy wallpaper, and floral carpets. I knew that Olivia wanted to go through this house like a storm, sweeping out all the knickknacks, stripping the walls, rolling up the carpets, laying modern linoleum, installing furniture with smooth, sleek lines and satin upholstery, clearing all surfaces of clutter. Very modern, very efficient. I knew this because this is what I would have done, if this were my house.

I was not happy in the house where Mr. Lee and Iris and I lived in Oakland. The *feng shui* there was very bad. The house was situated on an incline so that our luck rolled downhill. A room had been added sometime in the past, changing the floor plan from a pleasing square to one that "dangled." Iris's bedroom had originally been that added room, but when she was an infant and we realized she was not developing normally, I moved her out of that bad luck bedroom and into our room. The living room was L-shaped, signifying a sense of incompleteness, and when I saw how my daughter was so slow to learn, so slow to walk, that her mind seemed lacking in places, I knew it was because of that bad luck living room. I wanted to buy a house in San Francisco. But my husband was Chinese, we were restricted; in Oakland the property laws were more lenient.

Gideon's house had good *chi*, except that the flow was blocked by so much dark wood and clutter. Olivia knew this, just as I knew it. Which was how I knew what she would do to change the house, to bring in luck and prosperity. And perhaps a second child.

Olivia had miscarried twice and had been warned against getting pregnant again. I gave Gideon a bottle of Golden Lotus Wine to give to Olivia, but I do not know if she ever used it. As for my own childlessness with Mr. Lee, Golden

Lotus could not help. I had often thought of him, in our years together in Chinatown, as a gentle soul who belonged in a monk's scriptorium, laboring over a mystical manuscript. And on our wedding night, when he wept softly in my arms as he confessed that he could never give me a second child, I had consoled him. I was going to have Gideon's child. It would be enough.

But now I knew how Olivia felt. I sympathized with her most deeply, although she did not know it.

There were only four of us in the study. Either by design because she knew I was coming, or by coincidence, Fiona Barclay was not at home that day. She had taken her grandson, Adrian, to the park, along with the daughter of a friend of Olivia's, a little girl the same age as Adrian, Margo, who was spending a holiday with the Barclays.

When Mr. Winterborn, Gideon's attorney and a man well respected in the legal world, had finished reviewing the papers I had been served with, he said, "This does not look good, Mrs. Lee. Not good at all." He peered at me over bifocals. "Did you say these things in front of witnesses."

Besides Mr. Osgood, there had been the caretaker, who had heard every word. "Yes."

"You say that your accusations are true — the stolen formulas, the fire at Huang Trading Company. Can you prove any of it?"

I glanced at Gideon. "The fire, no, no proof."

"What about the accusation that Red Dragon makes toxic products that hurt unsuspecting people?"

"That is true. I have been at the bedsides of Red Dragon's victims."

"I have some knowledge in the area of pharmaceuticals, Mrs. Lee, and as you yourself already know, herbals aren't federally regulated. There are no laws that say warnings have to be put on labels. So, essentially, it's let the buyer beware." He removed his spectacles and laying them on the small table beside his chair, said, "There's a lot of money at stake here, Mrs. Lee. Your firm has been doing extremely well, considering the rest of the economy." The world was, of course, in a serious depression, many people were out of jobs, many people had lost entire bank accounts. Even the Barclays had suffered, having lost nearly half of their investments. But *my* company prospered because when people are unable to afford a doctor, they turn to self-medicating. "This man is going to go after every penny you've got. He can take your company, your house, your car, even your teapot."

"What about us?" Olivia interjected as she fitted a cigarette into a long holder and lit it with a gold lighter. "Can they touch us?"

When I had telephoned Gideon and said, "I need you," he had said, "Come over right away." I had interrupted a tennis game. Olivia was still in her white skirt and blouse, as if this were a brief diversion before she went back to her game.

Mr. Winterborn said, "You and your husband are not named in the suit, Mrs. Barclay, and most likely won't be. Because your partnership in Perfect Harmony Chinese Herbal Company is restricted to the export division, which is located in Hong Kong, you are not connected to the San Francisco holdings."

Our contract with Titan Mining Company had led to others so that soon we were distributing my remedies all over Southeast Asia. Since we had been importing the herbs from Hong Kong, making the compounds here, and then shipping them back, it had made sense to have a plant in Hong Kong. Gideon was the director of Harmony-Barclay Ltd.; it was what had helped make him rich and successful by the age of thirty-four.

"So far, Mrs. Barclay," Mr. Winterborn said again to Olivia, "it doesn't appear you and your husband can be touched."

She sat back and blew out a long, thin stream of smoke.

And behind that smoke I saw her eyes settle on me. As I
watched the way she sat in the high wingback chair, one
tanned leg crossed casually over the other, I remembered a
time when Olivia had been kind to me. But that was before
Gideon had asked me to marry him, before he had then
asked *her* because I had married Mr. Lee instead.

I looked away from Olivia and gazed through the open
doorway into the large living room. On the far side, huge
windows looked out over the northern curve of the city and,
beyond, the Bay. It was possible to just see the new bridge,
partly under construction — the two towers and suspension
cables holding up half-completed decks that seemed to
strain out to meet each other. I remembered the night
Gideon and I had stood on that promontory, and he had described his dream to build a bridge that the world had never
seen before.

The Golden Gate *was* going to be a monumental bridge,
but it was not Gideon's.

"Mrs. Lee," Mr. Winterborn was saying, "how many formulas would you say Red Dragon stole from you?"

I brought my attention back. "Four that I know of for cer-
tain. Perhaps five or six." Why, Gideon? I wanted to ask.
Why is that bridge not yours? Did the state reject your bid?
Did someone with a bribe or a relative on the commission
get the job instead of you? Gideon never spoke of the
Golden Gate bridge again after that night under the stars, so
I did not know what had caused his dreams to die.

"We are going to need solid, tangible evidence, Mrs.
Lee."

I listened to the ticking of the ornate grandfather clock.
whispering away the minutes. I thought of the two decks of
the bridge, stretching to join each other, the way I sometimes sensed Gideon and I did, during captured moments
when, as we discussed shipments and costs and profits in
our Asian concern, I would see him looking at me, and our

eyes would meet and for one instant we would feel each other's longing. I suspected he was not happy in his marriage.

"Olivia," Gideon said, as he stood up abruptly and raked his hair back. Like his wife, he was dressed in white: slacks, sweater, shoes. But with Gideon I did not sense he was anxious to get back to his tennis game. "Could we have some coffee, please?"

"Certainly," she said as she unfolded herself from the chair. She turned to me, and said, "Would you like coffee, Mrs. Lee?"

I read her meaning clearly: I was not part of Gideon's *we*. "Thank you," I said.

She went to a corner of the study and tugged on a bellpull. When a maid appeared, Olivia ordered coffee and sesame seed cake. As she returned to her chair, flicking ash in a crystal ashtray, she said, "Really, Gideon, do you think it's wise for you to connect yourself with this case at all? I mean, think what it would do to the Barclay name."

He kept his yes on my papers, flipping through them, frowning. "For God's sake, Olivia, what a thing to say."

She smiled at me. "I'm sure Mrs. Lee would agree that we should protect the Barclay name."

She kept calling me Mrs. Lee as though I were an older woman, yet we were both twenty-eight. It was to remind me of my Chinese name, I knew, and that I had not gotten what I came to this house for nine years ago — the right to carry my father's name. It was to remind me also that *she* was Barclay, that this was *her* house, that Gideon was hers. Olivia had somehow triumphed in a race I hadn't even known we were running.

"Your wife has a good point, Gideon," Mr. Winterborn said. "Right now you are not connected with this case. But Red Dragon Company is powerful and has a lot of money. If they decide to go after you as well, you might not win."

Gideon handed the papers back to the attorney. "I am standing by Harmony," he said quietly, "no matter what happens."

"Very noble, I'm sure," Olivia said with a fixed smile.

"Mrs. Lee," Mr. Winterborn said, also standing up to rise to his full height — he was a tall man, lean almost to gauntness, with white hair and sharp blue eyes — "you can be sure that Red Dragon is going to build a strong case against you. We are going to have to build a stronger one. First, I want to see your production logs. We'll compare the dates of when you experimented or manufactured your formulas to when Red Dragon came out with *their* formulas."

"I have no production logs, Mr. Winterborn."

He paused, looked at me, then at Gideon, then back to me. "Well then, any notes or letters in which you mention formulas, any written records at all that are dated and verifiable."

"I have my mother's recipe book. It contains dates and formulas."

He unbuttoned his dark blue jacket and slipped his hands into the pockets of his trousers. Careful gestures, while his mind worked. "I guess that will have to do," he said, "if that's all you have. I will also need the names of all the people who have worked for you over, say, the past ten years." He paused again to give me a questioning look. "You do have records of people who have worked for you?"

"Mr. Winterborn," I explained, "Chinatown is not like the rest of San Francisco. A girl comes into my factory and tells me she is hungry, she needs money, she is in trouble. I take her into the packing room and ask one of the others to show her how to put labels on boxes. At the end of the day, I give her money. Perhaps she comes back the next day, perhaps not."

"You made some very damaging remarks about Red Dragon, Mrs. Lee, and unless we can find a way to back them up, you are going to lose everything. You do understand that, do you not?"

"He stole from me."

He ran a hand over his white hair. "Yes, I realize that. But we need *proof*. If we can find at least one incidence in which your proprietary rights have been violated — proof of just one stolen formula . . ."

There *was* one formula which I knew for certain Red Dragon had stolen from me, and I had written evidence to prove it. But how could I speak of it here, with this man whom I had only just met, and in front of Gideon and Olivia?

"I will give you Mother's recipe book. Some of the formulas have dates recorded."

He rubbed his chin. "It might not hold up in court. Records can be falsified. Do you have any letters in which you describe a formula?"

"There is one," I said reluctantly. "It was a secret formula that I made from an ancient recipe on a papyrus. No one knew I was working on it. And Red Dragon did not possess that papyrus . . ."

"Go on."

I glanced at Olivia, but did not meet Gideon's eyes. "There was a problem with the formula, so I sent it to a chemist for analysis. He wrote back that I should remove one ingredient, which I did. A week later, Red Dragon introduced a new product. It was the same formula I had found in the papyrus, and it contained the ingredient which I subsequently removed from mine."

"Indicating," Mr. Winterborn said with a delighted smile, "that the formula had been stolen *before* you received your reply from the chemist. Do you still have those letters, Mrs. Lee?"

"Yes."

"All right, it's a start!" He rubbed his hands together. "By the way, what is the medicine?"

"It is called Ten Thousand Yang."

"That's an unusual name."

"It is a very good name in Chinese. Ten thousand is a magical number in Chinese calculations, very powerful. And *yang* is the masculine principle. Ten Thousand Yang is a potency tonic."

"Potency tonic?" His silver eyebrows arched. "Good Lord, do you mean to say . . . ?"

"It is an aphrodisiac."

The day the trial began, I felt hopeful, even though afraid. Mr. Winterborn and his staff had worked tirelessly to build a strong case in my defense, which in actuality was an offense — against Red Dragon Health Company. Mr. Winterborn's staff had tracked down girls who worked for me years ago and obtained their depositions. They combed through my mother's recipe book and compared formulas and dates with those of Red Dragon products, coming up with eight instances in which I created a remedy and a week later Red Dragon had it on the market. We also had Mr. Huang's testimony that after our verbal rental agreement, he had been approached by a representative of the Red Dragon Health Company to rent the same space.

With luck, Mr. Winterborn assured me, Red Dragon Company would drop the lawsuit and the whole matter would be resolved, quietly and out of court, in a few days.

I prayed for luck as I left Iris in the care of one of Mr. Lee's female cousins, whom I had helped bring over from Hawaii. We both pretended that Iris waved good-bye to me, although in truth her hand was chasing something seen only to her busy eyes.

The sun was shining on the first day of the trial. And when I paused to look up, on the steps of the courthouse, and saw a long-necked bird fly up from the roof, I took it as a good luck sign.

The man I had come to think of as the Dragon arrived at the courthouse dressed modestly and with a serious demeanor. In his sixties, with shoe-blacked hair and an unlined face, he was a handsome Chinese known for his charisma and generosity, and also for his penchant for nightclubs and white women. As if to offset his playboy image, he arrived in the company of his eighteen-year-old son, who sat behind him on the other side of the railing, a quiet, long-faced boy in a dark suit and starched collar.

I was pleased to see that there were four women on the jury, which Mr. Winterborn told me was highly unusual and assured me would help my case. I took this an another sign of good luck. I was also relieved to see that the courtroom was almost empty, except for Gideon and Olivia sitting in the front row, and Mr. Lee a few seats away. There would be no audience to witness this loss of honor, and when the attorney for Red Dragon stood up to make his opening remarks, his voice echoed in the large room.

Mr. Osgood, the real estate agent, testified first, and then the elderly caretaker, who offered me an apologetic look as he verified Mr. Osgood's testimony. But Red Dragon did not stop there. They paraded witness after witness through the courtroom, all testifying that they had heard me make disparaging remarks about Red Dragon. Some were valid, most were falsehoods.

And then they proceeded, over the next few days, to break down my allegations one by one: they produced records and logs for the past ten years, with formulas recorded, their dates of manufacture. They were the formulas Red Dragon has stolen from me, but their records were dated earlier. I knew the records were false, but I had no way of proving it. They produced women who had worked for me who testified that at no time was there a spy from Red Dragon among them. Finally, evidence was provided that the Dragon had been out of the country when the fire broke out in Mr. Huang's warehouse.

They discredited my own witnesses most brilliantly. Mr. Winterborn called Mrs. Po to the stand, and under his questioning she glowingly told the court of the new ointment I had given her in the pretty jar, and how it had cured her chapped skin, her insomnia, her husband's headaches. And yes, she remembered exactly when I had given it to her, just two weeks after Chinese New Year because she had just installed a new steam press in her laundry. This was weeks before Red Dragon came out with their own ointment, the exact same formula as mine, also in a pretty jar.

I felt a small thrill of triumph. But then the Dragon's attorney stood up and said, "Mrs. Po, can you tell us who the president was at the time of this incident?"

"What?" she said. "President?"

"The president of the United States."

I knew that Mrs. Po did not concern herself with affairs beyond Chinatown. I knew why he had asked this question. When she said, "George Washington?" the court erupted in laughter.

By now there was an audience. I believe they were workers from the Red Dragon factory, for they cheered each little victory on the Dragon's side, and booed my own.

My mother's book of remedies was handled, read, copied, photographed, passed around, and examined until it began to fall apart. Mr. Winterborn produced witnesses who testified as to when I had created specific formulas. Red Dragon brought in experts who proved that the formulas were a thousand years old. The fact that Red Dragon did not manufacture those compounds until I had made mine was not proof that they had been stolen.

It finally became apparent that the trial was not going well for me or Perfect Harmony Chinese Herbal Company.

* * *

Mr. Winterborn had said he hoped we would not have to introduce Ten Thousand Yang, due to the delicacy of the nature of the product. But when it became apparent that I was losing the battle, he warned me that things could get a little rough. I had no choice. I was unable to find any more witnesses who would support my claims. Many who had worked for me over the years were either afraid or perhaps they had been bribed. It was no secret that the owner of Red Dragon Health Company was thought to have ties with the Chinese underworld.

"The most damaging allegation," Mr. Winterborn explained one evening after another devastating day in court, "is *not* that Red Dragon stole formulas or had a spy planted in your factory, but that he knowingly manufactures and sells lethal medicines. If we can get him on this, then we might win. But to do that I'm afraid we shall have to bring in Ten Thousand Yang."

"Then we shall do it," I said.

"We are going to have to do more than that, Mrs. Lee. Can you find any of those people who were made sick from the Strong Man?" This was what Red Dragon called their Ten Thousand Yang formula: Strong Man Tonic. "Can you find any widows who will testify?"

Gideon said, "My God, you can't ask some poor woman to sit on that stand and tell the world that her husband died because of taking an aphrodisiac."

"I will find them," I said.

Every night during the trial my husband and I would go home to our house in Oakland, where I would feed Iris and bathe her and put her to bed, and then review my notes of the day's proceedings, and review what was going to happen tomorrow, while Mr. Lee retreated to his study to work in silence on his painting.

The next morning, we would read in the newspaper a strangely distorted report of the day before: they seemed to focus mainly on me, describing my "Chinese dresses," what I had for lunch: "steamed dumplings and chow mein noodles brought in from Chinatown." they called me a "wife and mother who runs a business" but they did not refer to my adversary as a husband and father who owned a business. Even my moods were recorded — "Mrs. Lee looked sad" — and sensational elements were hinted at: "the beautiful young Harmony Lee looking longingly at Mr. Gideon Barclay."

Finally, it could not be helped, Ten Thousand Yang was introduced into the trial.

I took the witness stand despite Mr. Winterborn's recommendation that I not do so. He warned me that the advocate for Red Dragon would use it as a chance to humiliate and embarrass me. But it was my one chance to speak up for myself and let the jury, and the world, judge my honesty for themselves.

"You claim that your tonic is safe, Mrs. Lee," the lawyer for Red Dragon declared. He was a large man who wore loud, checked vests and was fond of making dramatic gestures.

"It is."

"You will have to speak louder, Mrs. Lee," he nearly shouted. "So the court can hear you." I understood his strategy. He shouted to make himself and Red Dragon appear strong and myself weak. "It is," I repeated in the same voice, because I knew the court could hear me and I would not let it seem that he could manipulate me.

"What makes your tonic safe if it is the same formula as Strong Man?"

That was when I saw a woman standing at the back of the courtroom. She seemed familiar to me, but I could not recall where I knew her from. She seemed nervous, fearful. When her eyes met mine, I heard a silent communication: *I am sorry*.

"It isn't the same formula. Red Dragon's product contains one extra ingredient that mine does not."

"Ah yes, this interesting contradiction — you claim that Strong Man is your formula and then you say it is not!"

A murmur rippled through the crowd.

"I created my tonic for a particular customer — I do that in special cases, when other remedies fail. I put together customized formulas to suit a unique case."

"How did you come up with this particular formula, Mrs. Lee?"

"I found a recipe on an ancient papyrus and made the compound myself."

"An ancient papyrus you said? Meaning this recipe is . . . how old?"

The courtroom was hushed as everyone hung upon my reply. "The recipe is over a thousand years old."

"Ah, so then you did not really invent it!" he said theatrically, and another murmur rose up, causing the judge to bang his gavel.

Mr. Winterborn questioned me next. "The recipe is old, Mrs. Lee, but did you change it in any way?"

"Yes, I *customized* it, making it uniquely mine."

"And what happened after you made this unique formula?"

"My client fell ill after sampling it, and when I saw what his symptoms were — the rapid heartbeat, the elevated blood pressure — I suspected it was due to one ingredient in the recipe. I wrote to a chemist who had done analysis for me in the past, and requested his opinion. He wrote back that it was indeed the ingredient which I suspected, and that I should remove it from the formula. Which I did."

"What ingredient was that, Mrs. Lee?"

"Ephedrine."

"So you don't use ephedrine in any of your products?"

"I use it in my Golden Lotus Wine. Ephedrine relieves asthma."

"So it is not a toxin?"

"In large doses it is fatal to healthy people. In lesser doses it is fatal to people with weak hearts or who have high blood pressure."

"But how does the customer know this?"

"There is a warning on the label that says the wine contains ephedrine, which should not be taken by people with heart conditions."

He handed me a bottle of Red Dragon's Strong Man. "Will you read the label, please?"

"It says this tonic restores virility, vigor, and potency."

"Is there any mention of ingredients?"

"No."

"Is there a warning against taking too much?"

"No."

"Your Honor, I have here reports from independent analyses done on the contents of this bottle. Both conclude that Strong Man contains a quantity of ephedrine that exceeds safe limits."

The courtroom erupted, and I saw Gideon smile and wink at me.

Over the weekend, a headline appeared in the newspaper — "Manufacturer Accused of Selling Lethal Sex Tonic." There was an artist's sketch supposedly of me, but it looked like Anna May Wong, the Chinese film star. On Monday morning the street and sidewalk and steps of the courthouse were so mobbed police had to come in to control the crowd. Reporters were there, and Movietone News cameras, people trying to get a seat in the audience.

Now I knew why Mr. Winterborn had not wanted to bring Ten Thousand Yang into the case.

"What is your tonic for, Mrs. Lee?" Red Dragon's attorney boomed in his theatrical way of facing the audience when he was addressing *me*.

"Male vigor," I said, not wishing to respond to such rudeness, but knowing I must appear cooperative. It was difficult to read the mood of the courtroom and the jury. I hoped they were on my side, but so far I could not tell.

"You mean strong muscles?"

"Virility," I said.

"As in it puts hair on a man's chest?"

I glanced at Gideon. He sent me a supportive smile. The audience stirred. I sensed their excitement as everyone waited for me to speak the forbidden words. Suddenly I was angry. Why was I being punished when I was the victim? "Ten Thousand Yang is a formula for improving sexual performance. And that man," I said, pointing to the Dragon, "stole my recipe and left in an ingredient that is lethal — an ingredient that I removed from my final recipe. That man's drug is poison."

The Dragon shot to his feet. "It is not poison!"

"Then drink it, you bastard!" Gideon suddenly shouted, also jumping up. "Drink a bottle of it right here and prove it's safe!"

"I have no need of the tonic," the Dragon shot back, "but perhaps you do?"

The courtroom erupted in pandemonium. The judge banged his gavel but it could only barely be heard over the noise.

After order had been restored, the Red Dragon attorney said in a loud voice, once again talking with his back to me, "Now, Mrs. Lee, you stated that you made this formula at the request of a particular customer. Was this customer a man?"

"Ten Thousand Yang is a compound made especially for men."

"Then will you please tell the court one more thing, Mrs.

Lee? Who *was* this customer for whom you made the potion?"

Mr. Winterborn stood up. "Objection, Your Honor. The identity of the customer is of no relevance here —"

"I believe it is, Your Honor. It is my client's opinion that there has been a conspiracy against him. The name of Mrs. Lee's customer is of direct significance."

"Objection overruled. Answer the question, Mrs. Lee."

I had not thought they would do this. I had thought the names would remain confidential.

"Mrs. Lee?" the lawyer said. "Would you please tell the court the name of the customer for whom you created the aphrodisiac?"

I turned to Gideon. He had a stricken look on his face.

"Mrs. Lee?"

"I made the formula," I finally said in front of all those gawking strangers and reporters and movie cameras, "for my husband, Mr. Lee." And as I spoke those words, as the courtroom erupted in chaos, with bulbs flashing and reporters running out of the room, I looked at my husband, who sat with quiet dignity in the front row, his head held high.

I had never seen Gideon so angry. "They are *crucifying* her in there!"

Mr. Winterborn shook his head. "Our hands are tied, Gideon. Harmony has failed to come up with proof to back her allegations. Now it's up to the jury to decide and I don't think they are on our side."

Gideon glared at the lawyer. "I thought you said that having women on the jury would help."

"I thought it would, but those women have turned out to be a big mistake."

"Why?"

"Because Harmony is young and beautiful and she sells sex tonics to their husbands. She is a threat to them."

"Look," Gideon said, "we've got signed affidavits from chemists stating that Red Dragon's elixir is dangerous. That backs up what Harmony said, doesn't it?"

"Anything is toxic in a large enough quantity. Besides, Gideon, there is no proof that anyone has actually *died* from ingesting Strong Man. That's the problem. We're traveling on assumptions here, not proof."

"But Harmony produced names —"

"Of men who were sick or died. But of what? No autopsies were performed. We don't know the state of their health when they died."

He turned to me and released a ragged sigh. "Mrs. Lee, I think you should prepare for the worst."

I would not give up hope. "Mr. Winterborn," I said, "there was a woman in the courtroom the other day. She was there for only a few minutes. I think she was afraid. She left as soon as I saw her."

"Who is she?"

"At first I could not remember. And then it came to me: she is Betty Chan. She worked for me nine years ago. And I am almost certain she is the one who stole my ideas and gave them to Red Dragon. If we can find her, and persuade her to testify . . ."

"I'll get my private detective on it."

That night I lay in bed and cried. What future was I going to give to my daughter now? A mother without honor? A family without fortune? Mr. Lee took me into his arms and comforted me. Even in bed I called him Mr. Lee. He held me until I fell asleep in his gentle embrace.

When we arrived at the courthouse the next morning, Mr. Winterborn had good news. "My detective has found the whereabouts of Betty Chan. He's on his way now to talk to her."

"Do you think he can persuade her to come forward?" Gideon said. As usual he was at my side as we made our way through the mob, while Mr. Lee and Olivia followed behind. The newspapers had picked up on this and made references to "the constant company of Mr. Gideon Barclay." Mr. Winterborn had suggested Gideon physically distance himself from me, but of course his advice fell on deaf ears.

"It depends. But my man can be fairly persuasive," Mr. Winterborn said with a smile, "especially with the ladies. I also instructed him to let her know in veiled terms that she would be recompensed for her efforts. Not exactly ethical, but then this whole trial has been a farce."

Mr. Winterborn requested a recess while we waited for the arrival of a new witness. The judge granted us one hour.

It was the longest hour of my life as we paced in the hallway, watching both entrances, checking our watches, while the Dragon and his now considerably larger entourage sat on benches beneath the high windows, talking softly and occasionally laughing out loud. Once in a while he glanced my way, sending me a triumphant look, and I wondered what I had ever done to this man to deserve his animosity.

Betty Chan never arrived.

"Where is your witness, Mr. Winterborn?" the judge asked as the packed courtroom settled down.

"Your Honor, if we could just —"

"Mr. Winterborn, do you or do you not have a witness to call at this time?"

"Your Honor, I request a —"

"You are trying the patience of this court, Mr. Winterborn."

The double doors opened just then and Mr. Winterborn's private detective hurried in. The audience stirred and shifted, sensing high drama as the man came up to the railing behind us and said quietly, "Betty Chan is dead. They just fished her body out of the Bay."

I must have cried out, because the judge had to bang his

gavel again to maintain order in his court, and I saw Gideon's pale face, and then I saw the vast empty edge at the end of the world, opening up, about to swallow me. I was going to lose.

My company, my honor, my dream.

When my husband slowly rose to his feet, I thought it was to leave the courtroom. Instead, to my great shock, he said in an uncharacteristically loud voice, "I am the witness, Your Honor." He turned to Mr. Winterborn. "I am ready to testify now."

My attorney gave him a puzzled look, then turned to me with a raised eyebrow. But I had no idea what was in Mr. Lee's mind.

I watched as he approached the bench, this tall, reed-thin man who had always seemed to me older than he was, of a quiet disposition that made me think of cloistered scholars in mandarin robes. When he reached the witness stand, Mr. Lee produced an envelope and handed it up to the judge. His voice rang out over the hushed audience: "This contains a certificate attesting to my perfect health. The physician who examined me is here today." Then, to my further shock, Mr. Lee reached into his pocket and brought out a bottle. "I purchased this bottle of Strong Man at Fen Yuen's Market on Grant Street. I asked the owner to seal the bottle." Mr. Lee handed it up to the judge. "As you can see, the bottle is still sealed. The owner of the market is also here today."

The audience stirred, murmured, everyone talking, wondering.

I sat frozen as my husband asked the judge to open the bottle. With bulbs flashing and the Movietone News cameras rolling, the judge did so, handing the bottle back to Mr. Lee.

With a flourish I had not known my husband capable of, he turned to the audience and, before I could react, drank down the entire bottle of Red Dragon's Strong Man Tonic.

"No!" I cried.

The courtroom exploded. Cameras flashed, people shouted, reporters dashed out for the telephones. The Red Dragon attorney, looking furious, was trying to say something to the judge, while the gavel came down again and again as I flew to my husband, who stood there with the empty bottle in his hand.

He had taken the medicine on an empty stomach. He felt the effects almost immediately. By the time the doctor reached him, Mr. Lee was sitting on the floor, his back propped against the base of the judge's bench. His heart was racing so fast I could not count the pulse; his face was pale, his skin drenched with sweat. I feared he was going to die right there, his life slipping through my helpless fingers.

I gazed at him in speechless wonder, barely aware of Gideon keeping the onlookers back, shouting, "Give him room!" Men with cameras pressed in as close as they could, I heard women sobbing.

Mr. Lee was rushed to the hospital. "Why?" I said as I rode in the ambulance with him. "Why did you do it?"

He took my hand between his, smiled softly, and said, "Because my painting is finished."

He died that night at the hospital, and the doctors decreed it was the Strong Man that had done it. People came forward after that, reporting their own injuries and losses due to using Red Dragon products. Workers at the Red Dragon factory made anonymous tips to the police; a subsequent investigation revealed that the production records had indeed been falsified. When police questioned employees about whether they knew Betty Chan, whose poor body lay unclaimed in the morgue, they testified that she had indeed worked as a spy for Red Dragon.

An investigation by the Internal Revenue Service produced false books and evidence of tax evasion, money laundering, and connections with the Chinese mafia. The plant was shut down, the Dragon was arrested without bail, pending the investigation of reported deaths due to his products. He died before he went to trial, of a heart attack it was said, although there were rumors that he had committed suicide due to loss of face.

To my surprise, sales of Perfect Harmony remedies did not suffer; in fact they increased. The publicity attending the trial had generated an interest in my medicines so that people who had never tried them sampled Beautiful Intelligence Balm and Bliss, and became regular customers. Because of this, and for my daughter's future, although I was in mourning I went ahead with my plans to purchase the factory in Daly City. Mr. Lee would have wanted me to.

I hired a geomancer to inspect the *feng shui*. She found a leak in a pipe — "Your money will dribble away" — and a door that blocked the flow of *chi*. We repainted the buildings with colors that brought them into harmony with their surroundings, we hung wind chimes to capture and radiate good *chi*, and when I saw that the address was 626 — which adds up to fourteen, a very bad luck number meaning "guaranteed death" — I changed it to 888, to bring good luck and prosperity.

The day of the factory opening, an auspicious day chosen by a soothsayer, we hired lion dancers to invoke the goodwill of the gods. We all stood for a group photograph, including Gideon and Olivia, who had brought their son, Adrian, and the little girl who was their houseguest, Margo.

I also arranged, through Mr. Winterborn, to give anonymous financial assistance to the Dragon's eighteen-year-old son, Woodrow Sung, for he was now without mother and father, and I did not think he should have to suffer for his father's sins.

It was months before I could bring myself to go into Mr. Lee's study. I had not seen his newest painting since the day he started it. I had no idea what it was he was creating, all those silent nights during the trial. But I had to face it, I had to see if it held the answers to why Mr. Lee had killed himself.

The painting was where he had left it. I saw at once that it was not his usual pandas and horses and temple dogs. Human beings were the subject and it was a vast scene, with hills and clouds and an ocean in the distance. It took my breath away. Never had I seen so beautiful a painting.

And then I recognized the subjects, I began to see their story, and I understood why Mr. Lee had drunk the potion.

I was at the center of the scene, there was a red dragon breathing fire at me, and I appeared to be running, with my arms outstretched, toward a man who was not Chinese. In the background, barely visible, as if he were a ghost, was the image of my husband, watching me run to Gideon. In the foreground was a little girl with butterflies for eyes. And next to her was a ghost-baby.

The baby he could never give me.

38

3:00 A.M. — Palm Springs, California

Charlotte flew into the office, breathless. "You're not going to believe what I found!"

Jonathan was on his back under the desk. "Half a mo," he called out, and she heard the sound of something being snipped. "Right," he said. Pulling himself out from under the desk, he sat up and, setting aside the wire cutters and screwdriver, brushed the light dusting of plaster from his forehead.

Charlotte held the newspaper up to him. "I found this in

one of the displays. Jonathan, Mr. Sung is the son of my grandmother's competitor, the man who tried to destroy her company!"

He saw that it was the front page of the *San Francisco Chronicle*, dated 1936; the headline read: Dragon Beaten by Willow.

Charlotte summarized the trial briefly, adding, "Mr. Sung's father heavily laced his products with *ephedrine*."

Jonathan got to his feet, brushing himself off. "So you're saying Mr. Sung is using ephedrine as some sort of ironic justice?" He gave her a dubious look. "It could just as easily be someone who wants to make it *look* as if Sung is the guilty party."

"Maybe. But I do know one thing," Charlotte said as she folded the newspaper and carefully slipped it into her leather tote, where she had packed as much as she could, including a fresh box of tea from her office and, as a last-minute impulse, the 1981 book of prize-winning poetry. "Rusty Brown could not possibly have been hired through normal channels. Our personnel department runs thorough background checks. And yet that man was arrested for tampering with formulas at a drug company! He not only was arrested, he was put on trial! There is no way Mrs. Ferguson could have missed that. So someone above the personnel director got him in. And Mr. Sung has that authority."

Jonathan slipped his hands into tight black gloves. "If Sung is our man, then why did he give you the puzzle box that led you to search in the museum in the first place? If he was guilty, why would he do that?"

"I don't know. My head is swimming." Charlotte massaged her neck as she surveyed the small office that she had closed up six months ago, when she had thought she would never set foot inside it again. But now she saw the dishes from the cafeteria, the packets of tea, Jonathan's raincoat hanging on a hook, the coffee cups, the electronic gear, the floppy disks and pages of computer printouts. Her grand-mother's small office, intended for the modest use of an el-derly Chinese lady and her memories, had become a battle command center.

And now Charlotte would be closing it up again. With the threat of Valerius Knight arriving any minute, possibly with a warrant for her arrest — there was no way she could con-vince him that her knowing all *three* victims was only a co-incidence — she and Jonathan were preparing to make a hasty departure and find a place to hole up until they trapped the killer.

As she thought about the news article she had just read, a shocking account of a trial that had taken place over sixty years ago, Charlotte conceded that maybe it *was* too easy to think that Mr. Sung was their killer, just because his father had used ephedrine. However, Charlotte was certain about one thing: despite Jonathan's suspicions, Naomi definitely was not the killer.

What did holding shares in a rival company mean, any-way? Moonstone was a solid corporation with a future of growth, and Naomi's fiancé was, after all, an investment broker. If Harmony ever went public, Charlotte had no doubt that her friend would buy shares in it as well. The fact that Naomi hadn't mentioned buying Moonstone stock, an outlay of over thirty thousand dollars despite her mentioning only a few weeks ago that money was tight — well, Naomi was sometimes absentminded. And anyway, friends didn't always tell each other everything. It was monstrous to think that Naomi would burn her own house down for the insur-ance, and it was equally monstrous of Jonathan to suggest it.

Because of this, and the possibility that Naomi might be further victimized by falling under Knight's suspicion, Charlotte was more determined than ever that she would find the killer in her family's past, and that was why, while Jonathan rewired her grandmother's computer for remote access, Charlotte had hastily packed her leather tote with items from the museum — documents, letters, newspapers — anything that might give a clue as to who could be out to destroy her company.

Jonathan consulted his watch and then glanced at the security monitor. "We have to get to that network hub and then get out of here before Knight shows up. Our intruder has been accessing the system through an in-house terminal, and most likely still is. I have to reroute the path so that the next time he logs on to copy a formula, he will come straight to us, and then we'll grab him by remote access from our new location."

She looked at the computer screen. "But if he is rerouted, he won't find the formulas and he'll log off."

"Take a closer look."

Her eyes widened. "Fake formulas?"

"With invisible tags on them, silent strings of codes which I have attached that act sort of like homing beacons. All he has to do is download one, and I can run a trace. We'll have his location in minutes. But we have to hurry."

Jonathan turned to the security monitor — the parking lot was in view, a few cars standing in the pouring rain. He hit a key on the console and the third-floor offices came into view. "He's still there," Jonathan said, referring to the federal agent who had been assigned to guard the network closet. "I need about ten minutes with the network server. The question is, how do I distract him?"

Charlotte looked at the man on the screen: he was large, with a blond military cut, and the neck and arms of a football player. Charlotte doubted he would be easily distracted. "I can do it," she said.

"No. You have to stay hidden until we leave. We can't risk you running into Knight."

"It's only ten minutes, you said. And I'll keep a watch out. The first sign of Knight and I'll run."

He gave it thirty seconds of consideration. "All right, but only if you promise to run like hell at the first sign of Valerius Knight."

39

"Hello," she said, smiling as she walked up. "I'm Ms. Lee, I believe you know who I am?"

The agent rose from his chair and positioned himself between Charlotte and the door to the network. "Evening, ma'am," he murmured. "Yes, I do."

"Such a terrible mess. I can't tell you how much I appreciate the quickness of your team's response. The sooner we catch the person who is sabotaging my company the better!" She held out the tray she had picked up at the cafeteria. "I thought you might like something to eat." At this hour there hadn't been much of a selection, and the hot food service had long since closed down. But she had been able to find coffee and the raspberry jam doughnuts looked relatively fresh.

"No thanks, ma'am, I'm fine."

"But you've been sitting here for four hours. You must be hungry."

"I'm fine, thank you."

Despite his rejection of her offer, Charlotte saw how his eyes lingered on the plump donuts, which she had displayed as enticingly as possible, with the jam oozing out. "It's a long time till morning," she said, setting the tray on the nearest desk and holding out a Styrofoam cup. "Cream and sugar?"

"No, thank you, I'm fine," he said, holding up a hand.

Charlotte surveyed the tray. "Well, if you don't mind, I

happen to be ravenous. It's been a long day and a very stressful one."

Selecting one of the doughnuts, she turned and faced him just as she bit into it, making sure jam spurted out the other side. "Oops!" she said, grabbing for a napkin. "I always do that!" She laughed with her mouth full and then wiped off her chin. "Oh boy, these are fresher than I thought. Our kitchen makes the best doughnuts. They deep-fry them first and then fill them with custard or chocolate or jam, and then dust them in cinnamon and sugar. Try eating them when they're still warm. . . . The outside is just a little crisp and the center just melts in your mouth."

She saw his tongue make a quick appearance on his lips.

"Are you sure?" She held the plate out to him. "Just one doughnut isn't going to hurt. I won't tell anyone if you don't," she added with a wink.

He still declined, but not without hesitating, Charlotte noticed, so she continued eating the doughnut, commenting on every bite, declaring how she was going to have to go on a diet for a month the pastry was so rich and sweet and delicious. When she saw his eyes glance quickly at the plate and then away, she offered yet again, and this time he said, "Well . . . ,"

"Save me from myself!" she said with a laugh as she nearly nudged him with the plate.

"I think one would be all right," he said. "Much obliged, ma'am," he added as he accepted a cup of coffee.

When the overhead lights flickered, Charlotte said, "What a night out! It doesn't rain much in this area, but when it does you expect to see Noah go sailing by!"

"Yes, ma'am."

Leaning against the wall opposite the computer room, Charlotte folded her arms and said, "It can't be much fun sitting here alone all night."

"I guess not," he said, polishing off the doughnut and wiping his lips with a paper napkin.

"Have another," she said, pointing to the tray.

He did not need to be persuaded.

Charlotte glanced down the hall to where Jonathan was waiting. Then she watched the agent make quick work of the second doughnut. When he had downed the rest of the coffee, she said, "Don't you get bored? I mean, just sitting here all by yourself. Do they let you read magazines? I'll be glad to get you —"

"I'm fine, ma'am. Thank you for the coffee and dough-nuts."

She continued to lean against the wall, arms crossed. She looked up at the clock. Only two and a half hours before the six o'clock deadline, and she could only guess how long they had before Knight showed up. As she reached into the pocket of her jacket, she was aware that the agent closely watched her. She didn't look at him as she produced the small puzzle box and began slowly turning it over and over in her hands.

With her fingers working to find the first panel and slide it open, Charlotte started to hum softly. The agent kept his eye on her hands as she found the second panel, slowly slid it to the side, humming as she did so. The tune was simple, a lul-laby she remembered from her childhood and she hummed it absentmindedly as she slowly worked the box, this way and that, rhythmically, hypnotically. The storm raging outside could barely be heard within these expensively decorated and soundproofed walls. The interior design of Harmony Biotech's corporate offices was the work of Margo Barclay, who had personally chosen the thick, pale blue carpeting, the beige grasscloth on the walls, the blue-and-silver partitions around the secretarial cubicles, and the soft, recessed light-ing. The idea had been to create a subdued, tasteful am-biance. On a stormy night, it felt like a cocoon.

The first time the agent yawned, hiding his mouth behind his hand, Charlotte didn't look at him. With the next wide-mouthed yawn she gave him a surreptitious look. The third yawn was accompanied by a rapid blinking of the eyes — a man trying to stay awake.

It took a few minutes longer than she had expected but the syrup that she had injected into the raspberry jam finally did its job. Although not federally approved to manufacture opium products, Harmony Biotech's lab had a plentiful supply of *Papaver somniferum*, more commonly known as the poppy, for research purposes (*"somniferum"* meaning "sleep inducing").

While the agent sat slumped in the chair, snoozing with his chin on his chest, Jonathan materialized. Telling Charlotte that he would meet her back at the museum in ten minutes, he quietly slipped into the network closet and got to work.

40

Charlotte watched Jonathan vanish into the network closet, checked once more to make sure the agent was deeply asleep, then hurried toward the stairs on the southeast side. As she reached the top landing, the heavy metal door whispering shut behind her, she almost screamed when someone suddenly stepped out of the shadows and blocked her way.

"Desmond!" she said, her voice echoing in the deserted stairwell. "Don't sneak up on me like that! You almost gave me a heart attack."

"Wanna drink?" he said, holding out a silver flask.

She smelled the liquor on his breath and saw his disheveled appearance. Desmond looked as if he hadn't shaved in twenty-four hours, his hair was uncombed, and there was a dried glob of what looked like mustard on the front of his black V-neck sweater. Very unlike Desmond, who was almost as obsessive about his image as his mother was. The alcohol was especially surprising.

"So, cousin," he said, "what are you doing prowling around here at this ungodly hour? I thought you'd gone home."

"I came looking for some information."

He ran a hand over his mouth. "So, dja find it?"

"Desmond," she said, closely watching his face, "do you know where my grandmother heard about that rare herb in the Caribbean? Do you know who told her about it?"

He shrugged, leaning against the wall. "The old dame and I didn't talk much."

"Do you know how Rusty Brown managed to get hired?"

He looked at her with unfocused eyes. "Who?"

"One of our production technicians. The police arrested him three hours ago."

"Oh. Him. Don't know a thing — *hic!* — about him."

"You're drunk." She started for the stairs but he caught her arm. "Not drunk enough," he said with a lopsided smile. "Do you know what's happening, Charlotte? My father is about to lose millions of dollars. In fact, I wouldn't be surprised if he went to jail for playing around with investors' money. They thought they were going to get rich on GB4204. Instead, the FDA is putting their approval on hold, so it will never pass, will never be released, and voila! My father is a convicted man." He laughed. "I kind of like the idea."

Charlotte studied him. His handsome face seemed to have collapsed, the attractive features no longer so perfect, as if he had gotten tired of trying to hold it all together. "Desmond," she said slowly, observing him for a reaction, "you've changed. What happened while I was away last year?"

"Last year?"

"I went to Europe for a month. Did something happen while I was gone?"

"Something happen? Hm, let me see, what happened. . . ." He jerked his shoulders. "Nothing I can think of. Why?"

"Are you sending me e-mails?"

"Huh?"

"Have you been sending me e-mails?"

He blinked at her. "What would I do that for?" He helped himself to a swig from the flask. "I think my father would look good in stripes, don't you?"

"I've never heard you talk this way before."

He leaned close and whispered in her ear, "That's because you haven't been listening." Releasing her arm, he stepped around and put his hand on the wall, blocking her path. "I'm going to tell you a secret."

She turned her head, the fumes were so strong.

"When I was a wee lad of fourteen, I was given to snooping. I was going through Mummy's desk one day, when I found a letter written to her from Daddy. Don't you find that odd? A spouse writing to his spouse at the same address? Anyway, it was all this 'I love you' crap and something about 'I'll always be there for you' and 'You make me feel ten feet tall.' I have no idea what *that* was all about, but I found one sentence an absolute riot. In fact, it's such a gem that I memorized it. Daddy said, and I quote, 'It's a terrible thing when a father has a total loser for a son.' "

Desmond leaned away and ran a hand through his unruly hair. Charlotte noticed sweat stains under his arms. "So whaddya think of that one? Grandmother Olivia was obsessed with having a real grandson, a *real* Barclay, as she put it. As if my father were one! Ha! Gideon was adopted, but Olivia seemed to forget that little fact. So, from the day my father was born, Olivia hammered it into her precious

Adrian that he was a Barclay and that his sole purpose on earth was to produce future Barclays. Well, it didn't happen. They got *me* instead. Ha!"

Charlotte reached for the flask. "Let me take that," she said.

But he eluded her grasp and took another long drink. "Did you know that the night Grandmother Olivia died, she called her son to her bedside, and this is what she said. She said, 'Adrian, you let me down.' A mother's last words to her son. Adrian Barclay, son of the great Gideon Barclay, didn't have the *cojones* to produce an heir."

He staggered back and bumped against the metal railing. Charlotte made a grab for him. "Des! You're going to fall down these stairs. Give me that flask."

"And then, of course, there's my mother. Now *she's* a pip."

"Don't say that. You always worshipped her, Des."

He released a loud, resounding belch. "Sometimes even the worshipper's eyes get opened."

"Something *did* happen while I was away last year. When I came back, you had changed. Mr. Sung, too. What was it, Des? What happened?"

"Ah, Mr. Sung. The great inscrutable Woodrow Sung." Desmond smothered a belch. "He handled my adoption, you know. Sung's signature is on all the papers." He took another swig from the flask, holding on to the railing as if he were on a rolling ship. "Did you know that my father and mother didn't get married out of love? They'd been living together since they were seven. Apparently my maternal grandmother dumped her daughter with the Barclays and never came back for her." Desmond frowned. "Do you think they ever did it? You know how you can't imagine your parent having sex? Well, I think in this case it's true. My mother is such a castrator, I'll bet my father never got it up once with her."

"Desmond," Charlotte said, "let me get you into a taxi. You need some sleep."

"And then of course there was the House. Capital H. Olivia was obsessed with that house." He hiccuped and wiped off his chin. "Didn't you ever think it odd that my mother was over there so much? Frankly, I preferred our own swimming pool, it was a lot newer and it was heated. That old Barclay pool had been built at the turn of the century."

"Then why did you come over so much?"

"Olivia insisted. She would come over and say, 'Margo, when was the last time you and Desmond went to the House?' How your grandmother put up with it I'll never know."

"My grandmother was a generous woman, her house was always open to friends and visitors."

"We were there every week, for Christ's sake. What was that all about?"

"We are family, Charlotte-ah. *This is their house as much as it is ours."*

He took another drink. "Christ, Olivia was obsessed about it. She would spend hours at her desk churning out letters — reams and reams of them."

"Letters? To whom, about what?"

He shrugged. "She had this godawful stationery — with a big obscene crest on it. It used to be Fiona's. I guess Olivia thought it was classy." He tried to take another drink, but the flask was empty. Tipping it upside down, he dropped it to the floor. "I always felt inferior to all of you, you know," he mumbled. "The more my mother bragged about me, the more worthless I felt. See, I wasn't really a Barclay. Well, neither were they, really, but I was" — he leaned closed and whispered — "*adopted.* I was an Outsider. Olivia had been friends with Fiona, and then Margo became Olivia's protégé. A nice tightly knit little group, I should say. And then on the other side of the street there was you and your grand-mother. The real Barclays!" Desmond threw back his head and laughed.

His laughter died after a moment, and his eyes clouded with a saturnine mood. Staring at a spot above Charlotte's head, he said quietly, "Do you know what it's like to imag-ine your father looking at you as if you were something he tracked in on his shoe?"

He lowered his gaze, focused blurry eyes on Charlotte. "Oh, I forgot. You don't know what it's like to have your fa-ther look at you at all. You never had a father, did you, Charlotte?"

"Desmond, call a taxi and go home." She started to walk past him, but his hand shot out, his fingers curling around her arm in a tight grip.

"Let me see, he was supposed to be some sort of scuba jock, wasn't he? Strange how your grandmother never had any pictures of him. You ever think about that?"

"Let me go, Des."

He leaned close again, engulfing her in bourbon fumes. "Didn't you ever wonder? About your mother, I mean? There's all this secrecy wrapped around her, like cotton wool. You know what I think? I think there was something weird about her."

She wrestled against his painful grip. "I don't have to lis-ten to this."

"No one believed for a minute that Mr. Lee fathered your mother. Did you know that? There was some kind of trial back in the thirties — it came out that Lee was impotent. So guess who your mummy's daddy was? You know what I heard?"

"Desmond —"

"I heard that when you were fifteen, you resembled your grandmother when she was that age, when Gideon first met *the* Perfect Har-mone-*ee*."

"What are you implying?"

"You disappeared that summer, for three weeks. So did my grandfather. He wouldn't tell anyone where he had been, not even his own wife, Grandmother Olivia. And you wouldn't tell *me* where *you* had been."

"It was none of your business. Besides, Gideon was my uncle."

"And *my* grandfather — your grandfather, too, if the rumors are true. I'll bet you told Braveheart where you went."

"Yes, I told Jonathan. So what?"

"So where did the great Gideon take you? He did take you somewhere, didn't he? Everyone knew that my randy old grandfather had a taste for Chinese."

"You're disgusting."

He laughed. "So, is Braveheart still here?"

"Stop calling him that!" She yanked her arm free. "And what do you have against Jonathan, anyway? He never did anything to you!"

"No, except steal you away from me."

"Desmond, you never *had* me. I told you that a long time ago. We're cousins —"

"Not really. Not flesh and blood. I'm adopted, remember?"

"It doesn't make a difference, Des. We grew up together. You're more like a brother to me. I can't feel about you that other way."

"How do you know till you've tried it?" Suddenly he was pressing his mouth to hers, forcing his tongue between her lips.

She pushed him back and slapped his face. "Desmond, go home. You're drunk." As she turned and fled down the stairs, she heard him shout, "Think about your idiot mother, Charlotte! *Think* about her!"

41

As Jonathan made his way back through the rain, he thought of another rainy night, back in Boston, when he and Charlotte had snuggled beneath the blankets, weaving a tapestry of dreams.

It was the next night that he had written the poem, right after she left from the airport. He had returned to his small apartment and sat there in the semidarkness, amid the lingering traces of Charlotte's fragrance and laughter, and composed the poem straight from his heart onto the page, changing not a single word or comma from the first line to the last.

When he had sent it off the next day to an East Coast university that annually held a prestigious poetry contest, he hadn't told Charlotte. He didn't even know why he was sending it, because he knew they wouldn't choose it; he was no poet, just a computer jock with aspirations to be an elite hacker. For an entire year he didn't tell her about it: not about the fact that his poem was chosen out of over five thousand entries, nor about the prize money he had received, nor about the fact that his poem was going to be published in a book along with the other winners. He didn't tell her any of this because he had decided to let his poem do the talking. The poem was far more eloquent than his own words could ever be.

And then the book had arrived. It was the spring of 1981. He had mailed it to her and waited the agonizing days for her response.

And then she had telephoned. . . .

"Charlotte?" he called out as he entered the museum. "Charlotte, are you here?" He went around the display cases and then looked in the office. She wasn't there. But she had left the main building ten minutes ago.

Going to the security monitor, he rapidly hit switches, bringing up scene after scene: the federal agent waking up and looking at his watch; the cafeteria, deserted; the production plant, where a janitor in coveralls was mopping the floor. But no Charlotte.

Where *was* she?

"Damn it, Charlotte," he whispered as he hit more keys, bringing up the shipping dock, the main lobby, the parking lot. "Where are you?"

He paused when he saw a figure stumbling through the rain — Desmond, without an umbrella or jacket, weaving among the parked cars. He slipped at one point, crashing against a minivan, grabbing the handle before he fell into a puddle. Then he hauled himself around and managed to make it to a black Cadillac, where he propped himself up as he fumbled in his pockets. A minute later he was behind the wheel and starting the engine.

After watching Desmond leaving the parking lot, brake lights on the whole way, Jonathan switched views on the monitor, his anxiety growing as he still saw no sign of Charlotte.

He had to get to the communications array, and then the two of them had to get out of here before Knight showed up. Where had she gone?

Going to the computer, he clicked on the e-mail icon and then *"Check host for new mail."*

Nothing.

He went back to the security monitor and hit switches until he was back in the main building, where he saw the federal agent shaking his head and looking sheepishly around. Jonathan watched the man quietly dispose of a paper napkin and Styrofoam cup, brush off his clothes, straighten his tie,

and then resume his post in front of the network closet as if
nothing had happened.

Jonathan continued his search, his worry mounting: the
packaging plant, the research lab, the control room and visitor center.

No Charlotte.

Seizing his raincoat, he began to head back out into the
storm, when the alert sounded on his laptop. He was getting
a phone call.

He hesitated for an instant, then he quickly punched a key
— with luck it was a response to calls he had sent out to various friends he still had in the Agency. But, to his surprise, it
was Adele, her soft, round face regarding him with a sad
smile. "Do you know yet when you are coming home,
Johnny? I have to send an R.S.V.P. to Buckingham Palace.
What should I say?"

The look in her eye and the tone in her voice stabbed him
to the core. He knew how much Adele had been hoping for
this royal invitation. She had worked on it for months —
Adele's father might be a lord, but he didn't have royal connections. It wasn't easy getting an invitation to the Royal
Box. Adele almost looked like a child at Christmas.

He felt wretched. Since coming back to California and
being in Charlotte's constant company, Jonathan had seen
his old demons resurface, hobgoblins that had once plagued
him night and day with nightmares and bouts of guilt that he
had worked hard to suppress. They were vanquishing him
again. He knew that the next time he fell asleep, the nightmare would be back — the dream that was in fact a memory
of an unbearable reality. The Amsterdam Eight, two lying in
unnatural positions, blood pooling around their bodies. The
third — Jonathan couldn't even think of the third.

Adele had married him because she thought he was a hero.
But Jonathan knew he was no hero. Adele, Quentin, the
NSA, even the president of the United States, who had given

him a special commendation for bringing down the notorious hacker gang, were wrong. Jonathan Sutherland was a fraud, and he was the only one who knew it.

"I'll have some news for you in a few hours," he said now, wondering if, now that the demons were loose, he was ever going to find peace again.

"Shall I accept the invitation?" Adele said.

He hesitated for only a fraction of a second before saying, "Of course you must accept it. We'll go, naturally." But she had seen the hesitation. And in the next moment something seemed to fall behind her eyes, like wings gracefully collapsing.

"Adele —" he began, but then something stopped him, nailing him to the spot as he stared at the screen. A sound in the background.

"I have to ring off, darling," she said quickly, glancing over her shoulder. "The gardener is here with a million questions. I'll ring you later. Be careful. Love you."

42

Charlotte rushed inside the museum and went straight to where an enormous piece of furniture stood by itself under a gentle spotlight and roped off by three velvet cords. *"The Elaborate Art of Chinoiserie,"* the placard read. And underneath: *"Secreatary, circa 1815."* It had stood in the library of her grandmother's house for as long as she could remember, and then Grandmother had had it shipped down for her museum.

Charlotte unhooked one of the velvet ropes and stepped onto the small square of gray carpeting.

Taller than a person, the black lacquer desk cabinet was

covered in stunning gold-and-bronze motifs and made up of myriad drawers and cubbyholes, with the fold-down desk laid out with antique pens, blotter, old-fashioned spectacles. The cubbies held stationery, and one of the drawers was open to reveal sticks of sealing wax and string.

Desmond had said Olivia had an obsession about something, that she had spent hours writing letters.

Charlotte reached up and pulled down a bundle of envelopes bearing an ornate crest and tied together with a ribbon. She had always thought they were just a prop. But now she saw that the letters were real.

She quickly tucked them into her leather tote, along with everything else she had gathered up that she thought important, including the antique diary she had found in one of the kitchenette drawers. And then she saw the note from Jonathan: "One last adjustment to make at the main outdoor communications array. I'll meet you at my car."

His gear was gone; he had taken everything with him, even his raincoat. But there was his jacket, still draped over the chair. He had clearly left in such haste that he had forgotten it. Charlotte picked it up and folded it over her arm. His wallet slipped out, falling open when it hit the floor. As she picked it up, Charlotte saw a piece of paper sticking out from the billfold compartment. A familiar symbol caught her eye: the moon with a cat face in it.

Pulling it out, she saw that it was a sheet of notepaper, folded several times, addressed to Jonathan. Charlotte recognized the personal stationery — Naomi's.

"My dear friend," she had written. "It's been such a long time since we last saw each other. I wanted you to know of my change of address. We mustn't lose touch! Peace and love, Naomi."

Charlotte looked at the date. Three years ago.

Jonathan knew Naomi.

Hearing voices, she turned and saw on the security monitor Valerius Knight and his men stepping out of two dark sedans in front of Harmony's corporate headquarters. Knight was giving his men instructions: to find and detain Charlotte Lee.

She was about to be arrested.

Looking at the note in her hand — Jonathan knew Naomi, he had lied to her, possibly even betrayed her — she felt a rare anger surge through her. It blew like the fireball at Naomi's house, and raged like the inferno that had destroyed the Chalk Hill Animal Lab.

How could he not have told her? Why the secrecy? Why all the questions about Naomi when in fact *he already knew her?*

Charlotte blindly threw the note down. Jonathan could wait for her at his car until he dropped. Let him explain her disappearance to Knight. Charlotte was on her own, as she had always been, relying only on herself.

Damn you, Johnny, for letting me down.

She started to leave, when the hail sounded on the computer. She wanted to put her fist through the monitor. Instead she paused long enough to recognize what she was looking at: a video transmission of a tall black metal box. It was attached to a beige cinderblock wall, with wires entering at the top and emerging from the bottom.

The communications array panel.

Frowning, she approached the monitor. Was Jonathan transmitting this?

The lens zoomed in. Someone was there, operating the camera!

And then she saw what she was obviously meant to see: a small box on top of the panel, higher than a man's height, and back toward the wall, so that it was out of sight of anyone approaching. The small box was green, with red-and-blue wires protruding. A red light flashed.

Text appeared across the bottom of the screen, scrolling

like the Times Square marquee: *Smaller than the one that blew up Naomi's house but just as effective. All he has to do is open the door* . . .

A bomb.

"My God," she whispered. "Jonathan!"

He hadn't gotten there yet. She had to warn him. But how? Hitting buttons on the security panel, she scanned view after view of the whole park — offices, doorways, corridors, parking areas —

There he was! She recognized the spot as being one of the employee picnic areas, where they ate lunch or dinner outdoors. Jonathan was talking to a man wearing a Harmony Biotech security uniform. Jonathan was shrugging and shaking his head as if he was being questioned. Charlotte wondered if Knight had called ahead and instructed her own security staff to search for her.

She tried to think. The only way to warn Jonathan was to be at the communications panel before he got there. But where was it? There were several, serving each of the various buildings of the sprawling facility.

He said he had gone to the main trunk.

She quickly looked around the office, but Jonathan had taken the blueprints with him. Trying to picture the plans as they had lain spread out on the desk, with Jonathan marking various spots, tracing a line with his pen from the museum to —

It was behind the warehouse.

Without further thought — forgetting the letter from Naomi and her anger, and ignoring the threat of being arrested by Valerius Knight — she ran out into the storm, her leather tote bag slung over her shoulder, her thoughts drumming in time with her heavy footsteps: *Wait, Jonathan, wait, wait.* . . .

There were federal agents everywhere, but she had the advantage of being familiar with the grounds. She knew the hidden pathways and the unexpected open spaces landscaped with boulders and trees and benches. Sticking to the covered walkways as much as she could, pausing frequently to be sure she wasn't seen, she hurried as fast as she could to the communications panel.

When she flew around the corner of the building that housed the cafeteria, lunchrooms, and employee recreation rooms, Charlotte collided with a solid object that nearly sent her flying off her feet. A large fist grabbed her arm and steadied her.

"Ms. Lee!" Valerius Knight said. "Here you are! I have been looking for you."

"Please," she said breathlessly, "let me go. Jonathan Sutherland is in trouble."

"Ms. Lee, I have a warrant for your arrest —"

"You don't understand," she said, yanking her hand free. "He's about to be seriously hurt, probably killed! You've got to help me."

"All I've *got* to do, Ms. Lee, is take you in on charges of murder —"

"Oh for God's sake, Yes, I knew the first two victims, I've already told you that."

"And you also knew the third. Quite a coincidence, don't you think?"

"You can't arrest me on coincidence, Agent Knight."

"As it happens, we have a bit more than coincidence to go by. In the third victim's home we found a letter, written on your stationery, signed by you."

"What!"

"It's your signature all right, we had it checked out. The letter offers a free sample of Bliss, which was supposedly enclosed with the letter."

"That doesn't mean I sent it."

"Ms. Lee, where were you ten days ago?"

"What does that have to do with anything?"

"On the ninth of this month, where were you?"

"I was up in northern California, inspecting one of our farms. Agent Knight, we have to find Jonathan."

"The one near Gilroy?"

She stopped. "Yes."

"Ms. Lee, the envelope that contained that letter and the tainted Bliss bears a Gilroy postmark, dated the ninth."

Her stomach did a somersault. "But I've been a target, too! Do you think I staged that accident with my garage door?"

"Well," he said as he produced a pair of handcuffs from under his trench coat. "I do find it interesting, Ms. Lee, that this one night you chose to drive your other car. That certainly was lucky for you, wasn't it?"

Charlotte's heart raced at the sight of the handcuffs. "Listen," she tried to say in a reasonable tone, "you've got to believe me. Jonathan is in danger! A bomb is about to go off!"

"I recall you saying something similar when you insisted your housekeeper was being poisoned." He took hold of her wrist and snapped one handcuff around it.

"Do you really think I could kill three people and try to murder my best friend?"

He reached for her other hand. "I'd say a person who could cold-bloodedly bludgeon a defenseless dog to death is capable of anything. What was it you so eloquently said? 'If this is the only way we can get ourselves heard, then this is what we will do.'"

Something inside her snapped. Before Knight could get the second handcuff on her, Charlotte twisted away from him and then back, swinging her heavily laden tote bag with all her might, slamming it square into the startled agent's face. Knight flew back, stumbled over a curb, and crashed back against a wall. Charlotte heard a crack as his skull met concrete block.

She stared at the agent's crumpled body for a fraction of a second, then she bolted.

The quickest way to the communications panel was through the processing plant. She would avoid the agents swarming over the grounds and reach Jonathan by way of the maintenance road.

When she arrived at the large building, she slipped under the yellow police tape, cautiously pushed open the door, and looked in. The outer corridor was deserted. Ignoring the racks of paper coveralls and hats, she delivered herself to the silent laboratory.

At the other end, she hurried through the visitor lobby, down another corridor, and into the control booth of the main processing plant. Just down some steps and a few yards was the exit. From there it was a short distance to the communications panel.

Before she could reach the door, she heard a sound behind her. She started to turn. A hand suddenly clamped over her mouth. Charlotte struggled. And then she recognized a smell: chloroform.

No!

She saw the white handkerchief; the fumes stung her eyes. She held her breath as she struggled against her attacker's strong hold. Her lungs felt as if they were going to burst. Finally she had to open her mouth. She gasped and gulped in air.

And then darkness swallowed her.

43

The nausea was the first thing she noticed. And then the throbbing in her skull. As she struggled back to consciousness, Charlotte tried to gather together the pieces of her shattered memory.

Where was she? Why did she feel so sick? And why couldn't she move?

Sensations began to return: something hard beneath her back, sharp lights overhead, pain in her wrists. She opened her eyes to see the vast ceiling of the packaging plant, with its catwalks, spotlights, ducts. She realized she was on her back, her arms stretched over her head, pinned down. Across her back she felt a sharp metal edge digging into her, as if she hung over the side of a steel table. Her buttocks and legs swung free. She couldn't feel the floor.

When she rolled her head to the left, she saw a metal panel with wires and cables. She looked to the right. It took a moment for her eyes to focus, and when they did, she realized in dawning horror where she was.

She was handcuffed to the Computerized Ampoule Measured Dosing System — the very fluid injection and package delivery system she had installed recently and was so proud of and which she had demonstrated to Jonathan only a few hours earlier. She was just a few feet from the robotic arm, her body lying on the belt where bottles of empty, open-topped ampoules were lined up, ready to be filled and sealed.

But why was she here? And who had attacked her?

She suddenly heard a sound that startled her. A motor turning on. Rolling her head to the right again, she saw the robotic arm of the liquid delivery system come to life. It started to move.

She watched in bewilderment as the assembly began its three-step procedure, starting with the needles shooting down into the ampoules and squirting fluid. She instantly picked up the fragrance of rose oil. Then the arm moved, the needles withdrew, and three flames burst out, heating the tops of the ampoules. The flames shut off and down swung three savage-looking pincers, closing the molten glass and cutting off the tops of the vials, sealing them.

The arm then shifted to the left.

And continued to come her way.

Charlotte realized then what was happening, and what was the intent of her assailant. With her hands pinned over her head, handcuffed together and hooked over what felt like a metal post, her lower body swinging free, her feet not touching the floor, it was impossible to free herself, or even to move. The weight of her body kept her stretched across the belt, in the path of the oncoming robotic arm.

Three needles, three flames, three pincers.

Her head lay directly in its path.

"Help," she said. Louder: "Help!"

The motor was quiet; she could hear her voice echo over it, but the processing plant had been constructed with extra insulation so that the various machines and conveyors would not disturb this peaceful Palm Springs neighborhood. Not only would no one hear the CAMDS in operation, Charlotte knew they wouldn't hear her calls for help, either.

Nonetheless, she called out. "Help! Oh God, help!"

Three needles, rose oil injected into the ampoules; then hot flame melting the glass; then sharp, heavy pincers — *pinch, snap*.

The robotic arm shifted to the left.

No, she thought. This could not be happening. She frantically tried to free her hands. But she couldn't get purchase, she hung as helplessly as a rag doll. If only she could reach the floor. But when she tried to stretch her legs, the sharp edge of the conveyor gouged into her spine until she thought it would snap. The only thing she could move was her head, and that only from side to side. She had a choice: either look away or watch the liquid injection system inch slowly and unstoppably toward her.

Her eyes grew wide with terror as she saw the needles shoot down again, with such ferocity, she thought now. Had they always looked so lethal? When she had proudly watched her new acquisition in action, Charlotte had beamed

at such efficiency. The system could produce hundreds of
vials in an hour, each containing precious rose oil that was
shipped all over the world.

Now she saw three sharp spears shoot down, like something from a horror film, ejaculating a sweet-smelling fragrance with the lethality of a hypodermic filled with poison.

And then the flames, shooting downward like the needles,
searing, torching the delicate glass until it folded in on itself,
lifeless, malleable.

Finally the pincers. Snap! Spit! Retract! Perhaps the most
brutal step of all.

Coming straight toward her face.

But first they would go through her arm, which was protected only by the flimsy sleeve of her white blouse.

When had she removed her suit jacket? She hadn't. She
was sure she had had her jacket on when she was on her way
to warn Jonathan about the bomb. Had her assailant removed
it to make her more vulnerable?

Jonathan? Oh God. The bomb. Had it already gone off?
Was he dead? Was she about to join him, all their efforts for
nothing as she died in this hideous, ignoble way?

A sob escaped her throat. Please don't let Jonathan be
dead.

The assembly shifted closer. Three more ampoules were
penetrated, filled, seared, and sealed.

She felt perspiration break out on her forehead. She struggled with her hands, as the handcuffs tore into the tender skin
at her wrists. The metal edge of the conveyor dug into her
back.

"Help!" she screamed, and heard her voice echo mock-
ingly off the high ceiling and walls. "*Help!*"

Six ampoules left.

The rose fragrance was overpowering, sickening. Charlotte could almost feel the heat from the flames. She heard
the snap of the pincers sealing the glass.

First it would go through her arm — needles injecting rose oil. Then the flames would descend. Would they set her blouse on fire? And the pincers, would they seize only fabric or would they find the tender flesh on the underside of her arm?

"Oh God," she cried out.

The sobs came freely now, as she frantically worked to free her hands, her legs kicking uselessly in the air.

Three ampoules left.

And if she survived the attack on her arm? Her eyes would be the next target. First the needles — no, she couldn't survive that. Rose oil injected directly into her brain. Would she remain conscious long enough to feel the flames scorch her eyes? Would she feel the pincers as they descended —

"Help! Please, oh God —"

No ampoules left.

She watched in horror as the assembly regrouped, shifted to the left, and began the cycle. First the needles would shoot down with such force that she knew they would strike bone. At this proximity she could read the fine print on the side of the casing: *Manufactured in the United States, Kansas City, Mo.*

Oh God oh God oh God oh God oh God.

She heard the subtle shifting of delicate mechanisms deep in its machinery, old-fashioned gears and cogs and wheels turning at the command of impersonal computer code, a robot that didn't know the difference between a glass ampoule and human flesh.

Sweat ran into her eyes as she heard the final click that meant the sequence had begun.

The needles first —

She squeezed her eyes shut tight. *Jonathan!*

And she braced herself for the pain.

She waited.

She opened her eyes. The assemblage hadn't moved.

And then she heard the silence. Someone had shut it down.

In the next instant she felt hands on her wrists, lifting them up and freeing them from the post. Then she felt arms go around her waist as she was lifted up from the conveyor, her legs numb. She threw her arms over his head, held on to him as she cried.

He ran with her, away from the metallic monster that had been about to destroy her, out of the echoing plant, into the rain and into the night.

44

"You're alive," she sobbed as Jonathan gently placed her in the passenger seat of his car.

She saw him hurry around to the driver's side. The door opened and he jumped in on a gust of cold, wet air.

He paused before starting the motor. "Christ, Charlie," he said, smoothing the hair back from her forehead. "Are you all right?"

Except for pains in her back and shoulders and wrists, she was all right. During their flight from the processing plant to where he had hidden his car, through the cold rain and exhilarating fresh air, Charlotte had felt her head clear and her terror subside into fury. Rage, she knew, had the capacity to vitalize. But she felt unbelievably weak, as though her bones had melted.

"Who did it to you, Charlie?"

She regarded her raw, skinless wrists, still shackled in the handcuffs. "I don't know. I didn't see him."

"Him?"

"I think it was a man. I'm not sure. Thank God you shut the machine off in time. One more second —"

"But I didn't."

"You must have!"

"I got there just as the machine stopped. I didn't do it, Charlotte. I didn't have time."

She rubbed her forehead and pressed her fingers to her eyes. "Did the killer just want to scare me?"

"Or maybe it was someone else who stopped the machinery, someone who didn't want to get involved."

"Jonathan," she said, suddenly remembering. "Agent Knight, I hit him —"

"He's all right. You didn't kill him. I saw him with an ice pack on his head and not in a good mood."

"There was a bomb on the array panel —"

He started the engine. "I know, I saw it. Rather amateurish job. I was able to disarm it with one snip. We'd better get out of here."

As the car squealed out of the space, Charlotte looked ahead into the rain, and then at Jonathan. Now that the terror was subsiding and her brain was clearing, other memories returned. She thought of the note she had found in his wallet. "You know Naomi, don't you?" she said.

He didn't look at her. "Yes," he said as the car sped out of the lot, "I do."

45

1942 — San Franscisco, California

"I'm sorry, Mrs. Lee, but I am going to have to ask you to move out."

As I surveyed the broken glass on my living room floor,

caused by a rock that had been thrown through our window, I wondered if the whole world had gone insane.

War on all continents, and now here in the city, where hooligans smashed the windows of people with different-shaped eyes.

"If it was up to me," my landlord continued apologetically, "well, I mean, some of my best friends are Chinese. But the neighbors are complaining. It makes them afraid that they'll be targets, too."

"We will move out, Mr. Klein," I said. "My daughter and I do not stay where we are not welcome."

And so once again I was without a home.

When I sold our house in Oakland after Mr. Lee died, I returned to San Francisco, where I found I could not purchase a home, even though I was an American citizen, because I was a woman without a husband, and the law required husbands' signatures. Gideon offered to buy a house for me, but he had done enough favors for me over the years, and I wished to remain independent. I was content to lease, I told him, thinking it would be the same. I had not anticipated a world war, I had not seen the coming storm that would soon disrupt my life and so many others. I had not known the hatred that blind prejudice could generate.

Chinese who lived outside of Chinatown had put signs on their houses: "Not Japanese, We Chinese." Some even wore signs on their backs to prevent being accosted in the streets. I had no such signs, and so we were accused of being the enemy.

But we shared that enemy. When I read about the fall of Singapore and all the Chinese being rounded up, I recalled that day when I was sixteen and a dignified gentleman had stopped on the sidewalk to give us money. My grandfather. Had he managed to escape before the Japanese invaded? And the rest of my mother's family in the big house on Peacock Lane — Golden Elegance and Summer Dawn, wives of my mother's two brothers, First Young Master and Second Young Master, and her half sisters, Moon Orchid and Moon Cassia? Had they escaped, or did they become victims of war?

At my factory, I had comforted workers whose female relatives had been raped and murdered by Japanese soldiers. I had organized events to raise funds for United China Relief. I had sent my medicines to the war-torn areas of China. I had urged my workers to boycott Japanese goods. And then my living room window was shattered by a rock wrapped in a note that said, "Filthy Japanese."

It was not going to be easy, I knew, to find a place for me and my daughter to live.

"I don't know where they will be sending me," Gideon had told me the night he enlisted. "Because of the nature of what I'll be doing — building bridges and roads — it's classified. But when I get there, the army will inform my wife and mother. So if you need me, go to them, Harmony, and they will tell you where I can be reached."

I knew I could not go to Olivia; she would not tell me where Gideon was stationed. I also suspected Fiona would not help me. But I had to think of Iris. She was thirteen now and had to be watched constantly. She had blossomed into a beautiful girl who drew the stares of men and boys wherever she went. Iris did not know about danger, about men. She was still locked inside her prison; she had never learned to speak; she existed in a world of her own.

"Have you thought of putting her in an institution?" Gideon had asked one day when we were going over the books for Harmony-Barclay Ltd. But I could hear in his voice that he didn't mean it. He loved Iris as much as I did, and couldn't bear to have her locked away. But he was worried, too, as she approached young womanhood. He knew how men would look at her, how they would try to take advantage of her.

I kept Iris with me at all times wherever I went. She was a familiar sight at the factory in Daly City, where the workers fussed over her and gave her sweets. She traveled with me when I visited herbals shops and chemists and local farms where I purchased some of my herbs. She went with me to the movies, although we usually left in the middle because she could not sit still; we listened to the radio together at night and although I knew she did not understand, she laughed at Jack Benny and "Amos 'n' Andy."

I needed to find a safe, permanent home for my daughter.

I still had my father's letter, in which he told my mother that he was going home to get a divorce. I was sorry that Mrs. Barclay would have to see that part, but in order to show her proof that Iris was her husband's granddaughter, she would have to read the whole letter. If she would not be willing to help *me*, surely she would want to do something for Richard's descendant.

I stood again between those magnificent columns, but I felt more assured this time than I had when I was nineteen and had come here to ask for my father's name. I had my daughter to think of now.

"I wish to see Mrs. Barclay, please," I said to the maid who answered the door.

She led me inside, through the grand entry I remembered from six years before, the last time I was here, during my battle with Red Dragon. But the interior had changed. Gone was the heavy Victorian furniture and flowered wallpaper. There was space here now, and light.

I was taken to the downstairs library, where I saw that the tufted sofas had been removed, and the busy writing desks. Now the room was sparsely furnished with aluminum chairs and new tables made of plastic. The only clutter was blueprints pinned to the pale yellow wallpaper, showing where walls were going to be removed and added, how the floor plan was going to change. There were large books of fabric samples, and piles of carpet and drapery samples, and as I walked through the door, Olivia was holding up a swatch of pale pink satin and saying, "What do you think, Margo dear?"

They could have been mother and daughter. Margo, at thirteen, had grown tall and reedy. Her hair was the same pale yellow as Olivia's and was worn in a matching pageboy. Both wore calf-length straight skirts and sweaters, both watched me with round blue eyes.

Thirteen-year-old Adrian was in the library as well, lying on his stomach and flipping through a magazine. He looked up as Iris and I entered, and I saw him exchange a glance with Margo. When Olivia said, "What can I do for you?" in a tone that indicated I had interrupted something important, I saw Margo make a quick gesture that sent Adrian into giggles: she put her fingers to her temples and pulled her eyes back.

"I came to see Mrs. Barclay," I said. "Gideon's mother."

"Fiona isn't to be disturbed. She isn't well and can't receive visitors." Olivia's eyes slid to Iris and remained there for a moment. Although my daughter could be taken for Chinese, the American influence was evident in her features. I wondered if Olivia was searching for signs of Gideon. I wondered if she found them.

"The maid will show you out," she said, and returned to her drapery samples.

But I remembered where Fiona's bedroom suite was from fifteen years before, so I took my daughter's hand, led her from the library and up the grand stairway.

Up here, I saw that the Victorian influence remained. And when the maid led me into the room and I saw Gideon's mother, and the frail state of her health, I realized how Olivia had gotten away with the changes she was making. Fiona Barclay did not go downstairs. She did not know what her daughter-in-law was doing, that Olivia was gradually moving Fiona's furniture out of the house, and with it, Fiona's spirit.

Fiona Barclay was sitting in a chair beside the window, gazing out at the Bay. She was sixty years old but she looked eighty.

"Mrs. Barclay," I said, wondering if the lifelong imbalance in her lungs was taking its toll at last.

She turned to me. "You," she said, "go away."

"I need your help, Mrs. Barclay. I need to know where Gideon is stationed."

"You were mistaken if you thought I would help you."

"Why do you despise me so?"

"Because you came between me and my son."

"I didn't marry him."

"All the same, the damage was done. When he returned from Panama fourteen years ago, on the day of your wedding, he said terrible things to me. He accused me of turning you against him. My son and I have been strangers ever since."

This was when I should have brought out my father's letter and shown her the proof. But this was also when I noticed the bluish tinge to Fiona's lips and fingernails, and I knew she had a failing heart and did not have long to live. So I left the letter in my purse and decided to find out where Gideon was through other means.

As I started to go, I saw her eyes shift to Iris. "What's wrong with the child?" Fiona said. "Is she backward?"

Before I could respond, Mrs. Barclay pulled herself out of her chair and, with the help of her cane, moved laboriously to an ornately carved armoire of dark, heavy wood. Opening the glass doors, she reached inside and brought out a small, square wooden box with inlaid marquetry. As she walked with it, I heard something rattle inside.

To my surprise, she tried to hand it to Iris. Of course my

daughter didn't see it, or if she did, she didn't know she was supposed to take it.

Mrs. Barclay rattled the box in front of Iris's face, and when she had her momentary attention, she did a curious thing. Holding the box up for Iris to see, keeping it before her wandering eyes, Fiona took the little box between her hands and seemed to move one of its sides.

I realized what it was: a puzzle box. They were a Japanese invention and were sold all over Chinatown, but I had never tried to work one before.

I was about to assure Mrs. Barclay that my daughter would have no idea what to do with a puzzle box, when all of a sudden Iris's eyes caught and focused on the box. Fiona had slid open a second panel, just a fraction of an inch, and now her fingers were pressing down on the other side of the box and a third panel moved. Then she slid all three panels back to their original positions, in the order they had been opened, so that the box was a single, seamless piece again.

Immediately Iris seized the box, turned it over and over in her hands, and, to my astonishment, began swiftly and with ease to slide the three panels open in the right order, as if she had worked that box a hundred times, and then, to my further astonishment, continued on — panel number four, number five, six, seven — not hesitating as she pushed one way and then another, not stopping to examine the wood, to plan ahead. Her hands and fingers flew as if they had minds of their own until, before my startled eyes, she had the box all the way open, the lid pushed back, revealing a piece of candy.

I was speechless, I had never seen Iris sit so still for so long; I had also never seen her eyes remain on one object for such a length of time. I had never seen her do anything, least of all open a puzzle box.

"The girl can keep the box," Fiona said as she sank back into her chair. "And now I shall have to ask you and your daughter to leave. I am very tired. I am sorry that I cannot help you."

"Look at this!" Mrs. Fong thrust a jar at me.

I looked up from my desk and frowned at the greenish substance. "What is it?"

"It supposed to be Beautiful Intelligence Balm, that what! Mrs. Lee, we got to nip this in the butt. This no good." Mrs. Fong was one of my inspectors, a perfectionist who took her job very seriously. This was the third time within as many days that she had brought a defective product to my attention.

"Sloppy work," she said. "*They* don't care." She nodded in the direction of the main factory building, where work was going on around the clock, now that the war had increased the demand for medicines. "They get paid. They go home. They don't care." *They* being the three hundred people I now employed at Perfect Harmony Company.

The sight of a ruined batch of Beautiful Intelligence Balm distressed me. If it weren't for Mrs. Fong, this might have been shipped, and who knew what harm it might have done to an unsuspecting customer?

I left my desk and went to the Chinese lacquer sideboard that stood beneath my window. Here I had an electric hotplate, a tea kettle, three red earthenware teapots from Yixing, and a variety of teas, each to suit a required need. My need today was to calm my floating *yang* energy. I had been suffering from insomnia and anxiety, for Iris and I still had nowhere to live. Those landlords who would rent to us had houses in bad luck areas or even dangerous neighborhoods. Good luck places in the city, where positive *chi* flowed and the address numbers were filled with luck, were also places where whites did not welcome Chinese.

As I poured a cup of tea and dropped into it two capsules of Bliss, I looked out over the compound of Perfect Harmony Company and I wondered: was my company becoming so big that I was losing control over it? Golden Lotus Wine and Ten Thousand Yang were selling so well all over Asia that our offices could hardly keep up with the demand. The two remedies had become cure-alls among the poor, and were being used for first aid in war regions. Here at home, medical supplies were low because everything was being funneled into the war effort, and so more and more non-Chinese were venturing into the herbal shops, looking for home remedies. When I had seen the clouds of war gathering, I began to stockpile large reserves of imported ingredients, so that when the Japanese attack on Pearl Harbor shut down all commercial shipping to and from Asia, my warehouses were full. Production at my factory had never been so high.

And, despite the conveyor belt and new copper vats, every stage of manufacture was still done by hand, such as the jar of balm Mrs. Fong had brought to me — that single jar had gone through over a dozen stages before it was ready for the shop. Where, along the way, had it been corrupted?

The compounds were made in enormous vats and then dispensed into jars and allowed to cool and solidify. These were then taken to the long workbenches where women capped the jars, after which another group of women labeled them. The next stage involved wrapping the jar into a leaflet of warnings and instructions for use of the medicine, and, finally, a colorful blue-and-silver-willow wrapper was rolled around it. A seal resembling a postage stamp, bearing the date and lot number of the compound, secured the final wrapper.

And that was for just one jar of Beautiful Intelligence Balm. Perfect Harmony Company also produced pills, poultices, teas, elixirs, ointments, tonics, powders, fragrant oils, and healthful spices for cooking. How could I possibly oversee every step of every operation?

I sipped my tea and tasted its soothing flavor. Was the whole world filled with bad luck? Was there any good luck left?

Yes, there was, for I saw at that moment, reflected in the windowpane, the image of my daughter as she sat quietly in the corner of my office, working out a new puzzle box. I would never forget how still her head had been that first time, when she had worked Mrs. Barclay's puzzle box, how at rest she had seemed as her eyes had focused, for the first time in her life, on one thing for a long time. After that I bought her more boxes, as many as I could find — although they were growing scarce, since they were made in Japan — for they seemed to bring her such delight, as though her mind were finally at rest, all its wandering components working together in harmony at last.

She was a marvel to everyone. I could not solve the simplest puzzle box, not even one that had only eight moves. Mr. Winkler, my company accountant and a man proud of his sharp mind, had taken all day to finally solve what Iris could do in minutes. I had taken her to another specialist, who confirmed that somewhere in my daughter's brain there existed what might possibly be a brilliant intellect, but that it was hampered by an unknown handicap that perhaps might never be found.

I set my tea down and finally looked at Mrs. Fong. "Let us go see," I said.

Leaving Iris in the care of my secretary, a capable, middle-aged woman had grown children and who was very fond of my daughter, I accompanied Mrs. Fong to the large, barn-like structure where Beautiful Intelligence Balm was manufactured. As soon as we stepped inside, the din assailed my ears, starting at one end of the vast room, where workers noisily filled jars from steel cauldrons filled with liquid balm, to the workbenches in the center where rows of women laughed and talked as their nimble fingers sorted, organized, and capped the jars, the sound of rattling glass mingling with their voices. Thousands of jars were being capped and labeled as workers moved quickly among the tables, picking up and depositing, calling out, the air filled with the smell of glue prepared from rice flour, and cigarette smoke from women in the corners taking a break, and the pungent aroma of tea and steamed noodles.

Gideon had once teasingly described my factory as an insane asylum. He tried to persuade me to "Westernize." But I visited a modern pharmaceutical plant and I was appalled by what I saw. Where was the *feng shui?* Where was the incense, and the prayers to the proper spirits? Where was the care taken to prepare herbs only on propitious days? That lab that I visited manufactured its compounds every day without first conferring with a soothsayer to see if that day were auspicious. Those Western scientists mixed good luck with bad, they allowed water to run in sinks so that their profits drained away, the walls were white and the lights were too bright, so there was too much *yang*, no balance.

No, I would not modernize. Not even for my beloved Gideon.

With Mrs. Fong accompanying me, I inspected the vats and found an inconsistency in the formula from one batch to another. I also found women smoking at their work stations, which was forbidden. Lunches were also being consumed, so that egg rolls and bean sprouts shared space with Bliss and Golden Lotus Wine.

Mrs. Fong was right. The workers didn't care.

We retreated to the relative quiet of the central yard, where trucks pulled in and out all day long, bringing in fresh herbs and carrying out my medicines.

"What we do?" Mrs. Fong said, clearly upset. Loyal employee that she was, she took personal responsibility for the sloppy behavior of those under her.

"I suppose we shall have to hire more supervisors," I said, although I was not sure it would help. If a hundred employees were making sloppy mistakes, I would need a hundred supervisors to watch them.

"Punish the slackers," Mrs. Fong said.

Then that would mean firing a hundred workers.

"Have everyone watch everyone else," Mrs. Fong said.

That would mean a hundred spies.

I could not think of a solution to the problem.

"May I make a suggestion?"

Mrs. Fong spun around. "Who you? How you get in here?"

I looked around her and saw a young man standing behind us.

"I think perhaps I can help," he said, so softly spoken that we could hardly hear him. The young Chinese held his hat in his hands as he stepped forward, and in the sunlight I saw two things: that his clothes were clean but shabby, and that he walked with a limp.

He also looked familiar.

"You get out," Mrs. Fong said. "We got guards here." Mrs. Fong had been with me since our days behind Mr. Huang's warehouse on Grant Street.

"How can you help?" I said to the young man, who appeared to be in his early twenties.

"Offer your products free of charge to your employees for their personal or family use."

"What!" Mrs. Fong cried. "You crazy? Reward those slackers?"

"The products are to be distributed," he said, "upon request at a central supply. When the employees go to pick up their free supply, they will not know which batch they are going to receive, one they had personally worked on or another."

Mrs. Fong sucked on her lower lip and said, "Hmmm."

"The employees might not care about strangers," the young man added, "but they do care about themselves and their families."

I knew why he had come. "Do you need a job?" I asked.

"No one will hire Chinese. Not even Chinese with a law

degree from Stanford," he said modestly. "I remembered you. I thought you might help me."

"Why you limp?" Mrs. Fong said.

"I was wounded. I have my army discharge papers."

"*Aii-yah!*" she cried, and I saw Mrs. Fong's maternal instincts suddenly rise up.

And then I remembered him from the long days during the trial, when he had sat quietly behind his father, the Dragon. I recalled that he had an unusual name, Woodrow, for a president of the United States. "I would think you would not want to work for me," I said with caution.

"What my father did was wrong. He dishonored our family. I am his only son. It is up to me to restore honor to our name."

I believed him.

While I left Mrs. Fong to take young Mr. Sung around the plant, I returned to my office, where a formidable amount of paperwork awaited me, as well as rental listings, and messages from the few real estate agents who were willing to help a Chinese find a home. When I stepped inside and saw Gideon standing there, so handsome in his uniform, my heart nearly burst with joy.

I took him into my arms, and he took me into his; we held each other for a very long moment, not speaking, letting our hearts do the communicating. When he finally drew back, he said, "My mother has passed away."

I hadn't known.

"The will is to be read tomorrow. Mr. Winterborn says you are mentioned. I imagine Mother left you your father's ring."

I went the next day to the big mansion on the hill, taking Iris with me, so that there were seven of us gathered that afternoon in the study, which was now half Victorian, half Danish modern: my daughter and myself, Gideon and Olivia, and their son, Adrian, and Margo.

I had difficulty keeping Iris still. She seemed agitated. I wondered if perhaps she remembered coming to this house weeks ago. When she reached out and started to grab for a vase, Olivia snapped, "Don't touch that!"

I felt Olivia's rancor at our presence as strongly as the solid chair beneath me. She did not trouble to disguise her resentment. She had lived in that house for fourteen years, her son had been born there, she was mistress of it at last and wanted me to leave.

While the fortune and family business went to Gideon and Olivia, Fiona Barclay left Richard Barclay's ring to me, as Gideon has surmised. She also left the house, and all its contents, to me.

The night before Gideon was to set sail for the Pacific, where a terrible war was waging, he came to me and said, "Olivia and the children will move out right away. You can take over the house as soon as you want."

"There is room for all of us."

He shook his head. "I could not live in the same house with you, Harmony. It would be more than I could bear. And besides, Olivia won't live there. She wanted to contest the will, but I said no. The house *is* rightly yours, Harmony."

"But it's yours, too," I protested.

"No, it isn't. It was Richard Barclay's and you are his flesh and blood." He smiled sadly. "It's ironic in a way. We are Barclays and yet have not a drop of Barclay in us. While you, Harmony and Iris Lee, are the only true Barclays."

We all went to the dock to see him off, where there were other wives and mothers, and families with tears on their cheeks. We all held the same thought in our hearts: Bring him back safely to me.

I watched Gideon embrace and kiss Olivia, and then hug

thirteen-year-old Adrian. He even hugged thirteen-year-old Margo, who impulsively threw her arms around his neck and kissed him on the cheek. He then took my hand, and looked for a long moment into my eyes, silently communicating his love. He tired to do the same with Iris, but her head was not still, and she looked this way and that, up and down.

Recalling how, for a few minutes that day in Fiona's bedroom, my daughter's eyes were still and her mind focused, I can only imagine what had gone through Fiona's heart as she watched my daughter swiftly open the puzzle box. "Although I suspected you were indeed Richard's child," she had written in the letter Mr. Winterborn gave me after the reading of the will,

I was never certain. But when I saw your daughter, I saw the truth. Richard's sister was the same way. It's a trait that runs in the family. So you *are* Richard Barclay's daughter. And as I loved him with all my heart, and continue to do so to this day, then I pledge to you that your birthright — his home, his name — will be yours. And I ask your forgiveness, and God's, for the way I have treated you.

When Gideon's ship was finally heading out of the Bay, Olivia turned to me and said, "My son and Margo and I will be out of the house tonight."

"There is no hurry," I said. "Please stay, at least until Gideon returns."

But she looked at me with a hard eye and said in a tone that left no doubt as to her feelings: "That house is mine. It belongs to me and my son. I intend to have it back. And if it's the last thing I do, I am going to see to it that you will wish you had never come to this country."

46

4:00 A.M. — Palm Springs, California

Beep! Beep! Beep!

Charlotte's head snapped up. The alert was sounding on Jonathan's laptop. Dropping the letters she had been reading — threatening letters from Olivia to her grandmother — she ran to the coffee table where he had set up his equipment. She saw a red light flashing on the screen.

The intruder was in the system.

Quickly picking up her cell phone, she dialed Jonathan's pager number. When she heard the tone, she typed in *S.O.S.* — their prearranged signal that the rerouter had delivered the intruder to the fake formulas. She prayed he heard it. In these mountains above Palm Springs cellular signals were sometimes dicey. And when he got it, how long before he would be back? Jonathan had gone down the road in search of a diner or café that might be open at this hour. It had been a long time since they had eaten; at the least, they needed coffee.

After they had sped away from the Harmony Biotech facility, Jonathan had guided the car up into the mountains, where, on such a rainy night, it had been nearly impossible to find a motel that was open. When they were just starting to think it was hopeless, they had spotted the small Vacancy sign over a cluster of rustic cabins named Tiny's Mountain Retreat. Once they secured the room, Jonathan had wasted no time in setting up his equipment on a knotty pine coffee table that stood on a braided rug, and establishing remote access into Harmony's internal system. In the meantime, Charlotte had searched the modest bungalow for something to cook with, at least to boil water, but aside from the flagstone fireplace that looked as if it hadn't been cleaned in decades, there was nothing. So Jonathan had gone back out into the night, leaving Charlotte to watch the computer.

Her heart pounded as she quickly sat down and began to type. "Control plus alt plus insert," Jonathan had said before leaving. "Strike them simultaneously. That will send the signal back, along with my string of code that will act as a probe. By the time I return, we'll have the source of the break-in."

Her hands were no longer handcuffed, having been freed by Jonathan shortly after they left Harmony. He had pulled off the road and expertly picked the lock with a microinstrument, then he had resumed driving. Charlotte had tended to her raw wrists by applying ointment obtained from the rental car's rudimentary first aid kit, and then wrapped them with sterile gauze. She had waited several miles before asking Jonathan what she desperately needed to know.

"Why didn't you tell me you know Naomi?"

"Because I felt such a fool. Besides, I don't really know her, not in the way you think."

Charlotte had kept her eyes on the rain-swept road as they searched for a motel. She had no doubt that Knight had alerted the local authorities about a woman, wanted for questioning in three murder cases, who had resisted arrest and assaulted a federal officer. Knight would probably add tampering with evidence, obstruction of justice, and a string of other offenses. The Palm Springs police most likely had an all points bulletin out on her right now.

"Tell me how you know Naomi," she had said, as if that was all she cared about in the world. Maybe it was. Jonathan's lying to her seemed more important in that moment than anything else, including her near misses with death.

If she couldn't trust Jonathan, then what was left?

His eyes had remained fixed on the road. "After I saw the

Chalk Hill incident in the news, I subscribed to a clipping service. I wanted to keep track of you."

"You were married."

"And *you* were still my best friend." He took his eyes off the road long enough to send her a glance that punctuated his sentence. "And then five years ago I received a clipping about a convention of psychics that was going to be held in Sacramento. I was sent the article because you were referenced in connection with a Miss Naomi Morgenstern, who was going to chair the conference."

Charlotte picked at the edge of her bandage. "Our names became linked after Chalk Hill. Any time Naomi got a mention in the press it was 'Naomi Morgenstern, who made national news when she and Charlotte Lee, of Harmony House pharmaceuticals, were arrested. . . .' Was it something like that?"

"Yes."

"So you attended a convention of psychics?" She couldn't keep the astonishment out of her voice.

"I was hoping you would be here. I thought I'd run into you accidentally."

"Did Naomi know?"

"God no."

"Then how did she get your address?"

"To register, we had to show a form of ID, so I left my business card. Obviously it found its way to a mailing list, and that was how I ended up receiving that friendly note from Naomi. I imagine she sent out hundreds like it. I did meet her at the convention, we even shook hands. But there were so many attendees, she would never remember me."

"Why do you carry her note around with you?"

"Because she's my only link to you."

Charlotte hadn't known whether to laugh or cry or be angry, and even now, half an hour later, her nerves were still so savaged from her close call in the bottling plant, and their hasty flight into the storm, as well as the emotional shock of discovering Jonathan had been keeping track of her all these years, that her fingers trembled badly as she tried to type the three hot keys. She hit the wrong combination, missing one key altogether. "Damn," she said and started again. But before she could execute the command, the window snapped closed and another opened instantaneously, startling her.

And there, on the screen, was Adele Sutherland's face.

For a moment Charlotte thought a call was coming through. And then she saw the message at the bottom of the screen: Recorded, and the date and time of the call.

When she saw the time, just over an hour and a half ago, she realized the call had come through while she had been having her encounter in the stairwell with Desmond.

She contemplated the word *Recorded*. And then, hesitating long enough only to hit the three keys to send Jonathan's beacon back to the intruder, she hit Replay. And Jonathan's wife began to speak. . . .

47

As Jonathan left the all-night diner at the truck stop and hurried back to the car, first checking the mountain road for signs of a police car, he looked at his watch. Less than two hours till the deadline.

He tried to keep calm. Charlotte's pager signal meant that the intruder had logged in again and had been rerouted to his laptop. They were going to know within minutes where the log-in took place. And then they would have the son of a bitch.

When he saw headlights approaching, Jonathan ducked into a phone booth and forced himself to hold back.

While he watched the car go slowly by on the slick road, his mind was a kaleidoscope of roiling thoughts and emotions, all out of sequence, all clamoring for his attention: Charlotte, handcuffed to the ampoule apparatus; Quentin, calling from London, lying about his flat being redecorated; Adele, with the hurt in her wide, trusting eyes, talking about the gardeners, while in the background —

A groan escaped his throat. *Adele . . .*

Jonathan had met her at a time when his heart was in two broken pieces, hurting and hungry for love. It had been five years since he had sent his poem to Charlotte, sixty long months since she had called and said, "I need my space, Johnny. There's just so much I want to do that I need to be alone."

He recalled mumbling something like, "Yes, I understand, Charlie. Me, too. And anyway, there's three thousand miles between us, it's just too much. . . ." He felt as if he had been hit by a fast moving snowstorm. It had rolled over him, flattened him into a frozen shadow, devoid of warmth or feeling. Charlotte had left him. She was no longer in his life — she was no longer his *life*.

He had gone through the motions of living after that, plunging into his studies at MIT with an almost maniacal purpose, and then, later, with the NSA, volunteering for jobs in far-flung locales, jobs with long days and nights of surveillance, assignments that required nonstop analytical thinking, dangerous missions that forced him to stay on his toes. If he filled his hours, he decided, he wouldn't have to think about filling his heart. And then Amsterdam happened and Jonathan's life was sent into another lethal spiral. He had left the NSA and set up a private consulting firm with Quentin, Quentin doing the up-front, "people" work, while Jonathan did the thing he did best — the solitary, behind-the-scenes technical work. They were a good team and Jonathan was able to keep himself emotionless and cold — his only defense against the nightmares and the demons. And then he met Adele.

Almost at once, her softness and warmth began to thaw him; her lack of drive and ambition created a cushion for his own restlessness and hard edges. She would listen for hours to accounts of his exploits with Quentin, and she would ask nothing in return except for his opinion on a flower arrangement, or whether he thought the garnets were better with this blouse or the pearls.

Adele did not collide with him as Charlotte had; there were no exhausting passions or expectations that took you up to the stars only to drop you to earth like a cold stone. Adele was steady, dependable, and always there for him. And if she took hours dressing, deciding what to wear, choosing her "look," he told himself that he loved her for it, because she was dressing for *him*. She never once asked him what happened in Amsterdam.

But now he thought of her last phone call, the one that had come just over an hour ago and the sudden sick feeling that had risen in his chest as he had heard the sound in the background just as she was saying something about talking to the gardeners.

And he had felt his world tilt, like a carnival ride, until the sick feeling rose in him again.

48

Charlotte was just watching Adele say, "The gardener is here with a million questions," when Jonathan came into the cabin. When she saw how pale he was, and the wintry bleakness in his eyes, she said, "I'm sorry. When I sent the signal code back, I hit the wrong keys. I really didn't mean to pry."

His eyes flickered to the face frozen on the screen. Charlotte saw pain ripple across his handsome features in a way she knew so well — Jonathan trying to bridle his emotions. And she understood the real reason why he was so pale; it wasn't because he had caught her snooping.

She waited for him to say something, and when he didn't she said it for him: "I heard it, Johnny," she said, referring to the noise in the background while Adele was talking. *Ka-chunk, ka-chunk. . . .*

"I didn't believe it at first," he said in a tight voice, his Adam's apple going up and down in a painful swallow. "After she hung up, I ran a caller ID. The number is the Four Seasons Hotel." He turned his pain-filled eyes to her. "My partner isn't getting his flat redecorated and my wife isn't at home talking to the gardeners."

Charlotte stood up from the coffee table. She saw tears in his eyes. "I'm so sorry," she said.

"No, it's all right," he said, turning away from her sympathy. "I had it coming. It happens to all heroes, at one time or another." He handed her the brown sack that contained coffee and bear claws. "I'd better check on the tracer."

The hardness in his voice made Charlotte want to reach for him. But she heard the bitterness, too, and the strange reference to heroes: she had heard the same thing ten years ago, in San Francisco, when he had told her he had resigned from the NSA. "A very nasty break," he had said just a while ago. What really happened with the Amsterdam Eight?

"Johnny," she said. Then she stopped. They had less than two hours to the deadline. He was right. They had to stay focused. Adele and Quentin and the rest of the world would come later. "I found something in Olivia's letters," she said instead.

She held up the bundle of letters that she had stuffed into her tote beg before leaving the museum. By some miracle, when Jonathan was searching for her, he had found the tote bag lying in the control booth of the processing plant from which Charlotte had been abducted. Her assailant had clearly had no interest in it.

"Olivia was obsessed with getting the house back," she said, as she opened the paper sack and brought out two Styrofoam cups. "All those letters from 1942 to 1957 threaten my grandmother, giving her no peace. They are literally a one-woman terrorizing campaign! I don't know how Grandmother could have stayed silent about it all those years."

Jonathan picked up one of the cups, pulled off the plastic lid. "So you think our killer is connected to Olivia? Maybe her son, Adrian? Or Margo? Maybe all of this is some sort of revenge for them not getting the house?"

She regarded the steaming coffee in her hands. "I don't know what to think. An hour ago I suspected Mr. Sung. Maybe I still do." She reached into the tote bag and brought out the carefully folded *San Francisco Chronicle* from 1936. "This article reads like something in a supermarket tabloid," she murmured. "They describe everything my grandmother was wearing, right down to her earrings, her facial expressions, whether she looked angry or sad. All these references to Gideon Barclay! And do you know what it says about my mother? They call her retarded."

Jonathan looked up from the computer. "Did your grandmother ever say she was?"

Charlotte started to shake her head, but stopped.

"What?" Jonathan said.

"I'm not sure. But I seem to remember now . . . whispers behind closed doors. I always knew there was something special about my mother, something different. Maybe I overheard it, maybe I just sensed it. But, Jonathan, it didn't occur to me that there was something *mentally* wrong with her. I thought maybe she had been gifted, like her father, Mr. Lee."

"Except that now you know Mr. Lee wasn't her father."

"No. My suspicion is correct. *That,*" and she angrily threw the newspaper down, "certainly confirmed it!"

Jonathan retrieved the newspaper and placed it out of sight, hiding from Charlotte the hurtful and offending words about Mr. Lee's impotence, the lurid account of Perfect Harmony concocting an aphrodisiac for her husband.

"I used to wonder why I didn't look more Chinese," Charlotte said. "I would study pictures of Mr. Lee and wonder why my mother and I didn't look more like him. Grandmother used to tell me it was because Richard Barclay had strong *yang,* that my physical makeup was ruled by my great-grandfather. But that's not so. I did not have a Chinese grandfather. I had an American one." She placed the untasted coffee on the table. "My God, Jonathan, it's just beginning to sink in."

He got up and went to the fireplace, contemplating its cold, black interior. He turned and looked at Charlotte. "What is?"

She regarded him with clear green eyes filled with wonder and bewilderment. "That summer," she said. "When I was fifteen. . . ."

It was a hot July Sunday and her grandmother was having a barbecue on the terrace. The Barclays had come, of course; skinny Desmond was in the pool, showing off, while his mother, Margo, wearing a racy black and gauze bathing suit cut high at the hip, bragged loudly that one of her son's teachers had declared that Desmond was the brightest fourteen-year-old he had ever met. Uncle Adrian was just inside the house, on the phone as usual, while Aunt Olivia, wearing a Hawaiian sarong, was helping Charlotte's grandmother with platters of ribs, pork tenderloins, and chicken wings, all marinated in soy sauce and ginger root.

There were over fifty people at the party, laughing and drinking and talking about Vietnam and Watergate, but

Charlotte had thought it was the loneliest place on earth — because Johnny wasn't there.

Uncle Gideon had found her up on the roof in the gazebo, crying her eyes out. "Why does Johnny have to leave?" she had sobbed when he asked what was wrong. "He doesn't have to go to Scotland every summer. He's American. He should stay here."

"Has he told you why he goes?"

Charlotte blew her nose into the handkerchief he had given her. "Johnny doesn't like to talk about his feelings."

"Have you asked?"

She mutely shook her head, thinking that September was so far away and that she would just die of loneliness until Johnny came back.

"What does your grandmother say?" Uncle Gideon asked.

"Oh, it's not something I can talk to Grandmother about! She wouldn't understand!"

"You think not?" he had said with a patient smile. "She strikes me as being a very wise woman."

Charlotte gazed morosely at her hands in her lap. "I can't talk to her about this. She wouldn't understand."

"Hmm," he said. "Are we referring to matters of the heart here?"

"If Grandmother knew, she'd kill me."

"I don't think she's killed anyone yet. Certainly not because of love."

Despite herself, Charlotte smiled. Uncle Gideon had always had a way of cheering her up, for as far back as she could remember. That was why she adored him so. It also helped that he was so terribly handsome with his tan and his broad shoulders and silver-gray eyes that matched his silver-gray hair. Even though Charlotte knew he was way old — in his sixties — she thought Uncle Gideon was very sexy.

"Grandmother's just so strict," she said with a sigh. "If she knew I had a crush on Johnny, she wouldn't let me go over to his house anymore."

"And Johnny . . . how does *he* feel? About you, I mean."

She shrugged. "He thinks we're just friends."

"So you haven't confessed *your* feelings?"

"Oh no! And I never would! Not until he did first!"

"Sometimes that's not always the best, Charlotte. Sometimes, if you wait for the other person, you can wait too long and you lose everything."

"Then I should tell him? Tell Johnny that I love him?"

"Well, that's not exactly what I meant. You have to be careful how you do it."

"I'm so confused! I have these feelings . . . when I'm with Johnny . . ."

"Charlotte," Gideon said gently. "Is there something you want to tell me? Have you and Johnny . . . ?"

It took her a moment to grasp his meaning. "Oh no, Uncle Gideon! Nothing like that!" And then she had looked at him with eyes full of innocence and said, "Would that make him stay? If I let him kiss me?"

Gideon had rubbed his jaw and then the back of his neck. "I don't think that's the way to find your answers. You don't need to rush into those things yet, Charlotte."

"My friend Melanie has a boyfriend and they kiss all the time."

"Charlotte," he said slowly, as if choosing his words with care, "has your grandmother discussed . . . er, things with you?"

"Things?"

"Well, about life. Love." He held out his hands. "Boys."

"Why would she?"

"Ah," he had said. And then again: "Ah," thoughtfully.

"Why does Johnny go, Uncle Gideon? Why does he leave me every summer?"

"Maybe he's trying to figure something out."

"Like what?"

Gideon had sat there on the wooden bench, the wind tousling his graying hair, thinking, while Charlotte had waited for his wise words to mend her heart. He said exactly what she wanted to hear: "I tell you what. How about a picnic? Just the two of us. In the park? Tomorrow?"

He came for her the next day, right on time. Charlotte had thought it was strange that her grandmother was still at home. It was Monday and the middle of the day — Grandmother was always at the factory then. And usually in the evenings as well, and on weekends, too, because there was always something that needed looking into, or correcting, or fixing, or planning, and Grandmother could never just leave it to her staff to do.

But she was there that noon when Uncle Gideon arrived to take Charlotte on a picnic in the park. And to Charlotte's further amazement, as they were about to walk out the door, her grandmother had taken her into her arms, hugging her tightly, murmuring, "Have a good time, Charlotte-*ah*."

There had been tears in her grandmother's eyes, and Charlotte hadn't understood until much later — years later — what those tears were for.

"Jonathan," Charlotte said now as she watched him start to build a fire using logs and old newspapers that had been stacked in the brass hod, "if my mother was retarded, how did she grow up to get married? Was she cured? Or is it possible she was never married and the story of a young husband dying in a scuba accident was a myth made up to hide the fact that I was illegitimate? I'll bet Margo and Adrian know. They're my mother's age. I had always imagined they were her friends. But that newspaper article —" Her voice broke. "It says Iris Lee was too simple-minded to even sit still, that she had to be taken out of the courtroom. How could I not have heard something after all these years? And how did she really die? All these secrets and lies! Grandmother told me my mother died when she fell down the stairs. But did she, Jonathan, *did she?*"

Resting back on his heels, Jonathan regarded the poker in his hands. Someone had thoughtfully polished it to a clear shine. "I don't know, Charlotte," he said quietly. "It seems that the more information we uncover, the more in the dark we are."

She finally picked up the coffee and tasted it as she listened to the wind rattle the old windows of the cabin, and rain pelt the roof. She closed her eyes, remembering what Desmond had said: "Everyone knew that my randy old grandfather had a taste for Chinese." Oh Desmond, you have it so wrong. You and everyone else, so wrong . . .

"The park isn't this way, Uncle Gideon," fifteen-year-old Charlotte had said when they were heading south on the Embarcadero.

"Oh, we aren't going to Golden Gate Park, Charlotte."

She hadn't pressed. It was to be another of Uncle Gideon's surprises.

He had surprised her a lot over the years, with special presents and outings, but this time, she realized as they took the turnoff for San Francisco International Airport, it was going to be something very special. And then when he produced two suitcases from the trunk of his car, and two passports with a first-class ticket tucked inside each one, she realized this was going to be an adventure with a capital *A*.

He didn't have to tell her where they were going. They were flying Singapore Airlines, after all. And after twenty-one and a half hours of playing cards, watching movies, sleeping and eating, they arrived in a sultry, Technicolor paradise.

They checked into the Raffles Hotel, two rooms adjoining, and then plunged without delay into the colorful, lively city, where policewomen in white uniforms directed traffic at intersections, and onion sellers squatted on the sidewalks, their produce spread out for inspection.

As Charlotte and her uncle left the skyscrapers and modern roads of Singapore behind, they explored the narrow streets and alleys crammed with small shops, food stalls, and boutiques. Gideon explained that he had been to Singapore twice before. "The last time," he said, "was when your grandmother brought me here to show me where she was born."

They had paused in front of a tiny store with a sign that said: "Wah's Silks, est. 1884." Uncle Gideon explained, "Your grandmother was born here, in a room upstairs."

Charlotte had already heard the story from her grandmother — such a romantic tale, Mei-ling coming to the rescue of the handsome Richard Barclay, who had been attacked by thieves, nursing him here in secret, taking care of him, falling in love. When Charlotte had once brought Johnny home to tend to a cut on his forehead, she had wondered if that was what it had been like for Mei-ling, to have someone you love sit so quiet and still while you applied gentle ointments and balms. Johnny had watched her with such trusting eyes. Had Richard Barclay looked at Mei-ling the same way?

"I'll let you in on a little secret," Gideon had said as they stood before the silk shop. "Your grandmother isn't as old as everyone thinks she is. She is actually two years younger. Ask her sometime to tell you the story of her faked immigration papers."

"When was the *first* time you were here, Uncle Gideon?" Charlotte had asked, and his look had darkened with hidden memories. "Thirty years ago, during the war. I was a prisoner at Changi Prison, where men did inhuman things to their fellow men. The only thing that kept me alive through the hell was thoughts of the woman I loved, and that I had promised I would return to her." At the time, Charlotte, remembering the war medals she had seen, had thought he was referring to his wife, Aunt Olivia.

He took her to the Temple of One Thousand Lights, where they saw a replica of Buddha's footprint. They visited the statue of Sir Stamford Raffles on the east bank of the Singapore River, marking the spot where the Englishman first landed in 1819. They attended an Indian festival where holy men in loincloths paraded about with hooks and spikes and skewers piercing their flesh. They snacked at food stalls on rice and kung pao pork; they attended an outdoor Chinese opera in which actors and actresses in brilliant costumes and elaborate makeup dazzled the crowds with performances of ancient legends and myths. They went to Tiong Bahru Road and listened to songbirds in elaborate bamboo cages warble melodies for the delight of passersby.

Finally they went to Jurong Bird Park, where they feasted on a picnic of chicken curry with Padang rice while they watched brightly colored parrots swoop in and out of the mist of a waterfall.

This was when, beneath the sultry blue sky, Uncle Gideon had said, "You know, Charlotte, relationships aren't always easy. You'll discover that as you get older. People don't always tell the truth. Sometimes they'll try to deceive you. Especially," he had added with a smile, "if you happen to be a beautiful young girl and a boy is very interested."

"But how do you know," she began, "I mean how does a girl know . . ." And her voice had faded on the mist of the waterfall because she didn't know what she was trying to say. Only that morning, in the hotel dining room, she had been admiring a doll Uncle Gideon had bought for her the day before, and in the next instant she was admiring the young man sitting at the next table. Was life always going to be so confusing?

"If you tell a boy you love him," Gideon said, "and he says he won't believe it unless you prove it physically, then he isn't worth it. It means he doesn't respect you. And without respect there can't be love."

She confessed to him that she knew girls who had already gone all the way. Some of her friends were even on the Pill. The information seemed to baffle him, and then make him sad. "Women's lib and Woodstock," he said, shaking his head. "It's a new age. But some things remain timeless, no matter how old they are, Charlotte. And one of them is, if a boy loves you, truly loves you, he won't force you to do anything you don't want to do, he won't make you 'prove' your love for him with your body. And sometimes," he said, "a boy will tell you he loves you so that he can get what he wants, but he isn't sincere. But on the other hand, sometimes a boy *does* love you but can't say it."

"How do you tell the difference?"

He laughed. "I don't think anyone has figured that out yet." And then, more seriously, "Promise me one thing, Charlotte. When the time does come and you decide you want to be intimate with a boy, promise me that you will make very, very sure that it is what you want, and that *he* is the one you want to do it with."

She could have promised him right there and then, because Charlotte was already very sure that it was what she wanted, and that Johnny was the one she wanted to do it with.

Gideon then took her to a horticultural and botanical garden on Peacock Lane, where thousands of varieties of flowers were on display, and as Charlotte had marveled, walking hand in hand with Uncle Gideon, at the beautiful courtyards, moon gates, curved-eave pagodas, wooden bridges, and tranquil ponds, he had said, "This used to be a private residence. This was where your great-grandmother, Mei-ling, was born."

That was all he had said. He hadn't been obvious about it, he hadn't lectured or said, "See, Charlotte? This is your ancestral home, this is where your roots are." He hadn't hit her

over the head with: "This is why Johnny goes home to Scotland every summer." Because Charlotte had walked along
those tiny paths and stepped under graceful arches and moved
through rooms resplendent with orchids and lilies and birds-
of-paradise and she had thought: "My great-grandmother
walked along these same paths and looked through these
same windows. She slept here, ate here, got sad here, was
happy here." And Charlotte had felt something she had never
felt before, a sudden connection, a sudden sense of belonging.
She thought of the room above Wah's Silks, where her grandmother had been born, she pictured the many faces she had
seen, resembling her own, with high cheekbones and almond
eyes, and the dialects she had heard — Cantonese, Mandarin,
Shanghainese — and the many statues of Kwan Yin she had
seen, and it amazed her to think: This is where I began.

Finally, Uncle Gideon had taken her to a small shop on
Orchard Road, where he had bought her a necklace — a
silver-and-amber drop-pendant on a silver chain strung with
amethysts. Gideon had showed her how to open the locket.
"See? You put something inside it, a keepsake."

She already knew what was going to go inside. Herself
and Johnny, forever.

Jonathan had the fire going, bright and hot, casting golden
reflections into the room, filling the air with a comfortable
roar dotted with crackles. As he joined Charlotte on the
couch, feeling springs as he sank into the old upholstery, he
saw something catch the fire's glow on Charlotte's chest, just
below her collarbone — the Shang necklace. It made him
think of the day he had first seen it, the day he had returned
from summer vacation when they were fifteen. In June he
had left behind a sullen and morose Charlotte, but the girl
who greeted him that September afternoon had undergone a
miraculous transformation. "Oh Johnny, you're back!" she
had cried, giving him a hug. And then, before he could even
say anything, she had recited a breathless account of a trip

she had taken with her uncle — "To *Singapore!*" — ending it, to his amazement, with a pronouncement that she *understood* now why he had to go away every summer.

It had baffled him because he himself didn't know why he went to Scotland every summer; he only knew why he came back.

"I truly am sorry I never told you about Naomi," he said. "I know how it must have looked when you found her note in my wallet."

"It's all right. I can understand." She looked at him, let her eyes feast on his profile. Suddenly, within the cocoon warmth of this mountain cabin, the world seemed no longer to exist. It was as if everything that had happened in the past ten hours had taken place long ago in another world; the old rules no longer applied, the barriers didn't seem necessary. "Jonathan, when you saw the news about Chalk Hill, eight years ago, what did you think?"

He turned honest eyes to her, an open look that reminded her of days in San Francisco, before they had each lost their innocence. "That you had been misrepresented in the media. I knew there was a real story behind the one the world was shown."

"The voice-over, where I say, 'If this is the only way we can get ourselves heard, then this is what we will do' — I spoke those words while standing in front of the FDA offices in Washington. Jonathan, I was holding a picket sign! But they played it while showing that picture, to make it look like I'm saying that if I have to slaughter animals I will. It wasn't true!"

"I know that, Charlotte."

She spoke with passion. "They made me look like I would sacrifice innocent animals for my own gain. There *is* a real story, as you say. I am opposed to animal testing, you know that. But I also think that in our fight against animal testing we have a responsibility to those same animals. Bless the

Beasts was an irresponsible group. They would set animals free and not think how the poor things were going to survive. I was tipped off about a planned attack on the Chalk Hill Labs. I and some others went there hoping to prevent it. We were too late. The animals had already been set loose and the lab was on fire.

"Jonathan, Chalk Hill is in northern California, in redwood country. Those animals had either been born in cages or had lived in cages for most of their lives; they didn't know how to survive in the wilderness. And it wasn't as if healthy animals were being set free, but poor beasts with diseases, tumors — That picture of me, kneeling over the German shepherd . . . , yes, I killed him. I had his blood on my hands. I bashed his head in. Jonathan, that poor dog had electrodes in his head. I saw him running from the lab, his eyes filled with terror. It was such chaos, with rats and monkeys — the animals were running every which way, sick, frightened, helpless. We couldn't round them up and take them back to their home because the lab was on fire. We couldn't take them to a vet — the lab was in the forest, miles from civilization. And then I saw that poor dog stumble to the ground and start to convulse." Her voice dropped to a horrified whisper. "I had to put it out of its misery. I couldn't just let it lie there —"

Jonathan put his arm around her, drawing her to him.

"Naomi was a member of Bless the Beasts," she continued in a tight voice. "She went there to set the animals free. But then she saw what the result was — that we had to kill them with our bare hands. Wring their necks. Bash their heads in. Otherwise, they would have suffered long, lingering deaths." She lifted moist green eyes. "She was as horrified as the rest of us, and she blamed Bless the Beasts for the disaster. She left the group. And that was when everyone started pointing fingers at everyone else, calling one another names — it's an episode in my life I prefer not to think about."

"*I* think you're a hero," he said softly.

She searched his face, marveling at the new lines she found where once there had been smoothness. She had known Jonathan's face in its many permutations — the ghastly pimple era, the months of soft new beard, the peeling sunburn, the scab that threatened never to heal, taco sauce clinging to the corner of his mouth, tears spilling from his sad brown eyes. She searched this older face for the one underneath, and she found it — she found the young Johnny again.

"What happened in Amsterdam?" she said.

He withdrew his arm and leaned back, dropping his hands uselessly in his lap, a gesture of resignation. He had known he must tell her eventually. It was only fair that he disabuse her of any thoughts she might be harboring of a noble, heroic Jonathan Sutherland.

"Eight hackers, top-notch types, had every government in Europe quivering with paranoia, including banks, defense plants, politicians with their private records. We didn't have their identities, we knew absolutely nothing about them. And although the gang never really *did* anything — mostly they were an information-gathering group — they had enough authorities and big corporations adequately frightened to want them found and locked away. I headed a special unit comprising agents from all the European governments. The Eight led us on a merry chase all over Europe; they seemed to regard it as a game. They would make appearances in highly sensitive computers, leave mocking messages, and then vanish. After a while, the press started to wonder why we couldn't catch them. People began to question our abilities. The Eight made us a laughingstock.

"When they posted the launch codes of U.S. missiles on the Internet, the pressure came down on us. I don't know what happened. I've run that night through my head a thousand times, trying to see what went wrong. Was it lack of sleep? Too much stress? Not enough resources or man-

power? Whatever the cause, it all boiled down to me. I was
responsible because I was, after all, the technological expert.
So what if these hackers had obtained two hundred thousand
credit card numbers? They never used then. And those
launch codes? They couldn't have used them, not in a million
years. I should have seen their actions for what they were —
not the work of deadly international terrorists, but the scare
tactics of a handful of misfits craving attention."

He drew in a deep breath and released it as a ragged sigh.
"But paranoia was rampant in the land, and I suppose that finally I was infected as well."

"What happened?"

"By the time we located them," he said softly, "holed up
in a farmhouse outside Amsterdam, my agents and I were
pumped up with anger, adrenaline, and thirst for revenge
against this mob that had made a dog and pony show of our
elite unit. I suppose we were also blinded a little by our own
self-importance, our own sense of celebrity. I was the only
one who didn't go in with a gun. But that doesn't exculpate
me. I should have stopped them. I was the one who knew the
mind of the hacker. I was the expert. It wasn't until I saw the
first body fall that I realized my horrendous mistake. By
the time I saw the boy on his knees, pissing his pants in fear,
two more had already been gunned down."

He stared into the flames in the fireplace. Charlotte
reached for his hand.

"That was when I managed to take control. I came to my
senses and ordered my agents to stop. By then it was too late
for the two who were killed, ages sixteen and seventeen, and
for the third, who took a bullet in his neck, leaving him paralyzed. He was fifteen."

"Jonathan," she said, "you couldn't have known. No one
knew who they were, how old they were."

"No, Charlotte," he said, withdrawing his hand from hers,
"I should have known better. I know the profile, remember?

Christ, these kids were bloody stereotypes! Walking clichés of the typical harmless antisocial hacker! I was blinded by my own arrogance and ambition."

He shot to his feet. "They called me a hero. The president of the United States shook my hand. I received book and movie offers. My partner got jealous. All because I had allowed a couple of kids who weren't old enough to buy cigarettes to get killed."

"They were a danger to society, to the world, Jonathan."

"Like hell they were. They didn't commit one single act of violence. All they did was shake up the establishment, convince the world that they had power." His voice fell quiet. "That was the turning point in my life. I'd always loved hacking, treated it as an art, always admired anyone as skilled as myself or better. I decided to get out of the game, get into corporate security, go after the white-collar bad guys, collect a paycheck and live safely. Two kids dead, Charlotte, and a third paralyzed from the neck down for the rest of his life."

"They were still wrongdoers, Jonathan," she said softly.

"Yes, but they didn't deserve that kind of punishment." He looked down at her. "Did that German shepherd deserve what *he* got?"

She stared mutely at him, her lips a tight line.

"We are the ones in control, Charlotte. *We* are the ones who must be careful and act responsibly. If I had kept my wits about me that day, I could have walked into that farmhouse, shared their coffee, told them some tales of real hacking, had the lot rounded up and thrown into jail for a year maybe. And probably even stayed friends with some of them."

When she saw a wintry bleakness enter his eyes, Charlotte knew he wasn't finished. There was more to come . . . and worse.

He went to the fireplace and stoked the logs. Flames and

sparks shot up. Resting the poker on the hearth, he leaned one arm on the mantel and gazed for a long time into the fire.

Charlotte waited.

Finally he turned around to face her. "I married Adele because she was there, Charlotte. It's that simple. The first night I slept with her, I slept through the night without waking up screaming. She softened the nightmare, Adele was like the guardian angel of my sleep."

Charlotte could barely find her voice. "She was *there?* That's all you have to say for marrying another woman — that she was there?"

"It's a shitty reason, maybe, but it's the truth."

"Jonathan, *I* could have been there. All you had to do was ask."

"And you think that would have been so easy to do after you had made it very clear that you wanted to be alone, that you had things to do?"

"You said it first!"

She stood up abruptly. "You have no idea how it hurts, Jonathan, to know that you were in such pain, so much suffering, and yet you didn't come to me."

"Did *you* come to me after Chalk Hill?" he said suddenly.

"You were married by then! Oh God, I knew this was going to happen. You're using me again. You come to me and bare your soul, cleanse yourself and then leave, while I'm left with the debris of your conscience and feeling abandoned again. Damn you, Jonathan. I should have sent you packing the minute I saw you standing in my office doorway."

"Charlotte, what are you so angry about?"

"What I'm angry about is the way you breeze in and out of my life as though I were some goddamn battery charger. I'm not going to be your listening post any more. My heart can't take it. Don't leave your fucking demons at my feet and then go tap-dancing back to your wife."

She flung open the door and ran out into the rain.

Jonathan ran after her, into the cold darkness and the merciless downpour. He grabbed her arm, spun her around. "Charlie, listen —"

"You bastard!" she cried. "You want to know what I'm mad at? Ten years ago, that's what! The way you kept your precious news to yourself while I sat there blithering like an idiot, stupidly hoping you were going to ask me to come back into your life. And then you dropped it on me, just that! 'Charlotte, I'm getting married.' What was I supposed to *say*, Johnny?"

"I don't know, goddammit, but I expected you to say something!"

Her green eyes blazed with fury. "I was supposed to follow some damn script that you never even *gave* me?"

"Well, I didn't think you would get up and walk out!"

She struggled against his hold.

"And why couldn't I get married?" he bellowed. "You're the one who said you wanted your freedom!"

Sixteen years suddenly fell away as if the ground were dropping from under her; Charlotte saw herself briefly suspended in a void, and when she crashed back to earth, it was 1981 again and Johnny had sent her a book of poetry. She had flown up to her room without even saying hello to her grandmother, slammed her bedroom door shut, flung herself on the bed, and opened to the title page, where Johnny had written, *This is how I feel. Page 97.* She had frantically turned the pages with shaking hands because it was happening at last, Johnny was breaking out of his mute shell and telling her how much he loved her.

And then the dream had shattered as phrases leapt off the page — ugly, cold, hurting words: "go my separate way," "space and solitude are my bread and light," "a soul alone, a lonely soul."

Words about wanting to go away, to remember "the au-

tumns of our love," *friendship*, "for that is the warp and weft
of my heart."

Nothing about love.

Nothing about lovers.

She hadn't even cried, the words had left her so numb. She
had telephoned him in Boston: "I want us to be friends,
Johnny," she had said. Saying it in a way that made it sound
as if it were her idea in the first place, because that spared her
the humiliation, helped cover up the pain of rejection. "Yes,
three thousand miles between us . . . , yes, your work, and I
have mine. . . ." Each word cutting her like a knife as it sliced
Jonathan bit by bit out of her life. She would never let him
know how the poem had hurt, she would never bare her feelings to him, or to anyone, ever again.

"Charlie, listen!" he said to her now in the rain, reaching
for her through the years, through the storm.

She was sobbing, gulping in air and rain. "Go back to
Adele! Leave me alone!"

"I'm not going back to Adele."

"Don't lie to me! Why are you here, Jonathan? Why did
you come?"

"I came because you were in danger —"

"Why do you care?" she screamed suddenly, her tears
joining the raindrops on her cheeks. She put her hands to his
chest and shoved him back.

"Charlie, you know why I'm here! I care about you!"

She broke away. "You said you read about my grandmother's death. Would it have been too much trouble to call?
Or just send a card? I needed you. I waited . . ."

"But I sent a telegram! And flowers!"

She thrust out her chin as the rain poured over her, sending her loose hair streaming like black ribbons down her
cheeks and over her shoulders. "There were no flowers from
you."

"Charlie, I got a receipt," he said, hands held out, pleading. "I was in South Africa, I tried to leave but couldn't. I made sure the florist got a signed receipt at the funeral home. And I did call you. I left dozens of messages. You never called back."

They regarded each other through the downpour.

"Someone must have intercepted them," he said. "Someone who didn't want you and me to get together again."

"Johnny" — she sobbed suddenly — "Grandmother and I had an awful row the night she left. I said terrible things to her! She was going after another herb, something she was going to make into a tea. I told her we should study it, analyze its chemical structure. She said no. She never liked her precious herbs to be analyzed. She didn't want to hear about molecular structures and base chemicals and enzymes. I told her that it was analyzing her precious herbs that led me to formula GB4204, and then I said that she couldn't have really cared about Uncle Gideon . . ."

"Don't, Charlie. You didn't know."

"Why didn't she tell me about her and Gideon? And why did she just turn away when I offered her an ice-cream sundae? Why couldn't she just have said, 'No, too painful, memories.'"

"She had her price, Charlie. Just as you have yours. You clam up just like your grandmother did."

She turned away. "I don't know what you're talking about."

He took her arm. "Yes you do and it's time we faced it!"

"Let go of me!" She broke free and started to run.

"Charlie," he said as he ran after her, grabbing her wrist, making her turn around. "We have to face it. We have to talk about what happened."

"You said you wanted to be alone!"

"After *you* said it —" The memory suddenly overwhelmed him, like a tidal wave in the rain: how he had agonized waiting for her phone call, imagining her excited reaction to his poem, thinking how she would get on a plane and fly to him, and they would never be apart again.

"You said it first!" she cried. "And you were such a coward about it, sending me a goddamn book instead of telling me to my face!"

"What the hell are you talking about?"

"Let me refresh your memory!" She spun about and ran back to the cabin, where she reached into her leather tote bag and brought out the book.

She threw it at him.

"*You* did it," she said, her chest heaving. "*You* ended our friendship."

He stared at her, the book lying on the floor at his feet on the braided rug.

"All right, then," she said, picking it up. "If you're too scared to read your own cowardly words —" She frantically turned the pages, and then she read: "'Space and solitude are my bread and light.'" She gave him a challenging look. "If those words aren't a good-bye, then what are they?"

He frowned. "But that isn't my poem," he said, taking the book from her. "This isn't the one I wrote."

She blinked at him. "What do you mean, the one *you* wrote?"

"Well, of course, why do you think —" He turned more pages. "Here."

She took the book back and stared at the page, her eyes riveted to the dedication: *For Charlotte, by Jonathan Sutherland.* "I don't understand. You never told me you wrote a poem."

"I wanted it to be a surprise," he said simply.

"Johnny, I didn't know! I thought you had just found a poem in a book!"

"But even so, Charlie, that's not the one I told you to read."

"Yes it is." She flipped back to the title page, where he had written: *This is how I feel. Page 97.*

When she read it out loud, he said, "My God, Charlie! That's not a seven, it's a one!"

"*What?* You mean I read the wrong poem? But why didn't you tell me! You just sent the book to me! No explanation. I didn't know!"

"Well, maybe it was like you said — I had a script, except that I seemed to have forgotten to give it to *you*. Read it now, Charlie, read what my heart says to you."

I am a thousand miles above the earth,
The cold expanse of space yawns as if to swallow me
whole,
I know why I am here,
Wings are stretched, taut wires awaiting,
You!
There, the earth's revolving curve catches the first yellow
bar and holds it for the briefest second,
A bar of pure yellowness, the curve of life itself.
My breathing slows as you break free and rise,
Glorious and Godlike towards the racing stars.
I scream as the warm touch upon my feathered sails,
Dispels doubt as futility,
Below, the tiny sparkling waves are diamonds on velvet.
I spin and tumble as if new born,
And drop like stone,
Wings in tight, I am the rocket,
I am faster than you.
You are majestic: I am speed itself.
I level out and hurtle breakneck between white-flecked
canyons.
I beat you here, it is still dark,
But I know you rise still.
Three years will pass or more,

It seems,
But I will wait and you will find me,
Among the rolling, crested waves,
Head over heels.
Godspeed, my love,
'til then.

She was silent for a long moment, then she lifted tear-filled eyes. "Oh Johnny, it's beautiful! And all this time wasted!"

"It's my fault. I should have said something. But when you called that night and said you just wanted to be friends . . ."

"Because when I read that other poem and it said things about wanting to be just friends — I was in such pain," she said.

"Not half the pain *I* was in. My God, I love you, Charlie, you know that. I have always loved you."

Suddenly they were reaching for each other, pushing aside the past and the pain, arms and bodies finding each other, connecting, until Jonathan and Charlotte were kissing with all their pent-up passion, a kiss that had been waiting sixteen years to happen.

Charlotte closed her eyes and surrendered herself to Jonathan's embrace, her arms around his neck, her hands on his wet hair, her tongue in his mouth, tasting him, feeding a hunger she had carried for too long. While Jonathan held her so tightly neither of them could breathe, bending her to his body, his hands on her hair, her back, her waist, wanting to feel all of her at once while he feasted hungrily on her mouth.

"Johnny, Johnny, I love you —"

"Charlotte, my God —"

He undid the clasp at her neck and released her hair, driving his fingers into it, pushing it to the side as he kissed her neck wet with rain. She felt his harness pressing into her thigh.

And then they heard a sound, small and faint against the roar of the fire, but persistent, a steady rhythm. They both turned to the computer. "It's the tracer!" Jonathan said. "The tracer has found the intruder!"

And then suddenly there was a massive crack of thunder.

The ground shook, and all the lights in the cabin, all the power at the mountain retreat, went out.

49

1957–1958 — San Francisco, California

I had never seen Mrs. Katsulis so distraught.

She had been in my employ for eight years, and in all that time she had been nothing less than solid, stable, and level-headed, qualities for which I had hired her in the first place.

Mrs. Katsulis was Iris's companion, a registered nurse with experience in dealing with developmentally impaired adults. This was what Western doctors called it; they said my daughter was "developmentally impaired." Chinese doctors said that there was a blockage of flow between her fifty-nine meridians. Gideon listened to the Western doctors and wanted Iris to try medications with bad luck–sounding names such as methylphenidate and chlorpromazine. But I calmed my daughter's blood and soothed her *chi* with decoctions of chrysanthemum flower, lady's slipper, and fossilized dragon bone. In her bedroom I placed pillows filled with lavender and bowls filled with orange blossoms; I removed all mirrors that reflected her bed so that her spirit didn't receive a shock when it saw itself while she slept; and on the walls I painted eight good luck symbols in turquoise, which is the color of the northeast, also a good luck symbol. In time my daughter's untethered mind found tranquillity, so that when she was not involved with one of her enormous and complex jigsaw puzzles, which she completed with astonishing speed, she could finally sit quietly for long periods of time on our rooftop or in our garden or by the pool. At such times she looked normal, and new visitors to my home believed she was simply shy.

And then one day Iris began wandering off. That was when I had new locks put on all the doors, but, like the puzzle boxes and jigsaw puzzles, there was no lock Iris could not eventually figure out. For this reason Mrs. Katsulis took to sleeping in Iris's bedroom. My daughter had grown into a beautiful young woman, and men who did not know her mistook her demeanor as coyness, an invitation to seduce.

Why Iris felt this sudden compulsion to wander, I do not know. I have no idea what vision drew her out of the house, for she did seem to be searching. I followed her once, when an episode came over her, and I observed that she walked with the manner of someone who had lost her way and was looking for signs pointing home. When I stopped her at the corner, she merely smiled and came back with me. But I wondered how far she would have gone, what she would have seen that would have made her think: I have arrived.

I had no other children. Mr. Lee had been unable to give me a baby, and after he died, I saw men only as friends. Gideon Barclay had my heart, he would forever be the only man I would ever love, and Iris was the child we created together. This was enough for me. If at times I thought of grandchildren, or saw the grandchildren of other women my age, perhaps I felt a pang. For Iris could never marry, and at forty-nine and widowed, I knew I would have no more children. Richard Barclay's line stopped with my daughter.

And so when Mrs. Katsulis came to me, wringing her

hands, her face as pale as the white clouds scudding in over the Bay, I was of two minds when she told me what she had discovered about Iris. I was at first angry and outraged that someone had touched my precious daughter, and ashamed as well that such dishonor had fallen to us. But then I thought: Iris is pregnant and it doesn't matter who the man was, because the bloodline that started between Richard and Mei-ling is going to continue after all.

I told Gideon, of course, and he was outraged, as I had expected. Being her father, he wanted to find the man who had done it and exact punishment. But that was something we could never find out, because Iris had left her room one night without waking Mrs. Katsulis, and we found her the next morning, asleep in the gazebo on the roof. We all thought she had merely gone up there to look at the stars. But now I knew she must have gone out into the streets as well. It was only good luck and the watchful guidance of Kwan Yin that my daughter did not suffer a worse fate.

Gideon wanted to tell the police. That was his way of doing things, through official channels, the American way. But there were *family* ways of doing things, the Chinese way. I had to protect my daughter's honor.

"I am going to take her to Hawaii," I told Gideon. "She will have her baby there, away from prying eyes. When we return, I will tell everyone that Iris got married, but that the boy died in an accident."

"Harmony," Gideon said to me in such a gentle way that I yearned for his arms around me, "no one is going to believe that."

"Of course they aren't. But everyone will be polite and feel they must uphold my daughter's honor. It will be an open secret, shared by all, whispered by none."

I had to make many arrangements before I took Iris to Honolulu, for I was still the sole person in control of my herbal company, which was now called Harmony House.

The factory in Daly City had undergone expansion and renovations several times, and upon Gideon's advice, I had finally switched to automation. I had learned that to heed advice could be beneficial, for when I followed the advice of young Mr. Sung that I offer free products to the employees, quality instantly went up, as he predicted, as no one knew which batch they would be drawing from, and so we never had a problem again, and my company continued to grow. In 1949, when an embargo was placed on imports from the People's Republic of China, which drastically limited the supply of herbs, we shipped through Hong Kong, using our own company, Harmony-Barclay Ltd., as our supplier. The growth continued, and as people became more health conscious, and aware of the importance of vitamins and herbs, my mother's recipes began appearing in places outside of Chinatown, in drugstores and markets and a new phenomenon called a health food store.

It was while I was drafting lengthy and detailed instructions for my supervisors, for I expected to be gone for nearly a year, that I received an unexpected visitor.

Olivia Barclay had not set foot in the house since the day she moved out, fifteen years before, and I had seen little of her in the years since — once, at Margo and Adrian's wedding, because Gideon had invited me, and once at the hospital where Gideon had been recuperating from surgery on his knee. I knew from Gideon that she was not a happy woman, despite being very rich and the queen of her social circle, despite being a Barclay and having married handsome Gideon. These seemed not enough. I still had the house.

This, of course, was the reason for her letters to me, sent over the years, filled with angry and poisonous words, threats to leave me homeless, promises to make me wish I had never left Singapore. I had told no one about the letters, not even Gideon, until eventually they came less frequently, became shorter and less vehement, until finally they stopped altogether.

As I led Olivia into my living room, I knew what she saw as her eyes moved over the walls and floors and furniture. She saw insult, and the desecration of her dream. There was no Victorian age left, but I had also not left any of Olivia's ultramodern world. I had brought Chinese into my new home, so that when she looked around, she saw carved furniture in exotic dark woods, black-and-gold lacquer screens, scroll paintings on the walls, sparse but meaningful works of art such as the cloisonné imperial dragon standing on a rosewood chest, the enormous melon jar lamps painted with Mandarin ducks against a red background, and, dominating the living room, a trio of life-sized brass cranes standing among lifelike verdigris reeds and bamboo. While I served tea in a cloisonné set of cobalt blue decorated in butterfly and peony accents, I saw the undisguised judgment in Olivia's eyes. You would think I had strewn rubbish in my house.

"This is not a social visit," she said, not touching the jasmine tea or my almond and sesame cookies, not even bothering to add politely, "I am honored but too full to eat."

She said, "I would like to come straight to the point," in a tone that was as sharp as a sword. She opened her purse and produced two envelopes, one sealed, the other not. As she handed me the latter, she said, "Read this one first."

More letters, I thought. And these so important that she must deliver them in person.

As I opened the first, carefully withdrawing the papers inside, I felt my heart flutter anxiously like a bird in a cage. I knew at once that Olivia had come with bad news, that she had come with bad luck, for this letter had not been written by Olivia — the return address on the envelope was the name of a private detective agency in Hong Kong.

"It has taken me fifteen years to obtain this information," she said, retrieving a cigarette from her purse and lighting it without asking permission. "I didn't believe that you were Richard Barclay's daughter. Or, if you were, that he was ever married to your mother. It took a lot of money and a lot of footwork to get this information — the war caused a lot of records to be lost, a lot of people, too. But the man I hired was finally able to find out what I needed to know."

I did not look down at the papers. I kept my eyes on hers. "And what did he find?" I asked softly.

"That I was right. Your mother and Richard Barclay were never legally married."

"No," I said, "not legally. Nonetheless they were husband and wife."

"Not in any way that would stand up in a court of law. Your birth certificate is a fake, as are your citizenship papers. I'm sure the courts would find it very interesting, Mrs. Lee, that you entered this country under false pretenses. I imagine you will be sent back to Singapore."

"And this?" I said, looking at the sealed envelope.

"My man included it with his report. It's marked personal to you."

Why had she not opened it, a mere piece of paper sealed with glue, when she had torn open my entire life? It contained a letter from Reverend Peterson, the man who had helped my mother and me so many years ago. "Forgive me, Harmony," he wrote.

The man tricked me. He pretended he was also a man of the cloth, and so when I later found out that I had been duped and had confided in him information not meant for anyone else, I sought him out and asked him at least to forward this letter to you, if he at all could. I do not know where you are, Harmony, but certainly this detective's client knows you, else why is he or she searching into your background? Since I revealed to this man the truth, then I must, for your own sake, reveal the truth to

you as well, lest it be used against you — a truth, my
dear Harmony, I had sworn long ago never to reveal.

Your mother did not die the year you sailed for
America.

The rest came to me in images instead of words, leaping
off the page like movie scenes on a screen: my mother hearing about the new Immigration Act that was about to be
passed in the United States that would bar even the children
of American citizens from entering the country; Mother
going to Reverend Peterson for help; the two of them con-
triving a plan that involved changing the year of my birth so
that I was eighteen instead of sixteen and therefore able to
travel as an adult; my mother feigning an illness, pretending
to be near death so that I would leave and start my new life
with my father in America.

"I told this charlatan," Reverend Peterson had written,

of Mei-ling's and my deception, the falsifying of official papers, and now it can be used against you. For this
I am truly sorry. But I am not sorry that I broke my
promise to your mother, because in writing to you now,
with this news, I am free to write to you with other, hap-
pier news. I said that your mother did not die the year
you left Singapore. She did not die in the next year, nor
the year after. She came to me one day, a few months
after you had set sail for America, to tell me a most
wondrous story: her father had come for her, she said.
He had sought her out on Malay Street, where he told
her that by casting herself out, by becoming a nonper-
son, she had brought honor to him, and so he had asked
her to come home.

I visited them there, Mei-ling so lovely in her father's
garden, serving us tea and those divine cakes she was
known for. I had never seen a woman so happy. I knew

why it was: it was because, Harmony, you were going to find your father.

I asked her why she had pretended she was going to die. She said because otherwise you never would have left. If *she* could not be with the man she loved, then it was enough that her daughter was.

And then, when she and I were alone and out of the hearing of others, your mother told me the most extraordinary thing. She said that soon after she returned to her father's house, she set about searching for your whereabouts in America. She had to do it on her own without her father's help, for you were an unspoken secret between them; you, Harmony, were the shame upon their family. But Mei-ling needed to know that you were all right, that you had found your father. These questions burned in her heart as she wrote letter upon letter to San Francisco and waited the long weeks for responses. She finally received news in the form of a newspaper clipping, announcing your engagement to Gideon Barclay, adopted son of Richard Barclay. She was going to write to you at once.

Her father — your grandfather — discovered this and reminded her that she had restored honor to the family by banishing her illegitimate daughter sired by a foreign devil. But to bring the daughter back to Singapore would be to bring dishonor back into the family. Mei-ling did not know what to do. She could not go to America and be with you because of the laws forbidding Chinese to enter the United States. She could not ask you to come back to Singapore.

She prayed to Kwan Yin, and the reply came in the most remarkable way. Your mother told me that the goddess spoke to her through *her* mother's voice! Mei-ling's mother died many years ago when Mei-ling was only a child. The voice said: "'Harmony does not belong to this world anymore, she has work to do in the New World. Leave her to her destiny."

Mei-ling never wrote to you, even though it pained her with every beat of her heart to be separated from you. She knew her mother had spoken wisely, for if Mei-ling had written to you, you would have come back, and two lives would have been ruined.

I looked at those words and was moved to tears by my own mother's wisdom. She was right. If I had heard from her, I would have gone back. Even if I had not, would not my letters to her have carried shame and dishonor with them each time they entered her father's house?

Reverend Peterson had added words at the end of his letter, which I read through tears:

I am sorry to say your dear mother passed away only a short time ago, but it was a peaceful passing, she had lived well and contented for thirty years in her father's house, making her medicines, taking care of people. When she died, she had a bottle of Perfect Harmony's Golden Lotus Wine in her hands, the beautiful silver-and-blue-willow label resting on her bosom. She was proud of what her daughter had accomplished. And I know that not a day went by in which she did not think of you living in the house of *your* father, Richard Barclay.

I laid the letter in my lap and regarded Olivia. She had come with the intention of frightening me. Instead she had given me back my mother's life. She had come with the intention of taking this house away from me. "You can do what you want with the information the detective gave you," I said. "But you are never going to have my father's house."

Gideon appeared at my door that same evening, as I was

packing our suitcases. "Olivia just got home. She was very upset about something. She told me she had been to see you. Harmony, what happened? Why did Olivia come here? What did she say to you?"

I showed him Reverend Peterson's letter and then I wept in my beloved's arms — for joy, for sadness, for my mother's happiness, for her death. He stayed with me that night; my darling Gideon stayed with me, leaving just before dawn while I slept.

And the next day as Iris and Mrs. Katsulis and I were about to board the Pan Am flight to Hawaii, I saw Gideon hurrying toward us through the crowd. I thought he had come to see us off, but he was carrying a suitcase. "I've told Olivia I want a divorce. I'm coming to Hawaii with you and our daughter."

We returned ten months later with Charlotte, who had been born in Hilo, a quiet town where no one knew us. As I had predicted, no one at home believed my story of the young man, Iris's new husband, who had died in a diving accident, but everyone accepted it nonetheless, and the secret was kept.

While we were in Hawaii, Gideon and I spun dreams of our new life together. But when we returned to San Francisco we learned that it was not to be.

Olivia would not grant Gideon a divorce. I had not thought she would. Why relinquish both house and husband to me? But there were also problems now in the family, and Gideon's strength and guidance were needed. At the core of the tempest was Margo's inability to get pregnant.

Margo and Adrian had been married for seven years and still had produced no child. Now Margo wanted to adopt an orphan but Olivia would not permit it, insisting that her daughter-in-law go to a specialist and find a way to produce an heir. Olivia wanted her grandchild to be a Barclay. "I have tried to point out to her," Gideon told me one day, "that we are not true Barclays, that Richard Barclay adopted *me*. But she conveniently forgets that fact as she coerces Adrian into intervening each time Margo goes to a lawyer or an adopting agency."

The two were fighting constantly, mother-in-law and daughter-in-law, no longer enjoying the close relationship they once had when Olivia had still lived in the big house and showed young Margo samples of drapery fabric. Adrian, nearly thirty and holding a high position running the Harmony-Barclay Ltd. office in San Francisco, found himself caught between obeying his mother and pleasing his wife, and so began escaping more and more to yacht clubs and golf courses and, Gideon suspected, Nevada bordellos.

I was troubled by what I heard, for I knew how much Gideon longed for grandchildren, and I knew that such disharmony was disturbing Margo's inner harmony and *yin-yang* balance, and blocking the flow of her *chi*, diminishing her chances of ever getting pregnant. Gideon asked me if I could help, if I had a cure. I reminded him that my medicines did not cure, for that is not the Chinese way; they only restored balance and harmony to the body, so that the body could then cure itself. But this was what Margo needed — a restoration of harmony.

I gave him a bottle of Golden Lotus Wine, which I myself had taken every day for years. I was proof, I told him, of the balancing powers of my medicine, for although I was fifty, most people took me for ten years younger. The bottle I gave to Gideon to give to Margo was my own special supply. It did not come from my factory; I made it myself in my kitchen, compounding it the same way my mother had, and the way Lady Golden Lotus had a thousand years ago, by steeping the ingredients in a large ceramic vessel filled with the strong Chinese liquor *gao liang*, sealing the vessel well,

allowing the brew to sit for six months, then straining it, re-
freshing it with more *gao liang*, sealing it again and steeping
it for another six months. Among the powerful ingredients I
used were angelica, which regulates menstrual balance, powdered silkworm, which calms the blood, and dried human
placenta. These were strong rejuvenating and fertility agents.

Margo did not like me. She did not believe in herbal medicines, even though they were what made her rich. And so
when Gideon told me she was faithfully drinking the Golden
Lotus Wine and had requested more, I knew that her desire
for a baby was deep and genuine.

In the early spring of 1958, I discovered that Iris was pregnant again.

This time we did not go to Hawaii. I did not tell Gideon. I
kept Iris in her bedroom suite, informing Gideon and our
friends that my daughter had taken a fall down the stairs and
was confined to bed due to a temporary paralysis. I hired two
nurses to assist Mrs. Katsulis and to keep a round-the-clock
watch on my daughter. I provided Iris with as many puzzles
as were necessary to keep her occupied. And seven months
later, when the time came, I was midwife again to my own
grandchild.

I had already known what I must do. After I examined
the infant carefully in the light and satisfied myself that
there were no Chinese features, I took the baby from Iris
while she slept, bathed it and wrapped it in blankets, and I
went in the middle of the night to Margo's house. I told her
that I had been called to the home of a friend whose daughter was in labor. The daughter was unmarried, the family
did not want the child. I told Margo that if she wanted this
baby, it would be our secret, and that Mr. Sung, who was
my friend and could be trusted, would produce a birth certificate and adoption papers that would make the adoption
appear legal.

Margo took the stranger's baby with joy. Olivia was not pleased when told the news afterward, but it was too late by then for her to intervene. And Adrian was relieved that the squabbling had subsided. No one knew that the adopted child was the grandson of Gideon Barclay.

They named him Desmond.

50

5:00 A.M. — Palm Springs, California

"Johnny!" Charlotte said as she emerged from the bathroom, a book in one hand, a towel for her hair in the other. "I know who it is!"

"So do I," he said, as he hit Enter and the result of his trace came on the screen.

He turned away from the computer and looked at her, standing there in the doorway.

He wanted to take the towel and finish drying her long black hair, run it through his fingers, taming it beneath his touch. He ached to hold her again as he had briefly held her a short while ago, when they had realized the horrendous misunderstanding of the past sixteen years. As Charlotte had said, so much time wasted because a one looked like a seven.

"It's all in here! Read it!" She held out the antique book she had found in the kitchenette drawer. It consisted of vellum pages protected between two wooden covers and bound with twine strung through holes top and bottom. "I didn't know what was written inside," she said as he took the book from her. "It turns out it's my grandmother's diary from the early 1950s. I never even knew she kept a diary."

Jonathan carefully turned the brittle pages, his eyes following the precise, flowery script Charlotte's grandmother had learned long ago in a Singapore missionary school. He stopped suddenly and stared at the bottom of the page. "Desmond is your *brother?*"

"*Half* brother. I assume we had two different fathers. My suspicions about my own father are confirmed in there. . . . My mother was never married. The scuba diver was fabricated, it was all an elaborate lie that everyone was in on. Now listen," she said quickly, tossing down the towel and hurriedly gathering her long hair into a black silk ribbon. "Remember when I told you that something happened while I was away in Europe last year, that Des had changed? Well, I think that 'something' was that he found out the truth about his parentage. Johnny, a while ago, when Desmond caught me in the stairwell, he said strange things. He kept talking about my mother and making disparaging remarks about Margo —"

"You don't have to convince me," Jonathan interjected. He pointed to the screen. "It took me a while because of the power failure, but I was able to retrieve the most recent files that had been accessed, and sent out a trace on the last copied formula. My probe sent back an IP address, which I was able to cross-reference on Internic."

Charlotte peered at the screen. "Desmond Barclay!"

Jonathan reached for his black windbreaker. "We don't have much time."

51

They drove first to Harmony Biotech. "There's something I want to make sure of first," Jonathan said as he guided the rental car into a protected space.

They entered the main office building by way of the back stairs, and when they reached the third landing, Charlotte picked up the silver flask Desmond had been drinking from earlier and then thrown down. Lifting it to her nose, she said, "That's what I thought. There was no alcohol in this. Just plain water. Desmond was pretending to be drunk! He probably rinsed his mouth with some of Adrian's bourbon, or splashed some on his sweater. It was an act, Johnny, to make me think he was too looped to even stand up!"

"Too drunk to send e-mails, too," Jonathan said.

They hurried down the hall, pausing to make sure the federal agent sitting outside the computer room didn't see them, and that neither Valerius Knight nor any of his agents were in sight. Then they slipped into Desmond's office.

His computer, like all the others, had been tagged, labeled, and disconnected by Knight's team. So had his telephone and external modem. Charlotte and Jonathan searched under the enormous executive desk, opened drawers, checked in the wastebasket, and then moved to the mahogany credenza, the wet bar, the closet where suits and designer sportswear hung, behind the white linen sofa and matching chairs, the glass-fronted lawyer's bookshelves, even under the wicker basket that held an artificial palm tree, frantically trying to find where he could have hidden a modem.

"It *has* to be in here," Charlotte said. "This office is the only place in the building where Desmond could count on not being disturbed. He could lock the door and type away."

Jonathan returned to the built-in cupboard between the

bookshelves, and surveyed again the stereo equipment, CD player, color TV. "Here it is," he said, pulling the TV all the way out on its rolling shelf to reveal a laptop computer tucked behind it, and the external modem hooked to it.

"If nothing else," Charlotte observed wryly, "Desmond is not dumb."

"I'll bet you anything this number is a DDI."

"A what?"

"Direct Dial Inwards. It doesn't go through the main switchboard, so there's no way your system administrator can detect that dialing-in is going on. I also bet if we check the e-mail software in this laptop, we'll find a folder filled with some interesting messages sent through anonymous remailers."

Sliding the TV back in, leaving the laptop and modem in place, making sure they had disturbed nothing, Jonathan closed the cupboard and said, "Let's go pay Desmond a little visit."

Charlotte peered out at the rain, a worried look on her face. "He lives about ten miles from here. But he's up in one of the canyons. We'll have to be careful."

52

As they made their way along Palm Canyon Drive, the torrential rain prohibiting them from going too fast, Charlotte said, "I've uncovered so many secrets in the past few hours, Johnny, that my head is spinning. It's as if everything I thought I knew about my family has been turned inside out. What I once thought was black is now white, and vice versa. Uncle Gideon, who is really my grandfather! And now Desmond, my brother! It makes me wonder . . ."

Jonathan took his eye from the road for a split second to look at her. "Wonder what?"

"I told you that Grandmother believed her mother spoke to her from the afterlife. She said it happens to all the daughters in our family at least once in our lives."

"Yes? And?"

"But Johnny" — she regarded him in the darkness, her face catching occasional illumination from streetlights they passed — "it turns out Mei-ling wasn't dead when my grandmother heard her voice! So what about the voice *I* heard, Johnny, my mother's voice, warning me about the tea? Does it mean that what my grandmother had me believe all these years, about my mother dying after a fall down the stairs, is really a lie? Does it mean my mother is really still alive . . . ?"

They came to a flooded intersection where the raging water was already over the curb and washing the sidewalks. Jonathan slowed the car, guiding it toward the center of the road, where the water was shallower. He gripped the steering wheel and peered through the rain like a man focused on only one task: to get to the other side. Then he startled Charlotte by saying suddenly, "I don't know how you can ever forgive me."

In the darkness, the only illumination coming from the headlight beams reflecting off the rain, she saw the faint throbbing of a vein at his temple.

"I decided that I was the only person in the whole world who had ever been hurt," he said quietly, pressing on the gas and the brake equally as he inched the big car through the flood. "I was an arrogant bastard who peered at the world over a high wall that I had built up around myself. I placed all my feelings on a tall pedestal and dared women to reach them. Adele accepted the challenge and so I rewarded her."

She watched his profile, remembering the feel of his embrace an hour earlier, the taste of his mouth, and the dizzying discovery of their incredible misunderstanding over a poem.

Jonathan turned his eyes from the road for just an instant. "Yes, you were supposed to tell me not to get married, that day in San Francisco. You were supposed to read from a script that I never gave you."

"So you blamed me for your unhappiness with Adele?"

"We weren't unhappy. In fact we were happy at first. Content, I guess. And then it became a passive life and we just allowed things to happen." He looked at her. "I don't want to let life just happen to me anymore, Charlie."

She reached out and laid a hand over his, feeling the hard knuckles as his fingers gripped the wheel. "We just need to get through this night, Johnny...."

She didn't need to say the rest.

Desmond lived in the hills overlooking Rancho Mirage, in a five-million-dollar glass-and-marble home filled with expensive sculpture and paintings, a private gym and hair salon, and an indoor air-conditioned swimming pool.

A white-jacketed Filipino houseboy admitted Jonathan and Charlotte, and escorted them along split-level corridors until they came to the "game room" — a vast glassed-in area furnished with a full bar and eight bar stools, a billiard table, two giant-screen TVs, six electronic arcade-sized pinball machines, a computer game center, and a fiery barbecue pit sunk in the center surrounded by sofas built right into the floor.

Desmond was at the bar, pouring a ginger ale. "Hello," he said with a smile. "Beastly out, isn't it?"

The expansive view of the desert valley, observed beyond an illuminated rock-and-cactus garden, was ruined by the storm. Not even the struggling dawn could get through the black clouds and heavy rain.

Charlotte noticed that Desmond had changed out of his pretentious black attire to a pretentious all-white outfit of

Hugo Boss oversized pullover, white cotton pants, white buck shoes. But at least he was no longer wearing sunglasses. When Jonathan started to go straight for him, saying, "It's time someone wiped that smug look off your face," Charlotte grabbed his arm, feeling the hard muscles flex and quiver. "It's what he wants you to do, Johnny."

"Still resorting to brute force?" Desmond said. "I'd have thought you would have grown out of that, after all these years."

"Desmond, you're not drunk," Charlotte said.

"Two hours ago you said I *was*. Make up your mind, Charlotte. Or should I say 'Sister'?" He sipped his ginger ale. "Ah, I see you are not surprised that I call you that. Have you always known? Has the whole damn world known my nasty little secret except me?"

"I only just found out, Desmond. I didn't know." She watched him open the refrigerator beneath the bar and retrieve a handful of ice cubes.

Dropping the ice cubes into his drink, he said, "When you said a while ago that you regarded me more as a brother, I nearly busted a gut trying to keep from laughing. It's ironic, don't you think? I mean, I *am* your brother. Well, half brother."

He smirked as he stirred his ice cubes with a finger. "Do you know what makes this such a delicious secret? I don't think Mother dearest knows that Iris was my real mother. I'm sure Margo had envisioned some beautiful debutante seduced by a calculus professor from Stanford. Maybe it was an astronaut. On no, we didn't have those in 1957. Well, Margo would certainly have expected my daddy to be some sort of brilliant mind or American hero, and my mummy to have had the looks of Grace Kelly and the pedigree of Princess Di. I think it will spoil her day when she finds out that I'm the result of idiot Iris getting out of her kennel."

"Don't talk like that," Jonathan said.

"You will pardon me," Desmond said, shooting Jonathan a lethal glance, "but I can say whatever I damn well please in my own home." He turned to Charlotte. "I had a feeling Braveheart hadn't left yet. He still had work to do, didn't he?"

"When did you find out, Desmond, about my mother also being your mother? Was it last year while I was away in Europe?"

He raised his glass in a mock toast. "Full marks, sister dear. Yes, it was while you were away. As you can imagine, the news did rather take me by surprise. I tried to accept it with equanimity, but you are very observant, you noticed that I had changed. Well, wouldn't you if you just found out the truth about your parentage? Especially if it was such a *laughable* parentage?"

"How did you find out? Was it Grandmother's diary?"

"Diary? What diary? No, I found out because of Krista."

He leaned with his elbows on the polished mahogany bar and pointed to a wall covered with photographs of his family: his three wives, his daughter, Krista, by his second wife, his son, Robbie, by his first. Desmond shared custody of the teenagers with two ex-wives, keeping Krista and Robbie shuttling back and forth between homes.

"What about Krista?" Charlotte said, looking at the last photo in the series, of a pretty girl blowing out candles on a cake that said "Sweet Sixteen."

Desmond leaned back and took a long drink of ginger ale. "Just over a year ago," he said, "Krista started showing signs of a blood disorder. She would bruise easily, cuts wouldn't heal. When she had her appendix out, they had to give her three units of blood. Her doctor told us that the symptoms were indicative of more than one disease, and that they needed to pinpoint exactly which disease it was in order to start treatment. It was possible, he said, that Krista was suffering from an inherited genetic disorder called von Willebrand's disease, which would call for a certain course of therapy. If that wasn't the case, then the therapy could actually be harmful to her. What he needed, he said, was an extensive family health history. When I told them I had been adopted and didn't know my biological parents, he urged me to find out as much as I could because it was crucial to his treatment plan for my daughter."

"So you went to Grandmother," Charlotte said.

"Bingo," he said, saluting her with his drink. "At first the old lady told me she knew nothing about my real parents, but when I explained the urgency of the situation, and how vital it was that we rule out heredity, she finally confessed that although she had no idea who my father was, she could assure me that my mother had not had von Willebrand's. I asked her how she could be so certain of that. And that was when she dropped the H-bomb, the A-bomb, and the neutron bomb all at once." He released a short, bitter laugh. "I wish I had a photograph of the look on my face at that moment!"

Desmond walked around the bar and stepped down into the sunken center of the room. He paused to gaze into the barbecue pit for a long moment, his eyes held by the glowing embers and blanket of flames.

He turned to face Charlotte, his attitude no longer flippant. "That was when I remembered hearing something about why your grandmother inherited the house from Great-grandmother Fiona. Something about Iris having the same mental disorder as Richard Barclay's sister. So, my daughter did not after all have an inherited blood disorder, because it seems that the thing that runs in *our* family is idiots!"

"Iris wasn't an idiot," Charlotte said in a hard tone.

"She had bats in her belfry!" he shouted suddenly, and Jonathan took an instinctive step closer to Charlotte.

"Oh, look at the two of you," Desmond said. "Always so cozy."

"So you found out the truth," Charlotte said, wanting to keep him talking. "And then what?"

"You were away in Europe at the time, visiting all those fascinating pharmaceutical houses. Big shot Charlotte Lee from Harmony Biotech being wined and dined and escorted around Wellcome and Merck and Bayer while I was on my knees thanking God my daughter had a temporary, curable blood disorder and at the same time cursing Him for having made me the son of an idiot who didn't even know she was having sex."

"Did you tell anyone else? Adrian or Margo?"

"Are you crazy? Margo would have gone ballistic. Besides, it was around that time that my little plan began to hatch, and I knew that if Mummy and Daddy knew the truth about me, they would do something to foul up my nice little plan."

"What plan was that?" Jonathan said, and Charlotte felt him tense up, heard the dangerous edge to his voice.

"Don't you find it ironic, Charlotte?" Desmond said, ignoring Jonathan. "I spent all my life trying to please Margo because I knew deep down she was disappointed in me for not being a Barclay. And now I *am* a Barclay!"

"Did you murder my grandmother?"

His eyebrows arched. "No, I had nothing to do with her death. If the old lady *was* done away with, it certainly wasn't by *my* hand."

Lightning forked down from the sky and exploded, flooding the vast game room with blinding white light.

"God, you're despicable," Charlotte said.

Desmond winced. "Such talk."

"You tried to kill Naomi."

He shrugged. "Nothing would have happened."

"How can you say that?"

"She's a psychic, isn't she?"

"And you tried to kill me."

He held his drink up to the light, as if counting the bubbles. "I wasn't going to kill you. I just wanted to scare you a little. The garage door would have only damaged the Corvette. And I did shut down the ampoule assembly in time, didn't I?"

"You poisoned my tea, though," Charlotte said.

"Only enough to make you ill, to scare you. I didn't want you dead. I really do want you to make that press announcement. And you are going to, you know? There's no getting out of it, Charlotte."

"So you engineered it all," Jonathan said. "You somehow got Rusty Brown to tamper with the products, and then you planted evidence in his locker connecting him to the three deaths and to the explosion at Naomi's house. All very smart, Desmond, but why go to the trouble of tainting three large batches of products? Why not just the three samples you sent?"

Desmond spoke grudgingly. "Not that I'm admitting to anything you understand, just in case you are melodramatic enough to have a recording device on you. But surely you can see that three samples would be easier to trace to the person who did the tampering. By altering hundreds of bottles and capsules, the trail to the perpetrator is hidden. Speaking hypothetically, of course."

He turned to Charlotte. "The police can't link me to those three deaths. I have no motive in killing them. But you do, Charlotte. *And* you were in Gilroy that day the third sample was mailed from there."

He looked at his watch. "My my, look at the hour. It's almost six, Charlotte." He looked around. "But where are the reporters? Where is the minivan with the satellite hookup? I meant my threat, dear sister. I *will* kill thousands. I can do it."

"What I'm curious about," she said, "is that you don't seem surprised to see us here."

Desmond shrugged. "Once I realized you had called trusty

Mister Spock to come and save you, I knew it would only be a matter of time before you figured things out. And, of course, snooping in that museum. You didn't know I knew what you were up to, did you? You might have fooled Valerius Knight, but I know you too well, Charlotte. So you found out — in a diary, did you say — that I am your brother?"

He crossed the living room, walking around cushions and ottomans, and stepped up onto the other side of the room, where arcade pinball machines stood lined up.

"What a shock," he said and he snapped the flippers on the Star Trek Next Generation game. "I've lusted after my own sister for all these years. It seems to run in the family."

He turned to face the two across the room. "I remember overhearing Grandmother Olivia telling my dear adoptive mummy one day that she hated *your* grandmother because Grandfather Gideon was in love with her. Olivia told Margo that everything had been fine while Harmony thought Gideon was her brother. But then he spilled the beans about being Richard Barclay's *adopted* son and so they became lovers. Do you see the irony there, Charlotte?" He laughed. "It's just the reverse of you and me! You didn't know I was your brother and now you do!"

Rain slanted against the floor-to-ceiling windows, sounding like hail against the glass. "Isn't it a scream?" Desmond said quietly, contemplating the drink in his hand. "All my life I felt worthless because I wasn't a true Barclay. As it turns out, I'm the only Barclay in the whole Barclay family! Ha! Just like you, Charlotte, *my* great-grandfather was Richard! That makes us somewhat aristocratic, you know. All those years of growing up and feeling like an outsider, now it turns out it's my father and grandfather who were the outsiders!"

He pushed away from the pinball machine and went to stand at the glass doors, which gave out onto a waterfall cut into the natural rock of the hillside. Against the backdrop of the dark storm, Desmond's reflection was a ghostly white.

"Desmond," Charlotte said, "what is this all about? Why does finding out who you really are make you want to destroy the company?"

"And I meant it, too," he said evasively. "I intend to go through with it, Charlotte. Make those statements to the press and I won't kill thousands of innocent people."

"But *why?*"

He smiled playfully. "For me to know and you to find out."

She gave him an impatient look. "I don't believe you can do it."

"Trust me. I can."

"How? You might have been able to engineer those three deaths — you sent them free samples, didn't you?"

"Don't you think it was clever of me to target three women whom you had a personal beef against?"

"But there are warnings out now, our products have been pulled from the shelves. You can't force people to ingest something they've been warned against."

"Oh, I wouldn't be forcing them. They'll *want* this."

She stared at him while thunder rolled over the mountains, making the ground shake, the lights flicker. "It's the classified formulas," she said finally. "That's it, isn't it?"

He winked. "There's my clever sister. Yes, the classified formulas. The ones currently under development that could earn us millions, possibly even billions."

"So you intend to sell them to another company? To Synatech, is that it?"

"Oh, nothing so ordinary. It's a new age, Charlotte. Get with the times. I'm going to publish the formulas over the Internet."

"What will that do?" she said.

He looked at Jonathan. "Braveheart knows what I'm talking about, don't you?"

"Desmond, you bastard," Charlotte said.

He smiled. "Just because everyone says I'm a bastard doesn't mean I'm not."

"Tell me what you are planning."

"Do you know how many cancer victims there are in the world, Charlotte?" he asked. "People who are desperate for a cure . . . *any* cure? I distribute those formulas, and in the wink of an eye hundreds of little cottage pharmacies all over the world start cooking up the drugs in the hopes of making millions. And believe me, people will buy those drugs."

"But how will that kill thousands? Those formulas are categorized as experimental, but you and I both know some of them actually work while others are benign —" She stopped herself. "My God, you're going to alter them."

"You get smarter by the minute."

"You're going to make them *lethal?*"

"I've already changed them."

"It won't work, Desmond. All I have to do is post a warning from Harmony Biotech."

"Oh come now, Charlotte. First of all, you don't know which formulas I have altered, and which I plan to release. And how are you going to post your warning? To news groups? IRC? There are thousands of new groups, millions of chat rooms and millions of websites. Ask Braveheart, he'll tell you."

"Why are you doing this?"

"Because the company is rightfully mine!" he bellowed, startling them. "I am Richard Barclay's only male heir! Harmony Biotech was begun by his daughter. When she died, it should have gone to me!"

"My God, Desmond, this is twisted thinking! You're actually telling me that if you can't have the company, you will destroy it?"

He looked at his watch. "Make up your mind," he snapped. "It's almost six." He crossed the room to an old-fashioned rotary pay phone on the wall. "I'll make it easy for you. I've got the number right here of Channel Seven News. You can make your statements over the phone."

When Jonathan made a sudden move toward a cabinet next to the pinball machines, Desmond said, "I wouldn't try that if I were you. Just stay right where you are and my houseboy won't turn into Jean-Claude Van Damme. With knives." He added with a smile. "He might look small, but he has a black belt in several martial arts."

"Desmond," Charlotte said, almost pleading, "this doesn't make sense. What do you gain? Either way — if I make that statement or let you release those formulas — the company will be ruined. You'll lose your job, your investment, probably this house! Kill Harmony and you commit suicide!"

He lifted the receiver, looked at it for a moment, then hung up and said, "Well . . . , there *is* a third alternative."

"And what is that?"

"Turn Harmony Biotech over to me."

Thunder cracked and rumbled. The flames in the barbecue pit danced in an unseen draft. "So that's it," Charlotte said. "That's what you've been after all along. You want me to give you the company."

"It's mine."

"You are forgetting that I am also Perfect Harmony's heir. *And* I am the eldest."

"I am the son!" he shouted.

Glancing at Jonathan, Charlotte said, "All right, I won't argue with that right now. But, for God's sake, Des, why didn't you just come to me about this in the first place. Why kill innocent people? Why those ridiculous e-mails? Why this silly press conference and deadline?"

"Well, first of all, darling sister, I hardly expected you to say, 'Oh here, you're right. The company *is* yours.' I also did it because I wanted to make you suffer."

"*Why?*"

"Because you had everything that I didn't."

"How can you say that?" she cried.

"Your grandmother loved you, Charlotte. Do you know what my life was like with Margo? She went to such extremes to show the world how much she loved me. The big parties, putting only me on our yearly Christmas card, bragging to everyone how great her son was. For the longest time I thought my name was 'You're-adopted-but.' She would begin every sentence that way. Or she'd say, 'We love you as if you were our own.' I felt like a stray dog she'd taken in."

He looked at the drink in his hand. "I think," he said softly, "if she had known I was a real Barclay, the great Richard Barclay's son, I think she might have loved me."

He raised his eyes to Charlotte. "That house should have gone to me, too. Instead the old lady left it to you and you turned around and sold it to strangers."

"I offered it to Margo and Adrian," she said.

"You offered to *sell* it to them!" he shouted again. "You tried to sell to them what already belonged to them . . . to *me!*"

"Desmond, listen, we can work this out —"

"Don't patronize me, Charlotte. And, no, we can't 'work it out.' Turn all controlling interest over to me or I destroy you *and* Harmony."

"You know, Desmond," Jonathan said, keeping a careful eye on the houseboy. "As I recall, you never had much time for computers. I'm rather impressed. It seems you've been taking lessons. You are aware, of course, that to transmit even one formula over the Internet would take days or weeks in order to reach the number of people you hope to."

"Jonathan's right, Des," Charlotte said quickly. "You don't have the ability to do it."

He regarded first Charlotte, then Jonathan, and then slowly smiled. "Ah, and is this the point where I am supposed to say, 'As a matter of fact, I've arranged for a little demonstration?' I walk over to my computer and say, 'Observe!' transmit a formula, and the feds come barging through the door. Is that what you have planned? God, but you can be obvious sometimes, Charlotte. Have you ever heard of spamming? Hot keys? Macros? Cross-posting? I type a three-key command and before you can say, 'There go the profits,' Charlotte's precious GB4204 has hit half a million e-mail addresses."

Jonathan shot Charlotte a cautionary look. "I guess you have been taking lessons, Des," he said as he mentally gauged the distance between himself and the closed cabinet Desmond kept glancing toward.

"Well, it helps to have a seventeen-year-old son who has been glued to a computer since he emerged from the womb. Robbie has been a big help. First time in his life the boy is actually aware he has a father."

"You really don't think you'd get away with it, do you?" Jonathan said, his hand on Charlotte's arm, urging her to move slowly back a step. "Sending intellectual property such as a stolen proprietary formula over the Internet is a federal offense."

Desmond gave him a withering look. "And don't *you* patronize me, either. I know what's legal and what isn't. I might argue, of course, that since I have part ownership in the company, I would only be taking what is mine. And besides, once the formula is altered, is it still then Harmony's formula? An interesting question, I think. But we don't have time to bandy that about right now." He picked up a sheaf of legal documents, bound in blue covers and stapled together. "I've taken the liberty of having it all drawn up. All you have to do, Charlotte, is sign on the dotted line."

She stared at the papers as if he were handing her a snake. "You can't be serious!"

"As serious as the plague, dear sister. Sign the papers and

you and Braveheart can go home, happy in the thought that you have saved thousands of lives . . . and your own besides."

"I'm surprised you want the power that badly. I've never had the impression you were interested in running the company."

"I don't think Desmond *wants* to run the company," Jonathan said quietly, inching away a little more.

"What do you mean?" Charlotte said.

"Not a bad guess, Braveheart." Desmond gave a shrug. "No point in keeping it a secret I suppose. If you must know, dear sister, I intend to sell the company."

"Sell it!"

"You think I didn't know about Synatech approaching you about eight months ago with an offer to buy? An offer, I might add, that would have put a lot of nice spare change in our pockets. Well, as I told you, I've been talking to them —"

The door chimes rang suddenly throughout the house. As soon as the houseboy disappeared, Jonathan strode across the room to the closed cabinet. A moment later the houseboy returned to the game room. "Mr. Barclay," he began. Immediately behind him Valerius Knight appeared.

"Oh God," Desmond muttered, setting down his drink. "Elliot Ness has arrived."

Knight walked up to him, holding aloft a laptop computer. "Is this your personal computer, Mr. Barclay?"

"What are you doing with that?"

"Will you please identify it for us?"

Desmond hesitated. Then he said, "You've obviously already checked."

"Yes or no, please."

"Of course it's mine."

"Mr. Barclay, we are placing you under arrest on suspicion of product tampering and conspiracy to commit wire fraud —"

"What!"

Two agents in wet raincoats were immediately at Desmond's side, seizing his wrists and clapping handcuffs on them.

"We are also arresting you," Knight continued, "on suspicion of commercial espionage, business fraud, and piracy."

"Wait a minute! Show me your proof!"

"The proof is in here, Mr. Barclay," Knight said, holding up the laptop.

Desmond smiled. "Show me a single file in that computer."

"I can show you thirty-eight," Knight said as he held up a floppy disk. "These files were deleted from the directory, of course, but we found them. They were still on the hard drive."

"Looks like Robbie didn't teach you quite enough," Jonathan quipped as he ran his fingers over the cabinetry.

"So take the laptop," Desmond said with a shrug. "I don't care. You have no proof of anything. You can't connect me to the murders."

"Mr. Barclay," Knight said in a resonant voice, as if he were on camera. "Were you in the town of Gilroy on the ninth of this month?"

Some of the color drained from Desmond's face.

"We have the hotel record, Mr. Barclay."

Desmond leveled a deadly gaze on Charlotte. "Really," he said, "I am disappointed in you. I warned you not to tell the feds. Now I am going to have to make good my threat."

"Well, technically," Jonathan said, "it wasn't Charlotte who alerted Knight to your hidden laptop. It was me. It was also my idea that he have his technician run a utility to find deleted files."

"It doesn't matter," Desmond said. "Arresting me won't stop me. I'll be out in a few days, maybe in a few hours. And then I'll make you and Charlotte wish you hadn't — Hey, where are *you* guys going?"

Two more of Knight's men, receiving a signal from Jonathan, strode across the room to the cabinet, which they pried open to reveal a computer game center. They immediately began labeling the cords, ports, and cables, swiftly, silently, as they had done at Harmony Biotech's corporate offices. When they disconnected the CPU from the monitor, Desmond said, "Uh, you can't take that."

Knight strode up to him and held up a piece of paper so that Desmond could read it. "We have a warrant to seize all suspected equipment, Mr. Barclay."

Desmond laughed. "Be my guest. That hard drive is four gigs, by the way. A lot of files to examine. Let me see, maybe I stored the stolen formulas under 'Letters to Aunt Matilda.' Or maybe they're nestled somewhere in my AlphaWorld resource directory. Hey! 'Taxes for Years 1986–1996!' Now that's a big file!"

"Somehow, Desmond," Jonathan said as he joined the agents at the computer cupboard, opening drawers and inspecting shelves, "I don't think you're stupid enough to keep the stolen formulas on your hard drive."

"You want to examine my floppies?" Desmond said. "Open that closet. Yeah, that one."

Jonathan opened a door to expose shelves crammed with games, sports equipment, and, at the bottom, shoeboxes filled with floppy disks.

"Help yourself," Desmond said with a triumphant smile.

Jonathan exchanged a look with Charlotte — they were thinking the same thing: it would take weeks or months to search all those files.

Knight strode over, stopped, and peered down at the boxes. "Jesus," he muttered.

"God but I'm enjoying this," Desmond said.

Jonathan's eyes scanned the shelves, skimming over old Monopoly and Clue boxes, a five-hundred-piece jigsaw puzzle, Scrabble, and checkers. When his eye fell upon a box brightly decorated with dragons and wizards, he brought it out into the light.

"I see you play computer games now, Des," he said as he held up the box. "I recall how you used to make fun of me in the old days for playing Pong and Asteroids. So what level are you at?"

"Huh?"

Jonathan shook the box, opened it, dropped the floppy into his palm. "Have you reached Dragonmaster yet?"

Desmond cleared his throat. "That isn't mine. It belongs to my son. He plays it when he visits on weekends."

Jonathan turned the box over, pondered it. "You should get your son some newer software. This is an old version. Games don't come on floppies any more. Or did you know that?"

"Desmond," Charlotte said, "I happen to know Robbie conquered *this* game in the seventh grade. He wouldn't be caught dead playing it now."

Desmond shrugged, a quick, nervous gesture. "What do *I* know what the kid plays? Maybe he hasn't touched it in years. That closet is full of old games."

Jonathan turned the disk over in his hands, then held it up to the light. "I wonder if this has been written over. Doesn't appear to be write-protected."

"It's a goddamn *computer* game," Desmond said, a note of panic rising in his voice.

"Game disks can be altered," Jonathan said. "I wonder if those classified formulas might not be hidden somewhere in Mordred's Castlekeep? Or maybe they're buried under the Lake of Khalila's Sorrow?"

Valerius Knight reached out and took the game box and floppy disk from Jonathan. "I've always wanted to try a computer game," he said. "This one looks like it would be fairly simple to figure out."

"Now, look —" Desmond began.

The front door chimes sounded again, and a moment later Margo and Adrian appeared.

"What's going on here?" Desmond's father boomed. "We just received a call from Sung telling us to get over here right away. he said it was an emergency."

"Apparently I'm being arrested," Desmond said.

"What!"

"It's a mistake, Father. Not to worry."

"Arrested for what, for God's sake?"

"They claim that I'm the one who tampered with the products."

Adrian fixed an eye on his son. "*Are* you responsible for those deaths, Desmond?"

"Of course not," Margo said sharply. "The police have already arrested the man who is responsible for that."

"Yes, but *you* hired Rusty Brown, didn't you, Desmond?" Charlotte said. "I believe when we talk to the personnel director, she will attest to it."

Adrian scowled at the agents unhooking the computer and wrapping it in plastic. Then he turned to Desmond. "Are you out of your mind? You deliberately hired a man who had a criminal record? What the hell did you do that for?"

Desmond shrugged. "I wanted to give a man the opportunity to see the error of his ways, a chance to rehabilitate. He's a good technician, he knows his job well."

"Desmond," Charlotte said, "you purposely hired Brown because of his record. You read about him in the paper, you read about his arrest and trial, and when he got off, you called him and offered him a job. Did you make big promises, Desmond? Was that how you manipulated him? And then when he was drinking at the Coyote Bar and Grill after getting turned down for a raise, you planted the idea of revenge in his mind."

"An interesting fantasy," Desmond said with an unconvincing laugh.

Jonathan poked around in the closet, removing the shoe-boxes of floppy disks, shoving skis and soccer balls aside, until he saw something wedged in the back. "Are *these* a fantasy?" he said, holding up the false beard and baseball cap with a ponytail attached. "The night janitor described the man who bought drinks for Rusty Brown as having a beard and a ponytail."

"This is ridiculous!" Adrian said. "What possible motive could Desmond have for wanting to destroy the company?"

"Because," Charlotte said, "Desmond found out that Iris Lee was his mother."

The two Barclays looked at her for a moment. Then Margo said, "I don't believe you."

"It is true," came another voice in the room. "Iris was Desmond's mother." Everyone turned to see the newcomer in the doorway.

There was a collective gasp.

"Grandmother!" Charlotte said.

53

6:00 A.M. — Palm Springs, California

They all looked at me as if they were seeing a ghost.

Maybe they were. I had come back from the dead, I had given them no time to prepare.

Desmond, with his wrists in handcuffs, had turned as white as his expensive outfit, while his father was as red as a peony. Margo just gazed at me with an unreadable expression — the way Olivia had regarded me many years ago through cigarette smoke — while Charlotte stared at me in shock and Jonathan, recovering from the shock, started to smile.

He was the first person I acknowledged — Jonathan, who had turned into such a handsome man. I kissed him on each cheek and told him it was good to see him again.

He smiled and said, "I'm sorry I missed your funeral, Mrs. Lee."

I always liked his sense of humor. No wonder my granddaughter fell in love with him. He didn't seem as surprised to see me as the others were. I remember him telling me once that his grandmother had "the sight" — what I call the "third eye." Maybe he inherited this secret knowing.

"Charlotte-*ah*," I said next, embracing her as she stood there like a tree, her mouth a big round O, like a knothole in the bark. Charlotte has always known everything, from when she was very little; it amused me now to see her not knowing something for a change.

"Grandmother," she said again, stuck on one word, like those old phonograph records when they got scratched. She put her arms around me and said, "I thought you were dead and now you are alive." I felt her tears on my neck and her arms around me. I held on to her as she held on to me.

Adrian, who never learned graciousness, said, "What the hell! You're supposed to be dead!"

"Is it mandatory?" I asked as I stepped into Desmond's game room that had always made me think of a spaceship. "Have I broken a rule of etiquette, Adrian?"

"Harmony," Margo said, "what a pleasant surprise." She always was a bad liar, but I think that is because she had never had any intention of being a good one.

And then they all rushed toward me at once — the policemen, Desmond, his parents, the houseboy in his white jacket — hands outstretched as if I were a prize at the end of a race. "Grandmother" — "Mrs. Lee" — "ma'am" — "Harmony!" They called me every name they could think of as they

fought for the honor of escorting me to a seat. Could they not
see that I was not an invalid? Perhaps I was eighty-eight
(ninety as far as they knew), but I had my cane and the supportive arm of Mr. Sung, who led me to a sofa that was part
of the wall and part of the floor and impossible to sit in. As I
lowered myself, with assistance from the African policeman
and Jonathan, onto big cushions, I said to Desmond, "Bad
feng shui in here. People should not sit lower than their
knees."

Everyone laughed — a nervous laugh, for how does one
treat a ghost? They took positions as if they were actors waiting for the curtain to go up. Mr. Knight, whom Mr. Sung had
described to me, seemed to be pleased, angry, and confused
at the same time, as he leaned against a glass palm tree with
water bubbles floating up the center of its pink trunk. I met
his eyes and saw the sharp intelligence behind them, a mind
working quickly, sorting, making swift decisions. I saw a
man bent on revenge who was already seeing how this new
situation could be fitted into his private scheme to destroy the
medicines that had failed to save his son. I knew that once
again, as it had been back in 1936 when I had engaged in battle with Mr. Sung's father, my company was going to be in
newspaper headlines.

"Well?" Adrian said with his usual bluntness. "Aren't you
going to tell us what this is all about?"

I must confess that I have never liked Adrian, even though
he is the son of my beloved Gideon. Adrian is more Olivia
than his father. And I never liked Olivia, either.

Margo reached into her expensive alligator purse, pulled
out a gold cigarette case, lit a cigarette with a gold mono-
grammed lighter in just the same way I had seen Olivia do so
many times. "Do tell," she said after she had drawn in smoke
and released it, talking through the smoky screen. "This
ought to be a riot."

"Grandmother," Charlotte said, emerging from her

wooden stupor, "you lead us all to believe you were dead. I've never known you to lie."

"I have not lied, Charlotte-*ah*. I *did* die."

Someone made a soft gasp. But there was disbelief in it.

"I died during the storm on that boat in the Caribbean. I am told that when they carried me to the beach, there was no life in my body. But someone blew breath into my lungs. I do not know who, but he was a respecter of life, a man of faith, for even though I was dead, his breath brought me back to life. I coughed the water out of my lungs and then the islanders took me to a hospital."

I had never in all my decades heard such a silence as I heard in Desmond's spaceship room.

"I was very ill," I continued. "An old woman who drowns cannot have a smooth road to recovery. But the islanders took good care of me, they fed me special herbs, perhaps the same herb I went there seeking. And as I lay in the twilight realm between this life and that of my ancestors, I experienced such a clarity of vision as I had never known before. I realized I had been given a gift."

"A second chance at life," Charlotte said with wonder in her voice.

But the gift was not a second chance at life. The gift was a chance to save my company.

"Hell of a trick to play on us!" Desmond snapped, sounding just like Adrian, even though they weren't really father and son.

I paused to read the faces around me, to gauge the happiness on some, the anger on others. I felt the probing gaze of Valerius Knight, an intelligent, determined government agent who observed with a guarded expression this elderly white-haired Chinese lady in a modest blue *cheongsam*. I saw in his sharp eyes that he did not dismiss me as inconsequential, as others might.

"I needed to be assured that after I die the company will be

safe. And so I instructed Mr. Sung to inform the family that
I had died. Which was not untrue."

I turned to Desmond. "I did not trust you. That day when
I told you Iris was your mother, I saw a change come over
you that was like a creeping sickness, like the gangrene that
takes a limb. A badness had hold of you, Desmond. Now you
knew you were my grandson, now I knew you would expect
me to leave a large portion of the company to you. That I
could not do. You are irresponsible, you do not love Harmony House the way Charlotte does. If I had left a larger portion to you, would you have been willing to share the power
with Charlotte? I think not."

"You always thought you knew everything," this insolent
young man said to me.

So I told him what I knew: "It is my good fortune that Mr.
Sung enjoys a mutually respectful relationship with an attorney at a pharmaceutical company called Synatech Corporation. Perhaps you are familiar with this company,
Desmond?"

I saw by the tightness of his jaw that I had guessed cor-
rectly. My grandson had planned to sell my life's work to a
competitor who wanted only my name and my laboratories.
A company that would let Golden Lotus Wine and Beautiful
Intelligence Balm fade from the drugstore shelves.

"But why the charade, Grandmother?" Charlotte said.
"Why not just warn me? You could have taken me into your
confidence."

"What proof did I have that you or the company were in
danger from Desmond? Simply an old woman's intuition.
Desmond would have waited until I was dead to work his
greedy plan, but I could not wait that long. And also, I was
not certain the danger would come from Desmond. I also did
not trust Adrian or Margo. I feared also that another company, perhaps Moonstone, might find a way to take over Harmony. I had to know. Once I was gone and you were on your

own, I would not be here to help you. So I decided to stay
dead and accept the gift from the gods. This way I was able
to help you."

"With the help of Mr. Sung," Charlotte said.

"I am sorry," the elderly lawyer said. "It was difficult for
me. But I had given your grandmother my word."

"What about the casket that's buried in the cemetery in
San Francisco?" Margo said, with a look on her face as if she
had just tasted something bitter.

"It is empty of course, a symbol of my incomplete death."

"Jesus," muttered Adrian as he marched to the bar and
reached for a bottle of Jack Daniel's. He poured a small glass
of it and threw it down his throat, as if aiming for a target.
Then he poured another and aimed again.

"It's six o'clock in the morning, Adrian," Margo observed
dryly.

"Yeah, so? I come in here and see a dead woman walking
and talking — a woman, for crissake, whose funeral I attended —" He paused, met his wife's gaze, then meekly set
the glass down. I knew of Margo's aversion to alcohol, and I
knew why. Gideon had told me how when Margo was a child
she would wake up screaming. I knew of the pain and shame
that had been inflicted upon her, and that was why I tolerated
Margo, even though many times Charlotte declared that she
couldn't understand why I let Adrian's wife walk over me, as
she put it.

Margo slid her eyes to me. "I did think Mr. Sung's insistence on a closed casket rather forced."

"And then I find out," Adrian continued, "that my adopted
son is really my . . . wait, let me figure this out. . . ."

"Desmond," I said, "is the great-grandson of *your* grandfather, Richard Barclay."

"Isn't he also," Margo said through a veil of cigarette
smoke, "the grandson of Gideon Barclay, Adrian's father?"

I understood her meaning. I was tracing Desmond's line

through my descent from Richard Barclay. But there was the unspoken secret that Iris was not Mr. Lee's daughter, but Gideon's.

"This is making my head hurt," Adrian mumbled.

"Grandmother," Charlotte said, "the Chinese puzzle box Mr. Sung gave me, that was from you, wasn't it?"

"I wanted to guide you in the right direction."

"I could have used a little more help than that."

"How could I have given you stronger clues? Then you would have known I was alive and Desmond, or perhaps one of the others, would have hidden his sickness like a spider behind a rainspout, waiting. . . ."

"So what exactly do the charges against my son consist of?" Adrian said to Knight, and as the federal agent patiently outlined to Desmond's father the extent of his alleged crimes, I saw embarrassment grow in the son's eyes and admiration in the father's. "You did all that?" Adrian said with an astonished look on his face. Then he quickly held up a hand. "No, don't answer that, son. Not in front of these officers." A smile crept to Adrian's lips. "But my God, whoever did engineer all that must be pretty clever. We had — how many federal agents invading us last night?"

Desmond gave his father a startled look. I understood what Adrian did not: that Desmond had thought his parents would be ashamed and furious. And yet there were Margo and Adrian, smiling at their son with pride.

"Why aren't you mad at me?" Desmond said, sounding like a little boy.

"Why should we be?" Adrian said.

"Because this just proves to you that I'm a loser after all, just as you've thought all my life!"

Adrian blinked at his son in confusion. "What'd I ever do to give you that idea?"

"I read it in a letter," Desmond blurted. "You wrote it to

Mother twenty-five years ago! You said what a terrible thing it was for a father to have such a loser for a son."

A shocked silence rushed in behind his words as Desmond's parents stared at him, and then at each other. I saw bewilderment on Adrian's face, but after a moment it was as if a sunrise were occurring, as light flooded his tanned features and his eyes dawned with comprehension. "I remember that letter," he said. "But, Desmond, I wasn't referring to *you*. I was talking about myself!"

It was time now, I knew, for me to speak up, because I had known for years how Adrian saw himself against the backdrop of his father. "Gideon never thought of you as a loser, as you put it," I said. "That was your own perception. Gideon only ever loved you and was proud of you."

"Harmony," Adrian said, also sounding like a child again. "Do you know what happens to plants that grow in the shade?"

"Some flourish."

"When I was seven or eight, I was proud to hear how my father had built an emergency road to evacuate refugees. When I was ten and the reporters came to interview him, I stood like a peacock as he answered their questions. When *Life* magazine came to photograph him and I was twelve, I said to myself that I was going to be just like him someday. And then when I was thirteen and I understood the real significance of his war medals, I started thinking that I would *try* to be like him. When he was interviewed on television by Edward R. Murrow, I began to wonder if I could ever be like him. And finally I just started thinking that there was no way I ever could."

"It was not Gideon who did that," I reminded him, "but yourself in your own mind. Just as," I turned to Desmond, "you read a letter not intended for your eyes, and you read words not referring to you but you took them to mean you, and so upon those false words you built your life."

Another silence followed my words, this time filled with the mute question marks of a hundred unasked questions. Even Agent Knight, that rock-solid man, looked uncertain, as he searched among the floating pink bubbles in that ridiculous palm tree for his own place in this drama.

"Well, Mrs. Lee," Jonathan said at last, to break the silence, "it seems as if your charade was a success."

"Not that much of a success," Charlotte said suddenly. "Grandmother, I sold the house! I didn't keep it."

I could not help but smile. Had she not thought that through, my granddaughter who always knew everything? "*I* bought the house, Charlotte. I am the buyer you never met."

"So what now?" Adrian said. "Where does that leave ownership of the company?"

Margo joined her husband at the bar and put her arm around his waist. "It still isn't ours, darling," she said with a sigh.

Charlotte came and sat next to me on that low sofa. "I have so many questions," said my granddaughter who had once had all the answers. "What happened to my mother? Did she die after falling down the stairs?"

"No. That was another story to protect Iris's honor. Gideon and I finally had to put her in an institution."

"An institution!" everyone said, as if I had said, "We buried her alive."

"She was well taken care of by Catholic nuns, and I believe she was happy until she died."

"So she's dead?"

"Iris lived to be sixty years old."

"But . . . that was only eight years ago!" Charlotte said. "All this time my mother was alive and you never told me?"

"I wanted to, many times, Charlotte —"

She jumped up as if the sofa were suddenly on fire. "What is it with you and secrets, Grandmother?" she cried. She looked at me with eyes filled with reproach. "All these years you knew Desmond was my brother and you never told me."

Was I going to ease her pain by what I was about to say next, or cause more? It did not matter; the time had come for me to say it. "Desmond is not your brother, Charlotte-*ah*," I said.

"What!" Desmond said. "You mean you lied to me?"

I held up a hand. "I did not lie to you, Desmond. My daughter Iris was your mother." Then I turned to Charlotte and said, as gently as I could, "But Desmond is not your brother, Charlotte. He is your nephew. Iris was not your mother, she was your sister."

She frowned the way she used to over puzzle boxes, when she was little. "I don't understand."

"Charlotte-*ah*," I said, "*I* am your mother."

The silences of eleven people descended upon that room that made me think of spaceships. Even Mr. Sung, who had known and kept my secret all these years, was speechless. And the policemen, who didn't know our family story, were dumb with shock as they sensed a great revelation taking place.

"The night Gideon came to my house," I said, "the night before Iris and I went to Hawaii, he stayed with me and comforted me. And then, the next day, he went to Hawaii with us, where Iris's baby was born, and where we buried it after it lived for only two hours. Charlotte, I did not think I could get pregnant. But I could, as it turned out, and you were born two months after Iris's baby. When we brought you home, we told everyone you were my daughter's child."

I saw Charlotte's eyes fill with wonder — those green eyes she had inherited from Richard Barclay. "Then you mean my father . . . ?"

"Was Gideon. I remember, Charlotte, those years ago when you told me that I did not love you. Because I was strict and protective of you, you said I did not love you. But I did, and I still do, Charlotte, more than my own life do I love you, because you are the love child given to me by my darling Gideon."

I felt Charlotte's wonder-filled eyes travel over the hills and valleys of my face like a lost traveler searching for home. She was looking at me in a new way now, and spinning new threads to bind herself to me. What I had just told her was no easy thing for me to say, and so it would be no easy thing for her to absorb. She would not altogether grasp this today, or in the next few days. Perhaps she never would. Perhaps the look of shock and wonder in her eyes would be there from now on whenever she looked at me.

I held my hand out to Jonathan, who assisted me up from that bad luck sofa, and I went to Desmond, who stood between two policemen. "You are my grandson," I said. "I brought you into this world. My hands were the first human touch you felt. I loved you from the moment you were born. Perhaps I should have kept you, as I kept Charlotte. But I thought you would have a better life as a Barclay. Perhaps I made a mistake by keeping your true identity a secret . . . but I did it for your own sake, Desmond. There is Chinese in you, and those were still prejudiced times."

I reached up to touch the cheek that I had first touched thirty-eight years ago, when I drew him from my daughter's womb. "You have used my company," I said, "and my name for your own selfish gains. And you have taken innocent lives. I cannot call you grandson any longer."

I turned away. "And now the deaths of those three women are on *my* soul."

"I somehow think Desmond would have done it anyway," Jonathan said.

"Not if I had left the company to him. I did not know Desmond would resort to killing. If I had known, I would have handed him the company, like this." I spread out my hands to form a platter.

"But you didn't know that, Mrs. Lee. If you had really died on that island, not only would innocent people have died, but in fact thousands of them. But because you were still alive, you were able to guide Charlotte, to lead her to him, and we were able to stop him from killing those thousands."

I shook my head. "Mr. Sung did not tell me about the first two deaths — by Ten Thousand Yang and Beautiful Intelligence Balm — because I was still in the hospital, still weak. He was afraid the bad news would cause a relapse. But when he told me about the third, the lady who died from Bliss, then I knew I had to leave the island and come back here and stop this."

"If it isn't too much to ask," Adrian interjected, "what's going to happen now? Would someone please tell me who the hell owns the company?"

I looked at this man who was the son of Gideon, but who had none of his father in him, and I saw the life of unhappiness he had spent chasing riches because he thought himself inferior, and because he thought money would buy him stature. "You want to know what will happen to your investors' money. The money you stole."

"You just don't understand higher finance, Harmony. You never did."

I thought of that day on the dock when we saw Gideon go off to war, and Olivia promised me that she would take my house away from me. I remembered the look on her son's face, a hungry face even then, just thirteen years old but already believing that only the possession of other people's wealth would make him valued in his father's eyes. "Higher finance" was Adrian's word for stealing.

"The company belongs to my daughter," I said. "Together we will work to restore honor to Harmony House."

Valerius Knight and his officers took my grandson away, with Adrian and Margo following, assuring Desmond that they would hire the best lawyers. And after they were gone, Charlotte finally spoke. She broke her spellbound state and said, "Grandmother, I have a question."

"Only one?" I said with a smile.

"My Chinese name. I always thought Iris gave it to me. I hated that name."

"I know you did, Charlotte. When you showed me the storybook and said you wanted the name of that little girl, I said we could change it."

"Even though, I realize now, *you* named me."

I shook my head. "It was not I who gave you your Chinese name. It was your father, Gideon."

"*He* named me?"

"It was what you were to him. The night you were born, he held you in his arms and he smiled down at you and he said, 'You are my whispered joy.' This went on your birth certificate. It was a lucky Chinese name — Whispered Joy."

Her face was still a map of confusion. "Years ago, when you hit rock bottom in Chinatown, you heard your mother talk to you, remember?"

How could I forget?

"You thought it was proof that she was dead. And then you learned later from Reverend Peterson that she had been alive at the time. Last night, when I heard the voice warn me about the tea, I thought it was my mother's voice, speaking to me from the afterlife. And now I discover that my mother is alive, too! You warned me about the tea and you weren't even dead."

"I could not let you drink it."

"But how did you know?"

"I was on the airplane flying through the storm and praying to Kwan Yin. I saw a vision — it was you, lifting a cup to your lips. I knew the tea was poisoned. How I knew this I cannot explain. But I knew you were in immediate danger. And so I called out a warning from my heart."

We heard the thunder then, fading away like a grumpy guest leaving a party. I looked through those glass walls of Desmond's house and I saw that the desert storm was abating, and dawn was breaking through. It was daylight; we had made it through the dark night.

But there remained one last secret to reveal.

"Grandmother," Charlotte said with tears in her eyes that turned them to emeralds, "Mother — I said some terrible things to you before you went away. I am so sorry for what I said."

I turned back to my daughter and embraced her again, saying, "Charlotte-*ah*, I heard no words."

"Grandmother," she said softly, taking my hands in hers, letting the tears spill freely. "Mother. I don't know what to say, how to talk to you. I cried myself to sleep for weeks after the funeral. My grandmother, who had been like a mother to me, was dead. But now she is alive, my mother who was like a grandmother to me."

I said, "So many times it was on my lips to call you 'daughter.' And those many times you asked about your mother and I had to speak a lie ... each like a rock in my heart until my heart became too heavy for me to carry."

Charlotte looked down at our clasped hands. What was she thinking when she saw these aged fingers that had once mixed medicines, brought babies into the world, touched Gideon in love, and dried her own tears when she was a little girl? "For years," she said softly, "I looked at you as though you stood on the other side of a great chasm. I was on one ledge and you on the other. There was no bridge connecting us, no daughter/mother joining us. There was a step missing, and you seemed so unreachable." Charlotte lifted Richard Barclay eyes to me and when she spoke I heard the voices of many Charlottes — the little girl, the teenager, the young woman, the mature adult — all those daughters yearning for a mother. "Why did you never tell me?"

"And when would that have been?" I said. "When you were seven? How do you tell a child that her grandmother is really her mother and that her father is the husband of her Auntie Olivia? Do I tell you as a teenager when I am trying to teach you morals and honor and self-respect? Charlotte-*ah,* I kept the secret for many reasons. How could I have told you and not anyone else? Could you have carried the burden, while the Barclays did not know?" I withdrew my hands from hers and laid them on her cheeks. "Do you think it was easy for me? Do you know what it is like for a woman to hold her babies and know they can never call her Mother?"

"But we would have been closer!" she protested. "I always felt a distance between us. And you were always at the factory —"

Now it was out at last, Charlotte's deepest pain. And now it was time for me to reveal my final secret. "I have something to tell you," I said.

We returned to that knees-up sofa and when we sat, I turned to my daughter and said, "I know you resented the factory because it took me away from you. But I had to be there, Charlotte-*ah.* You see, when Reverend Peterson wrote me that letter about my mother, he forgot to tell me one important thing. He forgot to say that my mother did not die in Singapore."

I saw Charlotte's eyes on me, and I felt Jonathan's also as he came to sit on the other side of me, close, the two of them framing me like a rose arbor.

"When I got that letter in 1957," I said softly, reliving the bittersweet memory, "I knew I must go back to Singapore and search for what was left of my family. Of course my grandfather was dead, and many others, because of the war. But I found a cousin who told me a fantastic tale. She told me that when my grandfather, Mei-ling's aristocratic father, died, my mother made the decision to come to America and look for me. The immigration laws were still strict then, in

1953, but the tourist laws had eased. My cousin accompanied my mother, who was old by then, to California. My cousin gave me this." I reached into my handbag and brought out the old newspaper article that I had kept for over forty years. It was yellow and brittle and the picture was hard to see. I handed it to Charlotte as I said, "You hated that big factory in Menlo Park because it took me away from you. You said I loved it more than I loved you. I opened that big modern factory in 1953, four years before you were born, after Gideon convinced me that we needed big shiny vats and conveyor belts and test tubes. It was a big new modern factory that could make medicines a thousand times faster than the Daly City factory, curing a thousand times more people."

Charlotte frowned over the brittle newsprint with its faded photograph. "What am I supposed to be looking at?" she said.

I explained that when I returned to California, I went to the office of the *San Francisco Chronicle* and showed them the article and asked for a copy of the photograph. They sold it to me for two dollars and twenty-five cents. This, too, I had with me in my purse, and I gave it now to Charlotte. This glossy photo was much clearer and sharper than the one in the old newspaper article, so that now she could see clearly the faces of the people in the group as I am cutting the ribbon across the entrance of that new factory.

"This was taken on the day of the opening," I said. "Look here," and I pointed to a face in the background. "This is my mother. This is Mei-ling. She came to the opening of my new factory."

Jonathan leaned forward to look at the photograph while I sat back, recalling the day I had stood in the office of the *San Francisco Chronicle*, in 1958, looking at the face of my mother, just yards from me, being with me and yet not being with me.

Charlotte lifted wonder-filled eyes to me. "She didn't say anything to you?"

"How could she? My mother had promised her father never to contact me."

"But he was dead!"

"He was with our ancestors. She still must honor and obey him. But at the same time, she honored and obeyed her heart. My mother was there that day the new factory opened, and then, the cousin in Singapore told me, she died a few days later, there in San Francisco, and was buried in the cemetery where my empty coffin now also lies buried. Charlotte, when you attended my funeral, you walked on the grass of your grandmother's grave."

"But," Charlotte began, pain in her voice, "I still don't understand. What does this have to do with the factory?"

"Look at my mother's face," I said. "Do you see the pride in her eyes? Do you see how she looks upon her daughter with such joy? When I saw this, Charlotte-*ah*, and I realized she had stood only a short distance from me and yet kept herself from me, I understood about family honor, and about a mother's sacrifice. And that is why I went every day to the factory that you thought I loved more than you. Because my mother had been there. Because it had been the place of her final joy and happiness.

"My mother stood in the same space as I, and I didn't know it, just as you have stood in the same space as your mother and didn't know it. She stood close to me and yet could not call me 'daughter,' just as I have stood close to you and have been unable to call you 'daughter.' "

"Why didn't you ever show me this?" Charlotte cried. "Why didn't you tell me?"

"It was my mother's wish that I not know she had come. How could I dishonor that wish?"

I reached into my handbag again to bring out my final gift to my daughter. I wiped away the tears that were tumbling

down her cheeks and showed her the photograph that I had
carried with me for thirty-nine years. It was a small picture,
black and white, of an Asian woman sitting in a hospital bed
with a newborn infant in her arms. Next to her, with his arm
protectively around her, is a handsome American, smiling
into the camera. "This was taken the night you were born," I
said as Charlotte filled her eyes with the sight of Gideon, myself, and her own tiny form. "A nurse took this picture. She
had just brought you to me and I held you for the first time.
This is our only photo of you and me as mother and daughter."

Charlotte's voice was as fragile as glass chimes as she
said, "I don't know what to say."

"We have plenty of time to say things." I looked at
Jonathan and then at my daughter. "But I say this now: So
few of us are granted one great and abiding love in our lives,
Charlotte-*ah*. My mother found that love in Richard Barclay,
and I in Gideon. But we both lost that love. You must not
make our same mistake, Charlotte." I reached for Jonathan's
hand and entwined it with Charlotte's. "You have found that
love, daughter. Hold on to it. Open your doors."

I said: "Long ago I saw you close your doors, one by one,
until you were a locked-up house. You think that by locking
up you keep the bad luck out? You keep the good luck out,
too. Open the doors, Charlotte-*ah*," I said, smiling at her, and
then at Jonathan. "Open the doors and the windows, too. Let
the luck in. Let the *love* in."